DEEP SIX

MARK POWELL

DEEP SIX

Marshall Cavendish
Editions

Also by Mark Powell: *Quantum Breach*

© 2010 Marshall Cavendish International (Asia) Pte Ltd
Reprinted 2011
Published by Marshall Cavendish Editions
An imprint of Marshall Cavendish International
1 New Industrial Road, Singapore 536196

All characters in this book are fictitious. Any similarity to any person, living or dead, is purely coincidental

Other Marshall Cavendish Offices
Marshall Cavendish Ltd. 5th Floor, 32–38 Saffron Hill, London RC1N 8FH, UK • Marshall Cavendish Corporation. 99 White Plains Road, Tarrytown NY 10591-9001, USA • Marshall Cavendish International (Thailand) Co Ltd. 253 Asoke, 12th Flr, Sukhumvit 21 Road, Klongtoey Nua, Wattana, Bangkok 10110, Thailand • Marshall Cavendish (Malaysia) Sdn Bhd, Times Subang, Lot 46, Subang Hi-Tech Industrial Park, Batu Tiga, 40000 Shah Alam, Selangor Darul Ehsan, Malaysia

Marshall Cavendish is a trademark of Times Publishing Limited

National Library Board Singapore Cataloguing in Publication Data
Powell, Mark, 1963 May-
Deep six / Mark Powell. – Singapore : Marshall Cavendish Editions, 2010.
  p. cm.
  ISBN-13 : 978-981-4302-06-7
  1. Piracy – Fiction. I. Title.

PR6116
823.92 -- dc22   OCN630342815

Printed and bound in Great Britain by
CPI Bookmarque, Croydon CR0 4TD

For Freya

ACKNOWLEDGEMENTS

One evening over a chilled bottle of wine with my dear friend Nick, the plot for *Deep Six* was hatched. The very next day I started work. It is my ambition to one day produce a 'bestseller'—maybe this is it!

I have always endeavoured to learn, enhance and strive to perfect my writing style, and one thing I do know is that I owe a debt of gratitude to a few special people. Their support, energy, wisdom and, of course, friendship have helped me along the way. Writing a book, as any author will tell you, can be at times a solitary journey; a journey of self-discovery, learning and fulfilment. Completing the journey in some ways is not as important as starting it.

As such, the following people must be recognised, respected and thanked: Chris Newson, Violet Phoon and the team at Marshall Cavendish; Daphne Rodrigues; Linda Fulford and the team at Fulford Public Relations; Richard Mathews and the team at Design Print International for the awesome cover design; and my dear friends Nick Walker, Chris Knight, Gavin Rogers and Anita Green. Also to Khun Jong for her great support.

Denise Powell, thank you for being my best friend. Thanks also to David Axe and Mohamed Farid Aziz for providing 'intelligence' and to the unnamed pirates who granted interviews.

To the men of Echo Force—if you die, you owe me a beer!

Special thanks and respect go to:

Andrew Crofts, ghost writer extraordinaire and author. Your guidance, inspiration, wisdom, encouragement and friendship are indeed valued. You are truly a legend!

Matt Lynn, author of the *Death Force* series. Your words of wisdom, encouragement, support and friendship really made a difference. Above all, thank you for the great Foreword you gracefully provided. It adds so much to the book.

I have the deepest level of respect for you both; you are true gentlemen. Your help will never be forgotten. It is my hope that this book does you all proud.

Mark Powell
June, 2010

FOREWORD

by Matt Lynn, best-selling *Death Force* author

If you explore some of the dirt tracks that run along and around the craggy shorelines and through the coastal villages of Somalia, you may well stumble across groups of men whose bony shoulders carry not fishing nets as you may expect, but rocket-propelled grenade (RPG) launchers and Russian-made AK-47s. Their weapons are their trademark, carried in the same way a plumber carries his wrench, or a carpenter his saw. And their trade is among one of the oldest and most lucrative in the world—piracy.

Modern day pirates are well-funded and well-equipped. Their arsenal may well boast a buffet of weapons, from RPGs, AK-47s, M16s and an array of 9mm pistols to fast nimble RHIBs (rigid hull inflatable boats). Etched on their austere, dark, furrowed faces are the toils of civil war.

To most of the world and throughout the centuries, they have been viewed as menacing brigands and cut-throats. The truth, however (as it usually is), is more complex. The way these pirates see it, they are the victims in the story, as much as the villains. In the last decade, Western-flagged vessels have illegally dumped toxic waste and plundered the valuable tuna fish stocks that once thrived in their rich waters.

Is there any truth in that claim? Robbers and terrorists always claim to be victims. And yet there is some justification to the charge.

the crushing blow of a gun hard in his side. It sent shards of pain through his ribs. He collapsed on the deck and rolled over, seeing only the darkened sky, which seemed to close in on him as he blacked out.

A moment in time slipped by. When Goldsmith came to, he found himself looking up at a menacing figure.

'Who the hell are you and what do you want?' Goldsmith strained to get his words out. He noticed the savage scars etched deep in Mohamed's face and torso, then focused on the man's eyes, noting the intensity of his stare—the kind only amphetamines could induce.

'Money, of course. US$50 million.' Mohamed laughed. Then, his drug-induced state gave way to his alter ego. 'But, if you do not pay, we will not be responsible for what happens.' His eyes widened, exposing more of the whites of his eyes.

'My crew. Do not harm my crew. I will talk to my people.' Goldsmith pulled himself up and stood eye to eye with his captor. 'So you are one of the pirates we hear all about,' he said, careful to sound more collected but not sarcastic.

Mohamed snapped his teeth together like an angry dog, just inches away from Goldsmith's face, as if to bite him. 'Your crew, what's left of them, will not be harmed if you do as I say. Now head for Eyl and anchor, captain!'

Two battles were now raging within Goldsmith: fight and restraint. One thing he did know: never let your enemy see you sweat. He told himself to remain calm, which wasn't easy with the bloodied corpse of the first engineer sprawled on the deck in front of him.

'Drugs and guns are a lethal combination,' he cautioned himself. So he just nodded his obeisance.

Five days at anchor was long enough, but for Mohamed Aidid it had all been worth it. He had anxiously waited for the money to arrive. The air was warm and humid as he drew a deep breath. 'You see, my brothers! The rich pay!'

Delving into the sack—a sack filled with US$5 million—he scooped out a handful of bills and held them aloft in triumph. The money had been negotiated out of the US$50 million he had asked for—US$5 milllion was good enough. He then euphorically threw them to his men like raw meat to rabid dogs. This was a big payday, perhaps his biggest yet. Looking down at the smiles on his men's faces made him feel powerful.

Then, without warning, he raised his AK, aimed it at the men in the two waiting boats and opened fire, his laughter drowned out by the chorus of bullets and the wails of his dying men in the boats below. In seconds, the boats were awash with blood. The few men that had dived over the side in an attempt to escape felt the rain of lead from the other pirates. Bleeding and helpless in the water, they were left for the sharks.

As the smoke wafted away, Mohamed stood defiant. 'Only my true brothers will share in my spoils. These men were nothing but fools.' He spat.

Walking down the narrow gangway like a demented peacock, he stepped aboard the third boat and sped off, mission accomplished.

———

Goldsmith felt his ribs; the pain was intense. The blow he had received had broken at least two ribs, evident by the yellowish black bruising around his torso.

'Fuck!' he spat. He hated being injured.

He felt strangely hollow, a helpless feeling he hadn't felt before. He had failed his crew. Then, as if his brain had thrown a switch, a dark anger shot through his veins. Clenching his fists tight, he thumped the side of the bulkhead.

'Fucking vultures, they even killed their own men.'

Gonzalez looked at him, observing the anger in his eyes and the frown lines on his forehead.

'Nothing we could have done, sir.' He sounded passive and beaten.

'Oh, really? Give me a gun and I will show you nothing.' Goldsmith spat back, his pride now in tatters. 'I will tell you one thing—never again.' Then he walked into his cabin and slammed the door.

Gonzalez stood for a while, simply staring at the door. He at least was glad to be alive. The single gunshot that rang out said it all. For Goldsmith, now slumped over his desk in a pool of blood, it had simply all been too much. His pride had been ripped out of his soul.

ONE

June 2009. Northwood, United Kingdom.

Harry Ogilvy, known to everyone within the British Secret Intelligence Service (SIS) simply as Oley, hurried through the complex maze of underground passageways at the Allied Maritime Command Headquarters located at Northwood. Oley had been summoned by Dominic Langdon, commander-in-chief of the Royal Naval Command Task Force 151.

As he reached meeting room 5 which was located halfway down a long hallway, he paused, noting the illuminated 'Meeting in Progress' sign. He fiddled with the knot of his old boys Eton tie, more out of habit than a need to straighten it. Taking a deep breath and drawing himself up to his full height, he gently knocked on the door and swiftly entered.

'Sir, you wanted to see me.' He waited for a response.

Langdon was a man of few words, known for his brashness and intolerance of time wasters. He detested formal occasions and preferred to remain detached from any social obligations his rather bullied wife, Margaret, arranged for them. He would rather fight a tiger with a toothpick, he once said, than engage in social banter.

Langdon stood with his hands clasped firmly behind his back, at the far end of the long narrow room. There was no natural light, given they were at least two storeys underground. Only the integrated strip lights in the ceiling lit the room, their bright white glow making

Langdon look strangely pale and ghostly.

'Pirates. Are you aware of them?' Langdon launched into his line of questioning.

'Yes, sir. Somalia, South China Sea, … Hollywood.'

'Quite.' Langdon was not impressed by the cheap quip. 'Then, you are aware that I spend most of my damn time trying to stop these seaborne rats.' Langdon puffed out his chest.

'Yes, sir.'

Clearing his throat, Langdon continued: 'Well, another tanker has been taken by Somali pirates, this time off the coast of Kenya. Saudi-owned, I believe. The captain was American.' He paused and turned his back to Oley, who followed him with his eyes.

Oley noticed the woman sitting half in shadow in the far corner, her legs and arms defiantly crossed. Her sensible flat brown shoes caught his eye; that and her sharp grey suit and silver, almost metallic, hair, so neat it could have been fake. Her eyes were cold, her face showed not even the hint of a smile. The shadow gave her a menacing look.

'You said the captain was American, sir?' Oley asked.

'Yes, shot himself after the ordeal. Anyway, the main villain, we are told, is a man by the name of Mohamed Aidid, by all accounts an extremist and a cold-blooded killer. Even shoots his own men, we hear.' Langdon paused and took a sip of water.

'Thing is, we understand he is getting just too good at his craft, that is, hijacking ships, hundreds of them. The funding, we also hear, is coming from the damn Americans, which is ironic, don't you think?' Langdon looked at Oley, his eyebrows raised.

'Sir,' Oley acknowledged, indicating he was following the discussion.

'I want you to find out what is going on, why they would train and fund such a man.' Langdon paused again.

Oley, whilst deeply intrigued by the request, knew well enough not to question it. This was as good as getting an assignment from the head of MI6 himself. Not to mention Langdon was a personal friend of Prince Philip.

'That's all, man. Report back to me in a few weeks. Dismissed.' Langdon waved him out.

Resting his eyes once more upon the woman, Oley dared a smile, then turned and headed out. As he walked back through the gloomy corridors and eventually up and out into the daylight, Oley pondered Langdon's suspicion of an American connection with the hijacks. Above all, he wondered who the mysterious woman was.

There was one person he knew who could help establish some facts. As luck would have it, that man was already in Somalia.

———

'Can he pull it off?' the metallic-haired woman asked, leaning forward.

'Despite his arrogant charm, I hear he is good at what he does, so we shall see. Are you sure about what is going on? I mean, it's outrageous!'

'Oh yes. Very sure, Dominic. You have my word on that.' She smiled.

TWO

June 2009. Puntland, Somalia.

The midday sun made the wasteland look impossibly bright and lifeless. They crossed a ridge of mountains that gave way to a long empty beach and a vast expanse of teal blue water. They were about to enter Boosaaso, a booming pirate city and a portal to the chaotic underworld of Somalia. The town itself was perfectly positioned near the mouth of the Red Sea, at the crossroads of Africa and Arabia, to supply that lawless corner of the world with all its contraband needs: guns, drugs, expired baby formula, counterfeit electronics, counterfeit dollars, even smuggled human beings.

The airport in Boosaaso was, like most in the country, a strip of gravel with an outhouse and a corrugated-iron shack, where a few veiled women sat stirring a pot of murky tea. Outside, in the thin shade of some thorn trees, the *mooryaan* lurked. Half-starved young men with glassy eyes and loaded Kalashnikovs, the *mooryaan* haunt every nook and cranny of the country. Some of the ones he saw wore military fatigues that drooped from their shoulders, making them look like boys in men's clothing, which they were.

He grabbed his bags and stepped out into the crushing light and heat. He had been in contact with a young Somali journalist named Juno, whom he had deputised to line up security. Juno was wearing a polo shirt and wrap-around shades when they met on the airstrip. They shook hands and hugged Somali-style, shoulder to shoulder.

Juno led him to a 4x4 with tinted windows. It was gaudily decorated, with a feather boa covering the dashboard and gold-plated charms dangling from the rearview mirror.

The vehicle bumped along a dirt road through a field of garbage, where goats snacked on plastic bags and thin little boys with sunken eyes watched over them. Women, veiled head to toe, trudged along the road, hauling plastic jerrycans sloshing with water. Occasionally, a cart would pass, pulled by an emaciated donkey with every rib showing.

Puntland was lawless and he knew it. They were heading deeper into territory that no government controlled, though many had tried. Borders were simply ignored, nothing more than imaginary lines drawn in the sand. This was a desolate land, governed and controlled by pirates; the law, such as it was, was theirs and written in blood.

Every single muscle and bone in his body screamed with agony as he tried to sit upright in the rear of the bouncing Toyota Land Cruiser. Rocking from side to side, he eased up each side of his numb backside to stimulate the blood flow and find a more comfortable position. Even his head hurt from the occasional collision with the roof as they travelled down what seemed like an endless row of bone-shattering potholes.

Clouds of choking dust billowed in through the open windows that offered the only form of ventilation. As he blinked, he could feel the dust sink deeper into his eyes. Rubbing his eyes with his hands as he strained to look out through the dirty windscreen just made it worse. He pulled up the thin linen scarf around his mouth but that did little to keep out the dust. The thirsty 35-degree heat sucked moisture out of every pore of his skin.

Whilst disoriented by the harsh desert conditions and ill-informed as to their exact destination, he could see that they were navigating a series of narrow twisting tracks. He had started to make a mental note of every intersection they crossed, but soon each looked confusingly like the last. The journalist knew he would be in trouble if he needed to escape.

James Robert Cutter was a fresh-faced 35-year-old with blonde hair and piercing blue eyes. Having been afforded an education at Slough Grammar—better known as Eton—followed by Oxford, he believed the world was his oyster, and rightfully so given his grades were good: double firsts in Math and English. That, and the fact that his privileged, upper-class background assured him of an inheritance of a few million. He had had no idea what to do with his life, until the night he sat alone in one of the many student bars at Oxford, pondering his direction over a glass of flat beer. The men who approached him weren't dressed in dark suits and black hats, and it took less than an hour for the spooks to seduce him. The fact of the matter was that M16 had pegged him the moment he came to Oxford. Smart, affluent hungry men with no direction were just what they wanted; he could be moulded and trained. His double-edged journalist career had started from there.

Cutter's boyish face hid the anguish of the horrors he had witnessed over the course of his 10-year career. He worked freelance now, specialising in war zones. His current employer, who had called him at short notice and who seemed to use him a lot these days, was an exclusive stock image company, not that he had ever been to their offices. His commissions normally came via email, but they paid well and on time. This time, they wanted an urgent exclusive reportage. The subjects of the article were mysterious men; his client had referred to them as freedom fighters.

'Damn pirates, more like,' Cutter thought, having done some preliminary research. Lucky for one of his other clients, he happened to be in the area.

The list of questions they had sent him was, he thought, not only detailed but also extensive and strangely biased towards one man in particular. Still, the introduction to the company had come from a former friend at Eton, Harry Ogilvy. He knew instinctively not to probe too deep and, for the fee they were paying, he wasn't about to complain. They kept him busy and that was all that mattered.

Wiping the greasy sweat off his watch with his sweat-soaked shirt sleeve, he calculated, somewhat slowly because of his exhaustion and dehydration, that he had been battered and bumped around now for over 12 hours.

Their last rest stop, in the small town of Hobyo, had been all too brief. Or perhaps brief enough. He recalled the town's somewhat emaciated inhabitants glaring at him as he paced around in circles to stretch his limbs. 'Perhaps they were not familiar with or indeed fond of Western faces,' he thought now.

A painfully thin boy dressed in only a pair of filthy brown trousers that looked a size too big for him had dared to approach. He must have been no more than five or six years old. The boy had raised his cupped bony hands to Cutter, his big brown eyes screaming pity. His reward for such boldness had been a swat on the back of the head from one of Cutter's armed bodyguards.

That was two hours ago. Now Cutter turned his attention to the young Somali in faded ripped jeans seated opposite him in the vehicle. TJ seemed so relaxed, a stark contrast to his own frazzled state. Cutter watched the boy's rhythmic swaying to the vehicle's motion.

His gaze then fell on the AK clamped between TJ's legs. It was a grim reminder that bodyguards were an absolute necessity where he was. A wave of anxiety overcame him for a moment. He was alone, completely alone. But that was the deal, only him.

Shaking off the feeling, he knew he had no choice. He simply had to trust the men he had selected to protect him. TJ's toothy grin helped ease his uneasiness a little.

'So tell me, why do you do this?' Cutter settled himself back into his seat.

'Do it or starve. You have seen the state of my land. You think I have a choice? This is my choice.' TJ shook his weapon, his eyes for the first time angry. It was as if the question had insulted him somehow.

'Yeah, I know, but dangerous work, no?'

'Life is dangerous, is it not?' TJ returned to his smile, his point in his own way well made. Cutter found himself having to agree.

The sudden, sharp braking sent him flying hard against the back of the front seat as the tyres skidded to a halt in the sunbaked sand. They had arrived!

Cutter eased himself out of the rear door of the old cream-coloured vehicle, which was heavily scarred with dents and bullet holes. He felt exhausted, completely drained. As he stretched to get the blood flowing and relieve his aching muscles, he took in the barren landscape of jagged rocks that jutted out of the sand like evil fingers pointing to the heavens.

Then, he detected a slight scent of salt in the air. It brought back memories of long summer days he had spent as a child on the beaches of Cornwall, eating vanilla ice cream, Cornish pasties and pink rock. He winced as he remembered how his mother used to dry him off after a swim with a rough blue towel—fabric conditioner wasn't something she was familiar with. His father, a wealthy barrister, would be snoozing contentedly in a rainbow-coloured deck chair.

A welcome breeze across his face brought Cutter back to the present. It was coming from the Indian Ocean, not more than a few hundred yards away, he guessed. He could just hear the waves crashing on the shore. As he drew in the fresh salty air, he felt a light tap on the shoulder.

His guide, a small-sized Somali named Cassa, pointed to where they should now walk. Cutter readied his camera and followed, noticing that Cassa was barefoot, his leathery soles seemingly oblivious to the hot sand and the sharp stones that littered the path.

After 50 yards or so, they came across a skinny flea-ridden dog tethered to a tree by a long piece of frayed orange nylon rope—the type of rope Cutter used to find covered in tar on the beaches back home, along with a solitary shoe.

He broke into a smile as he watched the rather excited dog for a few seconds before snapping a picture. 'Male,' he thought, given the size of its bollocks. Looking closer, he realised the dog was frantically feasting on the remains of a large rat, caught presumably on the mounds of rotting rubbish that was its home, just outside the camp's entrance.

A sudden burst of gunfire stunned Cutter. The 'tat-tat-tat' ripped into his ears. He flung himself to the ground and the impact shot sand and dirt into his mouth. Instinctively, he brought his arms up over his head. His entire body tensed up as he lay face down, waiting for pain to surge through his body, but nothing.

Slowly releasing his grip on his own head, he looked up and squinted in the sunlight. He heard children laughing. Then, a hand reached out and pulled him to his feet. It was TJ, wearing a big smile.

'It's okay. Just kids firing at the rats. Come, we go.'

Cutter glared at the children, shaking his head to show his displeasure. They simply laughed back at him. He brushed himself off and followed TJ.

'They seem to think those guns are just toys.'

'Yes, to them they are,' TJ replied. 'They do not fear them. They learn fast here how to shoot. I shot my first gun when I was five.' TJ seemed proud of his achievement.

Cutter knew he should have been shocked, but he wasn't, and that said it all.

Entering the compound, which was ringed with barb wire, Cutter found the air of calm a relief after his experience just moments ago. Standing still for a second, he took in his surroundings. He studied the scattered open-sided huts with their rusty corrugated roofs through his lens and snapped away. There wasn't any of the chaos he had expected. No gunmen with black teeth, spitting tobacco. None of the dusty streets full of burning cars, bullet-riddled houses and blood-stained gutters he had seen in the Mog some 400 kilometres south. That was a place he was thankful to have left. But this was, as he well knew, Puntland, home to some of the world's most deadly and skilled pirate clans.

He felt a jab in his back, prodding him forward. Cassa led the way towards a hut on the far side of the compound. As they walked, Cutter scanned every face and every inch of the camp. He observed a few men posted on watch, more milling about than alert, blowing plumes of cigarette smoke into the late afternoon air. They were dressed in well-worn former Ethiopian camouflage fatigues and the well-used Kalashnikovs casually slung over their bony shoulders reminded him that these men were dangerous.

Others were far more relaxed. They were spread out in front of an old television set perched on top of a wooden crate and connected, it seemed, to a large satellite dish bolted to the roof. Cutter felt his throat tighten when he saw a few of the men sculling bottles of beer. 'Probably stolen booty from a hijacking,' he thought.

Reaching the hut, which was slightly larger than the others and built out of old driftwood and wooden pallets, Cutter saw the figure of a man sitting just inside the doorway. As Cutter stepped onto the narrow rickety decking at the front of the hut, he realised the man was casually seated with his back to the door, being tattooed by one of the local women. Craning his neck to get a better look, Cutter could make out the image of a rampant lion taking shape on the man's back.

Cutter winced each time the sharp stick jabbed into the man's skin. Yet, the pain seemed to have no effect on the man, whose head hung forward as if he was transfixed by the floor.

Cutter then noticed the pile of khat leaves by the man's side. He knew enough to tell it was a local herb that could induce a state of euphoria when chewed. Perhaps that explained why the man seemed oblivious to the pain as the tattoo was slowly completed.

Emerging from his trance, the man slowly lifted his head. He glared at Cutter.

'Sit.' His tone was firm as he gestured with a wave of his hand.

'Thank you.' Cutter obliged and took a seat just in front of his host, whose name he still didn't know. 'I am thankful you agreed to meet me. How should I address you?'

A deadening silence ensued.

Finally: 'Names are for friends. You are just a guest,' he said.

Undeterred by this reaction, Cutter leaned forward and prepared to start the interview.

'Okay, well, I would like to understand your motivations for being a pirate and what type of ship you prefer.' Cutter reached into his beaten-up blue backpack for his recording device.

This action triggered a sharp reaction from an armed man who had been standing in the corner. Only a wave from the tattooed man halted his advance.

'Sorry. Is it okay if I record our conversation?' Cutter asked nervously. His eyes were locked on the AK-touting pirate standing not more than 4 feet from him. He felt a bead of sweat trickle down his forehead.

'No. Just ask your questions.' The man's fluency with English did not escape Cutter's notice.

'May I ask, were you educated abroad? You speak with a slight American accent.' Cutter got down to the task at hand, not wanting to hang around too long.

'No,' came the short reply.

'Okay. So tell me about your agenda. Why has someone who is clearly educated turned to piracy? What is your view of how the West sees you?' Cutter wanted to get to the heart of what drove this man— a man who, by the look of things, was in charge and must have been the head of the pirate clan he had come to report on. These questions brought about a grimace on his host's face.

'First, do not think that those who follow me are not wise men. Just because I choose this path, do not infer I am stupid or, worse, ignorant. I have ambition. We are not pirates, Mr. Cutter; we are freedom fighters.'

Despite his reaction, the young Somali found himself reflecting for a moment. His ambition was, he thought, firm in his mind. He wanted to be the leader of all the militia groups in the area, pure and simple. He had already proven his skill in planning and strategising by leading his band of maritime freedom fighters—the MFF, as he called it—through a record seven successful attacks, and he had invaluable inside knowledge of ship routes. His reputation was beginning to spread to the other villages in Puntland.

Only one man stood in his way: the great Mohamed Farrah Aidid, who was currently on a mission to attack a French cargo ship some 20 miles off shore. The former warlord of Hobyo had fled his town just before its capture by the Islamic Court Union (ICU) on August 16, 2006. In an attempt to end piracy on the Benadir coast, the ICU had surrounded the town, a major port in southern Puntland, with armed pickup trucks and sent delegates to negotiate with the town's leaders for a surrender. After days of futile talks, the ICU took Hobyo, apparently without firing a single shot.

The good news for Cutter's host was that Mohamed's popularity amongst the pirates was waning. Apart from abandoning Hobyo to the ICU, he had also been losing too many men in his poorly planned and executed hijacks. Many of the pirate groups were now looking for a new leader.

Anxious to get out of there as soon as possible, Cutter coughed to regain his host's attention.

'May I ask, how many ships have you hijacked?'

Observing the man's dark eyes now burning into his, Cutter swallowed, sensing his interruption was not welcome. His stomach was so tense he felt sick. He could feel the bile in his throat. Worse, he realised now that more armed men had gathered in the hut and were looking at him.

'I have taken seven.'

'The average ransom would be … what?'

'One to five million. Why, you think I should ask for more?' His reply edged with sarcasm.

'Okay, I'm almost done. Can I ask if you are linked in any way to an Islamic extremist group and, if so, which one? I would also like to know if you have come across Mohamed Aidid?'

The man suddenly sat bolt upright. It seemed the last question alone sparked the biggest reaction.

'You ask too much. Be careful. I know Mohamed. He is not like me. He is nothing!'

The man's anger was now apparent. Unknown to Cutter, he had lost several men on a recent attack and knew Mohamed had executed them. Cutter decided it was time to make his move.

'Then, perhaps we can help each other. Where is he now exactly?'

The Somali was nothing if not sharp. He noted the change in Cutter's tone and sensed his guest was more than he seemed.

'Who are you and what is it you really want?'

'I am someone who can help you. If you tell me where Mohamed is right now and what he is up to, we can do a deal. You see, I know you would be better off without him.' Cutter leaned forward, as if to emphasise the importance of his words.

'A deal? You think I need one from you?'

'Let's just say my client would be grateful for any information you may like to share about Mohamed.'

The Somali paused, now seeing Cutter in a very different light.

'Leave us.' He waved his bodyguards away.

Cutter watched them leave. When he turned back, he found the muzzle of a 9mm pointed at his head.

'Okay, ghost, who are you?'

'Let's just say I'm a journalist with connections. Kill me and it ends here.' Cutter swallowed hard.

'Go on! Who sent you?' The Somali pushed the gun against Cutter's temple.

'I can't say, but my client needs your help.' Cutter slowly raised his right hand and gently nudged the pistol aside. 'I'm not armed. Don't think you need that.' Despite his calm bold move, Cutter was a wreck inside. He was not the best of spies and most certainly not James Bond.

'You have five seconds before I kill you stone dead.'

'We hear Mohamed and his men benefit from American funds. We are not sure why they would fund such a man. My client seeks to understand.' Cutter knew he had to talk now or lose his advantage. He noticed the Somali almost froze. The mention of Americans seemed to resonate.

The man finally lowered his gun. 'Yes, I hear that too. He is not a freedom fighter. He hijacks out of greed. He is out there right now.' His eyes gestured westward, as if to tell Cutter where Mohamed was. This was what Cutter wanted.

'Explain. Tell me everything.' Cutter eased himself back into his chair to listen. His host, it seemed, now wanted to talk.

———

Having answered Cutter's questions for almost an hour, the Somali agreed to a deal. As they emerged from the darkness of the hut, Cutter couldn't help but notice how athletic his host looked in the daylight. He had a rippling six pack and strong arms with symmetrical biceps.

'Any man that took this guy on would have to be fit,' Cutter thought. 'Either that or shoot him first.' He raised his camera and snapped a few pictures.

Hearing the camera, the Somali turned and looked at Cutter.

'That is all you get. Remember this moment, my friend, and tell your Western friends I fight for freedom, not to service your games. Now do as you promised.' He then turned away and started to walk towards the beach.

'Wait!' Cutter shouted. 'You called me friend. If I am now indeed a friend and you want me to deliver your message, may I at least know your name?'

The Somali looked blankly at Cutter, saying nothing. He seemed to be considering a response. After what seemed like an eternity, his face broke into a wide smile.

'My name is Abshir, Abshir Mohamed. I was once an American puppet. Now I am what I am.'

With that, he sauntered off.

———

Sitting alone on one of the many rocks that dotted the beach, Abshir looked out across the water. Tranquility was rare in his life. He enjoyed watching the sea birds dive for fish. He marvelled at the ease with which they operated and, in some ways, how simple a life they had.

A shout broke the moment of peace. One of his men was now running towards him. Seconds later, a rather battered yellow satellite phone was thrust into his hand.

Listening intently to the voice on the other end of the line, Abshir took in the news—news he had hoped long and hard would one day come. It seemed the young Westerner had fulfilled his side of the deal.

Now beaming, Abshir stood up and raised his arms euphorically in the air. He was a new man. The lion tattoo on his back, but a few hours old, seemed already to have brought him luck.

'I am king! I am strong!' he screamed.

Hearing the declaration from a distance, Cutter turned and smiled. He could see Abshir's men jumping around and shooting into the sky. It was clear he had done his job. The one call he had made to his client had changed everything.

TJ nudged Cutter forward. 'Come, we must go. It is their time now, not safe.'

THREE

June 2009. Gulf of Aden.

It was almost 6:00 a.m. when he finally mustered the energy to move. As he slid out of his bunk and stretched, he felt surprisingly sharp in spite of the numerous shots of whisky the night before, the evidence of which hung on his breath like a stale fog.

Stepping into the tiny rudimentary bathroom, he took hold of his toothbrush and vigorously brushed his teeth, spitting the foam into the basin. His eyes caught his reflection in the mirror—a tired-looking 49-year-old staring right back. He ran his fingers through his hair, observing that it was no longer completely dark brown but heavily streaked with silver grey. Not wanting to ruin his day, he convinced himself that it gave him the distinguished look of a ship's captain.

As he started to shave, he thought about that rainy November day when he had stood on the dock and looked up at his new vessel, named after the Nordic god Odin. It was so long ago. Turning his head slowly from side to side, he scrutinised in the mirror the deep lines of his somewhat austere face, a representation of the 20 years he had worked at sea. He was getting old.

Captain Karl J Vandenbrook knew the waters of the Gulf of Aden and the Somali basin well through years of ocean-bound experience—so well, in fact, he had defended his vessel against numerous pirate attacks.

Thinking of how people reacted when told of his encounters, he smiled. They expected Hollywood's swashbuckling 'Pirates of the Caribbean', with handsome actors and fake swordfights. Their jaws would drop when told that modern-day pirates brandished Russian-made AK-47s, darted around in nimble craft powered by twin Yamaha engines, owned top-of-the-range pickup trucks and, in some cases, lived in plush villas along the coast. The irony, he thought, was that the spoils of their attacks were the same: wealth!

Whilst rumours of pirates living in five-star luxury were somewhat exaggerated in his view, hijacking and kidnapping were indeed fast becoming a multi-million dollar business in the waters off Somalia—of that he was sure. The problem was now so severe that the grey ghosts of the various international navy armadas were now obliged to patrol these waters and escort vessels through busy shipping lanes, offering their protection.

But Vandenbrook knew the vast expanses of the Indian Ocean were about the size of Western Europe and could never be fully protected. That would be like looking for a man sitting in a wheelbarrow in the middle of France.

Enough contemplation, he thought, and got dressed. A few minutes later, he was on the bridge. As he stared out across the water to the distant horizon, he felt a twinge of guilt. He thought about the payment he had secretly received that morning and placed, as he always did, in the tiny grey safe hidden within his locker. He touched the key that hung around his neck as if to check that it was safe. Reminding himself that the sum covered his sons' private school fees for an entire year eased his conscience just a little.

The *Odin* was a moderately new and large cargo vessel weighing in at just over 65,000 tonnes. Its matte black body and bright red deck were beginning to show signs of wear from the harsh elements at sea. The ship was now positioned just 10 kilometres off the Somalian coast—and the arid beaches of Puntland. Looking through the light haze with his powerful binoculars, Vandenbrook could make out the coastal town of Bandarbeyla.

In his mind, he knew that his vessel's design gave it a low freeboard when laden with cargo. That alone made him feel uneasy, as it meant the decks came relatively close to the waterline, making the ship extremely vulnerable to pirate attacks.

He also knew, as he dropped his binoculars down to his chest, that the flat calm waters he could see with his naked eye were an ideal stage for such unwanted guests.

The fact that he had been encouraged to attract them by not deploying anti-piracy techniques and not joining one of the many navy escorts worried him even more.

He recalled watching a CNN report earlier that morning about an English couple who had been captured whilst sailing their yacht only a hundred or so miles west of his current position. The rather polished blonde presenter, with her shocking red lips and dimpled cheeks, had announced that they were now at the mercy of Somali pirates who were demanding a sizeable ransom. Somehow, her delivery of the news didn't seem very appropriate, given the severity of the situation. Her radiant face and light smile seemed out of place. 'God help them,' he thought, as he strode off in search of tea.

Despite the flat calm waters and the absence of white caps, Barry could feel his stomach churning. There was nothing left inside to vomit—his fried breakfast had been evacuated overboard a few hours ago.

Glancing at his watch, he realised he had been lying almost motionless on the cold hard deck for three hours. His clothes were soaked with sweat and sea spray. His eyes were sore, his legs numb and his fingers tingling. Then, reminding himself he had waited three agonising months for this day and paid a small fortune to make his dream come true, he decided he should just stop moaning.

At 31, Barry Caswell had never done anything exciting. In fact, the most daring thing he had ever done was to get a red devil with the number '6' tattooed onto his right upper arm. That was just a few weeks back. His staunch Catholic wife had not been pleased—she had sentenced him to one solitary week in the spare room. Barry grimaced at the memory of the piles of unwashed underpants.

Being a successful marketing executive with a large consultancy based in West London didn't afford him the adrenaline rush he craved. He had to lose himself in a virtual world of 'Hit Man', 'Wolf Sniper' and 'Call of Duty II'. Computer games had become his sanctuary from his dull corporate life and boring marriage. The reason he was lying here was to escape all of that. That made him feel better about the discomfort he was feeling now.

Unlike Barry, the man next to him, now looking intently at the horizon through his Leupold sniper scope, lived not in a virtual world of war but in a world of blood-soaked reality.

Louis Patron, or Bull, as he was known, was in charge of training this latest civy recruit for his mission. Forty-year-old Bull was a squat little man with a shiny bald head that seemed to grow directly out of a pair of broad square shoulders. He had the air of a rugged man who could handle himself well, and he had few words to say to anyone; it was just his nature. But he did have the experience young Barry had paid US$100,000 for.

Bull was a 22-year veteran of the infamous French Foreign Legion, having served as a sniper in Kosovo and Africa. But, despite his impressive service record, he was now a wanted man. The Legion had been on his trail for the past three years, most recently failing to capture him at a seaport in Turkey. His offence was the murder of his commanding officer in the French town of Marseille. His superior had battered his young wife to death after a drunken row.

Killing the man had not been the smartest thing to do, but it was personal. Bull had watched his own sister get beaten to death by his drunken father. As such, he had developed a deep hatred for woman beaters. After killing his father with a knife, at the tender age of 16, he sought refuge in the Legion, lying about his age. The skills he acquired during his years in the Legion now served him well.

Out of the corner of one eye, Barry noticed Bull tense up. Drawing away from his sniper scope, Barry strained his eyes and his ears to try and detect what had caught his instructor's attention. But blue water was all he could see, while the throbbing of the *Odin*'s engines drowned any distant sound.

'Stand to!' shouted Bull. A small boat had come into his view about 1,800 yards off and was heading at speed for their stern.

Barry quickly turned an eye back to the scope, now seeing the small boat bobbing around in his line of sight. Then, it disappeared behind the waves. Barry held his breath, waiting for the boat to pop back into view. When it did moments later, it seemed to be closer than before and he could clearly see the heads of the men on board— five, maybe six, he counted.

He felt his heart jump when he saw that two of the figures on board, seated towards the bow, were armed with AKs. Their faces were partially covered by scarves wrapped around their heads.

Barry's heart was now pounding in his chest. The pain he had endured lying on the cold hard deck seemed to be dissipating. The adrenaline racing through his veins like warm whiskey felt good.

He desperately needed to calm down and try to recall some of what he had been taught during his sniper crash course just before boarding the *Odin* eight days ago at the port of Salalah in Oman.

He took in a deep breath and then let it out slowly, trying to steady his breathing and settle his mind. The fact that nestling on his shoulder was a Barrett M107 .50 calibre sniper rifle suddenly struck home. Every nerve in his body was screaming and his mouth was bone dry.

Shaking his head to try and focus his mind, he narrowed his eyes and looked through the scope. There, in front of him, cut by the thin crosshairs, was his target.

'Eight hundred yards and closing,' Bull announced.

Barry started to run through in his mind what Bull had taught him—that the main forces acting on the bullet in flight were gravity, drag and, if present, wind. Gravity imparted a downward acceleration on the projectile, causing the bullet to fall from the line of sight. Drag, or air resistance, decelerated the projectile with a force proportional to the square of the velocity. Wind caused the projectile to deviate from the trajectory. All three forces had a major impact on the path of the bullet and had to be accounted for when taking aim. But knowing all that didn't help much, not when his mind was spinning.

'Seven fifty yards and closing. Wind speed four knots.' Bull rattled off the vital information. He moved over, pushed Barry to the side and started to fiddle with the Barrett's scope, making allowances for distance, wind and humidity. Then, he tapped Barry on the shoulder as if to let him know he had finished.

'Stand by,' Bull said.

Barry tried desperately to listen to Bull but also focus his mind on the job at hand. 'This is it, no turning back now,' he thought. He was sweating profusely, his senses heightened.

'Steady... NOW! Take the shot!' Bull shouted.

Barry drew a deep breath that filled his lungs. His right eye narrowed further. There was the target corralled in his scope. His finger hovered on the trigger. The masked man appeared to be glaring right back at him. Barry felt his right foot start to shake. His nerves were a mess, like tight bundles of steel wires. His heart was hammering like it was about to explode out of his mouth. His lungs were on fire. He tried to gather spit in his mouth, but there was none.

Then, as if realising it was futile to resist, his mind kicked into slow motion. His breathing seemed to almost stop as his finger squeezed the trigger. He felt the powerful Barrett push hard back into his shoulder as it spat out the round.

'Miss,' Bull reported almost instantly, his tone blunt.

Barry had sent the round whizzing right over the target's head. The sound of the .50 calibre round slicing the air at subsonic speed was enough to alert the pirates, who ducked down and returned fire.

'Four hundred yards and closing. Keep firing!' Bull's voice now sounded anxious. Barry drew another breath and fixed the crosshairs of his scope firmly on a man lying precariously at the bow of the boat. He eased his posture, focused his mind and squeezed the trigger. Once again, he felt the Barrett kick hard into his shoulder.

It was like a macabre movie. Barry took in the sight—the head of the man with the black woollen ski mask was now nothing more than vapour. Barry had hit him square in the forehead. Given the round had been fired from a weapon that would make a canon look wimpish, that meant only one thing: a shattered skull and instant death.

Before Barry could get another round off, the boat veered sharply to the left and vanished in the haze.

'Fucking hell! Awesome, I did it!' Barry screamed. He was practically rolling around on the deck—that's how alive he felt.

'My mates will eat shit when I tell them I did it. I shot a pirate! I told them I could do it!' Barry cried.

Bull slowly turned his head and glared at Barry. He knew what he had to do now. He casually stood up, shot a glance at the bridge and shook his head.

A tall, well-built man stood next to Vandenbrook on the bridge. With his arms folded in front of him, he looked relaxed, as if he had just been watching a cricket match on a Sunday afternoon. Seeing Bull's signal, he gave a thumbs up in return—a thumbs up that signalled the end.

FOUR

June 2009. Salalah, Oman.

Monday, just before midday. The sun was high in the sky and cast short shadows. He crept cautiously forward between the stacks of steel shipping containers, until he could see the wooden crates being unloaded on to the quayside. In his head, he counted each one. He needed to know that all 56 had made it safely, at least this far.

Each of the two-by-one-metre crates was marked with a bold red arrow indicating the correct way up. Much to his frustration, he noticed the instruction had not been adhered to in some cases. It had not escaped his attention either that there was a second mark on each crate, in the bottom right corner. In bold black type, it read 'SACAMO', the name of the factory he himself had stood in only one week ago.

He stepped out of the shadows to get a closer look, knowing his appearance would not draw any undue attention. Most men around the docks wore jeans, as he did, with a faded check shirt and a white safety hat. He looked perfectly at home. That is, apart from his rather polished brown brogue shoes.

But before he got any further, a yellow forklift thundered by within a few feet of him. Then it started beeping, the sound making him feel nauseous, as the driver began to load the crates onto a line of waiting trucks.

An obese scruffy man with small pig-like eyes, the driver looked as if he had been welded into his seat, a permanent feature of the forklift. He knew dockside activity was normally fast and furious. He also knew time was money and the longer a ship remained in port the more money got burned. Most of all, he knew he was paid not by the hour but by the number of ships he unloaded. As such, his foot was hard down on the gas.

The frantically waving arms of the small stocky customs official caught his eye. To ignore him would mean instant dismissal. Reluctantly, he pressed his foot down on the brakes, stopping the forklift mid-way through loading a crate. Only the amber strobe light continued to flash as he shut off the engine.

'Open the crate,' the customs official said, jabbing his finger at it.

The man in the shadows saw his opportunity. Stepping forward, he gestured to a dockside worker to open the crate. The lid was hurriedly levered off with a jemmy and the straw-like packing material removed. The customs official peered in.

'What is this?' he asked abruptly, examining the contents against a copy of the manifest.

'Machine parts used for distilling water,' the man from the shadows replied.

The official glanced down at his shoes and raised an eyebrow, then grunted.

'And you are who, other than being an American?' he asked.

'I'm from the shipping company.' The American deliberately avoided names.

'Are you planning to distil the entire ocean with this amount of equipment?' the customs official quipped, as he removed more of the packing material to get a better look.

'No, but our client has a big thirst.'

Not showing any sign of a sense of humour, the official looked at him with a steely gaze.

'Then you must pay the import duty.' A subtle smile formed on his chubby face.

'Of course, my friend.' The American then took a step closer, discreetly extracting a key from his pocket and passing it to the official. 'You will find everything is in order,' he quietly assured the official, then stepped back.

'Good. Then I think we are done here.' The official stamped the manifest, shot a last glance at the crate and calmly walked away.

'Okay, seal it up and let's get on with it,' the American instructed. As the forklift fired up and went back to work, he made one last count. 'Fifty-six,' he confirmed in his head.

Taking out his phone, he dialled an international number and waited as it rang. When the line connected, there was no hello, just the sound of someone breathing very slowly.

'The cargo is here and all accounted for,' he delivered his update. 'Is our man ready?'

A brief pause, then: 'Good. Make sure it gets intercepted as planned and delivered to our friends. Also, retire the good Samaritan. Is that clear?' The voice was monotonic, showing no excitement or satisfaction. But he knew it was typical of Johnson, his boss, an ice-cold operative.

'I will make contact with our asset and make sure it's arranged. The cargo will be delivered as promised. Anything else?' He paused, waiting for a reply.

The click of the phone told him the conversation was over. He dialled a second number. It barely rang before it was answered.

'It's me. Retire the Samaritan. Do it now and retrieve the payment, okay?' With that, he hung up and melted back into the shadows.

Abdul Kafka placed the key in the lock of the safety deposit box—it needed a slight push to see it home—and turned the key. Sliding out the inner steel box, he placed it carefully on the table behind him. The helpful bank officer who had accompanied him down to the vault nodded and left.

Abdul sat almost motionless for a few seconds, allowing his anxiety to settle. His fingers lightly tapped the box. Breaking the law was not a normal thing for him. He had spent 20 years as an obedient official, stopping those of a less scrupulous nature from smuggling arms and drugs.

Years of abuse from those he worked with had slowly shredded his character. His honesty, it seemed, had resulted in him being ostracised from the clique of customs officials who took bribes to fund their mistresses and expensive cars. Years of struggle had slowly eaten away at him. His plain apartment and humble lifestyle were now like a burning cross upon his shoulders.

His only luxury, his only guilt, was the occasional prostitute. He enjoyed the domination; it made him feel secure.

As with most weaknesses, someone will exploit it. The surprise offer of a very large payday was more than enough to crush his wavering morals. Perhaps that was why they chose him—they knew he would not be greedy. But everyone has a price.

Finally, he raised the lid of the box and peered in. It was empty, apart from a black velvet pouch. He opened the pouch and tipped out the contents. His eyes widened and a big smile formed across his face. His retirement from being an abused customs official was now assured. The heap of uncut diamonds he was looking at was enough to satisfy his needs for a long time to come.

He scooped them up and placed them back in the pouch, then got up and hurriedly left. The walk home was not at his normal casual pace; it was brisk, almost frantic. He felt vulnerable carrying such wealth. He started to sweat as he moved faster and faster through the narrow lanes leading to his home.

Trying to calm himself down, he turned his mind to more practical thoughts. He had an appointment first thing in the morning. One of his colleagues had given him the name of a reliable fence, one that could shift anything for a price. Turning the corner into a street lined with two-storey walk-up apartments, he bumped into a well-built man dressed in a dark suit.

'Sorry,' came his swift apology.

He could feel his heart racing, his entire body shaking. Pushing his way past, he continued on the last few yards. He fumbled for his key and placed it in the lock. 'Take it easy,' he told himself, trying to steady his hands. He unlocked the battered white gate, slid it back and stepped inside.

A wave of fear suddenly came over him. He quickly felt the inside of his left pocket and breathed with relief when his fingers touched the velvet pouch. For a split second, he had thought about the collision with the stranger. The streets around his home were notorious for thieves.

Not wanting to waste any more time, he hurriedly climbed the flight of steps leading up from the street to his apartment. He was starting to panic again as he placed the key in the lock and turned it.

The thud of a suppressed Ruger 9mm momentarily hung in the air. The force of the near point-blank round slammed Abdul against the door, then his limp body fell to the floor. Blood and brain matter coloured the walls. The second tap made sure he was dead.

The stranger in the dark suit retrieved the velvet pouch. Looking down at the body, he felt nothing, his hands still steady as he placed the Ruger back inside the holster under his arm. He was no amateur, after all; death was his trade.

Descending the stairs, he carefully closed the gate behind him. Hearing it lock, he slowly walked off, as if nothing had happened. His mind was now on meeting up with his employer.

———

Kevin noticed his dog go completely rigid for a second, its ears pricked up. Then it barked and frantically wagged its tail, before taking off across the wet sand.

'A strong scent must have grabbed his attention,' Kevin thought. 'Blue! Come here, Blue!' he shouted after the dog.

His calls were ignored. Blue disappeared over the rocks.

When Kevin scrambled up the slippery surface moments later, he found Blue yelping as a few pincer crabs nipped at him, forcing him back.

'Come on, boy. Here.' Kevin clipped back the lead and held Blue firmly. He could feel the dog straining on the lead.

As he looked around, he saw the waves washing over the smooth rocks that edged the pool and broad strips of reddish seaweed drifting gracefully in and out with the tide. He knew rock pools were always fascinating environments for a dog to explore; they often teemed with vibrant marine life trapped by the retreating tide.

His attention was drawn to the unusual number of pincer crabs that were scuttling around. Kneeling down for a closer look, he gently pushed aside a few strips of seaweed with his hand and instantly felt himself retch. A pungent smell shot into his nostrils and brought the bile up his throat. It was as if he had stirred up a pot of putrid soup.

Standing bolt upright, holding a hand to his mouth, he stared in horror at the tattered decaying human carcass that had bobbed up, distinctly bloated and black from the weeks it must have spent drifting at sea. Large chunks of the torso appeared to have been ripped off; there were no signs of the left arm and lower legs.

'Sharks,' Kevin thought.

A wave suddenly broke over the pool, causing him to step back as the body rolled over. He could now see the vacant eye sockets; the eyes had been removed by the crabs. The victim's right arm moved up and down as the tide lapped in and out of the shallow pool. The tattoo of a red devil and the number '6' was just visible on the blotchy skin.

Kevin felt the bile rising again and vomitted into the pool. He had visited the Sadha bay many times since arriving in Oman as a green expatriate, but he had never seen this.

Pulling the lead, he slid back down the rocks with Blue and started to run.

FIVE

July 2009. Singapore.

Twenty-eight-year-old Brit Daniel Spencer was on the phone. He was, after all, a 'rock star' commodities trader and being on the phone was what got him paid. His ego matched his oversized six-figure bonus, which seemed to get even bigger each year. He lived to make money, a fact his employer, the prestigious Burrows & Co bank, liked, of course.

Flinging himself back into his expensive ergonomic chair, he vigorously rubbed his face with his hands, trying to wipe away his frustration. He was annoyed at having wasted the best part of an hour with a bombastic client, who in the end had failed to close the US$50 million deal. Worst of all, he realised as he shot a glance at one of the many world clocks on the wall, it was still only 8:00 a.m.

He let out a sigh and allowed his attention to drift for a moment to the abnormal levels of chatter in the dealing room—chatter he had tried to ignore for the past hour.

Feeling a little more relaxed now, he mused at the banter running around the dealing room. It was like a bad attack of the shits, having caused the same level of distraction.

He noted that it was for once not entirely focused on the state of the world's markets or how Arsenal had indeed fared against Manchester United in the premier league. His eyes scanned the desks around him; to his surprise, most of the morning cups of bland, low-fat, foamless, mass-produced coffee were still untouched. Groups of noisy traders were huddled like old women around a few computer screens.

Listening intently, Daniel detected a distinct sarcasm and pure corporate arse-kissing in the chatter. He realised then that he had no idea what it was really about.

'Chris, what's the fuss all about, matey?' he asked.

'Blimy, mate, have you had your head up your arse for the past hour?' Chris quipped and turned back to his own screen.

'Haha. Seriously, what?' Daniel now felt he was missing out on something big.

'Internal announcement about Crick,' Chris fired back.

'Crick. What, has he quit or something?' Daniel was still not grasping the issue.

'No, you daft sod! David Crick, our long-standing chairman, has been knighted by none other than the fucking queen!' Chris replied in his best fake plummy British accent. Chris was a hard-nosed Aussie and he found it all highly amusing.

'God, they must be desperate!' Daniel said, sitting bolt upright in his chair. Turning to his own computer and scanning the vast number of unread emails in his inbox, he opened up the email regarding Crick. His eyes scanned for the reason behind Crick's sudden blessing from the queen. Daniel was, in fact, a staunch royalist.

As he read, it seemed Crick's sudden rise up the ladder of social standing was a reward for having expanded this most prestigious of British banks from its humble beginnings in London across Europe and then Asia, Africa and the Middle East. Daniel found it interesting that the article seemed to suggest Crick possessed some kind of Midas touch. Daniel smiled to himself, knowing as everyone did that the truth was far more basic: his wife was connected in the right political circles to some second cousin of someone with the title 'Lord' in his name. It was that simple.

'Mate, take a look at this.' Chris gestured for Daniel to come over.

There, in full colour on the computer screen now being tapped by one of Chris's sausage-like fingers, was a picture of the proud new knight of the realm in his top hat and tails, accompanied by his rather plain-looking wife, Pauline. The picture had been emailed to every employee within the bank's 56 global offices.

'What the fuck is she wearing?' Chris bellowed, drawing more traders around him.

Daniel smiled. Pauline was turned out in a rather heinous floral dress and bright red lipstick, with a disastrous floral hat to top it off.

'Where was that taken?' Barry, a yank with toxic breath, commented.

Daniel turned and looked at him in disgust. 'Clearly, that is outside of Buckingham Palace, you prat,' Daniel spat.

'Well, so much for his so-called Midas touch. Where was it when he married that monster? Bush pig in lipstick is what we Aussies would call that,' Chris joked.

'Easy, mate!' Daniel shot Chris a look. But he well knew the standing joke on the dealing room floor was that, if Greenpeace ever found Mrs. Crick on a sandy beach, they would immediately feed her fish and push her back out to sea.

Daniel wheeled his chair over the few feet back to his desk. 'What do I care about Crick and the fact he's been touched by the royal sword?' he thought.

His eyes darted around his computer screen, taking in the rows of finite information displayed in red, green and yellow. 'The markets are in a shit state.' Gold prices were tanking right before his eyes.

It hit him then just how important money was to him. He knew he had a massive overdraft to pay off. A chill ran down his spine and caused him to shiver as he thought of how much control money had over his life.

'Bloody hell, it's become my fucking life force, my oxygen and, by definition, my ruthless mistress,' he muttered. It made Chris look over.

'You okay, mate?'

'Yeah, just some days I hate myself.' Daniel carried on staring at his screen, his fingers drumming on his desk in frustration.

Leaning hard back in his chair, his favourite position when stressed out, he felt the chaos around him slowly fade away as the image of his parents appeared clearly in his mind. He recalled getting the news over the phone from some nobody at the British consulate. It was a Thursday morning. The man's tone seemed overly cold, he had thought.

'Mr. Spencer, we have to inform you that your parents have been killed in a yachting accident. You will be contacted with regards to identifying the bodies. We are sorry, Mr. Spencer.' Just that and a few questions to confirm his identity.

The recollection of the bitter memory made him jerk upright in his chair, then slump back down again.

It still made no sense to him. They had been killed almost two years ago, whilst on a yachting holiday in the Seychelles, by so-called pirates. 'Hardly an accident,' he thought.

Worst of all, they still hadn't captured the men who had done it. And, for what, a few quid and his father's gold Rolex. His fists clenched in anger, then thumped hard on the arms of his chair. 'What harm could my father have done anyone?' he thought. 'He was a retired banker.' His mind was spinning. He could feel the blood rushing to his face.

Daniel knew he was, in many ways, a carbon copy of his father. Ever since he could walk, he had looked up to his father and observed his skill at making money and excelling at sport. He recalled watching his father playing cricket on the lawns of Oxford in the summer, sailing his yacht to France and playing rugby for his old Etonian veterans. He marvelled at his father's effortless fitness and ability to always have time for him.

He still felt the loss. It then occurred to him that maybe this was why he had overdosed on work and junked up on sports. Maybe this was why he didn't care if his love of extreme sports killed him. His life was empty without his father's presence.

Daniel then felt a warmth flooding through him. He could almost feel his mother's presence. He missed her gentle nature and how she always made sure he was well looked after.

Daniel's fair hair, blue eyes, charismatic charm and athletic body, honed to perfection by years of extreme sports, made him popular, a fact he made sure he capitalised on.

He jumped as his phone buzzed. He picked it up.

'Burrows. Spencer here.' It was one of his best clients.

'No! I can't give you anymore. You either accept the price I gave you earlier or I close.' Daniel was firm. He stood up suddenly and paced around his desk. Standing up whilst negotiating made him feel assured and strong, more in control. At least that's what the book on assertive selling said, and it seemed to work.

His eyes followed every one of the 25 minutes that passed on the clock. He had tried to hold his ground on the deal for palladium, one of the many precious metals he traded for the bank. Sitting down, his face tight and showing his frustration, he eased back into the chair. Then, he rubbed his face with his hands and hung up.

'Fuck him,' he said.

It had been a really shit day. If he got fired, so be it. He already knew his commission would be zero today.

Daniel squinted as he stepped out of the office and into the evening light. His head was pounding and he felt like his eyeballs were about to explode. The nauseating phone calls and childish banter he had endured all day had gotten to him. As he walked sluggishly along the river, he knew the cure. He needed a stiff drink, and badly.

A few minutes later, he was outside BQ Bar, a bar he liked, given it was favoured by the banking set and he met many of his clients there. He didn't need much self-persuasion. He ambled inside.

The man seated outside with his legs crossed and nursing a bottle of beer had seen Daniel arrive. Not that he knew him, but he knew the type well enough. To him, Daniel may as well have had the words 'depressed banker' written across his sorrowful forehead. His body language screamed despair and frustration. Daniel was perfect in every way for what he wanted.

'Double shot of gin and easy on the tonic,' Daniel politely instructed the barmaid as he settled himself on one of the many bar stools.

He held the ice-cold glass against his forehead and immediately felt better. He saw that he was not alone. At least eight other poor souls akin to his own sat around, drowning their sorrows.

Sipping his gin, Daniel knew he only had half an hour of silent contemplation. After that, the bar would be a heaving mass of bankers, brokers and young females out for the night, all looking to get lucky. As his eyes wandered, his gaze stopped on Janette Peters. She was being chatted up by a young suit with a thin face and cheap shoes.

Daniel liked Janette. His eyes locked on her long legs and worked their way right up to her chest, pausing for a few seconds before continuing up, past her delicate freckles to her pouting red lips and matching hair.

'Red heads, sexy as,' he thought.

He recalled the less than flattering rumour about her that ran around the dealing room more often than it should—that she could make a dead man come in his pants with just a look. He felt the beginnings of an erection in his trousers as he continued ogling, but the sobering thought that he had tried his luck with Janette many times, only to be dismissed as too young and too flashy, stopped his growing penis. He knew she preferred older, more mature men. He quickly turned back to his gin and pondered what to do next.

'Bad day?' a voice said.

Daniel spun around with a start, not recognising the voice and having stared at the slice of lemon floating in his gin for far too long.

'Yeah, totally shit day. Still, this will help.' Daniel drained his glass in one gulp and indicated to the barmaid to get him another.

'Well, it can only get better. John Thirway.' Thirway held out his hand. Daniel hesitated, taking his time to size the guy up before extending his own hand in return .

'Daniel, Daniel Spencer. Nice to meet you, John.'

'Likewise, Danny. In the banking game, are you?' Thirway enquired, his body now turned towards Daniel.

'Yes, I am. That obvious, is it? And I prefer Daniel to Danny, if you don't mind.' He didn't appreciate being called Danny, especially by a complete stranger.

'No offence, mate,' Thirway replied, not really caring if he had caused any.

'Cool. So, what is it you do then, John, if not banking?' Daniel thought he would engage in polite chitchat. He took another large gulp of his refreshed gin. The drinks were sliding down way too easy and, as he had not yet eaten, he was feeling the effects.

'I run my own company, Force12,' Thirway proclaimed with a big smile on his face.

John Lucas Thirway was in his mid-40s, 6 feet tall and well-built, with tanned skin, dark brown close-cropped hair and green eyes. He had spent almost his entire career with the British Armed Forces, including 18 years as a Royal Marine Commando. After his retirement, he spent five years as an active mercenary, fighting other people's wars in Africa and the Middle East.

He now owned a part share in a private military corporation, which these days meant a bunch of mercenaries who disguised their special services with a polished corporate image and suits. The company made Thirway a cool million a year, such was the demand for his skills, which covered anything from executive protection to guarding a compound in Kabul. Thirway himself still engaged in fieldwork; he loved the buzz and the danger that made him feel alive.

'Force12?' Daniel enquired.

'We offer typically military-style services, close protection, the provision of a private army, if you like,' Thirway explained proudly.

'Cool, mercenaries!' Daniel's face lit up, now interested in the conversation. He had once considered an army career, after playing soldiers with a local branch of the Territorial Army near his home in Sussex, but stuck to his strategy and followed his father into the world of high finance.

'I was in the SAS myself,' Daniel proudly announced, sitting up straight with a cheeky grin on his face.

Thirway looked somewhat doubtfully at Daniel. 'Oh yeah?' he challenged.

'Yes! Saturdays and Sundays. Queen's own territorial regiment,' Daniel responded, now laughing his head off. With that, even Thirway laughed.

'That's funny, I like that.'

'Well, since coming out to Asia, I'm into all things extreme,' Daniel continued. 'That's how I get my kicks now. Hey, can I get you a drink?'

'Thanks, a pint of Heineken.' Thirway paused. 'Extreme. What do you call extreme?'

'Kiteboarding, rock climbing, fast motor bikes, that kind of stuff,' Daniel said.

Thirway was now looking intently at Daniel with somewhat of a frown on his face. 'Son, you have no idea what extreme is. I wouldn't want to scare you.' Thirway turned away and took hold of his pint.

Daniel was slightly taken aback by Thirway's brazen comment. He wanted to probe.

'Well, you tell me, then, what makes your definition of extreme?'

'Let's just say it may be out of your league, Daniel, no offence.' With that, Thirway sculled his beer and thumped the glass hard down on the bar, as if to emphasise the point.

'That's a bit bold, matey.' Daniel sounded annoyed, feeling judged.

'Listen, I have to run now, but if you're interested in something way beyond anything you've ever done, meet me here tomorrow, same time. But there is a catch.' Thirway stood up and looked at Daniel intently.

'What's the catch?' Daniel asked.

'You will need a hundred grand in cash,' Thirway said, deadpan.

'Ha, you're having a laugh, mate. Hundred grand, no way.' Daniel almost fell off his stool.

'I told you it was out of your league, but you did ask.' With that, Thirway started to walk out.

Daniel paused, thinking, then spun around on his stool. 'John, hang on. Okay, I'm intrigued. See you here tomorrow, but… well… can you give me a bit more of a clue?'

Thirway looked back with a wry smile. 'Put it like this, Daniel. You will never ever experience anything like this in your entire life. The extreme of extremes, a life-changing opportunity, Daniel.'

Thirway then walked off, still smiling to himself. He loved reeling in rich young kids who thought they knew what life was all about. To him, it was another hundred grand in his pocket. But he knew Daniel was just what his business partner, Stone, wanted.

———

After four more gins, Daniel staggered home along the river towards his condominium in the plush Marina Bay area. His head was full of thoughts, trying to work out what Thirway had on offer at such a heavy price tag. His fear was drugs, which was a no-go for him.

It was almost midnight, far too late to be out on a Tuesday. As he waited to cross the street, he remembered his close friend Michael, a 26-year-old foreign exchange trader in the prime of his life before he died of a heart attack caused by a cocaine overdose. Michael had been found dead in his hotel room, face down in a pool of vomit, while on an extended business trip in Tokyo. It seemed he had lost a few million dollars in a bad deal that day and needed a release—one that only a few snorts of cocaine could give him.

By the time he got home, Daniel was convinced Thirway had nothing to offer other than trouble and, with a price tag of a hundred grand, it could only be big trouble. After brushing his teeth, a nightly ritual no matter how late or how drunk he was, he climbed into bed.

Staring up at the ceiling, his expression vacant, he thought one thing was for sure: he needed an extreme adrenaline rush. It had been too long. As he turned over, the phone rang on the side table. He reached out and picked it up.

'Hello,' Daniel muttered, not bothering to check the number on the phone's display.

'It's me, Alexis. How are you, babe? Still awake, I see.' She sounded bubbly.

Alexis worked for the same bank as Daniel, although her father had wanted her to join the family business, promising her a director's position and a million-dollar salary. Intelligent and razor-sharp, the 33-year-old had risen to become one of the bank's top trade finance saleswomen.

Her father, Christos Pathos, was a Cypriot shipping tycoon. His net worth, according to Forbes, was estimated at US$10.8 billion. The Pathos estate, consisting of a fleet of luxury yachts and oil tankers and the odd hotel, had been painstakingly built up over two generations. Her mother, after whom she was named, had died of breast cancer when she was seven.

Not only was Alexis heir to a fortune, she was also stunningly beautiful, blessed with long curly brown hair, olive skin, green eyes and a trim physique. Needless to say, she was highly eligible and no stranger to the advances of rich playboys and film stars. Despite all of this, she was happy to play with Daniel, at least for now. The two had met at the company's Christmas drinks. Daniel launched his attack and won her over with his boyish looks, actor's charm and sharp wit.

Her father never interfered, but he strongly disapproved of Alexis hanging around with men he considered losers. He wanted better for her. Alexis, however, played the field, and her boss, a mysterious man, was the man who really amused her now. Daniel was nothing more than cover.

'Hi babe, just got into bed. Had a few drinks after work. Bad day, in fact.' Daniel slid down under his sheets and held the phone close to his ear.

'Oh, sorry to hear that. Hey, I'm back in town. Let's have dinner,' Alexis said.

'Sure,' Daniel replied, not really wanting to talk.

'Okay, so other than that, a dull day, then?' Alexis tried to engage him.

'Yeah dull, other than some weirdo I met in the bar. I think he was selling drugs or something. He claimed to run some kind of security company, Force12, or something like that. Anyway, best I get some rest. I'm knackered.'

'Oh, okay, goodnight then,' Alexis said and then hung up.

Placing her phone back into her expensive Prada bag, Alexis stood up and bid her companion goodnight with a passionate kiss on the lips.

'Who was that?' he asked.

Alexis looked back at him, her green eyes wide open. 'Oh, just a guy I see now and then. Don't worry, he acts as cover for us. If we get caught, I can get fired. You are my boss, after all.' Alexis gave him a cheeky smile.

'He works for us?'

'Yes, Daniel is one of our best dealers. Daniel Spencer. Really, he's harmless.' Alexis frowned at the inquisition.

'Sounds like he had a bad day. What happened?' he mused, then placed his arms around her, pulling her close. Alexis could feel his excitement pressing into her.

'Yeah, just some weirdo who runs a security firm bothering him. Nothing, I'm sure. Hey, see you tomorrow. We can finalise that deal you wanted me to work on, yeah?' Alexis smiled, pulled away gently and started to walk off sexily towards the lift.

'Hey, sorry, just out of interest, did Daniel mention whom he spoke to?' His eyes were now more intense.

Alexis turned slightly. 'Oh, Force12 or something like that. Why on earth would you want to know that?' She was puzzled at his question.

'No real reason. May be useful for the bank, that's all. I hear they are looking for security guys. Night then.' He sat back down and watched her walk off. He knew his line of questioning had gone as far as it could for now. He picked up his phone and dialled a number.

'Stone,' came the blunt reply.

'It's me. Find out what you can about a guy named Daniel Spencer. Seems your man Thirway is up to his old tricks. It may just serve a purpose for us.' All he got in reply was a mere acknowledgement.

Sitting back in his chair, he smiled to himself. Alexis and her toy boy had suddenly become of much more use to him.

———

Daniel was pleased to hear the loud ringing tones. It meant the markets were busy, so it was a far better day. He could hopefully make money and that, in his world, was a very good thing. He picked up call after call; he was on fire. The market had edged in his favour and it seemed every client wanted to deal his way.

'Burrows, Spencer,' he said in his normal polite but blunt tone. His standard greeting came automatically to him now. He repeated it many more times that day than any other day.

When the market closed four hours later, Daniel smiled like a cat with the cream.

'Eat my shit, Chris. I just made fifty grand today.'

'Good for you, posh boy,' Chris replied. His haul had not been as good.

Daniel stood up and switched off his computer, taking in the buzz around him. The dealing room had had a good day and that made him feel alive.

As he headed towards the bar, his mind started to focus on the meeting he was about to have with Thirway. Were his instincts correct? That the only thing Thirway had to offer was drugs? Reaching the bar, he stopped outside and settled himself, wanting to appear cool. Then, he walked in like a proud peacock.

———

It was almost 7:00 p.m. Daniel had eased down three double gin and tonics and was in desperate need of food. Getting up, his head somewhat light, he turned towards the door. Just then, Thirway appeared at his side, as if placed there by some form of teleportation.

'So, intrigue got the better of you, did it, Daniel?' Thirway said with a wry smile.

'You think? This is my local, so I may just be here for other reasons,' Daniel retorted. Thirway's cocky assumption had slightly jarred him.

'Good for you.' Thirway had noted Daniel's tone and eased himself up to the bar next to him. Daniel shot down the last of his gin, took a deep breath and then turned to face Thirway.

'Listen, John, I should say now. Drugs don't do it for me so …'

'Drugs! No, you have me all wrong. What I have to offer is way beyond that shit,' Thirway said, moving closer to Daniel so as to keep his voice low.

Daniel now felt somewhat perplexed. 'Oh! Go on, then, I'm all ears.'

'Okay, listen up. I will make this offer only once. If you say no, I'll respect that, but you only get one chance. Is that understood?' Thirway was now more serious.

Not really knowing how to respond, Daniel simply replied, 'Okay, agreed.'

'I can offer you an exclusive membership to a club, Daniel. A club so exclusive there are only six members at any one time,' Thirway explained.

'Club?' Daniel blurted out, looking decidedly unimpressed. 'I have more club memberships than I can shake a stick at, John.'

'You done? I said listen. This club is special.' Thirway's eyes bore down on him.

'Okay, well, tell me more then.' Daniel was impatient and wanted to get to the point. So far, the offer of another club membership did nothing to excite him.

'I run a club known as Deep Six. It's an exclusive club, Daniel, and I mean exclusive. A hundred grand gets you in and the opportunity of a lifetime. A spot has suddenly opened up. It's yours, if you want it.' Thirway paused and studied Daniel's face to try and work out his reaction.

Daniel played with his glass, turning it round and round. After a few moments, he asked, almost annoyed: 'What, is that it? You can't expect me to just hand over a hundred grand and not know what I'm getting?'

'Not asking you to. I am asking if you have a banker's draft or cold hard cash in local currency ready, to prove you are in the right league and not wasting my time. I will then tell you exactly what you get for your money and you decide on the spot. It is that simple.' Thirway patted Daniel on the shoulder and handed him his business card.

'Call me when you are ready, if you ever are.' Then he turned and left as quickly as he had appeared.

Daniel remained at the bar, wondering what on earth it was that Thirway was offering. He was intrigued. He studied the business card Thirway had handed him. It read: 'John Thirway, CEO, Force12 Security Services'. An email address and a phone number were printed on the bottom left corner.

Dismissing the idea for now, Daniel gestured to the barmaid to put his bill on his tab, placed the card in his wallet and headed home.

The rather sallow-looking bank teller dressed in a navy blue uniform that appeared way too small for her frame seemed to be on a go slow. Five minutes had passed already and Daniel was in a hurry. As her fingers tapped away slowly at the keyboard in front of her, Daniel tutted, willing her to speed up. She checked and rechecked every detail before finally handing Daniel the banker's draft. She didn't even smile as Daniel thanked her and left.

As he headed for the door, examining the draft made out to John Thirway, he started feeling stupid. The words 'One hundred thousand dollars only' were printed on it. Exiting through the large glass doors of the branch, he paused on the steps and took out his phone. He found Thirway's number and hit 'call'. After a few rings, a female voice greeted him: 'Good morning. Force12. How may I direct your call?'

'Yes, hi, John Thirway, please.' Daniel waited to be connected. After what seemed like ages, the woman came back on the line. 'I'm sorry, sir, but he is engaged. Can I take a message?'

Daniel was slightly disappointed. 'Yes, can you tell him that Daniel Spencer called and that I will be at BQ Bar around six this evening, should he want to meet? Thanks.' He hung up.

Entering BQ Bar, Daniel pushed his way through the heaving mass of bodies to get to the bar.

'Hello, Daniel! How are you?' One of his clients had spotted him.

'Yeah, good, mate. Bit busy, yeah?' he shouted back above the noise.

'Well, the markets are beginning to play again, so I guess everyone is celebrating.'

Thirway arrived at 6:00 p.m., bang on time, dressed in a pair of fawn-coloured shorts, a grey T-shirt and black flip-flops. Daniel was dressed far more formally in a Ted Baker shirt and navy blue trousers. From his seat at the end of the bar, he watched Thirway walk in, taken aback slightly by his casual appearance. He didn't comment though.

'So, John, here is my draft, as requested. It seems I am in your league, after all.' Daniel beamed and waved the draft around, feeling very cocky indeed.

Thirway looked at him, not reacting to Daniel's showing off. 'Good evening, Daniel. That kind of cocky behaviour in my game will get you dead.'

Daniel's smile vanished. He realised Thirway had a point.

'Now, if you have finished fluffing up your feathers, down to business. But before I accept your money, let me ask you, are you prepared to gamble with your life? If you ever divulge to another soul the code of Deep Six, you will find yourself in very deep shit, probably dead.' Thirway was very serious and he certainly had Daniel's attention; the latter's jaw dropped and he looked very alarmed.

'Wow, that all sounds a bit strong!'

'Well, if you hand me that money, Daniel, you will have to agree. Let me give you a taster of what you get.' Thirway finally sat himself down next to Daniel and waved for two beers.

'Twenty-three ocean-going vessels, mainly cargo ships and oil tankers, get hijacked each year. Many of them, Daniel, get taken right out there in the South China Sea.' Thirway pointed in the direction of Indonesia.

'One of the worst areas is off Somalia, in the Gulf of Aden. Those waters are infested with more than sharks—pirates, in fact. No, not pirates with eye patches and wooden legs. These guys carry automatic weapons or rusty old knives to slice your ears off.' Thirway then sat back and took a swig of the cold beer now in front of him.

'You okay, Daniel?' he asked, seeing that Daniel had turned white, his eyes looking blankly at him.

'Yeah, I'm fine,' Daniel lied.

'You watch movies, right? Action movies? Ever wonder what it would be like to shoot someone? Play judge and jury, pretend to be an assassin?' Thirway looked even more intense. He sat back, enjoying baiting Daniel.

'Deep Six can offer you just that experience, Daniel. We can place you on board a cargo ship bound for Somali waters. You will be trained by the best and armed with a state-of-the-art sniper rifle. You will have the opportunity to shoot any number of these bastards, none of whom the world will miss. You will also be assured of not being arrested for it; no one will ever know. Just accept the danger, put yourself in harm's way, Daniel. Now, that is extreme, my friend.' Thirway smiled.

Daniel sat frozen to his stool, his eyes and mouth wide open. After a couple of minutes and a few swigs of his beer, Daniel looked up at Thirway. 'Kill, you mean assassinate, no comebacks at all. I can really do that?' Daniel spat out, almost choking on his words.

'In short, yes, Daniel. You get to slot pirates,' Thirway responded and then paused. 'You would be doing the world a favour. No one cares, not even the navy. They may even thank you for doing their job,' Thirway finished his pitch.

Daniel sat motionless for a few moments, his face showing a mixture of bewilderment and excitement. It was as if he had been given the opportunity to avenge something. He slowly stretched out his hand, trembling; in it was the banker's draft.

'I'm in, no question about it. Bloody hell, I'm in.' Daniel then picked up his beer, toasted Thirway and sculled it down.

SIX

July 2009. Singapore / Sepang, Malaysia.

Having completed his personal regimen of calisthenics, which included a hundred push-ups, Mark McCabe took a long cold shower, pulled on his last pair of clean blue jeans and his favourite grey T-shirt, and headed for the door. He finger-combed his hair into his normal messy style as he walked off with purpose. It was his style; he very rarely ambled.

After 30 minutes of walking, he could feel the sweat running down his back. His T-shirt was soaked through. The 5-kilometre brisk walk in the humid heat had done him some good.

As he rounded the point, the plush beachside condominium loomed up in front of him. In his view, it was a statement of affluence. Despite the large hole it made in his wallet, it made Kelly, his ex-wife, happy. That meant he was, too.

Pausing for just a few seconds, he looked up and pinged the sixth-floor balcony. He could see a white towel draped over the rail. He smiled, recognising his daughter's secret sign that she was by the pool, should he suddenly want to drop by. Today, he did, and he knew that would please her very much. He strode off up the path.

The former SAS officer-turned-banker was now, in the words of HR, officially outplaced. 'Fired,' McCabe thought, 'fired with honey-coated benefits.' The payoff was enough to soften the edge, not that he really cared. At least, he felt alive now. He did muse at the irony of it all, though. He had saved the bank from massive fraud and national embarrassment but had in the process exposed his own true identity. It seemed the bank didn't want someone with his skills on the books.

Joy, the kind that makes you feel all gooey inside, was a feeling McCabe did not allow enough of in his life. Sitting relaxed on the grass, feeling the sun's warmth on his back and watching his daughter swim, he realised how simple, in fact, it was to feel it. He observed every movement she made—the smoothness of her strokes, the well-practised turns and the bursts of speed—as she tore down the pool. He loved it!

Seeing her athletic prowess, he realised just how much of her growing years he had missed. Just a few hours spent with her was like a gunshot in his head, shocking him back to reality, waking him up to the fact that he had been asleep for far too long.

He lay back and stretched his limbs, letting the sun's rays warm his face. He could smell the sea breeze as it blew in across the pool and over him, cooling his skin. He felt for once completely relaxed.

'Grown up, hasn't she?' It was a voice he knew better than his own.

Slowly opening one eye, he looked up at Kelly. 'She has indeed.'

'So, now you are a gentleman of leisure, what are you going to do with yourself? I hope you are done with chasing bad guys.' Kelly sat down next to him and crossed her legs.

'You mean ex-wives care about such things?' There was a touch of sarcasm in his voice.

'No, but I do care about her,' Kelly replied, looking at Elizabeth, 'and she loves you. She needs to know you will be around.'

Kelly had a knack of making a point without showing she cared at all, when actually she did.

'That last jaunt of yours nearly got you killed. Look what happened to Brian. I can't sit by and let you risk her happiness.' Kelly had a hint of fire in her eyes.

McCabe sat up. 'Would you rather I die of boredom?' he spat out. Any mention of Brian made him overly sensitive.

'Yes, if it means you are safe.' Kelly poked him hard in the shoulder and smiled. She knew well enough not to rile him too much.

'Speaking of boredom, how is that bald boyfriend of yours, anyway?' McCabe asked cheekily.

'He is fine and don't change the subject.'

'Kelly, I am who I am. If I stop being me, I may as well be dead.' McCabe said, more to convince himself. 'I love that girl, you know that.'

'You two okay?' Elizabeth was out of the pool.

'Yes babe, just talking to your wayward father, trying to get some sense into his thick head.' Kelly shot a fake angry look. Despite her frustration, she still loved him.

'Good luck.' Elizabeth smiled and shot a wink at her father.

'Yeah yeah, anyway, must be off. Meeting Mooney at the airport. Heading to Malaysia tomorrow.' McCabe kissed both of them on the cheeks, then sauntered off.

Kelly watched as he went. 'Mooney,' she thought, knowing that name spelled trouble.

———

He kicked down into third gear and felt the engine ease the bike back. He could hear the throaty groan from the bike's carbon fibre exhaust, a sound he loved; it was distinctly Ducati.

McCabe loved to get out on his bike. It allowed him to test his limits and blow off some steam, aside from mitigating his mid-life crisis. Track racing was marginally safer than riding on the roads, so whenever he could he came up to the Sepang circuit in Malaysia with his best friend, Nick Rogers. Unlike McCabe, Nick had no military background, a point McCabe liked, and it saved him from reminiscing about the old days and talking shit. Nick was a banker, honest, fun and, above all, a good listener. The two had been friends for five years. Nick also had no interest in McCabe's past, other than to sometimes just listen without judging.

He was now approaching the next tight left-hand bend. Dabbing the brakes with his foot, McCabe at the same time tweaked the throttle just enough to re-ignite the engine. Given the sensitivity of the bike, he could feel the broad rear tyre bite the warm tarmac below. As he leaned the bike hard into the corner, it glided around with minimal slippage. Then, shifting his body weight, he sat the bike up in its most aerodynamic position and barrelled up the narrow straight. He took in the streaked images of the crowd as he rocketed past the grandstand.

His heart was pounding in his chest and his warm breath fogged up his helmet visor, as the adrenaline surged through his veins and fuelled his desire to go faster. He was now pushing himself to the limit, increasing the adrenaline flow. He loved the intoxicating effects it had on him.

Kelly's words started rolling around in his head like marbles. But to give up his quest for action was to cease breathing. He wasn't much of a father, he knew that, but he knew who he was. He also knew that, despite his failings, his daughter loved him. There was almost a telepathic connection between the two of them, as if she understood him.

Clearing his head, he glanced at the speedometer. The digital display was rapidly climbing away from 85 miles per hour towards the century. Immediately adjusting his posture, he centralised his seating position to best align the bike. He could feel the brute force of the airflow around him, trying to rip him off the seat.

Turn three was coming up ahead fast, a tight right-hander, which he recalled kicked into a long sweeping left. Within seconds, he had reached the recommended braking point. Sensing the time was right, he dropped down the gears and touched the rear brake, again feeling the bike power down.

Easing himself over to the right, he forced the bike to lean. Then came a heart-stopping twitch as the rear tyre skipped a few inches underneath him. His entire body momentarily tensed up.

McCabe then eased around the turn and flipped the bike back up and then hard over as he prepared for the left-hander. Powering on, he barrelled down the short straight towards turn four. The distinctive growl of the engine echoed around the track.

He felt alive. The sense of freedom was electrifying and he felt in control. It was time to really test his limits; turns nine and 10 would be perfect for that. Just as he throttled up, seeing the digital display climb almost unintelligibly past 140 miles per hour, he felt a sudden blast of air as Nick rocketed past, the rear of his Honda Fireblade now vanishing around turn four.

'You bastard!' McCabe shouted into the inter-bike communication system. All he heard was Nick's heavy breathing coming back at him like a cheap chat line. McCabe knew that Nick was by far the more experienced rider and his fluid style set a high standard for him to reach.

As he navigated turn eight, he could feel the sweat run off his forehead. Then, a sudden burst of adrenaline coursed through his veins. He gripped the throttle and rolled it back, opening up the power; instantly, he felt the kick. Turn nine came into view. It was time to set a new record and this was as good an opportunity as any. As he punched down the gears once again to third, he leaned the bike hard over, his left knee carbon fibre slider block now in contact with the track. This was what he wanted, to finally slide the bike round a turn. He could feel the vibration at his knee.

Within seconds, he pushed down hard on his knee and muscled the bike back up to come out of the turn, tweaking the throttle to boost the power.

No sooner had he done that than he realised he had made a mistake. He had throttled up too much and the rear of the bike started to lift, twitch and skip until it finally slid; nothing could stop it now. McCabe knew he was riding a bucking bronco at 100 miles an hour. All he could do now was try to hang on.

The sudden impact against the tarmac jarred his body and he felt himself tumbling out of control, his limbs flailing helplessly, as he and the Duke slid along the track and finally into the kitty litter, eventually coming to a stop in a cloud of dust and grit.

McCabe could feel himself drifting off now, his mind spinning and his ears ringing. Images of tortured faces began to flit in front of his eyes, as if he were watching some kind of macabre movie of his own past. One face lingered. When its eyes suddenly opened and fixed its gaze on him, it mesmerised and paralysed him as he slipped into complete darkness.

'Would you like to fuck me? Drive a nail through my heart? Or maybe shoot me in the head?' Danny Murphy, a hardened killer and former PIRA marksman, whispered the taunts in McCabe's ear, as McCabe started to recall his worst nightmare.

The biting cold that night was so severe he could feel his skin tighten and begin to freeze. He had been en route back to his hotel along the river—a hotel so basic that even the soap was reused, with tiny hairs stuck on the surface.

It was meant to be a simple observation mission, nothing more than to gather intelligence on Murphy and report back. The spooks at 5 had run out of foot soldiers, so the regiment had been asked to provide someone. McCabe, being free, had been volunteered.

Having spent the day observing Murphy dart suspiciously in and out of shops, cafes and sordid nightclubs, McCabe had called it a day. He had each of the shady people Murphy met safely on camera.

That was as far as he could remember when the bolts of pain jolted him awake. Murphy was a sadistic bastard who enjoyed administering pain, the fallout from a childhood spent kneecapping people with Black & Decker drills for his PIRA lieutenants before progressing to guns. Capturing McCabe on his own, with no backup, pleased him. The old methods were the best; a lead cosh to the back of the head had been enough.

Murphy ran the sharp knife over and over again across McCabe's chest. The blood that ran from the deep cuts collected in a pool on the floor.

McCabe could see nothing but darkness. His lungs were working desperately, trying to take in air through the bag drawn over his head and suffocating him. His hands screamed pain as the six-inch nails that had been driven through his palms into the door ripped bigger holes each time he struggled.

For two days and two nights McCabe faded in and out of consciousness, clinging on for his life. He had been taught how to resist interrogation, but everyone had a breaking point and his was coming dangerously close. He knew his worst enemy was his own mind and tried not to let it turn on him.

At first he thought the loud bangs were a figment of his own imagination, and he was replaying his own training. Only when the combined SAS and Spetsnaz four-man extraction team came in hard and fast did he grasp that they were real. He was lucky that his abduction had been seen by an informer.

McCabe was taken down from the door and laid on the ground. Beside him, he could see Murphy—eyes wide open and the exit wound the single bullet had left in his forehead. McCabe would never forget that face, the blank stare and the cold hard eyes.

Yanking himself up, McCabe opened his eyes and flipped open his scratched visor. The bright orange light that hit his eyes forced him to close them again. Slowly re-opening his eyes, he could make out a sea of faces looking at him, and then Mooney's wide smile came into focus. Never had McCabe been so glad to see that ugly mug. He was indeed a welcome sight.

'You okay, mate?' Mooney was visiting from the UK on a sabbatical from his services to the crown. His voice sounded casual, as if McCabe hadn't just wiped out at well over 100 miles an hour and slid 30 yards across the tarmac. But for Mooney, who was built like a small train himself, that was as sympathetic as he got.

Just then, Nick arrived on his own death rocket and strolled over.

'That's more like it, buddy. Means you were trying harder,' he laughed.

Realising he was in one piece, McCabe tried to get up on his feet, helped by Mooney, who easily heaved him up with one arm. Seeing his now bent Ducati lying in the gravel was perhaps not the best way to end the day. But he felt fortunate to have suffered nothing more than the odd friction burn and a few scratches to his helmet and leathers. He would live to ride another day.

Alexis loved the night view from the lighthouse restaurant on the rooftop of the six-star Fullerton Hotel. It was majestic and, for her, the perfect place for a romantic dinner with Daniel.

A cool gentle breeze from the river carried the fragrance of the orchids that grew in the humidified boxes on the edge of the rooftop. She inhaled and smiled, feeling relaxed.

It was short-lived though.

'Daniel, have you gone completely mad? Have you lost your fucking senses?' Alexis spat out.

Daniel was seated now somewhat uncomfortably across the table, having informed her he was about to shoot pirates—not the average dinner conversation opener.

Alexis sat back and folded her arms, her face showing her shock. Despite the fact that Thirway had sworn him to secrecy, Daniel had to tell someone and Alexis was it.

'I really want to do this, babe. I know it seems odd but it's the adrenaline rush, the pure rush,' Daniel tried his best to explain.

'Daniel, you would be killing someone, or have you overlooked that minor detail?' The intensity in her eyes drove home the point.

'Yes, murderers, men who kill innocent people on yachts and ships,' Daniel fired back, his own temper fuelled by the fact that

Alexis had made him feel very guilty.

Alexis then fell suddenly silent. Daniel saw she was deep in thought. 'What is it, something wrong?'

'Nothing, just a bad memory.' She reached for her glass of wine, a subtle Pinot from Australia, and shot it down her throat. Daniel looked on with surprise; he had never seen her drink so fast.

'Okay, do it, damn it. I'm okay with it,' she replied, now looking at him.

'Really, I can? What...' Daniel started to ask what had changed her mind, but Alexis cut him off.

'Just accept my approval, no questions asked.'

Daniel knew when to quit; it was time to shut up. Alexis reached out and held his hand.

'Do you have the money to pay for this adventure of yours, Daniel? A hundred thousand dollars is a lot of money, even for you. I can ask my father for a loan, tell him it's for me.' Alexis now seemed almost happy at the idea.

'Really? You would lend me the money? I mean, I have it but it would clean me out. I have been spending way too much lately.' Daniel knew that, although he earned very good money, he was flat broke. It was not that uncommon amongst traders.

'Sure, why not? I will be seeing him in London soon; I have to go on business. But on one condition.' She glared at him. Daniel knew the look; it meant she was serious.

'Okay. What is that?' Daniel was cautious, expecting a condition far too big to accept.

'You take me with you.' She then leaned back, as if to say her request was not negotiable.

Daniel sighed and also sat back, his face blank, for once not knowing what to say. He recalled that Thirway had sworn him to silence and that taking a guest was far from an option. He was certainly not looking forward to asking Thirway about this.

'I will have to ask Thirway. He is the organiser,' Daniel blurted out.

'Then ask. Come on, let's go. I'm tired now.' Alexis gestured for the cheque.

SEVEN

Thirway, dressed casually in a light blue shirt and khaki trousers, had seated himself at a small table just inside the doorway of his favourite Australian coffee shop. Given it actually sold coffee that tasted of coffee and not day-old steamed milk, he frequented it often. The remnants of a curry puff and a cappuccino were an indication he had been there for some time.

Daniel arrived at 8:30 a.m. He was, in fact, a half hour late.

'Good morning, Daniel. How are we today?'

Daniel noted the hint of sarcasm. 'I'm good. Sorry I'm late,' he offered his apology all the same and took a seat.

'Okay, never mind, you are here now. We start your training in a few days, not far from here, in fact. Just out there on a secluded island. Something to break you in gently.' Thirway smiled, pointing in the general direction of Indonesia.

'Great,' Daniel replied, not really knowing what he was letting himself in for.

'If you pass the test, next, the gulf. Real action, Daniel! You will be taken on board a cargo vessel. Our course will take us right past Somalia. A member of my team will train you, teach you all he can about being a sniper. You still up for it?' Thirway asked, leaning forward.

Daniel didn't need to think about it. 'Absolutely, John, game on!' He was excited and could not repress it. Then a look of guilt crept over his face. Thirway saw it straightaway.

'What is it? Out with it!' Thirway was no fool. With his many years of training and experience, he could detect a lie or a show of guilt in a second.

'Well… my girlfriend wants to come along. Wait!' Daniel said, before Thirway could shut him out. 'She will pay her way, just to observe, I swear.' He then waited for what he knew would be a less than favourable response. It came within seconds.

'Do you think we are amateurs? That this is a bloody game, a paintball outing for yuppies? I should deal with you right here, right now, damn it!' Thirway thumped the table, his posture threatening and his eyes distinctly angry.

People at the shop shot a glance and then went back to eating their muffins, unaware of and not really caring about the seriousness of the argument that was unfolding.

After a brief pause, Thirway asked, 'Who is she anyway?'

Daniel felt his stomach churning. Thirway looked so intimidating that, for the first time, the weight of what he had signed up for hit him. He took a sip of water and composed himself.

'Alexis Pathos, the daughter of Christos Pathos, the shipping tycoon.' Daniel paused and waited for another barrage.

This time, strangely enough, Thirway said nothing; he just sat there, looking at him, his hands clasped in front of him. Then, after what seemed an eternity, Thirway spoke, this time in a softer tone.

'Tell you what. I will make an exception. Of course, Daniel, bring her along.'

Daniel let out a big sigh, and his entire body suddenly relaxed. 'Oh god, you had me really worried. Thank you so much.' He sat back.

'She will, of course, have to pay her way, not that it would be an issue for a member of the Pathos family. But, like you, she must keep her mouth shut, same deal.' Thirway reverted to a harsher tone.

'So you have heard of her then?' Daniel asked.

'Of course I bloody well have! Have to be stupid not to know who Pathos is, in my game. How did you meet her anyway?' Thirway was intrigued.

'At a bar. She works for the same bank. Something her father insisted on before she could join him, something about proving she could handle a real job. Anyway, you have a deal and my word that she won't say anything.' Daniel proffered his hand.

'No need for your word, Danny. I will have your balls if you fail me. Any Deep Six member who breaks the code of silence is in deep shit,' Thirway explained.

'Sure, understood. Is there some kind of initiation test?' Daniel enquired.

Thirway's face showed amazement at Daniel's question. 'This is not the bloody Masons, Danny, nor do you use a funny handshake and get a membership card,' Thirway fired back. 'Your money is your bond, your life the guarantee, and I'm not joking now.'

'Okay, understood.'

'Oh, but you do get this.' Thirway held out an image of what looked like a devil character.

'Cool, what is that?' Daniel asked.

'That, my boy, is a tattoo. Get it done. It's your badge.' Thirway stood up. 'I will call you in a few days and share with you the final plans. Take care, Danny.' With that, he walked off.

Daniel thought better of correcting Thirway again even if he hated being called Danny. As he started to walk back to his office, he couldn't help but wonder why Thirway had changed his mind so suddenly about Alexis. Whilst Thirway had army training and could smell a lie, Daniel as a trader could equally detect bullshit. He was puzzled, but had no idea why Thirway had suddenly softened his position.

McCabe felt his head throb as he slowly opened his eyes. He squinted to look at his watch on the small bedside cabinet. It was 9:30 a.m. Rolling onto his back, he stared at the ceiling and rubbed his eyes. The memory of yesterday's crash came back. He knew he was lucky to be in one piece; no broken bones and, better still, he felt very much alive.

He dressed and went to the spare room where he saw Mooney sleeping like a baby. He grinned at the sight of his buddy's large frame wedged into such a small single bed; the duvet was half on the floor, half clasped in Mooney's shovel-sized right hand, as if to stop it from falling onto the floor completely.

McCabe slammed a mug of steaming-hot milky tea down on the bedside cabinet and kicked the side of the bed.

'Wake up, fat boy,' McCabe greeted him and pulled back the curtains.

Mooney opened his eyes immediately and sat bolt upright. 'What the fuck?' he proclaimed, his eyes squinting to adjust to the light that suddenly burst into his room.

'Get showered and we can grab some breakfast. I'm starving.' McCabe instructed.

The two eggs over easy, pork sausages, rashers of bacon, mounds of baked beans and toast—and the copious amounts of sweet English Breakfast tea, hit the spot. Mooney sat back and stretched his legs.

'So, how is the shadowy world of MI5? Any work on?' McCabe enquired.

Mooney looked up at him. 'It's ok, just a few close protection jobs for sad politicians and the odd bit of tailing suspected terrorists around London, all of whom turned out to be just normal run-of-the-mill immigrants,' Mooney replied.

'Maybe you and I should start our own firm; we make a good team,' McCabe jested and sipped his tea.

Mooney leaned forward. 'You miss him.'

McCabe knew who he meant. 'Stowe, yeah, I do in a weird way,' McCabe replied, his face showing a trace of sadness.

'What happened to Ying? You still see her?' Mooney grinned, his head now filled with her sexy image.

'Nope, not much. I hear she is okay though.'

'You ever get that CD recovered?'

This question from Mooney took McCabe back to Mumbai.

After that mission, he had retrieved the CD Ying had left with the concierge at the Taj Hotel and headed right back to the airport. There was no reason to stay. As he studied the contents of the CD on his laptop, he immediately realised its value. Rows and rows of names were on it—sleepers within banks, all of whom, by the looks of the information, were in some way cleaning money through trades. Account numbers were listed for each name.

As McCabe scanned the list, he stopped at one name, Aziz. That name needed no introduction. McCabe recalled how the rogue Lebanese salesman had almost pulled off his mammoth money laundering scam. But how many, McCabe wondered, had ended up like Aziz—terminated by the Rain Angel.

Other tabs listed the names of what appeared to be business owners, CEOs and government officials. To McCabe's surprise, the names of CIA and MI5 agents were also listed. No wonder the infamous Rain Angel wanted the CD back.

Bringing the CD back had not been without incident. Whilst relieving himself in the toilet at the airport before his flight, he had been caught off-guard and suddenly felt himself pulled back by a wire cutting into his neck. Instinctively, he had heaved his body backwards twisting slightly, and dropping his body weight to knock his attacker off balance. At the same time, he had kicked his heel hard in the man's shin.

The man had winced in pain and relaxed his grip just enough for McCabe to slip his hand under the nylon wire. Driving his elbow into the man's ribs, McCabe then dropped his weight again; this time, the man stumbled and fell over. In one swift movement, McCabe had spun round, wrapped his arms around the man's neck, arched the man's body upwards and snapped his neck. He then quickly left the washroom and headed for the boarding gate.

'You okay, mate?' Mooney asked, bringing McCabe back to the present.

Rubbing his neck, McCabe finally replied, 'Yes, it's in a safe place. Not interested just yet to explore it.' He swirled the last sausage around his plate, mopping up the mixture of fat, beans and egg with his toast, and finished it off before sitting back and closing his eyes for a moment.

EIGHT

The alarm sent a shock wave through his system. Daniel slowly opened his eyes and tried to focus on the numerals that were flashing ad nauseum at him. With his right hand, he silenced the brain-numbing noise with a thump.

It was 4:00 a.m. He had just 45 minutes to get ready and reach the agreed meeting point. 'Bus stop number 66 on the West Coast Road,' he repeated the address over and over in his head.

As he dried himself off after one of the fastest showers he had ever had, he caught sight of his new tattoo in the mirror. He studied the bright red caricature of a devil with the number '6' in black; swollen, it looked all the more menacing. He smiled to himself, given it symbolised he was now a fully paid-up member of Deep Six.

Pacing up and down the pavement, he checked his watch, then looked up at the white sign above his head; it did indeed read '66'. He could feel his body tingling with an intoxicating mixture of excitement and nervousness in anticipation of the next few hours.

His eyes followed a woman walking her dog. She glared at him as she passed by, surprised to see a Caucasian man standing at a bus stop at such an early hour.

'The Ferrari is in for a service, dear,' he muttered under his breath.

'Don't be upsetting the locals, Daniel.' Thirway stepped out of the shadows.

'Jesus, Thirway, you scared me half to death.'

'Come on, 10 minutes this way.' Thirway marched off up the road.

Daniel followed, until he saw Thirway hold up the flat of his hand. They were, it seemed, now at the entrance of what looked like a private yacht club. Daniel looked in the window of the tiny guard hut. The old security guard was asleep in his chair. It seemed boredom had taken its toll on the old man and he had, judging by the loud snores, long since drifted off.

Thirway noticed a pair of scruffy old brown shoes by the door. He bent down, picked them up and tossed them over a small fence to his left.

'Can't have him running after us,' Thirway whispered.

Daniel couldn't help but feel a bit guilty as he watched the shoes sail over the fence. 'He probably can't afford new shoes,' he snapped. Thirway ignored him.

'Come on, this way.' Thirway waved him over and darted off into the shadows. Daniel followed him down a walkway located to the east side of the main club house. They passed the building and stepped out onto an open section of decking at the rear of the building.

'Shit, it's lit up like a fucking Christmas tree,' Thirway announced and disappeared.

Daniel stood rooted to the spot, taking in the sight of the official dock boundary to his left which was marked by high wire fences and powerful searchlights. An immigration checkpoint stood at one end of a caged walkway, a hundred or so yards onshore.

Suddenly, the lights went out and Daniel found himself in darkness. Thirway appeared moments later. 'That's better,' he said, 'Blew the fuse box. They will need a freaking genius to fix the mess I just made.'

Unfazed by what Thirway had done, Daniel focused on the docks. 'What is that?' he whispered, pointing.

'It's where the workers for the refineries and rigs board the boats out to the islands. Many of them are foreign workers.' It all seemed logical to Daniel now, as he looked at the lines of men in bright orange overalls.

Daniel then observed there was only a narrow expanse of water between the boat ramp at the club and the high fence around the docks, making the club very accessible. 'How did you know about this place?' he asked.

'One of the supply boat owners told me about this weakness. He used to smuggle in cigarettes and booze from Indonesia for me.' Thirway had a sneaky grin on his face. 'You see, every few minutes, boats loaded with supplies and men going to and from the refineries move in and out of this narrow inlet, making it extremely busy and, as such, difficult to observe.'

Daniel could already see lines of boats heading in to collect the waiting men.

'Come on, no time to daydream. We have to move.' Thirway headed off towards the ramp.

Daniel cautiously followed him down the ramp, trying not to slip on the seaweed and slime that covered it. To his left, he could see a long concrete jetty 50 or so yards away. Thirway stopped halfway down and lit a cigarette. Daniel remained silent as he watched Thirway take a few drags and then flick the butt into the water.

The man seated in the wheelhouse of a small blue supply boat next to the jetty also observed this and started to move his boat out and away from the jetty. As the boat started to turn, clouds of thick black diesel smoke billowed out, choking the air.

'We only get one shot at this, Daniel, so don't fuck it up,' Thirway instructed.

Daniel remembered what he was expected to do. He knew that he would have to make a small leap to board the boat, but it bothered him that they had to be so covert. He needed to put that aside for now and concentrate on what he had to do. He pulled himself together fast.

As the stern of the boat swung within a few feet of the boat ramp, Daniel drew a deep breath and leapt forward. Feeling his feet slip on the wet ramp, he braced himself to hit the water, clamping his mouth shut tight to stifle a yell.

Just as his feet touched the water, Thirway grabbed him by the arms. 'I got you,' he said, and hauled Daniel over the side of the boat as if he were nothing more than a rag doll.

'Jesus,' Daniel let out.

'Easy, Daniel, we are not safe yet. Stay down,' Thirway replied, holding Daniel down on the wet, oily deck. With a burst of the throttle and another billowing cloud of thick black diesel smoke, the boat eased away and headed out to sea.

After they passed a large refinery on their right and seeing no sign of a coastguard vessel, Daniel relaxed. As he popped up his head, he could see the sun coming up on the horizon. He could almost feel the warm orange glow hit his face.

'You know what they say, Daniel,' Thirway spoke up, 'Red sky at night, shepherd's delight; red sky in the morning, shepherd's warning.' He laughed and lit another cigarette.

Daniel felt a chill run down his spine. 'God, I hope not,' he muttered. Then, snapping out of it, he asked, 'Hey, how come we had to be so sneaky getting off the island? I mean, if it's a Singapore island we are going to, we are ok, right?'

'Well, not too many dive or tourist boats go out at the crack of dawn and, should we be asked by the coastguard where we are going, I'm not sure they will believe my bullshit. That and the fact I am carrying this.' Thirway lifted his T-shirt.

'Blimy!' Daniel took in the sight of what looked like a 9mm pistol jammed down Thirway's waistband. A wave of schoolboy excitement rushed over him and he asked, 'What is it? Can I have a go?'

'It's a Glock 18, one of the most reliable and accurate handguns in the world, a work of simplicity. No, in a word.' Thirway pulled down his T-shirt and leaned back against the side of the boat.

'Will we need that?' Daniel was curious about why Thirway was tooled up.

'I hope not, but you never know. If I get caught with this, it's a whole heap of shit.' Thirway then turned and raised a pair of binoculars.

'How long until we get there?' Daniel asked.

Not turning, Thirway patiently replied, 'Twenty, maybe forty, minutes. Now stop with the questions and relax.'

Thinking no more of it, Daniel tried to settle down, but the smell of diesel fuel and the motion of the boat made him feel a bit sick. The only food in his stomach was a rather stale curry puff that he had managed to grab from a street vendor near his home.

Daniel moved towards the bow, trying to avoid the drifting fumes. Looking at Thirway seated on a pile of old rope and smoking a cigarette, Daniel thought he looked like he hadn't a care in the world. 'Perhaps he hadn't,' he thought.

Tiredness took over as he looked out to sea. He needed some caffeine to jolt his senses. He turned his thoughts to what would be in store for him during his first training session. He knew, at least, he would be firing a weapon. This thought helped his weary mind a little as a trickle of adrenaline momentarily woke him up. Then, his eyelids felt heavy again. Resigning himself to the fact that coffee would not be on offer on this journey, he sat down with his back to the cabin, closed his eyes and got some sleep.

———

The sun was rising above the dozens of tiny islands, some of which were formed long ago by some ancient volcano. One island, in particular, now being observed on the horizon by a well-built man in his mid-30s through a Leupold sniper scope, stood out: the booming city-state of Singapore.

He hated the feeling of jet lag. After a short walk only an hour ago in the humid early morning air, across the tiny island he was now on, he was sweating like a pig. He felt annoyed, given he was used to the jungle and humid environments, but somehow today he felt crap.

Scanning the westward approaches to the island, he looked for the small blue boat he had been told to expect—the same boat, in fact, that had delivered him the day before. He could see nothing other than the giant oil tankers that dotted this part of the South China Sea.

He had read the brochures on the plane, all of which tried to entice tourists to visit the plush hotels and high-end shopping malls of Singapore. To him, coming from the brutal unforgiving back streets of Chicago, the metropolis looked like a floating image of the future. But he wasn't here for fun!

The island he was on reminded him of the others he had seen whilst on the final approach to Changi Airport. They seemed to be stuck in a distant past. Whilst lush and verdant, they looked like so many islands in so many places, with palm trees and sandy beaches lining their shores, sleepy, completely unaware of their own beauty. But he also knew some of these tiny islands hid secrets—the secrets of men who dared to smuggle and steal. Men he was now paid to hunt!

His eyes then caught the bow of the tiny blue boat as it came into his line of vision. Jerking the rifle a few degrees to his right, he aligned his position. Now, as clear as day, he could see Thirway in his crosshairs. Squeezing the trigger of the Barrett, he laughed out loud. He heard the snap of the rifle's action click home.

'Lucky for you, Thirway,' he muttered. The breech was empty. Getting up, he picked up the weapon and paced off towards the beach.

Reaching out his hand, he shook hands with Thirway. Daniel received a nod.

'Nice to see you, boss,' he said to Thirway.

'Likewise,' Thirway replied. 'Daniel, this is Troy, one of my best men.'

'Pleasure, Troy,' Daniel politely nodded.

'Okay, let's get down to it.' Thirway took the Barrett from Troy and walked off up the beach.

.
.

The kick from the Barrett M82 .50 calibre rifle as he squeezed the trigger took Daniel by surprise. He recalled the last time he had fired a rifle, during his days with the Territorial Army. He remembered the prickly heather he was made to crawl through on his stomach during pointless exercises in the wilds of Ashdown Forest. The ultimate weapon now cradled on his shoulder felt light years ahead compared with the old Belgian FN 762 rifle he had used then.

'That's enough of shooting thin air. No more cold bore. Move your rifle 45 degrees to your right,' Thirway instructed.

Daniel shifted his line of sight 45 degrees and froze. There in front of him, not more than 300 yards away, was a man tied to a tree. The man's face was partly hidden by a woollen ski mask, which was askew, making his mouth seem deformed.

What Daniel could not see was the wooden stick jammed hard across the man's mouth as a gag. It was held in place by a piece of wire wound around the back of his neck. The man could only bite down on the stick; he could make no sound.

Daniel then looked at the two men holding him against the tree. Both were fit-looking military types dressed in grey T-shirts and khaki shorts. As the man struggled, they tied a rope around his neck tight against the thin palm tree. They tied more rope around his chest, waist and legs. The volley of punches to his stomach ceased his fight.

Once they had secured him to the tree, the two men walked off towards an area of vegetation 50 or so yards away. Daniel instantly recognised one of the men. It was Troy.

'What the hell, you were not bloody kidding, were you?' Daniel turned abruptly to Thirway, his eyes clearly showing his surprise.

'What did you think, Daniel? We would be shooting at tin cans all day? Now shoot him.' Thirway then went back to his scope to calculate the exact distance.

'Who is he?' Daniel did not feel comfortable.

Thirway turned to look at him. 'A pirate, a filthy, dirty pirate, Daniel, who murdered a ship's captain three weeks ago. He cut the bloke's throat with a rusty old *parang* and threw him overboard. The captain had three kids all under the age of 10. Now shoot him, Daniel, or it ends here.' Thirway was in no mood for questions.

Daniel held his gaze. His mind was racing, his heart was thumping in his chest and his mouth was bone-dry. Finally settling back down, he brought his eye to the scope. He forced the image of a man being murdered into his head. The face of his father appeared clearly, as if he were standing right in front of him. His breathing slowed as the hate began to fill his heart and the adrenaline he craved started to flow. His aim was now rock-steady on the man still struggling in the distance.

'Three hundred yards, Danny. No wind, piss-easy shot. Just squeeze the trigger.' Thirway's voice was almost calming.

Daniel felt almost hypnotised. His crosshairs were now dead-centre on the man's chest, his finger gently resting on the trigger. His breathing was very shallow, his heartbeat a slow thump in his ears. As he tensed his body, he felt every nerve ending tingle.

Just as he started to squeeze the trigger, Thirway tapped him on the shoulder. 'Stand down.' Thirway had seen a wave from one of his men in the distance.

Daniel let out his breath, the tension in his body released. 'Christ, what is it?' He was annoyed at the interruption.

'Patrol boat. Hold until I give you the green light.'

As the minutes ticked by, Daniel could feel himself sweating profusely. He felt dehydrated. He was not even sure he could take the shot. Maybe it was all macho bullshit in his head. He had convinced himself he could do it, but seeing the man in front of him, tethered like a goat to a tree, it seemed very frightening now.

He reached over for a small bottle of water. He drank, then coughed as the water hit the back of his throat, the dryness reacting to the much-needed moisture.

'Easy, Danny boy, settle down. Take the shot when you are ready.'

Thirway had received the all clear.

Daniel focused again. He could see the man desperately struggling to get free, his neck now red and raw from rope burn. Slowly moving his finger on to the trigger, he felt himself ease, his breathing now back under control.

'Maybe I'm a natural,' he thought, as he squeezed the trigger.

The kick of the Barrett told him he had, in fact, fired the weapon. Even with his ear defenders, he heard the .50 calibre round burst from the muzzle. He then smelt the whiff of cordite as it wafted up his nostrils; it was a smell he enjoyed.

The exploding torso of the pirate confirmed where the round had struck. Daniel felt himself retch as he witnessed the impact of the round. He looked in horror at the sight of the limp body hanging by the rope that held it to the tree.

'Keep firing, Danny. Use up a few rounds,' Thirway instructed.

Daniel sent the next round wide. A split second later, after a small adjustment in his position, he fired again. This time, he saw his round tear off a leg. The next tore open the head like a watermelon. After a few moments, the shattered body fell to the ground.

'Awesome, fucking awesome!' Daniel screamed, adrenaline surging through his body.

Thirway just looked at him, his expression showing no emotion. 'Seems you have a taste for it now.' He then got up and started to walk towards what was left of the pirate.

Easing the weapon down, Daniel followed. As they neared the tree, he looked down and saw shreds of body parts. He felt himself retch again and what was left of his curry puff landed in the grass. Bent over with his hands on his knees, he felt his entire body shaking. The adrenaline was wearing off and reality was kicking in.

As Thirway walked by, he patted Daniel on the back. 'All part of it, Danny. You will get used to it. Next time, you could be a mile away; you won't see the blood and guts.' Thirway then waved his hand.

Looking up, Daniel saw three men—they looked local, maybe

fishermen from Batam who didn't care how they earned some cash that day—run out from behind some dense foliage. They started to pick up what was left of the pirate and stuff the body parts into a sack.

'Make sure these guys clean up the mess,' Thirway instructed his men. 'See you back in Singapore tomorrow.' He then turned to Daniel. 'Come on, Danny boy, time to go home before the patrol boat is back.'

Daniel, who was now white, finally straightened himself. 'Not sure I can do this again,' he said and started to walk off towards the beach.

The hand he felt spin him around was so strong it knocked him off balance and he fell backwards into the long grass. Stunned, he just sat there at first, squinting in the glaring sunlight. Raising his hand to shade his eyes, he now made out it was Thirway. He swallowed as he caught sight of the *parang* in Thirway's right hand, which had such a tight grip it was turning red.

'Make no mistake, Danny. You are in now, like it or not,' Thirway shouted, his eyes full of anger.

'You think this is easy? I have my reasons. Enough!' Daniel shouted back. 'I won't tell anyone, I swear.' He was shaking.

Troy stepped in. 'Give him a break, boss. He's just an amateur.'

'Get him out of my sight and onto that boat.' Thirway pointed his *parang* in the direction of the beach just off to the right about 200 yards away, then walked off.

'Don't mind him, mate. He just gets a bit edgy sometimes.' Troy held out his hand and pulled Daniel up on his feet.

'Thanks. Is he unhinged? He scares the shit out of me.' Daniel's face showed his concern.

'Unhinged, pure lunatic, that one,' Troy said and walked off towards the beach. Daniel hoped he was joking.

As he climbed aboard and sat himself down behind the main wheelhouse, Daniel contemplated the journey back to the Singapore mainland. His eyes followed Thirway as he walked towards the stern and sat alone behind a large blue barrel. Only the occasional waft of smoke from his cigarette told Daniel he was still there.

Daniel started to replay in his mind the shot he had taken and the sight of the pirate being torn in two by the .50 calibre round. Despite his initial shock, he had actually loved the rush it gave him. He also felt it had buried a ghost. Deep down, Daniel was looking forward to the next adventure and killing more pirates. A feeling of power and excitement took hold of him. Thirway had been right—it was extreme and nothing he had done before came anywhere close.

A sudden shout came from the boatman, 'Keep down. We come in slow.'

Daniel shook his head and rubbed his face. He felt dizzy and knew he must have drifted off. He then caught sight of Thirway, who had popped up from his position and was now waving for Daniel to come over and join him. The lights of the west docks loomed up in front of them.

'Too many police. You have to go over. If I turn around and head for the marina, it will draw suspicion,' shouted the boatman, as he turned the boat so as to obscure anyone on the port side from view from the shore.

Thirway calculated that they were about 400 yards from the jetty and the boat ramp they had left from earlier that morning. It seemed, however, that there were more police about now. He slowly got up and moved towards Daniel, taking him by the arm and forcing him to the far side of the boat.

'Come on, over the side. We have to swim for it.' Thirway climbed up on the side of the boat.

'What?' Daniel was taken by surprise.

'Get on with it. You want to end up in prison?' With that, Thirway dropped into the black water and started to swim in the direction of the jetty.

Not hanging about for another invitation, Daniel started to swim after Thirway, who was already 20 yards in front of him. Daniel knew he was a strong swimmer, so the short distance was nothing to him. Looking behind, he could see the boat move off and head towards the docks, its wake sending the oily water washing over his head. Shaking the water off his face, he could just see in the distance a line of workers dressed in bright orange boiler suits waiting to board and be taken to one of the refineries. He could also see what looked like two immigration officers scanning the lines of workers.

'Daniel, swim under the water as much as you can. We have to dive down for the last 20-metre distance,' Thirway shouted, his voice muffled by the waves splashing up into his face and mouth. Daniel raised a thumb in acknowledgement.

The light that suddenly flashed across the water just missed Daniel. He dived down quickly into the dark water, kicking with all his might to gain depth. He could feel the silt and mud swirling around in the water as he desperately kicked downwards, his water-logged clothing clinging to his body and making the swim harder. Shafts of light were chasing him. He dared not stop now.

He reckoned he had dived down at least 15 feet by now, so he levelled off and started to swim towards where he hoped the shore was. 'Where's Thirway?' he thought, as he swam against what seemed to be a strong current. His lungs were desperate for air and he felt himself almost blacking out, but he had to force himself to go on for a few more yards. Then, unable to stay under any longer, he surfaced. He jerked his head around, trying to get his bearings—but there was nothing, just darkness.

As his eyes grew accustomed to the dim light, he could see he had come up under a wooden jetty, the boardwalk only a few feet above his head. He slowly swam over to one of the wooden posts that held the jetty in place and clung on, the waves lapping hard against him. A sharp sting on his left hand made him draw it back. The razor-sharp barnacles on the post had ripped the skin.

'Danny, over here.' It was Thirway.

'Thank god!' Daniel responded, forgetting the pain in his hand as he swam towards Thirway's voice.

'You okay? Patrol boat came in almost on top of us. That was fucking close, Danny boy.' Thirway was beaming, as if it was all good fun.

'Jesus, John, what a day!' Daniel felt alive again, with the adrenaline rush. 'This is so awesome, worth every penny,' Daniel said.

'Glad you like it, Danny. More to come. Now, let's get out of here.' Thirway then swam off towards the shore.

———

Daniel collapsed on his bed exhausted. The same clock that had woken him up in the small hours of the morning now read 11:30 p.m. Squeezing out every last drop of energy he had left in his body, he heaved himself up and into the bathroom.

He turned on the shower and let the steam build before he stepped in. The hot water felt good on his skin as it washed away the foul-smelling oily seawater and eased his sore muscles. Thirway had indeed delivered on his promise of an extreme experience.

Daniel now focused on Somalia where the next hardcore sniper action would be, and he couldn't wait for it. He recalled Thirway's briefing—that he would be undercover, posing as a member of Force12, his legitimate and registered private military corporation.

According to Thirway, Force12 had a contract with Pathos Shipping to protect their vessels in the Gulf of Aden—at any cost. The odd civilian would go unnoticed. As such, Thirway could offer his Deep Six members all the extreme fun they could handle. Daniel smiled as he stepped out of the shower and towel-dried himself.

He then froze as he remembered Thirway had told him, in no uncertain terms, that anyone who opened their mouths about what went on would be dealt with. Replaying in his mind the incident on the island and the mad look on Thirway's face, he could well believe how Thirway would deal with such a person.

Daniel now also thought about the look on Thirway's face when he had asked during the taxi ride home how the vacant spot had come about. Thirway's eyes had been fervid, his face deadpan. The look was enough; Daniel knew not to ask again. Just stay silent and he would be okay.

With that thought, Daniel turned off the light and climbed into bed.

NINE

August 2009. London and Singapore.

Two million dollars in any font size is either impressive or suicidal, depending on which side of the balance sheet you're looking at. Given it shrilled profit, Alexis sat back and internally patted herself firmly on the back. She had spent all morning pulling the deal together, just as Kent, her boss, had instructed. A trade finance deal for close to US$80 million for a shipment of machine parts was a big deal, especially as the market was down. She smiled to herself, proud he had given her the deal.

She admired his intellect, his ability to smell a deal and close it. She liked his aloof nature and the fact that he was extremely charismatic—a rarity, going by her previous encounters with Americans.

'Yes, that's US$75 million. I need it in the client's account by end of day. SACAMO, thanks, yes, at today's rate.' She put the phone down; the deal was done. Getting up, she gathered her things and left for lunch. She had a date with a very special man.

———

Sipping his coffee, he observed on his computer screen that his deal had been done. He picked up his phone and made the call.

'We have another shipment,' he spoke into the receiver, 'due to be in Oman in a few days. From there, it will be loaded onto a ship by the name of *Odin*. Make sure your little pirate friend directs it as instructed, okay? I never had any issues with Mohamed, so sort it.

Oh and make sure that partner of yours doesn't screw it up with that sordid sideline of his.' He brushed his wispy hair out of his eyes and put down the phone. All the elements were now in place.

Stone got the message, but he hated the arrogance of the American.

The starched white tablecloth, polished silverware and crystal flutes, and chilled bottle of Dom Perignon vintage 2000 were the trappings of a normal lunch with her father.

As Alexis strode elegantly into Le Gavroche, the staff knew all too well who she was. She loved this part of Mayfair, and not only because it was minutes from her luxury flat. She never forgot the day her father had given her the keys to the flat and brought her to the very same restaurant to celebrate.

Alexis drew in her chair and waited patiently for her father to arrive; he was always late. As the waiters fussed around her, offering varieties of mineral water and draped a starched white napkin across her lap, her mind was on Daniel.

Impulsively reaching into her handbag for her phone, she started to dial Daniel's number, stopping halfway as she caught sight of her father briskly entering the restaurant. He was dressed, no surprise to her, in his normal Savile Row navy blue pin-striped suit, crisp white shirt and red Hermes tie. It pleased her to see him wearing that tie; she had given it to him last Christmas. His arms were held open in front of him, ready to embrace his beloved daughter, as he walked towards their table.

'Darling, please forgive me. Wretched meeting overran,' he explained, kissing her on both cheeks before giving her a firm fatherly hug.

'It's okay, father. Don't worry.' Alexis was always pleased to see him and well understood his busy schedule.

'Come, sit, sit, my dear. Now, tell me how you are.' He was

beaming, happy to see her.

'I'm great, no complaints. You're looking well.' She beamed back, then paused as a swarm of waiters descended upon them. She knew they considered having her father in for lunch a big deal.

'I've pre-ordered, darling. Hope you don't mind.'

They sat back and watched the food arrive in perfect timing. Alexis smiled as her father's favourite, steak tartare, was placed in front of him. Moments later, a rather delicious-looking sea bass was placed in front of her. The entire process was closely observed by not only the maître d', who was standing diligently to one side, just in case one of his staff fouled up, but also Nicolai, the 6-foot-tall wall of muscle that was her father's personal bodyguard.

Alexis gave Nicolai a wry smile, for which she received a gentle nod in return. She was always nervous around him, but she knew that the former Spetsnaz soldier, by definition of his elite training, was as tough as leather, as hard as nails and as smart as a fox. Perhaps it was his steely face, chiselled jaw and close-shaven head that unnerved her. She did, however, fancy his body; it was in excellent shape, as she ran her eyes over it.

She knew the story of how her father had met him. Pathos had been in Moscow on business. A shipping contract worth US$150 million was on the table with the Russians and he wanted to personally sign the deal. On his way back to the hotel, having signed the deal, his car was hijacked by gunmen, drug dealers looking for an easy target. At least that was the official police report.

His driver was shot dead and he was dragged out of his limousine. With a gun aimed at his head, Pathos was all but ready to accept his fate.

The first knife stabbed into the back of the gunman's head, scrambling his brains. The second man, who turned to attack, was rammed hard in the ribs back against the car by the dark shadow that had appeared on the scene; his neck was then snapped as if it were nothing more than a twig. A hail of bullets erupted from the remaining hijacker, hitting the hero of the hour once in the right shoulder and twice in the left leg. Despite his injuries, he managed to fend off the last attacker.

It took Nicolai six months to recover from his injuries. In the meantime, Pathos discovered that Nicolai was unemployed and heading for the gutter, riding the vodka express after his wife and 3-year-old daughter died in the crossfire between rival gangs on their way home from buying bread. Pathos offered Nicolai a job for life in gratitude for Nicolai saving his life.

'You okay, dear?' Pathos asked.

'Sorry, yes. How is business, father?' Alexis enquired.

'Not great. Fuel costs too damn high these days. Hard to make a profit from shipping. That and…' He stopped mid-sentence.

'What is it, father?'

'Nothing. Just an issue you have reminded me to deal with, one that is costing me millions. Pirates. Bloody vultures keep hijacking my ships. Anyway, nothing for you to worry your pretty head over.' He continued to eat.

Alexis looked at her father in surprise hearing the word pirates. She wondered whether to probe deeper but thought better of it, seeing her father clearly didn't wish to discuss the issue. She sipped her champagne.

'So, how is that chap you're dating?' he asked, changing the subject to one that, in some ways, concerned him more.

'Daniel? He's fine, father,' Alexis responded, emphasising the name her father couldn't bring himself to pronounce.

'Well, my dear, it's your life, but I do worry for you. I mean, so many fine men out there,' he said without even looking up from his plate.

Alexis just rolled her eyes. She was used to his view on Daniel. To him, Daniel was a go-nowhere trader not worthy of the Pathos empire. She admitted he had a point, especially since she knew where Daniel had been and what he was up to.

'I need some extra cash, if that's okay.' Alexis gave her father the sweetest smile; it always won him over.

'You have the account number, so take what you need, darling. No need to ask.' He returned the smile.

Alexis somehow hadn't thought of the account her father had flushed with a cool US$1 million in cold hard cash. It was sitting in a bank in Singapore, and the account number was fixed in her head. She knew it was intended for emergencies. She also knew it was small change for a man whose personal fortune was in the region of US$10 billion.

She felt a twinge of guilt as she thought about how she occasionally dipped into the account. She loved dabbling with the markets and had, in fact, never lost. On the odd occasion, she ventured into other lucrative areas, wanting to prove to her father that she was indeed a savvy businesswoman. She felt better this time, having asked for his permission.

Her mind then wandered to a man—not Daniel, but one of the executives she worked for at the bank. She deeply admired his business acumen and the fact he seemed different, almost as if he had a distinct sixth sense. He was unlike Daniel in so many ways. He was calm, older and very mature, and not controllable like Daniel.

Pathos broke her train of thought. 'Now, you must excuse me, darling. I have to travel to Dubai this afternoon, so I will be away for a few weeks. You know how to reach me.' He smiled and then stood up, placing his napkin carefully on the table. He signalled with a wave of his hand for the bill to be placed on his tab.

'Business or golf?' Alexis asked, tongue-in-cheek.

He wagged a gentle finger at her to let her know how cheeky she was. 'I'm buying another ship, nothing more exciting.' With that, he walked over and hugged her and kissed her on both cheeks. 'Can I drop you off anywhere?' he asked.

'No, thanks, I have the afternoon off. I feel like a walk. I'm staying at the flat. See you soon. Love you.' She blew a kiss at him. Pathos beamed and left, Nicolai following closely behind.

———

Walking along Park Lane, Alexis remembered she had wanted to call Daniel. She took out her phone and dialled his number. She knew he was a light sleeper and she needed to know he was okay.

After a few rings, she heard a click and his sleepy voice mutter 'Hello.'

'Daniel, it's me, Alexis. Are you okay? I have been worried sick.'

As if a switch had gone on, he answered excitedly, 'Yes, I'm fine! In fact, I had fun!' He realised immediately that that perhaps wasn't the most appropriate response, given he had just dismembered a human being with a .50 calibre rifle. But it had so excited him.

'So, what did you do?' Alexis wanted to know more.

'Not much. Just shot a few rusty cans, you know, to learn about the weapon and stuff,' Daniel lied through his teeth.

'Okay, Daniel, but please take care. Did you ask if I could come along on the next trip?' she enquired.

'Yes, Thirway said okay, it was cool!'

'Really? Cool!' Alexis smiled, surprised but glad.

'Yeah, he seemed fine. Listen, I'm really tired. See you in a few days. Love you,' Daniel said. He hung up and closed his eyes. Alexis thought nothing more of it and decided to enjoy the short walk back to her flat.

———

Alexis turned the key in the lock and opened her front door. On entering, she found a pair of polished black Church's shoes neatly placed in the hall. She smiled, knowing it was going to be a good afternoon.

As she softly entered the bedroom, she noticed the curtains had been pulled shut. She could see the figure of a man under the duvet. Slipping out of her clothes, she slid under the covers, placed her arm over him and kissed his back.

'This is a nice surprise,' she whispered.

'Yes, came over on business this morning. Thought I would surprise you.' His voice was calm. 'Is everything going to plan on the finance deal?'

'Don't worry. All done. The cargo is funded.' Alexis placed her finger to his lips, indicating that now was not the time to discuss business.

He then rolled over, pushing her underneath him. His lips met hers and they kissed. She felt him thrust into her, which made her moan loudly; she loved how big he was. The slow rhythm started to get frantic, as she ran her nails down his back and clung on with her legs. She became aware of her breathing getting shallower as she felt the rapid movements of his penis inside of her.

She loved making love to him; it was slow and sensual, unlike Daniel, who was rough and aggressive. Dismissing Daniel from her mind, she tightened her grip with her legs, as if to urge him on.

'You like this, baby?' he murmured into her ear.

'Yes, yes, harder!' she heard herself scream, almost breathless.

He drove slowly deeper into her, his rapid rhythm eventually making her orgasm.

'Oh god.' Alexis could feel the warmth of his fluids as they flowed into her. She then felt herself relax as he rolled off. Nestling on his arms, she drifted off to sleep.

Daniel could feel his eyes beginning to pop out of his head as he gasped for air. He stared desperately into the eyes of the masked man. He felt his life slipping away, as the hands around his throat squeezed harder and harder. Thrashing his arms and legs about didn't seem to help. The man was far too strong for him.

Then, he looked down and saw that the man's intestines were spilling out of him, like strings of raw sausages, and splotches of dark oily blood were all over him. He tried to scream, but the words choked in his throat. Then, release; he gasped for air, filling his lungs.

Daniel jumped up in his bed, his eyes darting around the room, his breathing rapid. He was hyperventilating, his heart pounding in his chest, beads of sweat running down the centre of his back. It took him a while to realise that the entire thing had been nothing more than a bad dream. Calming down, his breathing starting to slow, he slumped back into bed.

The dealing room was a hive of activity as Daniel took his seat. Phones were ringing off the hook, screens flashing commodity prices and stock yield curves. It was a few minutes before he could start to engage the market. His mind was still replaying the bad dream, seeing the eyes of the man behind the mask staring at him. He had lain awake all night and he was now desperate for sleep.

'Daniel, line 4,' one of his fellow traders shouted across the floor.

'Burrows. Spencer.'

'Danny boy, John. How the hell are you?'

'Oh, John, yeah I'm great,' Daniel replied.

'Okay, good. I need not remind you, Danny, not a word to anyone about yesterday, okay?' Thirway said.

'Yeah, of course,' Daniel replied.

'Okay, good. We leave for Oman on Sunday. You will need to take at least three weeks off. Meet me at Terminal 2, 9:30 a.m. on Sunday.' Thirway then hung up.

Somewhat surprised by the short notice, Daniel logged into his employee system and entered the dates he needed to take off. Despite the fact that he loved making money and the markets were running in his favour, the lure of an adventure was too strong. Nothing else mattered. He could make the dollars any day, but hunting pirates was not an everyday occurrence. He had to go and that was that. He then sent an email to Alexis, asking her to make sure she booked the same time. He knew she would check her BlackBerry before she boarded the Singapore Airlines flight back home.

Leaning back in his chair, he could feel the excitement welling up. Despite the bad dream, he felt alive, different. His thoughts then turned to the Somali pirates he would be tracking. He knew nothing about them, but maybe that was best. Thirway had given him enough insight and that was that. They were murdering bastards who hijacked innocent ships and no one cared if a few people were killed.

With that thought, he went back to work.

TEN

August 2009. Eyl, Somalia.

Abshir cut an imposing figure standing proudly on a dune, silhouetted against the backdrop of a rising sun in a deep-orange sky. His gaze was firmly fixed on the massive Ukrainian tanker that sat like a lumbering beast on the distant horizon. It was a ship now under his control. He would join his men on board in the morning, ready for payday. The ransom, all US$2 million of it, would be deposited then—dropped like a gift from heaven right onto the deck.

He laughed at himself, once a clean-cut 34-year-old US Marine, now an AK-touting Somali king in a land he knew to be unrelenting, populated by herds of nomadic camels and small groups of armed militia. But he was a pirate king, one who drew numerous fresh-faced journalists. They sought him out eagerly, expecting to find an illiterate blood-thirsty ape. Armed with expensive Japanese cameras and long lenses, they all wanted the same thing—to capture his image for all eternity. That and to sell it off as an expensive stock image to some stuffy ad or news agency. Yes, even they now seemed to accord him with a form of notoriety and respect.

Striding back to his hut, he smiled at the irony of it all. The news these days—at least any news considered exciting—so often favoured the devil.

Placing the satellite phone to his ear, he sat up and swung his legs over the side of the bed. The young girl with him simply pulled up the sheets and rolled over, not happy at all that her pleasure had been interrupted.

'Abshir, my friend, you have a prize waiting for you.' It was a voice he knew well.

'Go on.' Abshir stood up, pulled on a pair of shorts and ambled outside.

'The *Orion Star*, an aid ship, is right on your doorstep. On board is a cargo we want you to take care of for us. Arms. Hold them until I give you further instructions. What money you make from the ship is yours, same deal as we gave Mohamed, okay?'

It was just the news he wanted. His men were getting fat and lazy.

'Good, then I will take it and do as you ask. You want your cut?' Abshir knew the deal.

'A little reward is always good, my friend.' The click of the phone signalled the end of the call.

Abshir knew the strong winds of the monsoon had at last abated, which meant he could risk setting out to sea. Within an hour, the camp was alive; an energy coursed through it as streams of men ran past his hut preparing for the attack. He knew planning was key and he made sure his men were well-trained and, above all, disciplined. The bags of rice and tins of food that were now being loaded onto the support trucks were as important as the ammunition.

Turning around, he saw Cassia standing in the doorway. She was the 19-year-old girl he used to satisfy his needs. She was extremely beautiful. Her big round eyes were busy seducing him. She had been given to him by her parents, who had been desperate to see her looked after. The white sheet wrapped around her toned body hid what only Abshir could have; her virginity was lost to him alone. He went back in, pulled the door closed behind him and pushed her back onto the bed. He had at least two hours before he had to leave.

——— — —

The target was offshore, just as he had been told, 20 or so kilometres away, a sitting duck. The growling twin Yamaha outboards powered through the flat calm sea, eating up every mile with ease. For now, it seemed it would be the perfect day.

One man, however, sat alone, glaring up at Abshir. Teo, a staunch supporter of the late Mohamed Aidid, was not so assured; in his eyes, Abshir was an American, a corrupted infidel.

A second pair of eyes, eyes that were relatively innocent, were also fixed on Abshir, following his every move. They belonged to Asad, Abshir's 15-year-old brother. His hands were wrapped tightly around an AK-47 as if his life depended on it.

Having confirmed the ship's name, Abshir waved his hand to signal the attack. Then, he turned sharply to face Asad.

'Here we go, little brother.' His voice betrayed his excitement. It was Asad's first mission.

A macabre chorus of the clicks of so many automatic weapons signified the readiness of the men, now primed to board. Even Teo, for now, put aside his differences and crouched down, ready to spring into action. As they approached, the choppy wake of the *Orion Star* rocked their small boat from side to side; every man hung on.

'Easy, men, be careful,' Abshir announced, knowing that if anyone fell over now, there would be no time to rescue him.

As the boat slowed, one of the pirates rushed forward and skilfully deployed a grappling iron. He sent it up and over the guardrail in one move, as if practised hundreds of times. Abshir handed the controls to one of his men and stepped forward.

'Come on, brother, just follow me.' He took hold of the rope and climbed effortlessly, as if it were attached to nothing more than a tree firmly rooted in the soil. The pitching sea beneath him seemed to make no difference. Asad slowly followed.

'I can't make it,' Asad yelled out.

Looking down, Abshir could see his brother starting to slip, his eyes dark with fear.

'Come on, you can do this. Try,' Abshir encouraged his brother, knowing that, if the boy slipped now, there was a strong chance of him hitting the water and getting swept away.

Asad looked down. He too saw the water below, ready to swallow him up.

'I can't.' His foot slipped down the rope.

'Brother, do not make me look bad. Do it. Climb. You are a man now,' Abshir shouted, hoping he would not be heard by the other men above the roar of the *Orion*'s engines.

Slowly, Asad started to move; inch by inch, he shimmied up the rope, almost slipping again as he banged against the ship's hull. When he finally reached the top, Abshir grabbed him by the arms, immensely relieved, and hauled him through the guardrail.

'I told you so, brother. Well done.'

As the remaining men climbed aboard and melted into the shadows, the boat pulled away to a safe distance to await Abshir's signal.

A door opened just off the port side and a crewman stepped out into the night air, completely unaware of the presence of the pirates. Abshir moved slowly forward, using the shadows as cover. Once close enough, he delivered a blow, hard enough to knock the man out cold. Another pirate immediately dragged him off and hid him from view.

'This way.' Abshir started to move silently up a steel gangway towards the bridge. Reaching the bridge house, he carefully peered in and saw five men. Turning to his men, he signalled with his fingers. Then, as if propelled by pure adrenaline, he burst in through the door.

'No one move!' he shouted. Three of his men followed quickly behind, each brandishing a weapon.

'Look out!' Asad yelled.

Turning fast, Abshir saw a stocky man dressed in a pair of greasy faded white overalls rushing towards him with a large wrench.

'You robbing bit of filth!' The man swung the wrench. At that moment, Asad dashed forward, putting himself between the man and his elder brother.

'Asad, no!' Abshir shouted.

The wrench struck Asad hard on the shoulder and sent him spinning to the floor, screaming in pain.

Instinctively, Abshir brought the butt of his weapon hard up, under the man's chin, breaking his jaw and knocking him sideways. There was a sickening crack as the man's head struck the side of a control just before he hit the deck. Abshir then raised his weapon to finish him off.

'No, please don't kill him.' One of the crew moved between the man and Abshir. The glare of Abshir's eyes was so intense it almost froze him to the spot. Then, as if struck suddenly by his conscience, Abshir lowered his weapon. He moved over to check on Asad.

'Are you okay?'

'Yes, but it hurts.' Asad had clearly been injured.

'Why did you do that? You could have been killed.' Abshir's voice showed concern more than anger.

'To show you I am brave,' Asad smiled up at his brother.

'Who is the captain?' Abshir shouted. Silence was the only response he got. He counted four men on the bridge.

'Fifteen below. We have them all,' one of his men stuck his head in and announced.

'Good. Hold them and take care of my brother,' Abshir barked.

'I count to five and then I kill you all. Now, which one of you is the captain?' Abshir pointed the barrel of his AK at a thin balding man who was shivering against the back wall. He was angry and he could sense it in himself. The man trying to attack had really pushed a button, but the realisation that bringing his brother along had almost got him killed consumed him. Any peaceful agenda he had come on board with had now ebbed away. He preferred the crew to surrender.

'One... two...' he started to count.

'I am,' a voice spoke out.

A man in his mid-40s, with thinning brown hair, stepped forward. Michael Schmitt, a German, had been a merchant seaman for 25 years; in all that time, he had never been hijacked.

'Please take what you want; we will do as you say. That man was foolish. Please,' Schmitt blurted out his words, hoping to avoid bloodshed.

'How many crew?' Abshir demanded.

'You have us all, only 20 of us,' the captain spoke.

Abshir knew via his contact that the ship was registered to a Panamanian company, which was good news as it meant a US-dollar ransom of at least five million. Right now, he needed the captain to alert his company and ask for a ransom.

Schmitt could feel the gun in his back. His thoughts were with his wife, Charlotte, and his kids, Kurt and Helga. He had to stay calm. His voice over the radio sounded shaky as he delivered the terms. The response he received was not favourable. He turned to Abshir.

'You heard that. They said they will not pay. Please, we are just the crew. Let us go. Take the ship.' Schmitt hoped his pleading would save his crew.

'You come here.' Abshir pointed to a man in the corner. A rather short stout man with missing front teeth was pulled out by one of the pirates.

'Please, I don't want any trouble,' he started to plead.

'Shut your mouth, fool,' Abshir shouted.

'Please, this is not required.' Schmitt stepped forward.

Turning back to the captain, Abshir said, 'Now, tell your base to agree to the terms or I will order this man killed, right now. The Maritime Freedom Fighters demand ransom.' Abshir was now waving his AK in the air, his eyes angry.

Schmitt's face said it all as he stepped back and shot a glance at the shivering figure of his crewman. He picked up the radio and started to babble into it.

'This is the captain of the *Orion Star*. You have to pay or my crew will be shot.' After a few moments had passed, Abshir heard the second rejection as it broke the static silence.

'Please, I beg you, don't kill us,' Schmitt was on the edge of panic.

Then, as if he knew it had gone too far, Abshir lowered his weapon. 'I won't kill you, not in cold blood, anyway. I am not an animal. You tell your company that, unless I get the money, I will keep their ship under siege for weeks. That, I know, will cost them dearly.' He moved away and sat in the captain's chair.

Relieved, Schmitt let out a sigh. 'Thank you.' He started to speak into the radio once again.

Teo suddenly stepped forward and pointed his AK at Abshir. 'You coward, kill them all! Let the blood do the talking!' The look Abshir shot back was not one of fear, nor surprise; he almost expected it.

'Put your gun down. There will be no killing. Not unless I order it,' he barked and stood up.

'You are soft. Only blood will teach the foreigner.' Teo squared up. Abshir remained cool but kept his eyes firmly fixed on Teo.

'You men, are you with him or are you with me?' Abshir looked at the other pirates, who started to assemble around him. 'You see, Teo, no one supports you. You are a dead man.' Abshir's tone rang with confidence.

'I will take you all out with me. I am not afraid to die,' Teo replied, his eyes wild. He raised his weapon, aimed squarely at Abshir and eased his finger on the trigger.

A shot rang out. Everyone ducked down instinctively and covered their ears as the sound hammered around inside the bridge house. Teo fell to the floor. Looking around, Abshir saw Asad holding a 9mm pistol in his hands.

'Asad...'

Asad looked back at him, his mouth open and his eyes almost out on stalks. Abshir walked over and eased the pistol out of his hands and placed an arm around him.

'You, brother, are now a true pirate.' Abshir beamed with pride.

'God,' Schmitt muttered, horrified by what he had just witnessed.

'Do not be so surprised, captain. Even pirates fight amongst themselves. Be thankful we are not all like him.' Abshir gestured with his eyes to Teo's body. 'Get on with it,' he commanded, pointing to the radio, 'and, this time, tell them we have spared you.'

Picking up the radio one more time, Schmitt made his plea. 'This is the *Orion Star*. I urge you to pay the ransom. They will not harm us if the money is paid. They seem honourable, over.'

Schmitt looked at Abshir, somewhat shocked at his own comment. Honourable was not perhaps the best word to have used. But he appreciated the fact that Abshir had some moral code.

———

The boat came alongside the large orange dry sack that was bobbing in the water. It had taken only four days to reach an agreement. Abshir smiled, his arm around his brother's shoulders, as his men hauled the sack aboard in excitement. Then, they sped off.

———

Cutter tapped away at his keyboard in the soft glow of his desk lamp. Typing the opening of his report, which was initially so formal as to be boring, he decided to play with the words a little to better describe the man he had met.

A stream of whimsical words appeared on the paper: 'Beware not to scorn the weak cub, as he may become the rampaging lion...'

Cutter recalled every detail of his meeting with the man who was now king amongst his own people, thanks in part to Cutter himself. 'Funny that,' he thought, knowing the phone call he had made to Ogilvy that day had been as good as firing the bullet himself. The British had simply tipped off the French navy; Mohamed Aidid was a dead man.

Cutter had learned that Abshir had returned home from the United States three years prior, his heart full of disdain and hatred for the West.

As a child growing up in the slums of Mogadishu, he had endured the sight of Western wealth sailing past the shore whilst he and his family scavenged for food scraps in the rubbish dumps. He escaped the horrors of his childhood when he was only 15, working his passage on tankers and cargo ships around the world. The knowledge he gained of the ocean and of weapons served him well. Arriving in the United States when he was 20, he claimed asylum and managed to get a green card. He later joined the Marine Corps. The fake Kenyan passport he had bought from another seaman was never suspected. His Somali roots simply vanished.

Cutter had done his research and knew the facts, most of which now flowed from his brain to the paper. Finishing the last paragraph, he shot a glance at the photo lying on his desk. He would never forget the smile Abshir had given him when telling him his name. Cutter rubbed his eyes and sat back in his chair, glancing at his watch and noting the late hour. It took but a few seconds to email the report. His job was done.

ELEVEN

August 2009. Oman.

Stone wasn't hard to miss; his stocky figure and balding head made him stand out in the sea of Omanis. Thirway, having cleared customs, saw his partner talking to a man, who swiftly moved away and melted into the crowd.

'Who was that?' Thirway asked when he was with Stone, his eyes still trying to find the man amongst the milling throng of bodies.

'Just some tourist,' Stone brushed off the question instantly, pulling Thirway to one side, leaving Daniel, Alexis and another new Deep Six recruit, Jeremy Drake, to their own devices.

Thirway was less than happy as Stone broke the news to him. Mohamed Aidid was no more; Abshir Mohamed was the new king. He alone now controlled the various pirate clans, which Thirway knew could mean the end of his neat little sideline.

Mohamed Aidid had been more than happy to provide a few spent pirates for sniper practice in exchange for large numbers of greenbacks. Abshir, on the other hand, had morals. He also had a cause; his people, as such, would not oblige. This wasn't good news, especially as Thirway now had three new customers.

Thirway had little choice now; his cunning plan, only in part hatched in his mind, would have to be executed. Having Alexis on board, who he knew would be worth millions if ever kidnapped, would surely change the young pirate's mind.

That was the plan he put to Stone as they walked back to collect his guests. Thirway knew Stone was completely heartless and any sniff of money would see him onside. Stone also knew Abshir well; if anyone could convince the pirate to turn his hand to kidnapping people as well as ships, Stone could. All Thirway had to do now was wait for Stone to get the response.

'Just one thing, Thirway.' Stone grabbed his arm hard.

'What's that?' Thirway pulled his arm back.

'Do not let this little sideline of yours ruin the contract we have with the American. We need the ships to move his cargo. We need Abshir to make sure it gets diverted to the real buyers, just as Mohamed made sure. Get it? Alexis is a gift to keep Abshir happy, nothing more.'

Exiting Muscat International Airport, the new recruits knew they had no time for sightseeing. Thirway's brisk pace was an indication of his intent to keep things moving swiftly along. The fact that each aspect of the journey had clearly been planned and timed to perfection deeply impressed Daniel. His excitement was growing.

'This way,' Thirway instructed as they passed through the electronic glass doors, as if he was leading a bunch of schoolchildren. A white minibus was parked by the curb in front of the terminal, waiting for them.

Stone, who had only been introduced as 'my business partner' by Thirway, waved them off. Something about the little man didn't sit well with Alexis as she noted the cheap wink he shot her before they sped off.

'Where are we going?' Alexis enquired, having settled into one of the rear seats.

'Port Salalah, about an hour away, so relax.' Thirway turned and winked at her, not that she much cared for his overly familiar ways.

'But I need to pee,' she informed him.

'Cross your legs or go in this,' Thirway said, showing no sympathy and handing her an empty 7UP bottle. 'You should have gone at the terminal.'

'Charming, I must say,' she tutted, unamused, and turned to look out of the window.

'Is it a big port?' Daniel chimed in, more to change the subject, and trying not to laugh.

'What, you want chapter and verse? It's a multi-purpose port, with facilities to handle bulk cargo and containers. From there, we board a vessel named *Odin*, a 65,000-tonne Cypriot-registered cargo ship bound for London, travelling up through the Gulf of Aden and the Suez Canal. We set sail at 2100,' Thirway continued without a pause.

'Okay, just interested.' Daniel realised his question had somehow narked Thirway.

Pulling up at the dock almost an hour later, they hurriedly climbed out of the minibus and retrieved their luggage from the rear of the vehicle. Then, looking up at the huge vessel, Daniel took in the name: *Odin*.

Alexis was also looking. 'Hardly a luxury cruise liner, is it?' she quipped and walked off in the direction of the gangway, her bladder now screaming. Daniel followed.

Vandenbrook was happy once again to receive his cash from Thirway. He carefully opened the brown envelope to see the US dollar notes stuffed inside.

'It's all there, captain,' Thirway snipped, not liking the fact that Vandenbrook had to check. A slight nod was the only sign of Vandenbrook's gratitude as he tucked the envelope under his arm. Thirway walked on towards the ship.

The captain turned his attention to the cargo of machine parts now being loaded into the ship's vast hold, checking against the manifest that there were indeed 56 crates. Then, as he started back towards the ship, he stopped.

Something about the man standing some 30 yards off to his right got him curious. Dressed in a blue suit, with wispy brown hair swept back on both sides of his face and thin, almost hawk-like features, the man seemed somehow out of place.

The stranger had also noticed Vandenbrook looking at him, but that was secondary to something else he had just noticed. He moved forward just a bit, trying to make sure it was indeed Alexis he had seen.

Vandenbrook held his stare until he was interrupted by one of his crew; he was required on the bridge. Looking back, he saw that the stranger had vanished. Thinking nothing more of it, he walked towards the gangway. He had a ship to prepare for departure and that was all he cared about right now.

———

They moved down a steep stairwell and along a narrow dimly lit corridor, then stopped. The crew member who had led the way now had his arm extended towards the cabin they had reached, indicating this was where Daniel and Alexis would bunk down.

The cabin was small, with just enough space for a small side table, a battered grey locker and two apparently well-used grey bunks—the paint on the small ladder had been worn through to the shiny steel underneath by the many occupants who had climbed up to the top bunk.

Daniel scanned the array of nude pin-up posters that adorned the walls, most of them faded and tattered. He mused over the probability that the models immortalised in the aged posters were now either fat old barmaids or married to footballers.

Twitching her nose at the smell of diesel and cigarette smoke in the stale air, Alexis caught sight of the grey blankets that lay folded on each bunk. Clearly, they had seen better days.

'Oh god, look at this,' she said in a tone of disgust. The mattress on the lower bunk was stained with large yellowish patches. 'Is it urine?'

'Yeah, most likely the result of a drunken seaman. Or a wet dream,' Daniel laughed.

'Disgusting and not funny, Daniel,' she scolded.

Alexis tossed her bag onto the upper bunk, giving Daniel a look that told him she would not be sleeping in the lower bunk. Gingerly turning his mattress over, Daniel saw it was, in fact, only slightly better on the other side.

The solitary 60-watt lightbulb that flickered behind its glass cover did little to brighten the cabin's dreary atmosphere or Alexis's sensitive mood. Suddenly, Thirway poked his head in the door.

'Okay, you guys get settled in. See you in the galley in half an hour.' With that, he vanished, as quickly as he had appeared.

'It's not that bad, babe. At least, we're together,' Daniel said sheepishly.

'All luxury with you, Daniel!' Alexis retorted. 'My father owns a shipping company and I find myself on some old rust bucket.

'I'll sleep with my clothes on, I think. No telling who will pop in,' she added sarcastically.

It felt good sipping the hot sweet tea from the cup in her hands. She shot glances around the table; besides Daniel and Thirway, there were two other men she didn't know, not that she really cared.

Daniel was eyeing somewhat cautiously the man sitting next to Troy at the table; he had been introduced as Bull. A deep grunt was the only sound anyone had heard from him since. 'Clearly a man of few words,' Daniel thought.

Looking casually around the cafeteria, Daniel observed several members of the ship's crew, most of whom looked to him to be either Filipino or Dutch. The accents were a dead giveaway. One of them kept turning around and staring; given he was the size of a small village, Daniel averted his eyes.

Suddenly, the man blurted out, 'You pricks are the hired protection, right?' His voice was deep.

Thirway reacted first, slowly turning around in his chair. 'Yes, we are. Here to ensure your safety, in fact,' he replied curtly, shooting a thousand-yard stare along with his words. He then spun back around to face the others.

'Why the woman? Is she for us to fuck?' the man laughed, looking to his fellow crew members to join in on his joke. Daniel, who could see everything from where he was seated, noticed they remained silent, looking down at their food, clearly not wanting anything to do with what was unfolding.

'I said, who is the slut?' the man bellowed.

Daniel felt his anger boil over; he stood up. 'Look you—,' he started to say but felt himself being pulled back down fast by Troy. He then caught sight of Thirway looking at him, gesturing with a facial expression to let it slide.

Seeing this, the man pushed his chair back, scraping the floor. 'I said, is she for fucking?' He was louder this time.

After a few seconds, Thirway again slowly turned around; this time, he stood up.

'The lady is with us, so be polite,' Thirway said, trying to sound calm.

Out of the corner of his eye, Daniel noticed Troy and Bull tense up, as if ready to spring into action. He could sense the tension building in the air.

'Boys, come on, let's just all calm down,' Alexis piped in, trying to break the tension and hoping her female charm would have some effect.

'You shut the fuck up!' the man bellowed, pointing his rather large finger at her. He, too, then stood up, towering at least a foot over Thirway.

In a second, Troy and Bull were on their feet and moved in behind Thirway. Alexis moved closer to Daniel; she now felt very scared.

'Easy, boys, this animal means no harm.' Thirway gestured for

Troy and Bull to back off.

'Animal?' the man said angrily, drawing his arm back to take a swing.

Instinctively, Thirway lifted his right hand and jammed his forefinger into the crewman's mouth, fish-hooking him. He then turned, delivered a well-placed kick to the side of the man's right knee and pulled down hard, using his own body weight to bring the man down on his knees. Not stopping, Thirway connected his knee with the man's jaw and heard the jaw shatter in two. The man collapsed like a sack of shit and was out cold.

Alexis let out a scream whilst the other crew members hurriedly left the cafeteria.

'He will leave us alone now,' Thirway said calmly and simply sat back down and took a sip of his tea, as if nothing out of the ordinary had happened.

Bull produced a map and spread it out on the table. Thirway studied it intensely and ran a finger along the route the *Odin* would navigate.

'Here, this is where we are heading, Daniel,' he said, tapping his finger on a spot on the map. Daniel leaned over and looked. Thirway had placed his finger on the Gulf of Aden, near a coastal town named Berbera.

Just then, two members of the crew entered the cafeteria. Paying no attention to the group sitting around the table, they picked up the now semi-conscious man off the floor and dragged him out, without a word. As they were leaving, Jeremy entered and was confused to see the man being dragged out.

'Ah, Jeremy, you are late,' Thirway greeted the newcomer, less than pleased.

Jeremy had boarded with the team in Oman but needed more time than the others to unpack. In fact, he had spent the last hour chucking up.

At 35, Jeremy had a successful 10-year career as an oil broker. His last-drawn bonus, like Daniel's, was a six-figure number. Quitting his job in Hong Kong, he had moved to Singapore in search of a more relaxed lifestyle. He continued to live his single life in luxury, in a penthouse apartment overlooking the waters off Sentosa's eastern shore.

He loved Asia for its vibrancy and its food but even more for the girls—mostly bankers, lawyers and marketing executives—who escorted him around. His rule was six weeks, and then it was time for a new arm candy. Standing at 5 feet 8 inches and skinny, he didn't look the macho type, but his ease with spending made sure the bees visited his hive.

Joining Deep Six was his opportunity to buy the macho image he didn't have. He wrote the cheque the day he met Thirway at a charity dinner two months ago. Since then, he had overdosed on war movies, magazines and computer games with sniper scenes.

'Sit here.' Thirway gestured to an empty chair between Bull and Troy, and Jeremy quickly took his seat.

'Okay, now, listen up,' Thirway said. 'We are heading towards the Gulf of Aden, one of the most dangerous shipping channels in the world, apart from the South China Sea, that is. Once there, we will go fishing, our bait the very ship we are on.'

His eyes darted around the table. Everyone was listening, signalling their engagement with a subtle nod of the head.

'Bull and Troy will train you,' Thirway continued. 'Shooting out here is not like anything you will have ever done. Wind, sea spray, a moving deck and distance will all inhibit your ability to hit your target. Bull, here, is one of the best spotters in the business as well as a crack shot.'

Everyone turned to look at Bull, who remained expressionless.

'Troy, here, will help ensure we ourselves do not get boarded,' Thirway added. This comment made everyone sit up.

'Boarded?' Jeremy cried.

'Yes, you think they will just sit out there and wave their arms for us?' Thirway quipped.

'Will you not need more men?' Alexis enquired, trying to ask a slightly more intelligent question.

'We have four members of the crew, all trained in maritime security, so we have enough,' Thirway responded. 'Okay, Bull, get the Barrett.'

Bull got to work immediately. Daniel watched eagle-eyed as the M107 .50 calibre semi-automatic weapon came apart into an upper and a lower receiver and was reassembled in a minute. He knew and respected that the firepower of this particular model in the Barrett range was nothing short of incredible. He recalled the hours he had spent on the Internet researching the weapon rather than doing his job.

'To call this a rifle would be a gross understatement,' Bull explained. 'This is the ultimate weapons system.'

He paused to see if he had everyone's attention, then continued, 'The M107 can deliver 10 .50 calibre rounds at 2,700 feet per second in less than 10 seconds. Depending on what you aim it at, it can punch a hole through a wall, seriously damage a small armoured vehicle or even devastate a car's engine block. A human recipient of a round within its 1,800-metre effective range would stand no chance.'

Daniel and Jeremy looked on with their mouths open.

'This is it,' Daniel thought, his mind racing with excitement, 'the chance of a lifetime. Simply having the chance to operate such a weapon is awesome.'

The look in his eyes as he took his turn to adjust the sight, load a magazine and then handle the weapon did not go unnoticed. It excited Alexis.

Later that night, with Daniel's arms wrapped tight around her body as they lay in their cabin, Alexis felt good. The small size of the bunk they were sharing made it more intimate than a normal bed, whilst the gentle motion of the ship was making her feel sleepy. Even the smell of diesel seemed to have vanished, or perhaps she was just getting used to it.

Daniel was already out, his breathing calm. Thinking about what was to come, she suddenly felt anxious. Then, she smiled, her mind now on another man, who took her to sleep.

———————

The glowing tip of his cigarette in the dark would have made him an ideal target for any sniper. Leaning on the guardrail on the deck, Thirway gazed out to sea, his mind blank. He loved the sound of the waves breaking on the sides of the ship and the salty spray on his face; it was the feeling of freedom, almost isolation.

Hearing the thick steel hatchway door open, he snapped out of his reverie and turned. The bulky shadow of Bull emerged. Seeing Thirway, he walked over.

'You okay?' he asked in his dulcet tones.

'Yeah, I'm fine.' Thirway turned back to face the sea. Bull leaned on the guardrail beside him.

'So, which one will rat on us?'

'Not sure. Not Daniel. He seems okay,' Thirway pondered.

'The girl, who is she?' Bull enquired.

'The answer to that, Bull, would surprise you.' Thirway gave him a wry smile.

Never asking a question twice and accepting he was not going to get an answer yet, Bull turned to leave.

'Good night. See you in the morning.'

As he reached the hatchway, he heard Thirway shout, 'Her father owns the rusty bucket we're on. He is technically also our employer.'

Bull turned sharply and walked back.

'Are you serious?' It was rare for Bull to be surprised.

'Yup. Funny thing is, she doesn't even know it, nor Daniel. To them, it's just another ship,' Thirway laughed. 'It's not like she can tell her old man what she is up to when he finds out. So kinda funny.'

Bull shook his head and left, this time disappearing down the hatchway.

———

Seeing the shimmer of the sun on the water as it rose on the horizon could have been one of the most romantic moments Daniel and Alexis had ever shared. It was short-lived; Bull's dulcet tones reached their ears.

'This is not a bloody vacation. We have work to do. Meet me on the stern in 10 minutes.'

'Hey!' Daniel shouted back. 'We paid for this trip, you know. Don't scream at me like I'm in the bloody army!' Bull had pissed him off, interrupting his time to appreciate the sunrise with Alexis.

Bull stopped dead in his tracks, turned and walked over to Daniel.

'Lay a finger on me and I will report you,' Daniel got his words out before the big man could say anything.

'Report me. No one knows you are here, boy,' Bull boomed.

'Okay, just back off,' Alexis stepped in. 'Danny has a point. Don't treat us like shit. We paid to be here.'

Daniel stared at Alexis, shocked by the fact that she had placed herself in front of an express train with a bad temper.

'Discipline is what it is all about, miss, not being rude,' Bull retorted. 'You do not stroll up to a Barrett, pick it up and just shoot and hope to hit something a mile away, let alone not injure yourself. So, please take your time and enjoy the sunrise.' He turned and walked off.

Daniel and Alexis looked at each other. They both felt a little stupid. The big man was right—it was not a holiday, at all, but a premeditated killing spree.

Appearing at the stern, Daniel apologised, 'Sorry, Bull, it won't happen again.' He sounded like a naughty schoolboy. Alexis had gone off in search of hot tea and bacon.

'Get on the deck and listen up,' Bull said, pointing to the deck, where a Barrett M107 was already assembled on a large green groundsheet. Next to it, Daniel saw a couple of magazines. He assumed they were loaded with 10 rounds each.

'Run me through the parts of the weapon,' Bull ordered.

Daniel got down next to the weapon. 'Rear sight leaf, upper receiver, scope base, carrying handle, front sight, muzzle break...' he named all but one of the main parts.

'Not bad.' Bull seemed impressed. 'Now, load the magazine.'

Daniel picked up the magazine, checked it had a full clip and slammed it in; a few snaps and it was locked in place.

'Okay, now you will see straight ahead of you, bobbing about out there, an oil drum. Distance 500 metres and growing, hence my need for you to be here on time.' Bull made his point again. 'Now, shoot the damn thing.'

Daniel moved the weapon around on its bipod; all he could see through the scope was waves.

'Eyes on,' Bull shouted, which meant he could see the target through his own scope.

Daniel looked across at Bull, trying to get a hint as to the direction he was looking at, then turned back to his scope. It was there; he could just see the lip of the barrel as it lifted on a wave and then broadsided. He could now make out the name on the side.

'Shoot it!' Bull cried.

Daniel squeezed the trigger and felt the kick of the Barrett. Again and again, he let loose a round, feeling frustrated as he kept missing.

'Ease yourself. It's you, not the Barrett,' Bull commented.

Daniel drew a deep breath and once again scoped in the Barrett. He closed his eyes, cleared his mind and reopened his eyes; then, he squeezed the trigger.

This time, he saw the side of the barrel rip open. He quickly squeezed the trigger again and again, his mind focused. When he had finished all 10 rounds, the barrel was nowhere to be seen.

'It must have sunk,' he thought. 'No way it would float after that barrage of .50 cal rounds.'

Looking across at Bull, he was surprised to see a wry smile on his trainer's face. 'Good job.' Bull got up and started to pack up the gear.

'So, what now?' Daniel was ready to go again, feeling the adrenaline.

'Next, live bait.' Bull winked and strode off.

Walking into the galley, Alexis could see how excited Daniel was; his eyes were alive.

'Tea?' she asked.

'Love some,' Daniel responded, but his mind was still on the Barrett.

'So, how was it?' She set down a steaming mug of tea in front of him.

'Oh, it was awesome! You can smell the cordite and the thud in your shoulder is so powerful, it's just…' He was lost in his own world.

'Do you think you can do it for real, Daniel? Kill someone?' Alexis asked, looking very serious.

He looked up at her, his eyes suddenly growing dark.

'Yes, I can… I have.' A sudden pang of guilt hit him and he looked down at the table. Alexis read him like a book.

'Tell me, Daniel, what happened that night?' She placed her hands on his as he nursed his tea.

'I killed a man, a pirate. They tied him to a tree and I blew him apart.' He looked up into her eyes.

'Jesus, Daniel, what have you done?' Shocked, she recoiled.

'He had killed a ship's captain in cold blood. He was a murderer!' Daniel tried to justify his deed.

'That does not give you the right to act as judge and jury, Daniel.' She stood up and walked to the door. 'Stop now, Daniel, or lose me forever. I mean it, it stops here.' She stood in the doorway, looking at him.

Daniel remained seated at the table, staring into his tea.

'On deck now.' Bull stuck his head in the doorway. Alexis and Daniel shot each other a glance.

Daniel got up and walked over to Alexis, placed his hands on her arms, leaned in and kissed her gently on the cheek. No words were spoken. He just looked at her. Then, he carried on, heading for the stairway.

———————

The stranger with the hawk-like face dialled and took a deep breath. He somehow had to avoid showing his anger. The voice message that greeted him was not what he wanted to hear.

'Call me urgently. We may have a problem.' He then slammed down the phone.

TWELVE

September 2009. Gulf of Aden.

Men were running in all directions as Daniel stepped out on deck. It was a frantic scene of activity as reels of fire hoses snaked around. He then caught sight of Thirway and Bull leaning over the guardrail and looking out through their binoculars.

'Shit, is there a fire?' Daniel shouted across to Thirway.

'No, come over here.' Thirway gestured with a wave of his arm.

Joining them at the guardrail, Daniel took hold of Thirway's binoculars and brought them up to his eyes, squinting to adjust his vision. After a few moments scanning the waters, he locked onto two small wooden skiffs darting around about 800 yards off the port side. Then, suddenly, they veered off, seemingly on a course to cut right across their bow.

'Who are they?' Daniel asked.

'The welcoming committee, Daniel, and what you have come for,' Thirway jested.

Daniel dropped the binoculars from his face and shot Thirway a glance. 'Pirates,' he whispered, feeling the excitement already.

'Yes, Danny boy, pirates. They were checking us out,' Thirway responded.

'Are we going to take them out?'

Just then, Jeremy appeared and sauntered up to join them at the guardrail. 'So, what's with the fire hoses?' he asked.

'We use them to stop the pirates from boarding. The pressure of the water hits them like a sledgehammer in the head,' Thirway joked.

It all seemed to make sense now. 'Ready-made water cannons! Brilliant!' Daniel thought, glad Jeremy had asked the question.

'Okay, I'm ready when you are, Bull,' Daniel said eagerly.

'Not so fast,' Thirway cut in. 'These guys are just scouts. The real boys will hear about us soon enough. We wait for them. Patience, Danny.' He patted Daniel on the shoulder and strode off in search of some breakfast. Bull winked at Daniel and followed Thirway.

'Wait, you mean these guys actually conduct reconnaissance?' Daniel was surprised the pirates were organised.

Thirway turned back. 'Yes. In most cases, these guys are tipped off. They know which ships are heading their way well in advance. Did you think they were dirt farmers, Danny?' Thirway laughed and carried on.

Daniel began pacing around the deck, stopping every few yards to look out to sea. He was disappointed the men in the morning were not the real deal.

———

Alexis stood very still in the corner of her cabin, her back pressed hard against the steel wall. She had been trying for far too long to get a signal on her phone and had finally managed to, in her current position. This corner of the cabin seemed, for some bizarre reason, the best spot.

'Hi, it's me. How are you?' She pressed her ear hard to the phone. The static and echo made it hard to hear.

'Alexis, where are you exactly right now?' Kent sounded strangely anxious. And he had called her by her first name.

'Ehh, I'm on a ship. Took a few days off. Hard to explain.' She tried to think of how to explain her position.

'Never mind that. You have to get off. It's not safe. You are in danger. Trust me.'

'What do you mean? How do you know I'm in danger? It's just a ship. Don't be silly. Have you forgotten that I come from a shipping family?' Alexis wasn't getting what Kent was implying.

'Just trust me, okay?' he shouted.

Before Alexis could reply, the line went dead. She stood for a while, trying to piece together the conversation. Only the word 'danger' remained in her head.

Stepping out on deck, she caught sight of Daniel leaning on the guardrail. 'Daniel, are we safe?' she asked, placing an arm around him.

'You okay? Of course, it's not safe. We are hunting pirates!' He smiled at her as if the statement she had just made was almost silly.

'Daniel, I never want to stop you doing the things that make you happy, but this... I just worry for you. Someone just told me we have to leave.' Alexis rubbed her face into his chest.

'Who told you?' He looked down at her, surprised by her sudden concern.

'Oh, it doesn't matter. Just protect me, okay?'

Before they could continue, Bull appeared. 'Daniel, meet me at the stern in five and be prepared for a long wait.' He then vanished back down the hatchway.

'It's okay. You go. I will be fine.' Alexis gave Daniel a half smile and hugged him.

'Are you sure?' he asked, trying to look boyish and innocent.

'See you whenever.' Alexis walked off. She had far more important things to do. She needed a phone signal.

Daniel felt a high as he lay next to Bull on a green groundsheet at the stern. The Barrett had already been assembled and test-fired. The barrel was still warm to the touch.

Bull had his Leupold scope assembled on its tripod and trained out to sea. He took in the calm water, the clear sky and the warm southerly breeze. 'It's a perfect evening,' he thought.

Turning to Daniel, he said, 'We wait now. Any sign of movement, do nothing. Wait for my instruction, okay?' Daniel acknowledged with a nod and tried to settle himself down.

Thirway stood on the bridge, scanning the horizon in all directions through his binoculars. Glancing down occasionally, he saw an array of blips on the radar screen, each representing a ship close by.

Vandenbrook knew the drill. He simply observed Thirway from his chair and kept his mouth shut. Asking questions would only put a stop to the cash inflow from Thirway each trip.

With his ear defenders positioned slightly off his ears, Daniel could hear the waves breaking and the engine throbbing—and Bull's shallow breathing. All was calm, except for the occasional bang that jarred his senses every time a hatchway door closed.

As the 4x4 skidded to a halt, crowds started to gather around. Abshir smiled across at his brother.

'Today, Asad, you can take your first ship.'

The small village of Shilodo, located just south of Xiis on Somalia's northern coast, was an ideal base for hunting ships in the gulf. Abshir knew a ship with Asad's name on it was just offshore.

As Asad stepped out of the truck, his eyes widened. The crowd was surging towards them, chanting his brother's name. It was almost deafening. He knew Abshir was regarded as a king here—king of the pirates—and that made him proud. Raising his arms high in the air and holding aloft his AK, he joined in the chanting. Four of Abshir's best men moved forward and started to push everyone back and clear a path into the village.

One of his men ran up to him. 'Abshir, you have a message, to call Stone.'

'Later. I will call him later. For now, I have to teach my little lion to hunt.'

'Boss, he said it was important.' But Abshir and Asad had already disappeared into the crowd. Stone had called four times to warn Abshir that this ship was not like the others. It wasn't one he was to capture and divert. This was a sniper ship, one that carried customers who wanted a live kill.

The RHIB started to pitch and crash through the waves on the outer reef, sending salt water spraying in over the bow. Wiping his face with his hand, Abshir turned his head and took in the sight of his little brother at the helm. He felt good. He knew this was Asad's day; he would lead the attack.

Asad knew Abshir was looking at him. Inside, he felt scared, his stomach churning and twisting, but he dared not show it. He had to overcome his nerves and prove to his brother that he was worthy of being a member of the MFF. A steely look crossed his face as he recalled how his friends, blooded pirates, had teased him. Today, he would be king.

As the boat zigzagged further and further out to sea, one of the men suddenly signalled to Abshir that he had seen something. Abshir immediately gave the order to cut the throttle and allow the boat to drift.

'You take the controls,' he instructed one of his men. He then moved up the boat to get a better look. Asad followed his brother's every movement with his eyes, now wide with excitement.

Looking through his binoculars, Abshir could see it was a low-freeboard vessel. He wondered if it was the ship he had been informed of.

'Let's move in and take a better look,' he instructed his men. Then, he turned to Asad. 'Brother, this could be all yours, okay?' he shouted, as if already celebrating their triumph.

'I will take her, brother,' Asad replied bravely. 'I am the young lion.'

At 1,000 metres, Abshir once again signalled for the engine to be cut. Looking through his binoculars, he smiled. He could make out the word *ODIN* in bold white letters on the stern. That was indeed the name he had been given.

Scanning the decks, he could see only a few lights on; the rest of the ship was in darkness. The strong moonlight across the water, however, would make them an easy target, should anyone on board be looking out for them. Abshir knew this raised the danger level.

'Nine knots. We will go in under the stern and board her from there,' he told his men, his arm signalling to move forward. Various automatic weapons clicked in preparation for the attack.

Bull spotted the boat in the choppy water; his eyes missed nothing.

'Eyes on,' he informed, causing Daniel to tense up, his scope locking onto the approaching target. Daylight was fading fast, but the strong moonlight was sufficient for them to see.

'This is Bull. Dim all lights. We have a fish on the line,' Bull announced on his walkie-talkie.

Thirway responded instantly with a 'Roger that.' He then turned to Vandenbrook. 'Captain, tell your crew to lie low. We are about to have company.'

Vandenbrook just nodded as Thirway left. He knew his role, and that was to maintain a steady course and leave the pirates to Thirway.

Alexis was now completely frustrated. She had tried everywhere to get a signal. There was only one thing left to try, and that would mean approaching the captain.

She stepped onto the bridge wearing one of her biggest smiles; it normally got her what she wanted.

'Hi, captain, how are you?'

Vandenbrook turned. 'Fine, Miss Pathos. You?' He seemed overly polite and he knew her name.

'You know me?' she asked.

'Of course, miss. Can I help you?' Vandenbrook seemed puzzled.

'How did…' she began to ask, then stopped; it didn't matter for now. 'I need to ask a favour. My phone…' She didn't get to finish her explanation.

'Of course,' he interjected, 'you can place a ship-to-shore call over there.' He pointed.

'You don't mind? I will happily pay.' Alexis didn't really expect him to accept.

'Pay, miss? You own the ship,' Vandenbrook laughed.

Now, it was Alexis's turn to feel puzzled. 'Excuse me?' The look on her face said it all.

'You mean you didn't know this is your father's ship?' he looked more shocked than she did.

'No. Oh, god, I had no idea.' She went pale.

'You okay?' Vandenbrook was genuinely concerned. 'Get her some tea,' he barked at one of his crew, then turned back to Alexis and placed an arm around her. 'I must admit, I did wonder how you got mixed up with this, Daniel, was it?'

'Are we in any danger?' She looked up at him.

'No, miss, just a few pirates. All under control. I will let you in on a secret: they get paid to supply a few old men to shoot at. Not very nice, I know, but it's all a game, you see? Daniel won't know the difference,' Vandenbrook laughed.

Alexis felt marginally better, but what worried her now was her father.

Jeremy was on stand-down, much to his disgust. He had injured his hand whilst closing the bolt action of the Barrett; his shooting days were on hold. He simply stood behind Daniel, looking on as frustration grew within him.

Daniel maintained his visual on the pirates, like ghosts in the moonlight. They were visible enough to shoot at, and that was good news for him.

Abshir gave the order to cover up; in seconds, black ski masks and scarves hid the faces of his men. Despite the multiple hijacks they had executed, they knew the danger; it kept them sharp, tempered their hunger for wealth.

Asad moved to the front of the boat. He wanted to get a good look at the ship. His eyes from behind his mask glinted in the moonlight.

'Hold until I say. Eight hundred yards and closing,' Bull instructed. Time seemed to slow, each second ticking in Daniel's head like a drumbeat. He recalled how he had forced himself to calm down and breathe slowly on Junk Island, as he called it.

Daniel listened intently as Bull started to whisper the closing distance, 'Five hundred... four... three-fifty... Clear! Take the shot.' Bull turned sharply and tapped Daniel on the shoulder.

Seconds after Daniel squeezed the trigger, blood, skull fragments and brain matter sprayed all over Abshir and his men. One of them was down, his chest splayed open like a cheap can of tuna.

Abshir shouted to veer away and power up. 'Move it,' he screamed. The RHIB jerked sharply to the right, causing the men to fall over one another and one to fall overboard.

'Man over!' someone screamed.

'Leave him!' Abshir ordered, knowing he had to put distance between them and the ship. He felt his blood boil. He knew a sniper had hit them and that had not been part of the plan. More rounds whizzed past as they desperately tried to accelerate away.

'Move out of the way!' Bull took over the Barrett, his scope now locked onto the man splashing about in the sea. He fired; the shot took off the top of the man's head and the body sank out of sight in seconds.

As if it were all a dream, it was over. Bull turned to Daniel. 'Good shooting, boy.' Daniel knew, coming from Bull, that was special.

He felt himself relax, his body shaking as the adrenaline began to dissipate.

Thirway, who had observed the entire scene from the bridge, smiled. 'Another happy customer,' he thought.

'Jesus, I did it! Did you see that?' Daniel was up on his feet, pacing around in circles.

Jeremy grunted and stormed off to his cabin.

———

When they were 1,800 metres away, Abshir gave the order to stop. Looking around as the boat drifted on the waves, he started to take in the horror of what had happened.

Then, his eyes fell upon Asad lying in the front of the boat; bloody water sloshed around his body. Abshir froze as he noticed half his brother's head was gone. He knew ammunition well; it would have taken at least a .50 calibre round to cause such mutilation at such a distance. The round, having struck Asad, had continued and hit a second man in the chest with still enough velocity to nearly tear him in half.

The scream Abshir let out was enough to send fear through his own men. Falling to his knees, he cradled the corpse of his younger brother. After a few minutes, he drew a deep breath.

'I want them all dead!' he screamed. The hatred in his eyes said it all.

THIRTEEN

The small courtyard bordered by four small houses was hot, dry and dusty. A single orange tree, planted in the middle beside the old well, clung to life, its branches beginning to descend and wither. The tree and the well formed the only focal point in what was otherwise an empty space. The well was dry, its cavernous depths completely starved of water.

Each of the 60 or so weather-beaten faces now in the small courtyard was turned towards the formidable figure of Abshir. His powerful frame stood somewhat precariously on a wooden table at one end of the courtyard. He steadied himself, knowing he could not afford to show any sign of weakness as he addressed his clan.

'Brothers… our little brother has been killed, murdered by Western butchers, and I want revenge.' His voice was distinctly angry. Somalis grieved deeply and for long periods of time. Losing loved ones was a common experience; drought, famine and war made sure of that. It was all too familiar to Abshir as well. But something else now ran through his veins—hatred. His soul was at war, and he would not rest until his brother was avenged.

The imposing image of an enraged Abshir consumed the attention of the sole Westerner in the crowd. With his camera aimed at the pirate king, he kept clicking the shutter open over and over again. He was caught completely off-guard when a man behind brought the butt of his weapon down hard on the back of his neck, knocking him out cold. He fell to the ground, his face in the dust, and was dragged away.

Gunshots erupted and the fireworks of lead carried the mob's hatred up into the air. As adrenaline flowed through their veins, their jeering grew in intensity and the rhythmic stamping of their feet quickened, kicking up larger clouds of choking dust.

Jumping off the table, Abshir felt invincible. The atmosphere was intoxicating; he could feel the adrenaline charging through his body. His mind turned to the tip-off from his supposedly trustworthy insider a few days ago—the tip-off that had gotten his brother killed. He would not forget such treachery. YANIC AUTHOR.

He took in the sight of his men, all fired up and thirsty for blood. As the frenzy continued, he looked up and prayed to Allah that revenge would be swift. He would order his men to sea at first light.

Vandenbrook was getting impatient. He had steered his ship in figures of eights for over 12 hours now. They needed to get underway if they were to stand any chance of meeting the naval convoy that would escort them safely towards the Suez Canal entrance. Whilst it was all very well baiting pirates once, he knew there were many more pirate groups out there that would not play Thirway's game. That thought made him very nervous; the *Odin* was a sitting duck.

'Thirway, I will give you two more hours and then I will order full ahead. Is that clear?' he bellowed down the intercom.

Thirway was in the galley making tea. 'Wait, I will be up in 10 minutes,' he replied.

'When will I get my chance?' Jeremy asked, depressed about being passed over for a kill. Daniel, who was drinking hot chocolate on the other side of the table to replenish his reduced sugar levels, just looked on.

'You will get your chance,' Thirway assured. 'Have no fear. There will be more pirates. Don't worry. This time, you can kill at close range, see their eyes.'

'Yeah, that's more like it.' Jeremy seemed unnervingly happy about the thought.

'Nutter,' Daniel thought to himself. He also thought Thirway was just pacifying Jeremy.

'I have to go to the bridge. Get some rest, all of you.' Thirway dashed off.

——— —— ——

Alexis was bored, having finished her book, a thriller by Stephen King. She decided to take a walk and get some fresh air, despite the late hour.

Turning the corner towards the stern, she heard a raised voice from above. She stopped and listened, recognising Thirway's voice. He seemed unhappy about something, or at least he sounded like he was trying to calm someone down.

'How was I to know it was his brother? Calm down,' Thirway shouted, then paused, thinking he saw a shadow move below. 'I have to go. I will talk to you later.' He peered over the guardrail. Alexis quickly shrank back into the shadows to avoid being caught eavesdropping. Thirway shook his head and continued on his way to the bridge.

'Are you sneaking around?'

Alexis jumped and turned sharply towards the voice; to her relief, it was just Daniel.

'Jesus, Daniel, you scared me,' she breathed.

'Sorry, I was just getting some air.'

'Me, too. That cabin closes in after a while.'

'Hey, it went…' Daniel began but was cut short.

'I don't want to know. If you are happy, then okay, but spare me the details, okay?'

'Okay, agreed. Anyway, I'm done. Looking forward to flying home in a few days.'

'Really? You are?' Alexis was surprised.

'Yeah, I did what I set out to do. Time now for another adventure.' Daniel beamed, knowing it won her over every time.

'I'm glad to hear that. Come on, it's late. Take me to bed,' she said, her eyes now smouldering. With that, they both walked off towards the hatchway.

As they neared their cabin, the crewman who had been beaten up by Thirway emerged at the end of the hallway. Daniel observed the heavy bandage wrapped around his head. 'Most likely to hold his shattered jaw in place,' he thought. The man's eyes were intense as he started to lumber towards them. Instinct told Daniel trouble was coming.

'Listen, we don't want any trouble, okay?' Daniel tried to pacify him.

Seeing that the man was not stopping, Daniel grabbed Alexis by the arm. 'Come on, let's get out of here.'

They made just a few paces back towards the stairs before another crewman appeared out of a cabin.

'You are going nowhere, bitch,' the second man said. He spread out his arms to block the hallway.

'Listen, this is crazy! We had nothing to do with it!' Alexis shouted. Seeing the menacing look on the man's face, she drew a lungful of air and screamed, 'Help!' Her voice echoed through the lower decks.

The two men paused for a few seconds and then dashed forward. One grabbed Daniel by the scruff of his neck, slammed him against the wall and punched him in the stomach. Daniel doubled over, winded and unable to scream. Pain racked his body as the punch took effect.

Alexis grabbed the crewman's arm and tried to pull him off Daniel. 'Leave us alone, you thug!' she shouted, digging her nails into his forearm.

It was useless. The man simply pushed her, sending her falling to the ground. She looked up, dazed, and saw the man with the bandages staring at her. He grabbed her by the hair and dragged her kicking and screaming.

Seeing this, Daniel tried to get up on his feet. 'Get off her, you bastard!' he shouted with as much breath as his lungs could gather. A shard of pain pierced his guts again as a kick landed on his stomach. He collapsed, coughing as he tried to draw in air. As he lay there, he could see Alexis being dragged into a nearby cabin. Her screams were deafening and he felt completely helpless.

Vandenbrook had been alerted to the situation by a diligent crew member. Immediately, he bolted down the steep stairway, Bull and Thirway close behind.

Pushing past Vandenbrook like an express train, Bull charged at the man leaning over Daniel and slammed him against the wall. As if on autopilot, he wrapped his arm around the man's neck, twisted his body over and around, and heaved him upwards, snapping the neck instantly.

Thirway ran on whilst Vandenbrook helped Daniel to his feet. 'You all right, son?' he asked anxiously.

'Yeah, I'm okay, but Alexis... she got dragged in there.' Daniel pointed down the hallway.

Thirway burst into the cabin and saw Alexis pinned down on the floor. The man's overalls were hanging from his waist. Thirway pulled him off Alexis, slammed him backwards against the floor and delivered a brutal kick to the head. Given the man's jaw was already broken, this was sufficient to render him helpless.

'He won't bother you again,' Thirway assured Alexis as he helped her up. 'Get him on deck!' he boomed to the two crew members who had come in behind him.

———   —— ——

Standing on deck with his wrists tied, the man with the bandages swayed from side to side, his head bowed; he was clearly half out of it.

Vandenbrook walked up to him, looked at him and then walked

off. He had a logbook full of excuses to explain the loss of a crew member at sea, and he would use it; rapists were scum in his book. The fact that one of his own crew had lost control and degraded to the point of trying to rape a woman was enough for him to take matters into his own hands.

Alexis, wrapped in a blanket, her face bruised, could not bring herself to look at her attacker. Daniel had his arm around her, holding her tight.

'Daniel, your honour.' Thirway held out a 9mm pistol, cocked and loaded. Seeing this, Alexis turned her head away. Daniel gently moved away and approached Thirway. He took the pistol and walked over to the man.

'You piece of shit, not so big now, are you?'

Only a murmur of unintelligible noise escaped the man's mouth as he looked up. It didn't matter to Daniel what he was saying. Taking a step back, he aimed the pistol.

'Danny, no!' Alexis screamed. Bull turned towards her. 'Let it be, miss. It's done.'

Daniel fired. The round went straight through the man's forehead, felling him like a tree; his body was now twitching on the deck.

Thirway strode up to Daniel. 'Well done.' He then eased the pistol out of Daniel's hand and fired another round into the man's head. 'A double tap is always best, Daniel.'

'Get rid of him and the other bloke,' Thirway instructed Troy.

Alexis felt herself break. It had all become too much. She ran off towards her cabin. Daniel ran after her, reaching her just at the bottom of the stairs.

'Don't, Daniel! That was horrible!' Despite her ordeal, she was not impressed with murder.

'I just did the bloke who tried to rape you and that's the thanks I get?' He held her arms.

'Get off me! You are not the Daniel I knew. You don't take the law into your own hands and just shoot a man in cold blood. Police,

Daniel, that's why they exist. To deal with such shit. Not you, a banker.' She pulled away and vanished into the cabin. The slam of the door told Daniel he was not welcome.

'Women,' he muttered and headed for the deck.

———

Vandenbrook was now even more anxious to get underway. 'I need to speed up and get us away from here. We still have three to four days of sailing before we reach the Suez.'

'Not yet. Half speed for another day or so. Take us back and past Bandarbeyla. Then, my business is done, okay?' Thirway replied.

The look on Vandenbrook's face clearly showed he wasn't happy. 'Okay, but you had better protect us. We are sitting ducks out here.' He knew proceeding at anything less than full ahead made them vulnerable to further attacks.

Thirway patted Vandenbrook on the shoulder. 'Don't worry yourself. You are in safe hands.' His smile wasn't convincing as he ambled off in search of a cigarette.

FOURTEEN

Few scenes are as sobering as that of people standing around a grave.

Abshir now found himself gazing down at Asad's body wrapped in cloth—a sight he had hoped he would never live to see.

Shock still had its hands tight around his throat, making it hard for him to breathe. The past few days had seen him alternate between rage and numbness. Images of his brother lying in a pool of blood kept haunting his dreams, waking him up in a cold sweat every night.

Abshir knew his emotions well. The months he had spent in Afghanistan engaged in kinetic fights had honed his ability to search out his soul. Now that he had fought the bitter battle with hatred, managing to rein in his innermost demons, a new visitor arrived—guilt.

He had brought Asad's body back to this tiny village on the outskirts of Mogadishu. It was just a cluster of huts, with open sewers and no running water, but it was home—home to his people, whose salvation, he believed, lay in his hands. He believed he was acting on a message from Allah to feed and protect them. He only knew one way, and that was to fight.

Abshir was completely alone now. His mother and father had both been killed during an attack on Mogadishu by the Americans when Asad was only four years old. In fact, his entire family had been wiped out, all casualties of conflicts with devils from the West. His men were his family now.

Looking around Asad's grave, he saw only a handful of people—two of his most trusted men, who stood guard, and three of Asad's friends—all members of the MFF. Abshir had wanted it this way. It was personal and he would not have the rest of his clan see the tears running down his face.

Looking up at the sky, Abshir swore his revenge; he would not stop until his brother's killer was dead. The AK-47 he had given Asad as a gift now hung around his own shoulders; it would serve as a reminder of the deed he now had to perform.

A small wiry man with rather weather-beaten features now appeared amongst the small gathering of mourners. He was dressed in a dirty white shirt and a tatty pair of jeans rolled up to his knees. It was Dalmar, one of Abshir's men. He handed Abshir a satellite phone and stood back. Abshir took the phone, knowing it was Stone.

'You dare to call me? I will have your head for this.'

'Listen, I had no idea it would get out of hand,' Stone said quickly, trying to defend himself. 'It was an unfortunate accident. You know me; did I not save your skin once? Never mind that now. I have a deal for you.' He paused.

'I'm listening.'

'On the ship is something far more valuable than the cargo—a girl. Her father owns the ship. She is worth many millions.'

Abshir was silent for a few seconds.

'Who is this girl?'

'She is Alexis Pathos.' Stone smiled a sadistic smile.

'You are saying I can ransom this girl and forget to avenge my brother?' Abshir's tone was severe.

'No, I'm saying you can have that bit of information for free. Who you kill is up to you. Just make sure Thirway is one of them. I want him dead. He has gone too far this time. But the girl lives. Do we have a deal?'

Stone knew the value of keeping Abshir happy. He would make his money once the cargo made its way to Libya and then Iraq. The

Americans were trying to create another reason to invade, and who better to deliver the evidence than a bunch of Islamic extremists, or so it would seem.

'I will think about it,' Abshir said. He then handed the phone back to Dalmar.

'Come, please,' Dalmar pulled Abshir's arm. Abshir followed.

Cutter was seated uncomfortably in a small chair in the middle of a hut, his hands tied behind his back. He was completely in the dark; a bag had been placed over his head, which was still pounding from the blow that had knocked him out. Sweat had soaked through his clothing in the stuffy humid air.

As he swallowed, he could feel his throat swollen and parched. He was in shit order. He strained to free his hands and instantly felt a whack to the side of his head. It was enough to make him wince in pain. His ears then picked up the sound of faint footsteps. They seemed to pace slowly around him, as if the person were studying him.

The light that flooded his vision when the bag was removed was blinding, forcing his eyes to shut tight. As he slowly opened them, they began to adjust to the light, although his vision was blurred.

'Give him some water,' a familiar voice spoke. Cutter raised his head, squinting.

'We meet again,' he rasped and then drank from the cup now placed at his lips.

'Untie him,' Abshir instructed. 'What are you doing here, Cutter?' He pulled up a chair and sat facing him.

'You!' Cutter said, surprised to see TJ, who had stepped forward to untie him.

Abshir laughed. 'You know each other, I think. You see, my friend, TJ works for me.'

Cutter rubbed his wrists and sat forward. 'Listen, I came here to observe you, nothing more. I mean you no harm.'

'Observe me. You must have an objective, as to observe is to show interest, no?' Abshir showed his normal smarts. 'Come on, out with it. Why are you really here? '

'I'm not going to harm you. We're friends now. I heard about your brother. I'm sorry.'

'I won't talk about that now. Continue.' For a second, Abshir's eyes ran deep.

'Okay, my employers need you to help them stop the Americans.'

'Are you not both allies?'

'Yes, indeed we are, but even friends play games against each other and do things they don't agree on.' Cutter knew his Somali friend would grasp this concept.

'I see, British intelligence.'

'Listen, if you have any information, anything at all that will help us, please share it. We can reward you.'

'Really? What makes you think I have such information or that I need your money?' Abshir sat back.

Cutter put his best foot forward. 'Who helped you get to your current position? Do we not deserve a favour in return?'

Abshir knew the young Westerner had a point, and paying his debts was a matter of pride.

'Okay, you have a point. I like you. You have guts.' With that, he began to talk.

FIFTEEN

'God, this is so boring. How many times have we seen this film?' Daniel got up and stretched his arms.

'Shall we go for a stroll?' Alexis suggested, not that she wanted to admit she was also dozing off. An evening spent with a bunch of oily Filipino seamen watching *Die Hard II* was not her idea of fun.

Daylight was fading fast as they walked arm-in-arm down the port side of the deck. A slight breeze blowing in from Yemen in the north sent small sand particles into Daniel's eyes. He blinked and took in the calm sea; it could have been a perfect evening, aside from the fact that they were on a floating pirate trap.

Thirway appeared from around the corner; patrolling the upper deck was his routine now. 'Good evening,' he greeted. Alexis scowled and looked away.

'Hi John, all okay?' Daniel asked.

'Yes, for now. Enjoy your walk.' Thirway shot Alexis a glance and strode off.

'Has he pissed you off?' Daniel had noticed the cold shoulder she gave Thirway.

'I don't trust him. Come on, it's getting nippy.' She tugged at his arm and they headed back towards the stairwell.

Troy was getting some rest down below, spread out in his bunk, fully clothed and snoring lightly, his carbine beside him just in case it was called for. Bull had positioned himself near the bow of the vessel, his eyes scanning the waters for visitors through a night vision sight.

As Thirway burst into the galley, his face red from the wind, Vandenbrook noticed the 9mm pistol in his right hand. It was enough to freeze him, his spoon in mid-air. He stared for a while before going back to his soup, still keeping one eye on Thirway.

'I hope that is not required for me,' Vandenbrook said, raising an eyebrow.

'Relax, you know the score and I pay you well, do I not?' Thirway pulled up a chair and sat opposite him.

'So, what's the plan? Continue for the Suez?' Vandenbrook asked.

'No, actually! Change in plan. I need you to change course, head for Eyl on the south side. Once there, proceed at a speed of no more than 6 knots until I issue further instructions.' Thirway placed the pistol on the table, a deliberate gesture to unnerve Vandenbrook.

'What? I can't just change course. I have my orders.' Vandenbrook showed his shock by placing down his spoon hard. His face wore a big frown.

'You will do as I say, captain! That is, if you wish to continue receiving the kickbacks. I am sure you can think of a reason and inform your office.' Thirway tapped the table with his fingers.

'This is outrageous! You will not get away with it. Taking cash for the odd stowaway is one thing, even turning a blind eye to what he does, but this? Why would we want to head there?' Vandenbrook was flushed with anger. 'I can't just turn us around like a damn speedboat. Have you any idea of the cost this will incur?' He stood up and flung down his napkin on the table in disgust.

'Sit back down, captain.' Thirway paused. 'What will it take? How much?' Thirway knew he had to position a deal.

Vandenbrook hesitated and then sat down, his head shaking, trying to take in what Thirway was asking.

'No, I won't do it. You will have to find another ship. I have been accommodating for too long. I want you and your men off my ship. I have a cargo to deliver in London, in case that escaped your tiny mind. This is not your private yacht to go where you please.' Vandenbrook thumped his hand on the table.

'It seems you need persuading.' Thirway grabbed the pistol, which sent Vandenbrook jerking backwards as if expecting the worst.

'Easy, big boy, just relax,' the captain said.

Thirway produced a small video camera from a shoulder bag he had brought with him. Placing it carefully on the table with his free hand, he turned it on and faced it towards Vandenbrook. He then hit the play button and sat back.

The captain's face went pale. On the screen, he saw his family car arriving at what he immediately recognised as his home. His wife and two young sons got out of the car and entered the house.

Thirway watched Vandenbrook sink back in his chair.

'Well, captain, do we have a deal?'

It took a few seconds for the reality of what he had seen to sink in.

'You utter bastard.' Vandenbrook pushed the camera aside with his hand and stood up. 'Who took the film?' He was visibly shaken.

'Someone you need to worry about. Not a nice man, an evil little shit, in fact.' Thirway leaned in, his eyes on Vandenbrook, who just nodded.

'Good, then, it seems we have an agreement. Once at Eyl, I will warn my men off and your family will be unharmed.' Thirway stood up and placed the pistol in the waistband of his jeans.

'On your way, captain. I want to see this tub change course,' Thirway said firmly.

'One question, tell me what business we have in Eyl?' Vandenbrook was standing in the doorway.

'It's complicated. I have my orders, too. I have been told to make a course and ensure we arrive. My business will then be concluded.' In his head, he could hear Stone's voice.

Vandenbrook frowned, not knowing what to make of Thirway's response. But he did know that Eyl was hell.

'And I thought the Somalis were the pirates. How wrong was I?'

Vandenbrook sneered.

——— —— ———

It was half an hour later, as Thirway sipped his tea, when the announcement came.

'Men, listen up. We have a change in course, heading south for Eyl. I have been instructed by the ship's owner to divert the ship.' Hearing this, Thirway smiled.

'Eyl?' Hearing Vandenbrook's announcement, Daniel pulled out a chart from one of the drawers in the recreation room. He spread it out and ran his finger on it trying to locate Eyl. Finding it, he tapped it with his finger.

'What on earth would be there?' he thought, and went back to the drawers and rummaged around. 'Gotcha!' He found an old atlas, which was well-used, going by the stained dog-eared pages. Flipping through it, he found a page on Eyl. His eyes widened as he read what he could of the text, which was partly covered by brown stains.

'Eyl. An ancient town in northern Puntland, Somalia. The prominent Somali clans are Leelkase and Majeerteen, both sub-clans of the Darod.' He skipped a section that was unreadable through the stains. 'Eyl is situated near the Hafun peninsula. As of 2008, Eyl has become a pirate haven, with more than a dozen ships being held captive by pirate crews.'

Daniel could hardly believe it. 'Pirates!' he exclaimed, feeling the excitement welling up within him again.

——— —— ———

The room was full of men armed to the teeth and chewing khat. They jostled around, murmuring to each other, impatient to hear why they had been summoned.

Suddenly, one of them punched another in the face, breaking his nose. As the man cried out in pain, his nose covered in blood, a few others joined in, hitting him with the butts of their AKs.

Finally, he collapsed.

Abshir stood up. 'Enough!' The room fell silent, except for the moaning of the beaten man. 'Do not fight amongst yourselves. The enemy is out there.' He pointed to the sea.

'Listen to me, brothers. Many of you will die in this attack, but your lives will earn food for our families and milk for our babies. Let us not be afraid. Let us use both our wits and our guts. I promise you victory. I promise you respect. MFF, MFF,' Abshir began to chant, thumping his fists on the table.

As the men joined in the chanting, the noise in the room built up into a rhythmic roar. One man, however, did not join in but stepped forward to address Abshir.

'What will we get in return?' he shouted over the din.

Abshir raised his arms to silence the room. Slowly, the chanting ceased.

'This man asks what he will get,' Abshir addressed the room. 'I tell you—reward, money. This ship is worth many millions, my brothers.'

'And for those who die?' the rebel asked defiantly.

'Do not doubt me. This has been planned. Anyone who dies, who gives his life… I, Abshir, will make sure his family is taken care of.' His voice was deep and powerful.

'Planned,' the man spoke up again. 'Then, how did Asad die? Was that planned?'

The room went deathly silent; not the slightest murmur or shuffle of feet.

'You dare to mention my brother!' Abshir flew into a rage, which was exacerbated by the effects of the opium. His eyes, dilated and deep, he grabbed a machete off the table and raised it high.

The defiant man, as if unfazed, stood his ground and spat at Abshir. Without hesitation, Abshir brought the blade down, almost severing the man's head at the neck. Blood spattered across Abshir's face. He stood stone-still as the body quivered and collapsed.

Slowly, the chanting began again; no one would dare challenge
Abshir now.

Sketching with a stick in the sand, Abshir began to explain his plan,
which used military tactics he had learnt from his years with the US
Marine Corps. Unlike the other pirate leaders, he was extremely well-
trained and disciplined, which meant he had a strategy.

The men around him were divided into three groups: logistics,
muscle and technology. Abshir had trained them all. He knew poorly
disciplined men, no matter how well-armed, were a liability—
something Mohamed had not understood.

Twenty men would acquire from the locals boats, fuel and
provisions necessary to launch and sustain their attack. Another
20 were the hammer that would smash his enemy; these men were
trained to handle guns and RPGs and could kill, if required. Finally,
10 men would take charge of their communications; these men were
trained to use GPS devices and satellite phones. Gone were the days
when they were merely dirt farmers and fishermen.

Abshir was ready to strike. He just needed the word that the *Odin*
was offshore. He ran through the plan in his mind again and again.
He knew there were armed men on board, men who clearly had the
firepower to kill his men at a distance.

Despite having been told previously that his boats would not be
attacked, something had gone wrong. This time, there would be three
boats, each carrying seven men. The first boat would attack from the
port side, drawing any fire. The second would then attack the stern,
again drawing any fire.

Once the battle was underway, Abshir would approach in the third
boat head on from the bow. It was madness coming at a huge cargo
ship in what amounted to a rowing boat; he would not be suspected.
His boat would then skim down the starboard side of the vessel and
come in under the stern—a dangerous manoeuvre, but it was his only

chance. If Stone was correct, Abshir would find a rope ladder hanging at the stern, making it easy for his men to board. Stone hoped, this time, Thirway would do as promised.

Sitting on the beach, Abshir mentally prepared himself. One more day, or so, and he would avenge his brother's death.

His thoughts then strayed to his time in Afghanistan. He had been a US Marine then; it seemed so far removed from his life as a Somali warlord. He had been on a mission in the eastern part of the country near the Helmand River Valley, a vast province that was largely an arid dirt patch, save for a band of fertile land along the river.

His eight-man patrol was to take a small house in which a suspected Taliban leader was holed up; they wanted him alive. The house was bordered on three sides by open land whilst the river, although somewhat dry, ran across in front of the house, which made a daytime assault difficult.

Darkness had fallen as his patrol advanced. The only sounds they could hear were a dog barking in the distance and insects humming in the surrounding scrub. Abshir was the last to move out from cover and dash across open land to a depression just left of the house that was deep enough to hide in.

The patrol leader had kicked the door open and rolled flashbangs in before entering. Three men followed him in. Suddenly, there was an explosion and Abshir felt himself being pushed to the ground. It was as if the world had stopped. A dull hum in his ears told him he was alive as he lay in the dirt, stunned.

Five soldiers were killed that night; another was taken home in critical condition. The house had been a trap, set to explode upon entry. The bull-headed patrol leader hadn't checked for tripwires. Only Abshir and one other Marine escaped serious harm; that other man was Trevor Stone. He was the one who had pushed Abshir to the ground and saved his life.

Upon his return, Abshir was debriefed and subsequently discharged. 'Unfit for duty,' they said. The event sparked in Abshir a hatred so deep he loathed all things associated with the West—all things, that is, except their money.

SIXTEEN

September 2009. Eyl, Somalia.

Life, it is said, flashes before your eyes as you go towards the light. The past suddenly becomes clear.

Abshir had certainly had his share of close encounters. Now, he was prepared to die. The devil's own breath filled his lungs, and his eyes blazed like burning coals. He was the worst kind of enemy—one with nothing to lose.

Whatever games the British and American intelligence agencies wanted him to play were far from his mind. They would soon realise he was his own man, not a puppet in a play of secrecy and lies. His only agenda now was to take the *Odin* and kill those responsible for his brother's death. Asad would be avenged and that was that.

The news Abshir had been waiting for finally came at 7:00 p.m. The *Odin* was finally offshore. As if needing to release the demons within, he screamed his brother's name. Not a soul in the village could have failed to hear the anguish in his scream.

'Gather the men!' he instructed. 'We leave in two hours.'

The three boats pushed off from the beach, each carrying seven men armed with semi-automatic weapons. Their twin Yamaha 200hp outboards purred as they sped towards their prey. Abshir felt alive, powerful, almost invincible. His eyes were now locked onto the distant silhouette of the *Odin*.

The sea was calm and a warm breeze blew in from the south. The sun was giving way to the moon, its rays playing on the water's surface. Even the savage reefs, which had claimed so many lives, seemed gentle now, as if to allow Abshir to pass. This could have been a tropical paradise, but the hounds of hell were about to break loose on the horizon.

Abshir led the approach until their quarry was only 3 kilometres away. Then, the two boats behind him broke away. His plan had started to unfold.

Sleep is something you grab when you can, especially when you know you only have a while, which Thirway did.

Emerging from his cabin after an hour-long nap, he made his way to the bridge. He sensed something was up.

Vandenbrook gave him a cold hard stare as he stepped onto the bridge; as far as he was concerned, he wanted Thirway gone. Over the past year, he had witnessed Thirway and his men kill too many Somalis. He began to question the ethics. He knew things had gone too far and he simply had to stop it.

For now, he had to play ball. He had his family to think of. His wife's happy face popped into his head. Caroline was half his age. They had met whilst he was in Manila facilitating a course on navigation. Filipino crewmen were popular with charter companies as they spoke English, worked hard and, above all, came cheap. She was a maid at the hotel where he stayed. Romance blossomed and they married six months later. His job kept him away for months on end, but she was content and loved him.

Thirway looked out the large window on the bridge onto the huge expanse of deck in front. His mind was on his current predicament; only the thought of the money he made eased his anxiety.

'What's the harm? A few dead pirates,' he thought. After all, it did bring in, on average, US$700,000 tax-free a year. With that and the big legitimate contract he had with Pathos Shipping to protect their vessels, he did all right.

Now, Stone popped into his head. Something about him was off. The American visitors he received from time to time made Thirway uneasy. Then, suddenly, he stiffened, as if an electric current had fired through his brain. The man he had seen at the airport in Oman—he had seen him before, with Stone at the office. Thirway pictured the wispy brown hair and the hawk-like nose. It was him, no doubt about it.

What was the connection? He thought about how he had planned to abduct Alexis. But Stone knew nothing of that until Thirway mentioned it in Oman, so no connection there. Maybe he was, as Stone had said, just a tourist—who happened to bear an uncanny resemblance to the man he had seen at the office.

One thing was for sure: the money he would have made from Deep Six didn't matter now; Alexis would eclipse that once Abshir took the ship. Daniel and Jeremy would be nothing more than collateral damage.

Thirway had instructed Bull and Troy and a select few of the crew to put up a fake defence and make the theatrics look convincing. Daniel, Jeremy and Vandenbrook were to be killed in the crossfire. The fake defence, he secretly thought, would also be his cover story should anything not go according to plan.

The plan had one potential weak spot—Abshir. The fact that Daniel had shot his 15-year-old brother complicated matters. Thirway had no way of telling if Stone had convinced the Somali to take Alexis in place of killing him. He had a serious dilemma: defend the ship and protect himself from Abshir or take a chance and see if he can negotiate with the pirate? Or, worse, trust Stone?

The stress on his face told the story as Bull tapped him on the shoulder.

'You okay?'

'Yeah, just stand by,' Thirway replied. 'I think our friends will be here soon and not in a good mood.' Bull turned to leave.

Then, it struck Thirway—if it had been his brother, he would want revenge, and no amount of money would change his mind.

'Bull!'

'Yeah?'

'Change in tactics. Full response. We have no choice.'

Bull pondered for only the briefest of moments and then headed down the steep steel stairway to the deck.

Thirway drew a deep breath. It was going to be a long and bloody night.

Through his night scope, Bull saw the first boat emerge from the darkness about 700 metres off the stern. Jeremy lay beside him, just 12 metres from the guardrail on the deck area behind the towering accommodation block and bridge. With the M16 carbine beside him, Jeremy felt momentarily secure.

Suddenly, the boat veered right and another boat appeared, cutting across the wake in the opposite direction. Bull jerked his rifle from side to side. The first round he fired took out nothing but water; the boats were moving too fast.

He grabbed his walkie-talkie. 'Pirates! Eyes on!' he bellowed and turned back to his weapon. Jeremy was now on his feet and peering over the guardrail. 'Get the fuck down!' Bull shouted.

Then, as if taunting him, one of the boats cut across the wake again. This time, Bull was steady, his mind focused and his breathing shallow. He pulled the trigger and the round instantly struck one of the pirates. Instinctively estimating the boat's speed and direction, he fired again; another man went down before the boat zipped out of sight.

Hearing Bull's warning on the walkie-talkie, Thirway immediately told Vandenbrook to increase his speed to full ahead and alert the crew. They were now under attack; every tactical move he made could mean the difference between life and death.

Thirway also knew Abshir was no fool and would be playing out a strategy. Figuring out that strategy was of utmost importance. His only hope was for Abshir to be so fuelled by hatred he would make a mistake.

As he scrambled down the steel stairway towards the main deck, Thirway could feel his heart rate rising. He headed for the bow to join Troy.

Daniel and Troy had also heard Bull's alert. Both of them were now crouched down, taking cover behind a large steel box used to store equipment and life vests.

Alexis had sought refuge in her cabin down below after the horrors she had witnessed. The soothing classical music she was now listening to on her iPod was incongruous with the drama unfolding up above.

The second of the two boats was now safely under the *Odin's* stern overhang. Bull, looking further out from the stern, was unaware the small craft had slid in from the port side. Abshir's boat had also approached undetected and was now skimming down the starboard side from the bow.

Suddenly appearing at the base of the guardrail, the first pirate took Bull and Jeremy by surprise. He had climbed the 30 feet of rope dangling over the side, with ease. Thirway, in his sudden change of mind, had forgotten to remove it.

Jeremy let rip a burst of rounds from his M16 so sporadic it just peppered the guardrail and ricocheted in different directions.

'Calm the fuck down! Aim and then fire!' Bull screamed at his raw recruit.

As the sinewy pirate mounted the guardrail, he was struck in the chest by a single bullet from Bull's carbine. The force of the round threw him back over the side and down into the water.

'Get that rope!' Bull shouted.

Jeremy stumbled towards the guardrail and slipped, just as a second pirate reached the guardrail. Bull immediately aimed and fired, and the pirate fell out of sight as fast as he had appeared.

Jeremy froze; shock setting in. Bull made a dash for the rope; he needed to cut it to prevent any further attempts at boarding. As he reached the guardrail, he felt something hard hit him from behind, smashing him against the guardrail. From the excruciating pain, Bull knew the impact had fractured a couple of ribs.

A few of the *Odin* crew had heard the gunfire and were now rallying to help. Unfortunately, their ability to aim the high-pressure fire hoses left a lot to be desired; they ended up taking out the very men who were fighting the pirate assault.

This was the break the attackers needed. One after another, they climbed, boarded and dodged, as water shot all over the deck. A burst of automatic fire killed the crew members holding the hoses, which now wriggled like deranged snakes.

As Bull crawled on the deck, one of the pirates brought the butt of his AK down hard on the back of his head, knocking him unconscious.

Jeremy was desperately kicking to break free from the two pirates who were dragging him away. They struck him in the face and kicked him in the ribs until his body went limp.

Thirway and Troy were unaware of the chaos at the stern. They had heard the distinctive rattle of AK-47s but had to assume Bull could handle it. Leaving their position at the bow to help would weaken the defences for the rest of the ship.

A smoke grenade blast sent a cloud of white smoke into the air. Unfortunately, the wind direction was not in their favour. The smoke soon obscured any visibility they had had of the port and starboard sides of the ship.

The first pirate to board on the starboard side quickly positioned himself behind a container situated amidships. With a steel ladder running up that side of the ship, the climb could not have been easier. Abshir was next, his eyes blazing in his masked face.

Thirway fired first, hoping his round would find a target somewhere in the smoke. A second shot had more success, striking the silhouette of a man emerging from the now thinning smoke. It caught him in the shoulder and sent him spinning backwards.

A burst of bullets came back from the port side. Troy and Daniel started to return fire, hoping to keep the attackers down. Another pirate ran forward, only to be felled by a hail of bullets from Troy.

'Magazine!' Troy screamed. He was out of ammunition.

Popping his head above the equipment box, Daniel kept firing, but his shots just bounced off the boat's structure; the only damage they did was to the paintwork.

Thirway crept forward on his belly, putting down short bursts. He wanted to take the fight to them. Retreat was not an option, not that they had anywhere to go. A hail of bullets came down, forcing him back behind the large steel box.

'We are pinned down!' Thirway shouted.

Troy popped up and sprayed the port side. Two advancing pirates dropped back, returning fire. A second grenade went off, filling the deck with smoke. Thirway dashed forward, with Troy giving covering fire, and threw the grenade overboard. Then, he heard Troy yell; he had been struck in the shoulder by a ricochet.

Suddenly, silence, as if a ceasefire had been ordered.

Thirway stood up, gently placed his M16 down on the deck amongst the smouldering shell casings and raised his hands high in the air. Troy did the same.

Daniel shot Thirway a look that said, 'What the hell are you doing?' He then peered over the box and raised his weapon to shoot.

'Drop it, Daniel. I mean it,' Thirway snapped.

'Why?' Daniel responded sharply, not understanding what was going on.

'Look. Look up there.' Thirway indicated where with his eyes.

Looking up at the bridge, Daniel saw Alexis standing on the gantry, just outside the bridge house, with a gun held to her head.

Vandenbrook and several other members of the crew were now also being pulled out and shown off as trophies. The imposing figure of Abshir stood out amongst the hostages. Finally comprehending what was going on, Daniel lowered his weapon and, like the others, placed it on the deck.

Thirway's mistake was now glaringly obvious. He had left only two men to defend the stern, one of whom was not even a professional sniper but a rather unfit oil trader. The stern was the entry point to the massive accommodation block and bridge. Once Abshir's men had overpowered Bull and Jeremy, they simply had to take out the odd crew member and walk right up to the wheelhouse. That left Thirway, Troy and Daniel to defend the bow, which was in essence of no value. It was a mistake so careless Thirway knew his fate now lay entirely in Abshir's hands.

More pirates emerged from the port and starboard sides of the ship, their triumphant cries of 'MFF, MFF' now a deafening roar. Jabbing their AKs at Thirway, Troy and Daniel, they indicated for them to get on their knees. Others took the M16 carbines that had been abandoned on the deck; these would become proud additions to their own arsenal.

Abshir walked over slowly to his three new captives. He stood menacingly in front of Thirway. In his right hand, he carried the AK-47 he had given his brother as a gift. Thirway looked up at him, trying not to show any fear. At this point, he had no idea how Abshir would play his hand.

Pain shot through his head as Abshir struck him with the butt of his weapon, sending him crashing to the deck. He started to fade out, his ears ringing, as the impact of the blow took hold. He could feel the blood running down his face.

'Take this one to the galley and watch him like a hawk,' Abshir ordered. 'Lock the others away.' He wanted to make sure Thirway was separated from the others.

As they were dragged away, Daniel tried to get a glimpse of Alexis, but one of the pirates jabbed the barrel of his AK hard into his back, causing Daniel to wince with pain and drop his head.

SEVENTEEN

Vandenbrook felt his stomach tighten, the churning of its contents audible in his ears. He could even taste a hint of the acidic bile rising up in his throat. Such was the state of his nerves. The ransom demand he was expected to relay to Pathos Shipping was heavy indeed—so heavy, in fact, his voice shook.

'Yes, 50 million dollars, that is what I said. Five-zero, US bills, used, okay?' He then felt a metallic tap to the back of his head.

Slightly unnerved, he continued, 'The Maritime Freedom Fighters state that, in return, they will free all on board, most importantly, Alexis Pathos.'

The reply, to his dread, indicated he should stall for time.

'Finish it.' Abshir pushed the muzzle of his Beretta hard into the back of Vandenbrook's head.

Now desperately trying to keep his composure, the captain added, somewhat frantically, 'The money must be dropped by heli as close to the *Odin* as possible. Upon confirmation, they will leave the ship. Do you understand? Confirm, over.'

'Now, tell them what I will do to you if they fail.' Abshir gave his final prompt, then cocked his weapon. The sound made Vandenbrook's legs momentarily buckle under him. Gripping the edge of the console, he steadied himself.

'Any rescue attempt will result in all of us being killed. Is that clear?' Vandenbrook then gingerly put down the radio receiver and slowly turned to face Abshir. He glanced down at the pistol he had felt at the back of his head in Abshir's hand.

'I have done as you asked. Now, can you point that thing away?' Vandenbrook was nearing the end of his composure.

'They have 48 hours. Then, I start killing. Now, make way for Eyl,' Abshir growled and then left the bridge.

Vandenbrook remained standing for a while before his legs finally gave way. He collapsed into the captain's chair and stared blankly at the main control panel, taking in all that was going on. Whilst he had encountered pirate attacks in the past, the *Odin* had never been boarded. He felt helpless and, for the first time, very afraid. In his mind, he pictured his family—he would use that to keep himself alive.

Feeling more stable now, he turned his thoughts to Alexis. One thing puzzled him. How did Abshir know about her and who she was? He concluded it could only be one man—Thirway.

Thirway tugged at the ropes, but they were too tight. His hands were throbbing and his fingers were getting numb. Glancing at the two sinewy pirates, who looked like they needed a good meal and some intensive dentistry, he scowled. The air in the tiny room was stuffy and beginning to stink.

The footsteps he heard in the hallway told him he was about to have a visitor. He knew it wouldn't be long and his ears had been tuned in. He kept his eyes down as Abshir entered the room.

'Look at me, you pig,' Abshir snapped.

Slowly raising his head, Thirway inched his eyes up Abshir's towering figure, taking in the bare torso festooned with belts of ammunition and the ice-cold, piercing stare.

'You need to tell me what happened. I want to know who killed my brother,' Abshir said bluntly. 'You play your games shooting pirates.

Well, I am not Mohamed.' He punched Thirway in the face.

Wincing but not yelling, Thirway spat blood. His lip was bleeding.

'Tell me now or you will be the first one I gut and throw over the side.'

As Thirway looked up, he felt the second blow. This time, it shattered his nose. He choked on the blood in his throat and spat it out.

'Okay! Enough!' He knew he had little choice. One way or another, Abshir would get it out of him. There was no point in taking a beating to make his lie any more believable. He would just have to get on with it and hope Abshir swallowed the hook.

'If I tell you who it was, I want your assurance I will be set free along with the girl.'

Abshir narrowed his eyes and frowned.

'You do not tell me what you want. I tell you.'

Thirway sat motionless and just stared at him. Abshir moved closer.

'I am waiting. Who was it?'

Thirway could feel the warm breath in his ear. He could also smell khat on Abshir's breath, which meant he was high. Thirway swallowed.

'Jeremy. His name is Jeremy.'

Abshir knelt down and brought his face just inches away from Thirway.

'This Jeremy. You give him up so easily. Why?'

'I'm not the enemy here. He means nothing to me. He didn't follow my orders. He was only meant to fire over your heads to warn you off. It gives me no pleasure in keeping him from you.' Thirway did his best to make it sound convincing.

Abshir began to pace around Thirway, his steps slow and deliberate, his eyes locked onto his victim, scrutinising him for any sign of lying.

Thirway jerked his head as he heard a pistol being cocked and felt the cold muzzle against the back of his head.

'Are you telling me the truth?' Abshir said and then pulled the trigger. Thirway felt his heart almost stop.

'Christ!' he gasped, his breath heavy.

Abshir started to laugh, as did the two other men in the room. He knew there was nothing like the sound of a pistol being discharged next to your head to make you shit yourself. Russian roulette could break the most hardened of men.

'Okay, then let us see if you speak the truth. Get everyone on deck now.' Abshir waved one of his men off. 'Bring this one along.' He pointed to Thirway and left the room.

The air out on deck could be cut with a knife. Daniel, who was on his knees, shot a glance at Alexis. He could see fear all over her face. She returned his glance, her eyes big and round.

Abshir appeared and stood a few yards in front of the assembled crew.

'I know who killed my brother. I know he must pay with his own life.' He took a deliberate step forward. 'Give yourself up now and I will give you a clean death.'

Daniel felt warm urine soak through his pants. He started to shake as he looked nervously at Bull and Troy. Their faces were emotionless. Then, he looked at Thirway, who stared back, subtly shaking his head.

'Shit, is he telling me not to give up?' Daniel's mind was on overdrive.

'This man will pay for what he has done. He has taken my brother.' Abshir drew a machete from a leather holster strapped to his side. Seeing the blade, Alexis screamed and turned away, closing her eyes. The pirates started to wave their weapons in the air.

'Take him!' Abshir commanded. Daniel tensed up, closed his eyes and felt his heart almost stop. Then, he heard Jeremy yelling. Slowly opening one eye and then the other, he saw Jeremy struggling as two pirates dragged him towards Abshir.

'Stand him up and hold out his arms,' Abshir said.

Jeremy was hauled to his feet, his arms stretched out in front of him. He could barely stand.

'Help me, John! It wasn't me, I swear it! Please... Daniel, it was Daniel!' Jeremy screamed, jerking his head around to find Daniel.

'Wait!' Abshir shouted. 'Who is this Daniel?' Everyone fell silent.

'Who is Daniel?' he shouted again. Hearing nothing, he walked towards Alexis and raised the machete. She reeled backwards and screamed.

'I am,' Daniel spoke up, his voice dry and shaky. All eyes were now on him. He could see Thirway out of the corner of his eye. His face said it all.

'Did you kill my brother? Was it you? Does this man speak the truth?' Abshir walked over and bore down on him, placing the tip of the machete on his chin. Alexis was now crying uncontrollably.

'No, sir, I did not,' Daniel answered firmly, looking Abshir in the eye. He had mustered every ounce of courage he had and brought to bear every aspect of his experience as a trader to pull off the bluff of his life.

'You lying bastard, it was you!' Jeremy shouted and lurched forward.

Abshir stood stone-still, looking deep into Daniel's eyes, as if probing for the lie. Then, turning to Thirway, he asked, 'Does he speak the truth?'

Daniel now fixed his eyes on Thirway, his heart beating fast.

'Yes, he does. I told you it was Jeremy,' Thirway replied. Daniel tried hard not to gasp; he could hardly believe his ears. Why had Thirway covered for him?

After what seemed an eternity, Abshir turned and walked back to Jeremy, raised the machete and brought it down. The scream that followed would have sent a chill down any normal person's spine. Jeremy's left wrist was completely severed. He almost passed out as blood squirted from the stump.

The second blow took off his right wrist; even Thirway looked away at that point. The pirates went into a frenzy, poking and pulling at the other hostages. Alexis, after opening her eyes, vomitted. Jeremy was now floundering around, screaming, as he stared in horror at his mutilated limbs.

'Let that be a lesson to anyone who thinks of harming my family.' Abshir walked off.

Two pirates hauled Jeremy over the guardrail; his screams faded as he fell 30 feet down and hit the water. Only his hands remained on the deck in a pool of blood.

Thirway knew it was highly unlikely Jeremy would survive his injuries, let alone the shark-infested waters of the Indian Ocean. He would most likely bleed to death or, if he was lucky, drown before the sharks got to him. In any event, the problem had been solved; Abshir had executed his revenge.

Locked in the galley, each man sat in silence, the horror of what had happened a few hours ago still fresh in his mind.

'Why did you protect me?' Daniel asked Thirway, keeping his voice low just in case the pirate on guard outside the door could hear them.

'Simple, you are worth more alive,' Thirway replied.

'What do you mean?'

'Alexis is what they are after. They won't harm her. She is worth more to them than this rusty old tub. If she is happy, then it helps us all. If they had killed you, who knows how she would have reacted,' Thirway explained.

'Alexis... how on earth would they know who she is?' Daniel was now even more confused.

'I think the captain turned rat on us. Why do you think he is up there and not down here with us?'

Daniel paused, clearly in shock. 'Maybe he needs to manage the ship, that's why?'

'Yeah and my arse doesn't smell,' Bull chipped in.

'They won't hurt her, trust me.' Thirway smiled.

'You seem very sure,' Daniel said, noting Thirway's confidence.

'Not hard to work out. She is worth a small fortune in ransom.'

Daniel's face then dropped as the meaning of Thirway's words finally hit home.

———

Her eyes were focused on a nicotine stain on the ceiling. Slowly, it morphed into Jeremy's haunting face, staring at her and screaming. She closed her eyes, trying to think of anything else.

She recalled that day she had visited her father at his home in Knightsbridge. He was seated in his study behind a large mahogany desk with inlaid green leather, drinking Earl Grey tea. In front of him was a photograph of a ship. She remembered that he had a picture of every vessel proudly displayed on his wall. The 'Pathos wall of pride,' he called it.

When she asked what that photograph was, he explained it was the newest addition to his cargo fleet. She remembered dismissing it as just another ship, to which he responded, 'No, dearest daughter, this is *Odin*.'

The fact that she was on her father's ship sank in. Her only hope now was that he would know and come for her.

She was almost dozing off when a knock on the door woke her. Getting up, she walked to one corner of the tiny cabin and stood there.

'Who is it?' she asked.

'Captain Vandenbrook, miss.'

'Okay, come in,' she replied.

The door opened and Vandenbrook entered. Behind him was Abshir.

'I mean you no harm,' Abshir said, anticipating her reaction.

'You murdering bastard, let us go!' Her voice was strangely defiant.

'You dare to call me a murderer? I avenge my brother's death, nothing more. As for letting you go, you are worth money, Miss Pathos.' He gave her a wry smile.

'You know about this, captain?' Alexis turned to Vandenbrook.

'Yes, miss, I was made to contact your father's office and issue a ransom for you and the other hostages.' Vandenbrook moved over and stood beside her, placing an arm around her. 'Don't worry, miss, I won't let anything happen to you.'

'You will be set free once I get paid. Until then, you will stay here,' Abshir said.

'What about the others? Are they okay? Why can't I be with them?' Alexis asked.

'They are okay, for now. Best you stay here safe.' Abshir turned to leave.

'Captain, are they really okay?'

'For now, miss, but if your father doesn't pay within 48 hours...' He fell silent.

Alexis knew what he meant. She shot a glance at Abshir, who was now standing in the hallway outside the cabin.

'You are an animal!' Alexis yelled.

Vandenbrook placed his hands gently on her shoulders as if to ease her back. 'See you later, miss. I will have some food sent in,' he said and walked out.

Abshir glared at her, his eyes cold and dark, before Vandenbrook shut the door behind him.

EIGHTEEN

Pathos ran his eyes and fingers meticulously down the columns of large numbers. Should he agree with the forecast in bold type at the bottom of the page, another hotel would be acquired at the snap of his fingers. The sallow accountant sitting opposite him was tensely awaiting his decision.

Taking a sip of his favourite Earl Grey tea in the gold-rimmed china teacup, he raised his eyes. Just as he was about to speak, the door to his office burst open.

'What on earth is the meaning of this?' Pathos was clearly annoyed at the disturbance.

Justin Burrell, one of his shipping managers, had been tasked to break the news to his boss; he had agonised over it on his way up in the lift.

'Sorry, sir, it's very important,' Burrell spoke, entwining his fingers nervously and looking as if he was about to wet himself.

'Well, get on with it!' Pathos barked.

'It's your daughter, Alexis. She has been... well... kidnapped, sir.'

Christos dropped his cup, spilling tea all over his papers.

'Are you alright, sir?' the accountant asked.

'Of course, I'm bloody well not!' Pathos stood up, only to collapse back into his chair, his legs trembling.

Rushing forward, the accountant took his arm.

'Get out! I need a moment with Burrell.'

Not wanting to risk another dressing down, the accountant hurriedly left the room.

'Well, Burrell, what happened? Tell me.' Pathos glared up at his manager, his face ashen. Shock was taking hold.

Before Burrell could respond, the door opened and Nicolai strode in.

'What is it? What has happened?' Pathos's bodyguard enquired.

Burrell observed the anguish on his boss's face. He felt powerless to help.

'She is on board the *Odin*, taken by pirates yesterday, sir.' Burrell stood, waiting for the fallout.

'Pirates?' Nicolai asked.

'What... how can she be on the *Odin*?' Pathos was confused. He shot a glance at Nicolai, who simply raised his eyebrows. 'I want facts. Find out everything you can and report back in one hour, do you hear me? That means both of you. Now go.' Pathos waved his hands, gesturing for both men to leave and start digging.

'I want these people caught, do you hear me?' he shouted after them. 'If they so much as...' He stopped, not daring to say what he was thinking. He knew only too well what the Somali pirates were capable of doing.

An hour later, Nicolai returned, carrying a file. He slid it under Pathos's nose and stepped back.

Examining every page, scrutinising every detail, Pathos now knew something was very wrong. The cargo manifest he had just read made no sense at all. What he did know was who he now had to meet.

'Get me Burrell,' he snapped.

A few minutes later, Burrell walked in like a sheep heading for slaughter. Pathos did not even bother to look up.

'Since when have we shipped agricultural machine parts on this ship?' He looked up, his eyes probing.

'I will double-check, sir, and get back to you.'

'You have fifteen minutes to verify. Make the call.' Pathos wanted facts and fast.

Burrell made a few phone calls and came back with a reply that was not good. As he knocked and walked in, he could feel his stomach turning over.

'The manifest is correct, sir. I have checked many times now.'

'Really, well, if you are wrong, it will cost you your job. Now, who chartered the vessel and who is funding the cargo? Do we at least know that?' Pathos was agitated and not convinced.

'Yes, we do. Burrows & Co, sir,' Burrell answered, pleased he actually had some facts on hand.

Nicolai shot Burrell a look that didn't escape Pathos.

'What is it, Nicolai?' Pathos barked.

'Nothing, sir. Sorry, just trying to follow the conversation.' Nicolai covered his reaction.

'You get out.' Pathos had had enough of Burrell. He buzzed his PA. 'Get my plane ready. I need to fly to Singapore first thing in the morning.' He then leaned back in his chair, his mind on overdrive.

Stepping out of his Bentley, only 45 minutes after touching down in Singapore, Christos Pathos took a moment as he fastened the middle button of his tailored grey suit. The white handkerchief in his jacket pocket added a distinct touch of class; he carefully adjusted it with his fingertips.

A woman dressed as smartly as him brushed past, not even glancing at him. The beige file was so expertly passed it was almost invisible; even Nicolai missed it. Pathos turned just a little and saw the silver-haired lady vanish around the corner.

Entering the lobby of the 60-storey blue-glass bastion of banking that was Burrows & Co, he knew exactly what his agenda was. Today, he was particularly focused and that meant he would leave with exactly what he wanted.

A pretty young woman—he guessed she must have been no older than 26—with long flowing brown hair and big green eyes, dressed in a well-fitting charcoal grey suit and black patent heels, showed him into the opulent boardroom located on the 40th storey. He paused for a second as she left; she bore an uncanny resemblance to his daughter. He felt momentarily a rush of emotion.

After regaining his composure and taking in the panoramic views offered by that expensive piece of real estate, Pathos made his way to the nearest chair at the large boardroom table. He sat and placed his file on the table in front of him. A glass of chilled mineral water was dutifully served by one of the staff.

Seconds later, David Tate, a steadfast and athletic Brit, entered, looking every inch the stereotypical banker in his pin-striped suit that had been tailored to justify every cent of the three grand he had paid for it. He had to look smart; he was the chief executive officer of the bank's wholesale division.

With him was Timothy Kent, an American, the head of Trade Finance. His wispy light brown hair and bird-like features gave him an intense look. Unlike Pathos, who appeared relaxed, Tate and Kent seemed somewhat on edge as they seated themselves directly opposite him.

'So, gentlemen, it seems we have a situation on our hands,' Pathos started the discussion whilst flipping open the file in front of him.

Burrows & Co had served the Pathos family for the past 25 years, specifically supporting the large ship leasing and trade financing deals his company engaged in. More recently, they had agreed to finance, along with a Japanese bank, his new hotel chain in Asia at a cost of US$700 million dollars. As such, he was an extremely important client.

'Firstly, my apologies for being late. May we offer you some tea, Mr. Pathos, before getting to the point in hand?' Tate announced in his best clipped British public school accent.

'I'm fine, thank you.' Pathos had no time for tea. 'But I am interested to know how a number of gas centrifuges for separating uranium have found their way onto one of my ships.'

Tate and Kent looked at each other. Tate, at least, looked somewhat confused.

'Sorry, why would that concern the bank?' he had to ask.

'Because it was financed by Burrows & Co.' Pathos delivered the blow and sat back. Tate nearly choked on his water.

'You may also be interested to know,' Pathos continued, wanting to embed the harpoon well and truly in, 'that my daughter is on board with one of your staff, Daniel Spencer, a fact, gentlemen, that I find strangely coincidental.' Pathos brought his fist down on the table, causing his glass of water to jump.

After a pause, Tate said, 'Mr. Pathos, with all due respect, we have no idea how two members of our staff ended up on your vessel. We, too, would like to get to the bottom of this. But, you must understand, you walk in here and hit me with this. I must investigate.'

'How do you explain the cargo?' Pathos eyeballed both of them.

'As I have said, I will investigate the matter and inform you the moment we establish the full facts. What I can tell you is that I am shocked. The bank would not typically finance such a cargo.'

Kent then interjected, 'I was under the impression the cargo was nothing more than agricultural machine parts. So, I can't see what the fuss is about. Obviously, there is a mistake somewhere.' His tone was slightly aggressive and verging on sarcastic.

'Are you sure about this, Mr. Pathos?' Tate enquired, energised by Kent's response.

'Yes, I bloody well am!' Pathos was now enraged. 'I have my sources too, you know. One of my managers who loaded the cargo in Oman disguised it in the manifest as machine parts. He blew the whistle once he heard the ship had been taken. His mistake was, the *Odin* normally carries rice or seed oil.

'Needless to say, my people were able to extract the truth out of him yesterday. Maybe the fact that the customs official who saw the cargo arrive in Oman turned up with a hole in his head loosened his tongue. So, ask me again if I am sure, gentlemen.' Pathos stood up.

'Okay, let's all calm down,' Kent said. 'It sounds to me like this cargo manager is the issue here. He probably switched the cargo, hardly our issue, Mr. Pathos.' His tone was now more cordial.

'I agree, we need time to clear our name,' Tate chimed in, 'and I am sorry about your daughter, Mr. Pathos. I am sure the authorities will get her back safe.'

'May I make a suggestion?' Kent again spoke up.

'Please do,' Tate replied.

'Mr. Pathos is an important man, media material, shall we say. As such, we may want to keep this matter quiet. I mean, the daughter of a billionaire hijacked by pirates along with suspect cargo? It would be a media frenzy. Of course, we, too, as a bank need to clear ourselves and not be unduly involved in this, if you get my drift.' Kent leaned forward.

After a few moments, Pathos sat back down. 'On that we do indeed agree,' he said, his face still red with anger.

'So, how do we deal with this?' Tate asked somewhat anxiously.

Pathos looked at him. 'After this meeting, I will make some enquiries. There are men who can deal with this sort of thing and, I hope, rescue my daughter. Paying a ransom is no guarantee she will be kept alive, and that is my only concern, gentlemen.'

He leaned forward, now glaring at both men. 'You, my friends, will foot the expense for engaging such men. Is that perfectly clear?'

Tate looked shocked. 'We will have to take that under consideration, Mr. Pathos. As I have said, we may not be involved here.' He was trying to avoid making any commitment.

Pathos then decided to play his ultimate hand. He stood up. 'Please cut the bullshit, gentlemen. I am not wet behind the ears. You think I got to where I am without knowing certain things?' He slid two photographs out of his file and gently pushed them around on the shiny tabletop with his fingertips. Kent now looked decidedly nervous.

'You know it and I know it,' Pathos said calmly. 'You are in it up to your little starched white necks. Maybe I should be having this conversation with the bank's chairman, Sir David Crick, or maybe Scotland Yard.' He glared at Kent. He then flipped over the two photographs and sat back down, a wry smile on his face.

Tate and Kent took one photograph each and studied it. Kent's face turned white.

'Is that not you, Mr. Kent? Looks to me like you were overseeing the cargo being unloaded when it first arrived from Malaysia.' Pathos waited for their response.

'What is the meaning of this?' Tate turned to a now very uncomfortable Kent.

After a pause, he replied, 'Okay, I need to lay my cards on the table. What I am about to say does not leave this room. I ask this of you, Mr. Pathos.'

'That depends on your explanation, man.' Tate was very anxious.

'Allow me to explain.' Kent took a sip of water; his mouth had gone dry. 'One of my clients, wealthy like you, Mr. Pathos, I can't divulge who it is… the cargo was being shipped for them. I assisted with the financing of the deal. It's all perfectly legal. In fact, it was your daughter who closed the deal.'

He took another sip of water and continued, 'It would not be prudent for us to be associated with the funding of anything that can potentially be used to make nuclear weapons, hence the secrecy…'

'You got that right! What the hell have you done, Kent?' Tate was fuming and not fully believing what he was hearing.

'Listen, you don't complain when the revenues are up. The cargo is worth a fortune to us, so calm down,' Kent snapped back.

'Damn it, man, it's now in the hands of pirates. If this leaks out, we are done for.' Tate was growing more anxious by the second.

'Mr. Pathos, given what Kent here has just confirmed, I will authorise and underwrite the cost of the ship's safe recovery. Is that good enough, Mr. Pathos?' Tate then sat back in his chair, knowing he was now in no position to argue.

'You idiots! What were you thinking? You ship gas centrifuges made in a suspect factory in Malaysia and hope no one will find out? And you involved my daughter in the deal!' Pathos was enraged.

'What's this?' Tate was floored by this new information.

'Suspect factory? How on earth did you reach such a conclusion?' Kent snapped. 'It is perfectly legal, as I have said.' He then looked away.

'It's a restricted cargo, you fool,' Pathos fired back, 'that originated from a factory in Malaysia—a factory that is under investigation by MI6, or did you not know that? You have placed us all at risk. Do not take me for a fool.'

'You seem very well-informed, Mr. Pathos. Who is your source? If we go down, so will you.' Kent, shocked that Pathos had such information, was now in attack mode.

'Really? We will see about that. I will take care of the situation with pleasure, gentlemen. And you,' Pathos pointed a finger at Kent, 'don't ever take me for a fool again. I know people.' He stood up to leave. 'I suggest you leave it to me now to sort this out. Good day, gentlemen.'

When Pathos had left the room, Tate turned to Kent. 'I have no idea what you were thinking, Kent, but this needs to go away, and fast. I can't even fire you for fear of this entire mess blowing up in my own face. Get it sorted and fast.' He stood up, paced around the room and then turned sharply back to Kent.

'We cannot afford for this chap Spencer to walk off that ship. God knows what he has found out. How the hell did he get on board anyway?'

'I have no idea. But, yes, he must be dealt with, and the girl. Even if we deal with this Spencer chap, she is equally a risk,' Kent stated coldly.

'Oh god, that's just bloody great!' Tate now realised the full magnitude of the situation. Despite his anger at Kent, he knew the power of making big revenues. Keeping his job was all he cared about.

'I know of someone who can take care of it for us,' Kent said, his eyes intense.

'You do?' Tate looked up, both surprised and relieved at the mere suggestion that Kent could handle it.

'Indeed, I do. A woman, she works for the US government sometimes as an operative. As I recall, she has some weird code name… it escapes me right now. But let's just say a good friend of mine knows her and may just be able to put me in contact.' Kent had a sinister smile on his face.

'Sounds all a bit undercover to me. Is she a spy?' Tate asked, not really expecting a reply.

'Getting one over on that pompous arse Pathos would be good. He must be eliminated,' Kent commented.

Tate was surprised to see the hatred in Kent's eyes. 'You don't mean…' He could hardly bring himself to say it.

'Put it this way, if we get linked to that shipment, we are both dead. So, yes, he must be removed,' Kent replied.

'What a bloody mess! I want no part of it, but get it settled before we all go down,' Tate held his head in his hands.

Pathos was on the phone. The lady at the other end of the line was being, as she always was for her old friend, very helpful—not to mention the file she had slipped him before his meeting with Tate and Kent. She liked Alexis and was deeply saddened to hear of her abduction.

Her past stood her in good stead. The wife of a senior diplomat with the Lebanese government based in London, she had secretly served the British SIS and the CIA. In addition, she was linked to several organised crime groups. Her extensive web of contacts made her valuable to the governments of the world. She was known quite simply as the Rain Angel. As a friend, she was loyal; as an enemy, she was deadly.

Pathos said goodbye and hung up. He now had a name. Not just any name; this was the name of the man who was his best chance of getting Alexis back alive. His old friend never made a recommendation lightly. The fact that this man was right under his nose in Singapore delighted him even more. He would arrange a meeting as soon as possible.

Not long after she had concluded her business with her old friend Pathos and returned to her lunch, her phone vibrated again.

'Hello?' she said, not recognising the caller.

The conversation that followed deeply interested her. It seemed a Mr. Timothy Kent needed some help—help she could very easily provide. The man whose name she gave Kent would, she was sure, work out for himself who was, in fact, worth protecting. Hanging up, she couldn't help but smile at the irony of the plot that was about to unfold.

NINETEEN

September 2009. Singapore.

Having deposited the keys to his rather beaten-up old Series III Land Rover into the clammy hands of the shocked valet, McCabe, dressed comfortably in a blue cotton shirt and khaki trousers, breezed through the large revolving doors. The Fullerton Hotel was nothing if not opulent.

As he walked across the expanse of white marble towards the bar, McCabe studied his surroundings. It appeared as normal, with clusters of bankers and lawyers sitting around in the lobby, engaged in what he suspected would be money-driven conversations.

Pausing outside the bar, McCabe checked the time on his watch. It was indeed 1800; as always, he was bang on time. He entered and scanned for anything that might seem out of place—from habit rather than a case of paranoia.

He made his way to one of the small circular tables and took a seat, careful to face the entrance. This way, he could see who came and who went.

It wasn't long before a petite waitress arrived at his table, eager to please, and set down a bowl of sweet cashew nuts. Since she was cute, he let his attention waver for just a second.

'Can I take your order, sir?' she asked, beaming.

'Gin and tonic, thanks.' He delivered one of his cheeky smiles, which sent the waitress scurrying off, blushing.

Snapping back to the task at hand, he noticed Mooney lumbering into the bar. He walked right past McCabe; a slight turn of his head might have been the only indication to the trained eye that the two knew each other. He took a seat in the corner by the main bar. From his vantage point, he had McCabe's back covered.

Halfway through his drink, McCabe spotted Pathos. Immaculately turned out in an expensive grey tailored suit, with a white shirt and a blue tie, and very polished black shoes, his well-styled hair swept back over his ears, Pathos looked exactly like he did in the picture McCabe had seen on his Wiki page.

McCabe observed him for a moment, as if studying his form. Given the vacant look on his face, McCabe knew Pathos had no idea who he was looking for. As Pathos started to walk towards him, McCabe noticed his shadow—a tall well-built man who screamed ex-military. McCabe could spot the type a mile off; military men had a distinctive swagger.

'Mr. Pathos, I think,' McCabe said, smiling, as Pathos almost walked on by.

'McCabe?' Pathos turned, somewhat surprised, and held out his hand. McCabe leaned forward, still seated, and shook his hand, taking in the manicured nails and soft skin.

'Clearly a man who never had to indulge in manual labour,' McCabe thought; his own hands, in comparison, were rough and calloused.

'May I?' Pathos gestured to be seated.

'Of course, please.'

'Oh, and this is Nicolai. He looks after me, shall I say,' Pathos introduced his protection.

'Not sure you need him in here,' McCabe jested, sizing up Nicolai. In return, he got a cold stare. He sensed something off about the man but ignored it for now.

Pathos took a moment before turning to Nicolai. 'Very well, Nicolai, you can wait outside for me.' Then, he turned to McCabe.

'As can your man, Mr. McCabe. I assume you are also not alone?' Pathos was nothing if not sharp; his eyes indicated he had pinged Mooney.

'My man is more a team member. He can stay since it is you who wanted to see me.' McCabe stood his ground and took a sip of his drink.

Pathos looked at him, anxiety written all over his face. 'Very well, let me get to the point.' He leaned forward.

'I will assume you know who I am, so we can skip the formal introduction. I have a daughter, Alexis, a rather impetuous girl at times. Well, she is in a spot of trouble, very serious trouble, Mr. McCabe. She has been kidnapped by a bunch of people who call themselves the Maritime Freedom Fighters. Bloody pirates, in my view. They want a large ransom. They contacted my office yesterday.'

He paused and took a sip of water. 'The thing is, McCabe, the situation is tricky. She was captured on board one of my own ships in the Gulf of Aden.'

'When did this happen, exactly?' McCabe interjected.

'Four days ago, from what I can understand. I'm sure you are aware of how dangerous those waters are.' Pathos was fidgeting, clearly anxious, a far cry from the ice-cold billionaire in the Burrows & Co boardroom not 24 hours ago.

McCabe simply nodded.

'I fear her life is at risk.' Pathos paused.

'But surely you need to engage the relevant authorities,' McCabe jumped in, wanting to save Pathos the time. 'They have teams that specialise in hijackings.'

'Indeed, they do, but the last thing I need is press coverage. There is more, if you will allow me to continue, Mr. McCabe.'

'Please go on.' McCabe decided to let him finish.

'Aside from the fact that I own the vessel, the folks I had on board to protect the ship from these bloody pirates have failed me.'

'What's the name of this firm, if you don't mind?' McCabe knew most of the international firms and wondered who had cocked up.

'Force 12 or something like that. I have a man that arranges it.' Pathos seemed unsure. It wasn't a name McCabe recognised.

Pathos continued, 'I learned my daughter was on board with her boyfriend, a banker by the name of Daniel Spencer, a foolish idiot, in my opinion. I had no idea! So, you see, Mr. McCabe, I need your services and you have come highly recommended.' He sat back.

McCabe thought for a moment. 'I have some questions, as you would expect, Mr. Pathos.' He leaned forward.

'Firstly, this Force12 crew, never heard of them, but I assume they are some kind of PMC?' Pathos frowned.

'Private military company. Mercenaries,' McCabe explained.

'Oh yes, I see.' Pathos was none the wiser but decided not to show any further ignorance.

'How many of them on board?' McCabe asked.

'I'm not sure exactly, but the man in charge is a chap called Thirway, John Thirway.'

McCabe shook his head. 'Not a name I know. Where can I find him?'

'Ah, he is in fact on board, so a bit tricky,' Pathos explained.

'Okay, so they have asked for a ransom for your daughter. I don't need to know how much at this stage.'

'Yes. They have threatened to kill her if I don't pay within the week.' Pathos turned pale, clearly upset.

'Okay, well, we hope it won't come to that. But why not just pay? It's not like you can't afford it. You see, Mr. Pathos, any form of rescue carries a degree of danger. Trust me, I know first-hand.' McCabe looked him in the eye.

'I know, but if I pay, I send a message to every damn pirate out there that I have an open bank account. But, honestly, even if I pay, I think they will kill her. I simply can't risk it.'

'Okay, I see your point.' McCabe sat back and looked over at Mooney, who was trying to work out the conversation. McCabe waved him over. As Mooney approached, Nicolai appeared and also headed to their table.

'It's all right, Nicolai.' Pathos put up his hand. Nicolai slowed down but sat at the table all the same.

'Forgive me, Mr. McCabe, but he gets very anxious when people who look like your friend approach me.'

'Understood. This is Mooney. He's like a brother,' McCabe introduced.

'Pleasure, sir,' Mooney addressed Pathos.

'Okay, let's get back to it, shall we?' McCabe turned to Mooney. 'Mate, I will fill you in later, but Mr. Pathos here thinks he needs our help. His daughter is on board a ship hijacked by pirates.' Patting Mooney on the shoulder, he noticed his friend was focused on Nicolai.

'What is it?' McCabe asked.

'Your man,' Mooney said to Pathos, 'what's his history?'

Pathos looked surprised. 'Nicolai is a former Spetsnaz. I trust him with my life. Is that good enough for you?'

'Ex-Spetsnaz, I see.' Mooney turned back to the conversation.

'I have heard of you, Mr. Mooney,' Nicolai said; he was a man who didn't need to say much.

'Really? And how would that be?' Mooney was intrigued.

'Just have,' Nicolai replied.

McCabe wanted to move on. 'Okay, I have to ask,' he said to Pathos, 'what the hell is the daughter of a shipping billionaire doing on a rust bucket sailing through one of the world's known black spots?'

'Yes, indeed,' Pathos replied, 'I wondered the same thing. I have no idea, to be honest. Some kind of prank that has landed her in trouble. Can you get her back?' He looked extremely worried.

'Not sure I need the work, Mr. Pathos,' McCabe said. 'This is tricky stuff and I have long since retired from any active service.'

Pathos gave him as big a smile as he could in his situation. 'I hear very different. The lady who gave me your name said you are good.

You would be able to help me.'

McCabe and Mooney exchanged glances.

Dismissing what Pathos had said for the time being, McCabe proposed, 'If I accept, and it's a maybe, I will need help, more information, of course, like who on board can give me intel, the number of pirates on board, what weapons they have. I will also need some funds to purchase my own logistics.' McCabe looked at Mooney.

'Mr. McCabe,' Pathos spoke, 'please allow me to get to the point. I will pay you, in advance, one million dollars, and an additional half a million for each man you need. Upon the safe return of my daughter,' he paused, 'I will give you a bonus of another million. Will that cover it?' He then produced a chequebook and placed it on the table.

Shocked at the bounty, Mooney coughed rather obviously. McCabe looked at him as if to say, 'Act cool.'

'You think I can be bought, Mr. Pathos?' McCabe was also shocked but preferred to maintain some dignity.

'No, Mr. McCabe, I think not. But I think you of all people would understand a father's love for his daughter, that a father would do all he can.' Pathos knew this would strike a chord with McCabe, who now thought of his own daughter and how he would act in the same situation.

'I see you are well-informed. Who is she?' McCabe was done playing.

Pathos sensed the change in tone. 'Very well, she is a close friend, works for MI6 on occasion as an informer. She is a charming woman with class. I am sure you know who I mean.' He raised his eyebrows.

McCabe paused and then smiled. He knew it could only be one person. But, it also meant he would have to be careful.

'Okay,' he said, 'but let me make something very clear. I cannot guarantee your daughter's safety. It's a high-risk mission. But what I will promise you is I will do my best. Agreed?' McCabe held out his hand.

Pathos reciprocated. 'Thank you,' he said. 'So, how much do I write on this cheque, Mr. McCabe?'

McCabe looked at Mooney, trying to work out fast how many men he would need. 'I will go for four men, including myself,' he said. 'If I need more, I will hire them myself. So, I think we have a deal, Mr. Pathos.' McCabe smiled.

Pathos made out the cheque for S$2.5 million as if he were paying his electricity bill and handed it to McCabe, who studied it and placed it in his pocket.

'Keep me informed. Here is my private number.' Pathos handed him a business card.

'Leave it with us,' McCabe said. 'But give me the information I need soon. I will need to get going fast.' He stood up, pushing his chair back.

'Thank you. I will be in touch. Oh, and I have a plane at your disposal. It will take you anywhere you need to go.' Pathos then headed out of the bar with Nicolai close behind him.

'Well, oh buddy, what do you think?' McCabe turned to Mooney.

'How do we know it's not a trap? He meant the Rain Angel, didn't he?' Mooney pulled up a stool.

'Have no fear, my friend, I have a feeling I will be getting a call from her very soon. You let me worry about her,' McCabe replied. Mooney moved his large head up and down.

'So, who else do we need? How about Chaz? He did all right in Dubai,' Mooney suggested.

McCabe looked down, wearing a serious frown.

'You okay, mate?' Mooney tapped his arm.

'Yeah, I was just thinking about Stowe. Yeah, Chaz would be good. Give him a call, will you?'

'Sure. Maybe I will sweep the floor, too.' Mooney shot him a wink.

McCabe put down the phone and looked at Mooney, his expression somewhat thoughtful. 'Something seems off,' he said.

Mooney was stretched out on the sofa. He sat up, frowning. 'Go on,' he prompted.

'That was Pathos. The scoop is, he has just spoken to this Thirway guy on board the hijacked ship, ex-bootneck and head of Force12. See if you can get anything on him from your pals over at 5.'

Pacing around the room, one hand on his chin, McCabe continued, 'He claims there are only four guys on board armed with light weapons, the kingpin being a guy called Abshir Mohamed, some kind of pirate warlord. Best have him checked out, too. Anyway, Thirway confirmed Alexis and her guy, Daniel, are still unharmed.' He sat down.

'So, that all seems okay. What's the concern?' Mooney asked.

McCabe looked up. 'Instinct. Something about this doesn't feel right.'

'You think it's a trap?'

'Not sure, but we will find out.' McCabe looked serious—a look Mooney knew all too well.

TWENTY

The Penny Black was swarming with bodies jostling for space to enjoy a drink, whilst those stuck outside turned to their cool beers to beat the humid heat. A veil of cigarette smoke hung just in front of the entrance—given that smoking was prohibited inside. The five o'clock starting gun had gone off and clusters of bankers and lawyers now gripped the necks of their green beer bottles as if their lives depended on it. It was Friday, after all.

McCabe and Mooney were seated apprehensively in one corner, nursing their bottles of beer, when Chaz ambled in, pushing his way through the crowd, with a somewhat battered green canvas kit bag slung casually over his left shoulder. It took him less than 30 seconds to spot Mooney.

'Is this the section for old farts and wannabe mercenaries?' Chaz blurted out with a big smile on his boyish face.

'No, it's the section for macho men and tough guys,' Mooney responded, reaching out one of his shovel-sized hands.

'Good to see you, Chaz,' McCabe said.

'You, too. Looking good, man.'

'Okay, let's get you a beer, then down to business.'

McCabe called the meeting to order. The mission, as he explained it, was to head out to Oman, following the route Alexis and Daniel had taken. Despite the offer from Pathos of a plane, McCabe decided a normal charter flight would be sufficient; they would also avoid drawing any undue attention that way. From there, they would join a flight to Mogadishu, posing as journalists.

Once in the Mog, McCabe would make contact with the fourth man, who, as luck would have it, was working for the United Nations and had useful contacts. Given this was not a sanctioned military operation and Mooney was on sabbatical leave from MI5, they could hardly waltz in armed to the teeth.

'We are a man down,' Mooney reminded McCabe.

Looking at him and Chaz, McCabe smiled. 'You are going to have to trust me, okay? The fourth man will meet us in Oman.' Mooney and Chaz shot each other a glance.

'So, why can't you tell us now?' Chaz enquired.

'Simple,' McCabe replied. 'I have been asked not to divulge who it is and I respect that. You should both know by now I would not ask you to work with anyone I would not trust with my own life.'

Both men knew not to argue, but McCabe knew they would be bothered not knowing.

'Another round of drinks on me.' He waved to the barmaid, who dutifully brought over three more beers.

'I hope we are going to eat, too. I feel like a bear with its throat cut,' Mooney bellowed.

'I'm not your mother. Eat what you want.' McCabe stuck a menu in front of Mooney and then continued to explain the plan.

A night assault was favoured purely because the cover of darkness would give them an advantage. Getting close in daylight would require some kind of disguise, and McCabe was sure, even if they posed as a fishing vessel, they would draw attention. So, stealth was the elected option. Chaz and Mooney jotted down notes; they were nothing if not serious about their work.

It was as if someone had thrown a live grenade in the middle of the bar. People were moving away from a sinewy man who had shuffled in. His dirty old singlet and baggy blue shorts, held up with a piece of twine, did nothing to help his appearance—not to mention the self-made tattoos all over his body.

The barmaid descended on him as if he were nothing more than a cockroach. McCabe held out an arm.

'It's okay, miss. I need to speak with this man,' he said to her and quickly pulled the newcomer over to their table. Chaz and Mooney were clearly now wondering what McCabe could want with such a man.

'Who on earth is this?' Mooney decided he just had to ask.

'This, gentlemen, is Ponco. Despite his looks now, he was, not so long ago, a pirate operating just out there in the Malacca Straits.' McCabe pointed in the general direction.

Mooney and Chaz smiled. 'Nice going, McCabe,' Chaz commented.

'Yeah, this guy can give us valuable insight into how we can board a moving ship using alternative methods, as in, not military. May as well learn all we can. I know we have all done the tactical SBS-style training, but sometimes the more primitive methods can be the best.' McCabe sat back.

Ponco smiled, revealing a set of blackened teeth. 'Nice to meet you,' he greeted the others.

Ponco was 55 years old, although he looked more like 75. His father was from Batam, a small Indonesian island; his mother was Singaporean Chinese. His tanned and wrinkled skin, covered with self-made tattoos, was a storybook of his adventures. Carved on his back was a green mass of amateurly drawn images of ships, birds and flowers.

Having lived almost his entire life as a fisherman, he had in his later years turned to the more lucrative lifestyle of a pirate. He had been arrested many times and spent the past six years in prison. Subsequently, his poor health forced him to give up his life at sea and seek any work he could find. He now lived in Singapore, carrying baskets of fish in one of the wet markets. It did not pay well, but it was enough to feed him.

McCabe had found him via a chain of contacts in the British naval contingent based in Singapore. It seemed Ponco, in his day, was a force to be reckoned with; he could shin up a 40-foot bamboo pole and board most cargo ships in less time than it took McCabe to change his socks. It was this knowledge McCabe wanted.

Ponco was now busy devouring the basket of crispy chicken and calamari Mooney had ordered. Considering how useful he was going to be, Mooney let it slide.

'Hey, get that urchin out of here!' A young guy in a suit stood at the end of the table, his beer slopping over his glass; he had clearly had way too many. Mooney just stood up—he didn't have to say a word—and the guy nearly wet his pants and staggered off.

Having fed, Ponco explained as well as he could in his limited English and with an array of hand gestures how he used to board vessels out at sea. Chaz was surprised at how easy it seemed, at least from an equipment perspective. Armed with just a *parang*, Ponco would fashion a pole out of bamboo, lash a tree root to one end, hook it over a ship's guardrail and simply shin up.

Looking at Mooney, Ponco shook his head; he was not at all sure a bamboo pole would work for the big man. Noticing Ponco's concern, Chaz and McCabe laughed.

By the time they left the pub, Ponco was well-fed and S$50 richer. McCabe had pressed the handful of notes into his hand. It was enough to last him a few months.

As the three men strolled along the river towards the main road, nothing was said. Each was deep in thought, with images of the vessel, how they would board and the kind of defence they would face in mind. Tomorrow, they would fly to Oman; in essence, the mission had begun.

It took them more than 40 minutes to navigate their way at Muscat International Airport. Mooney cut a swathe through the crowd, Chaz and McCabe trailing in his wake. The Oman Air flight to Mogadishu would leave in two hours.

To the casual observer, the three men looked nothing out of the ordinary in their jeans and T-shirts, their camera equipment completing their journalist makeover. But their destination was far from ordinary.

Mooney was pumped; he loved action. Being in harm's way was meat and two veg for him. McCabe was happy his old pal was there. Mooney's ability to defend and attack was nothing short of awesome. Despite his size, he was nimble, fast with his fists and an expert marksman—not to mention he had been involved in eight or so hostage extractions. Chaz was the most inexperienced of the three, but he was young, tough, fast and fit.

McCabe was glad to get underway, but he still felt an undercurrent of fear, which heightened his senses. The money they had been paid for the job would certainly come in handy; that is, if they survived.

———

The sun was setting as the plane turned for its final approach. Looking out the window, McCabe could see the small streets of the Mog tinted with the sun's orange glow. Ironic, he thought, that such a lawless city was bordered by the beautiful turquoise Indian Ocean coastline.

Mogadishu is one of the most dangerous cities on the planet, with a fluid population of 1.5 million. Its thousand-year history, during which the Persians and Arabs built it into a thriving seaport, lies buried in the dust. Now a lawless place, a city of civil war and famine, it is most certainly not a tourist destination, unless one desires danger, or the risk of being kidnapped or killed. The maze of streets is stained with blood and the buildings bear bullet holes and the scars of regular mortar attacks. In short, it is hell and the devil hides in every corner.

As they stepped out of Aden Adde International Airport, McCabe and his men were on heightened alert. It was a hot evening and people were milling about, many of them looking for easy foreign targets to rob.

Mooney walked at the rear, his eyes darting everywhere, taking in their surroundings. McCabe, who was leading the way, spotted the man who had been sent to meet them.

'Mr. McCabe, over here!' A small wiry man, dressed in a starched white shirt and a pair of black trousers, was frantically waving a name board.

McCabe sauntered over to the barrier. 'I'm McCabe,' he told the man.

'Yes, good, I have car, this way, from Peace Hotel. Come.' He darted off.

The Peace Hotel, known as 'the best hotel in hell', was one of the few in Mogadishu that was safe for Westerners.

In Mogadishu, no one really expects anything from a hotel, but just a safe resting ground. The Peace Hotel is literally an oasis in the middle of hell. Mealtimes find the chef turned out in starched white cotton and waiting personally on his guests. He serves up a feast of curried fish, fries, camel meat and spaghetti with ground beef—all washed down with freshly squeezed orange juice, cold water and bottled beer. Dessert, if one is still hungry, is a bowl of fruit, accompanied with hot sweet milky tea.

McCabe noticed the hotel was located in a small building consisting of only a few storeys. It was clean. Palm trees swaying in the sea breeze around the hotel hid the true identity of the city, whose name had become a synonym for anarchy. McCabe and his team were reminded they were in Mogadishu rather than Bali when artillery shells and mortar rounds whizzed above like shooting stars and gunshots rang out from the nearby Bakara Market.

The hotel's most important service, which McCabe was counting on, was the provision of professional security teams, arranged by the hotel's owner, Bashir Yusef. The handpicked security staff got their basic military training on the streets of Mogadishu and carried small arms licensed by authorities from the interim government, although veterans of the last military dictatorship were also adept at using anti-aircraft weapons and tanks.

The two rooms McCabe and his men checked into would be their operations centre for the next few days as they readied themselves for the mission. The sweltering heat made them all sweat. Mooney thumped the air-conditioning unit, which sprang to life, only to clatter to a stop a few moments later. At least, they had electricity, which, in Mogadishu, was rare.

Having settled in, McCabe prepared to meet his contact, the fourth member of the team. Mooney would go with him as back-up, leaving Chaz behind just in case anything happened. The agreed meeting place was the Arba-Rucun Mosque, or Mosque of the Four Pillars, dating back to the 13th century.

In the morning, the four of them were to visit the notorious Bakara Market, located in the heart of the city. It was the biggest and busiest market in Mogadishu, although McCabe was not going there for fruit. He had his eye on the AK-47s, the 9mm pistols, the carbines and even the odd RPG—not to mention all the ammunition they could carry.

Mogadishu at night was even more sinister; gunshots and screams could be heard on most streets. The mosque McCabe and Mooney were heading for had a narrow courtyard that opened up via a central portico into a series of five bays. The central bay was covered with a fluted dome.

McCabe edged his way along the wall, the sound of his footsteps echoing off the stone walls. Mooney positioned himself a few yards away, behind a large pillar, but his shadow crept out across the floor. McCabe stopped just before the entrance to the vaulted room.

'It's been a long time, McCabe.' Bill Hadlow stepped out of the shadows.

'It has indeed,' McCabe whispered. 'Can we talk here?'

'Yes, no problem,' Hadlow spoke normally, smiling.

With that, Mooney appeared, his shadow smothering Hadlow before he could work out who it was.

'My god... Mooney!' Hadlow exclaimed, surprise evident in his voice.

'When McCabe told me we had a fourth man, I wondered who the hell it was,' Mooney jested.

'Yup, me.'

'Good to see you, old mate.' McCabe extended his hand.

Bill Hadlow was a living legend. A former officer with the Royal Marines Special Boat Service, the navy's equivalent of the SAS, he was literally a crack soldier who knew his craft. His skills, given all SBS officers were highly trained in maritime anti-terrorist tactics, were gold. He had met McCabe and Mooney during a training exercise in Canada and the three had just bonded. They were kindred spirits and had been friends ever since. When McCabe called, there was no hesitation.

McCabe had another reason for bringing him in. Hadlow, it was rumoured, now spent his time running a company that specialised in maritime security. This made him the most informed member of the team. He would know how the pirates operated; above all, he might just know about Force12.

Leaving the mosque, Hadlow led the way to a bar in one of the few safe areas in the city. Safe, as in the chances of getting abducted were lower—just 60 percent. The beer was cold and cheap; it didn't come any better.

The bar was located on one of the many small streets lined with white houses in Mogadishu's old town area, near the port. It was a good place to sit and talk. A few aid workers and a local businessman were the only other patrons, which meant the team could relax a bit.

'So, fill me in on the details,' Hadlow began. 'I know we are about to rescue the daughter of a rich bastard, but what else?'

'John Lucas Thirway. Ring any bells?' McCabe asked.

Hadlow shot him a glance. 'Oh yeah, nasty bit of work, ex-42

Commando turned bad.' He took a swig of his beer. 'He runs an outfit known as Force12, only a handful of guys, mainly former US Marines or Legionnaires. Not used by many companies as, I hear, they can be a bit heavy-handed.' Hadlow put his beer down on the table. 'So, don't tell me he is involved.'

'Yeah, he is. He has a contract with Pathos Shipping and he is on board our hijacked ship. In fact, he seems to be acting as a mediator between Pathos and the pirates,' McCabe explained.

'That means only one thing, we have to be careful. My guess is, he must be mixed up in it somehow, mark my words,' Hadlow jested. 'Listen, I don't want to jump the gun and all that, spoil the fun, but are you not better calling in the navy, let them use my old mob to sort this out? They do it all the time out here,' he explained.

McCabe and Mooney looked at each other and then back at Hadlow.

'It's complicated,' McCabe said. 'Pathos wants no press. The bank that is financing the cargo, I hear, also wants no press. So, that's why we are technically a black op.'

Hadlow pondered for a few moments. 'That means only one thing, McCabe. Trouble with a big T.' He stood up and paced around. Then, he sat down.

'Okay, what do we need?' he asked, his face lighting up. It was the sign McCabe had been waiting for. Hadlow was in, and that was very good news.

TWENTY-ONE

September 2009. London and Oman.

'Get up, for Christ's sake, you bloody pansy!' he spat. His eyes were glued to the rather poor-quality TV picture of Arsenal playing at home. The main striker, who had stumbled and fallen somewhat theatrically and was now play-acting on the grass, holding his knee, was pissing him off.

Nursing a pint of brown ale and taking the last few drags on his cigarette, he observed the scowls around him.

Inspector John Boyes was a 48-year-old flatfoot veteran with an unblemished 21-year record of service with the revered Scotland Yard. He was, some said, born with a whistle in his mouth, starting out as a beat officer in 1980.

At 6 feet 2 inches tall, with a mop of black curly hair and thick dark eyebrows, and his once toned physique now bulked up with perhaps more fat than was healthy, he was an imposing figure of a man. His 18-year marriage to Claire, a former nurse, had ended in a bitter divorce two years ago—so bitter, in fact, his home was no longer a five-bedroom house in London's Battersea but a one-bedroom flat above an off-licence.

Even his two sons had distanced themselves. Boyes blamed himself; too many late nights at work and his drunken rages had torn the family apart. Now, he lived a life of bad curry, cigarettes, beer and work—a lifestyle that would, if not stopped, choke his heart.

The brown buff file in front of him contained only a few documents, mainly because it was a new file. Thumbing through, Boyes came across the colour photograph of a young Caucasian male by the name of Barry Caswell. There was no criminal record on file. His wife had reported him missing two months ago. Investigations by flatfoots found nothing. His wife later noticed his passport was missing, along with a few pieces of clothing.

The only lead Boyes had was that Caswell had left the country via Heathrow on a charter flight to Oman. As a result, Interpol was now involved and the case was to be headed by Boyes.

Boyes looked at the note that stated Mrs. Caswell had called yesterday, having just discovered her husband's two-month-old voice message on her mobile phone.

'Then that is where I will start,' Boyes said to himself.

———

The house was situated on Radley Road, a street like any other in suburban Battersea, lined with large semi-detached Edwardian and Victorian houses. It was, as luck would have it, an area Boyes knew particularly well, given his ex-wife lived not more than two streets away.

The white picket gate in the laurel-covered brick wall surrounding the house opened onto a path that led up to a black-and-white tiled doorstep and a navy blue front door with a big brass lion's head knocker. The curtain moved as Boyes paced up the path; she knew he had arrived. As the door opened, the aroma of baking bread hit him in the face.

'Inspector Boyes, Scotland Yard, madam,' Boyes announced, holding out in front of him his warrant card.

'Yes, do come in, inspector.' Mrs. Caswell stood back and gestured for him to enter. She led the way into the front lounge, a nice room with two large white sofas, a large glass coffee table and numerous family photographs.

'Can I get you some tea, inspector?' she offered.

'Yes, thank you, very nice.' Boyes always appreciated a good cup of tea. He never made it for himself now; the milk was always off.

Sitting forward on one of the sofas, Boyes rested his teacup on one knee.

'So, Mrs. Caswell, can you take me through what happened exactly? I would also like to hear the voice message.'

'Yes, of course. Well, I never check my phone for voice messages, silly, really, but I did this one time and...' She needed a moment. 'I found this message.' She then handed the phone to Boyes. Putting the phone to his ear, he listened.

'Babe, it's me. Sorry I had to just leave, no time. But deep six is awesome. I get my first...' The message ended abruptly. Boyes looked up at Mrs. Caswell.

'I will need to get a copy of this, maybe something we can distil out of it. This 'deep six' he mentions, any idea what he means?' he asked.

'All I know is, he joined this club, no idea what they do. He seemed very excited about it. I didn't know he had gone away,' she explained.

'How would you describe your husband?'

'Just normal, I suppose. Hardworking, good with the kids. Oh, and he loves his computer games.'

'Computer games?'

'Yes, you know, war games, guns and shooting stuff. I keep telling him not to play them in front of the kids. They seem too real,' she replied, almost forgetting her husband was missing.

'Oh, and that stupid tattoo! I was so angry!' She recalled how she had banished him to the spare room for it.

'Tattoo?'

'Yes, a devil or something, not sure what possessed him.'

Boyes noted it down. Then, clearing his throat, he asked, 'Is there another woman?'

Mrs. Caswell shot him a look. 'No! No, there is not. Honestly!'

She was not at all impressed with the question.

'Mrs. Caswell, let me be frank. Was your husband prone to just heading off and not telling you?' His brow furrowed.

'No, not at all. Very out of character.'

'Any debts, worries you know of?' Boyes was now running through his standard questions.

'No, we are fine.' She was getting irritated.

Boyes continued to scribble notes. 'Okay, I think I have enough for now. Anything else you can think of?' He was now fishing.

No response came. Mrs. Caswell was visibly still annoyed at his earlier question.

'Okay, then I will leave you be. I'm sorry you are going through this.' He stood up.

'Are you... I have no idea what has happened, and you bring it down to a sordid affair.' She was upset.

'Mrs. Caswell, sorry, but I have to ask. Do you know most missing persons are eventually found to be husbands having affairs?' He headed towards the front door. 'I will be in touch and you have my card.'

Boyes was walking down the path to the gate when he heard Mrs. Caswell shout, 'Wait!' She was waving something in her hand.

'You reminded me. I found this in a pair of his jeans, not sure if it's relevant.' She held out what looked like a tatty old business card that had been through one too many spin cycles.

'It may well be.' Boyes studied the card as best he could. The words 'John Thirway, Force12' were just legible.

Boyes let out a sigh and sat back in his chair. He could tell from listening to the voice message Caswell left his wife that it had been made from a street full of people. The source placed Caswell in Oman, so that, at least, confirmed where he had placed the call.

What Boyes needed to know now was why a 31-year-old executive with a loving family would be in Oman—and not on company business, as his employer had confirmed.

Something else bothered him. Force12, the name of the company on the business card from Mrs. Caswell, was a private military company with listed offices in London, Oman and Singapore. How was Caswell linked to them? Clearly, he had to find out.

He put down his stainless steel scissors and nylon thread. The almost three-month-old human remains in the stainless steel tray in front of him were going to go back in the cabinet. For Dr. Mohamed Omar at the Omani mortuary, it was just another day.

The cause of death, in his opinion, was a shark attack. The savage bite marks still discernible on the badly decomposed torso and head were damning evidence. He would run the dental records against the Interpol database—along with a record of distinguishing marks, specifically, the tattoo of a red devil on the upper right arm.

Other than that, the case, in his world, at least, was closed. It had been a long enough day and he still had several other cases to handle. The case of a careless scuba diver did not warrant too much of his time. It did, however, catch Boyes's attention when he saw it on his Interpol alert.

'Caucasian male, age 31. Cause of death: Shark attack. Found south of Oman. Red devil tattoo on upper right arm. Match one Barry Caswell, 62 Radley Road, Battersea, London.'

This was the break Boyes had been hoping for. It seemed obvious to him now that Deep Six was some kind of diving holiday. Clearly, for Caswell, it had turned sour, most likely some shark feeding thing gone wrong.

Boyes sat pondering at his desk, which was covered with files and sheets of paper. The evidence seemed to suggest his conclusion was correct, but instinct—the instinct of a 21-year copper—was telling him otherwise.

He stood up and started for the door. Then, he stopped. 'The card,' he thought, and went back to his desk to pick it up. Something about it held his interest. A visit to the company was the only way to find out.

———

The offices of Force12 were located on the third storey of a run-down building near Soho. Having asked to see Trevor Stone, who was listed as one of the directors, Boyes took a seat and waited.

After a few minutes staring at pictures of oil tankers on the walls and enduring the musty smell that old offices seemed to have, Boyes was greeted by a rather tarty-looking woman dressed in a skin-tight blue dress and white stilettos.

'This way, inspector.' She led him into a small meeting room.

Boyes took a seat and waited again. This time, he found himself staring at pictures of what looked like special forces and attack boats hung almost anywhere a nail would go on the wall.

A few minutes later, a small squat man with a shaven head and blue eyes entered. He was dressed in a pair of jeans and a black polo shirt bearing the company insignia.

'Stone,' he introduced himself. He sat on the opposite side of the table and leaned forward. 'What can I do for you, Inspector Boyes?'

'John Thirway. Who is he?' Boyes was to the point, sensing Stone was also a man of few words.

'He's my business partner. He runs our Singapore office. Why?'

'His business card turned up in the pocket of this man.' Boyes slid a picture of the Caswell family across the table. 'He turned up in Oman two months ago.'

Stone studied the picture. 'Not a man I know, sorry. He may have worked with Thirway in the past. You would have to ask him.'

'Into marketing, is he?' Boyes quipped.

'Marketing?' Stone replied. 'No, he is in charge of recruitment for our protection team. He covers Asia, the Middle East and Africa.'

'Well, the closest this man came to that line of work was his computer.'

'Then, I have no idea.' Stone sat back. This was a sign of guilt, at least to Boyes.

'So, what is it you do, exactly, if I may ask?' Boyes enquired.

'No problem. We provide protection to a number of maritime clients.' Stone was calm.

'Protection?'

'Yeah, against pirate attacks, mostly. Gulf of Aden, South China Sea. Most, if not all, of our guys are ex-military, some coppers like you, ex-SO9 guys.' Stone seemed helpful, maybe too helpful.

'So, Thirway was what? How long have you known him?' Boyes was now taking notes.

'Listen, has he done something wrong? A lot of questions you have. If not, I'm busy.' Stone was losing his cool.

'I merely want to eliminate him from my enquiries. We can always go down to the station, if you prefer.' Boyes was in no mood for games.

Stone sat forward in his chair. 'Okay, look. Thirway, salt of the earth. We set the company up four years ago, that's it.'

'Okay, thanks. I appreciate your help. One last question, if I may. Who would your largest client be?'

Stone paused, looking at Boyes. 'Well, strictly speaking, that would be confidential. But, given who you are, I have no wish to play games, inspector.' He paused again. 'Pathos Shipping, based here in London. They give us about 70 percent of our income. Christos Pathos, wealthy bastard. You may have heard of him.'

'I think I may have read about him in the papers. Listen, thanks, I think that will be all for now. I will contact Thirway and just ask him a few questions.' Boyes stood up and shook hands with Stone.

'Don't mention it. But Thirway is away on a job, so he may not be contactable. If I can help in any way, give me a shout.' Stone gestured towards the door.

'Sorry, where would he be, exactly? Thirway, I mean.'

'Maggie,' Stone bellowed. The woman who had shown Boyes in

appeared. 'Thirway, where is he?'

'Gulf of Aden, on a job for Pathos,' she replied in one of the best cocky accents Boyes had heard in a while.

'Thank you. That could be very helpful.' Boyes showed himself out, his instincts once again heightened. Something was amiss and he couldn't place his finger on it. He also disliked Americans; Stone made his skin crawl.

No sooner had Boyes left than Stone placed a call.

'It's me, Stone. Some cop from Scotland Yard is sniffing around. Seems Thirway's little sideline may be putting us at risk.' He waited for the reply. 'Okay, then, he needs to be dealt with.' The line then went dead.

———

The offices of Pathos Shipping, located in London's affluent Mayfair, were a far cry from Boyes's at Scotland Yard. Upon entering through the glass doors that proudly bore the company's name in gold letters edged in navy blue, Boyes was greeted with a china cup of tea and seated on a cream-coloured leather sofa. A large glass vase of orchids scented the reception area.

'Good morning, inspector.' Samuel Teasdale held out his hand.

'Good morning,' Boyes reciprocated, standing up.

Formerly a defence barrister with top London firm Jud and Baker, Teasdale was the head of contract negotiations for Pathos Shipping. With brown hair, green eyes and a classic clean-cut appearance, he looked every inch the Oxford scholar. He had come on board three years ago, after successfully defending a case against Pathos Shipping for a contract breach. After that, it was a matter of how many numbers there were on his cheque that bought his loyalty.

'So, what can I do for you, inspector?' Teasdale sat on the sofa opposite.

'I understand you contract a company called Force12 to protect your vessels,' Boyes said.

'Indeed, we do. Why?' Teasdale was to the point.

'John Thirway. What can you tell me about him?' Boyes leaned forward and placed his cup on the table.

'Never met the man. I just review and sign the contracts. Not had any issues to date with the company.'

'I see. Well, I don't have any other questions for now.' Boyes stood up.

'Just one small thing, inspector,' Teasdale said, looking somewhat like someone in a Charles Dickens novel.

'And what would that be?' Boyes asked.

'I hear on the grapevine they run vacations—special vacations,' Teasdale replied in a hushed voice.

'Sorry, vacations?'

'Well,' Teasdale began to explain, 'a friend of mine was involved with a case a few years back. A man by the name of Brad Taylor had gone missing. He had paid a small fortune to Force12 to go on a vacation, some kind of extreme adventure. I don't know the full details, but strange they would offer that, right?'

Boyes thought for a moment. 'Okay, thanks, I will look into that.'

As he left the building, he was convinced Stone and Thirway had something to hide. He had to find out what.

TWENTY-TWO

Tears ran down Mrs. Caswell's face. Hearing her husband's body had been found was not the best news on a wet Thursday morning. Hearing sharks had enjoyed a meal out of him made it worse.

Boyes, not known for his delicate touch, broke the news by reading out the official cause of death from the coroner's report: 'Death by misadventure, most likely whilst engaged in the sport of scuba diving.'

'Can I ask why you seem so surprised about his diving accident?' Boyes enquired.

'Well,' Mrs. Caswell sobbed, 'for one thing, he couldn't swim, inspector. That and the fact he had a defective ear drum. I need to find out if it invalidates his life insurance. What will I do?' She was clearly in a state of confusion.

———

Boyes, too, was now more than a little confused. Back in his office, sitting in his chair with his hands behind his head, his brow furrowed, he tried to think where he could take his investigation next. Travelling to Oman seemed like a good idea, but it might not help any more than to see Caswell's remains in a steel tray. That is, if he hadn't already been boxed up and sent back to the United Kingdom.

As he sat there contemplating, the door swung open. 'You may want to take a look at this,' Smith, one of his detectives, announced.

'Another case, sir, just came up on Interpol.'

Boyes logged on. Then, his eyes widened. This surely had to be linked; it was too much of a coincidence. He scanned the report again. The body of a Caucasian male had been caught in a fishing boat's nets off the coast of Somalia. The fisherman had the common sense to contact a British naval frigate, the *HMS Devonshire*, which had been patrolling the area. The report concluded that sharks had damaged the remains, but there were suspicions as to how the body had made its way that far out to sea.

Boyes popped his head out of his office door. 'Smith, find out how I can get in contact with the frigate *Devonshire*. I need to know every detail of what they found and where they will send the body. I need it back here in London.' He knew he was about to hit something big.

His footsteps echoed down the narrow corridor as he followed the signs that seemed to be taking him through an endless maze of left and right turns towards the pathology lab. Two women wearing white hair nets clattered past, pushing battered aluminium trolleys loaded with tepid meals. They didn't seem to be in any rush.

The smell of disinfectant was all too familiar. It triggered memories of his visits to the same hospital; his father had been here for almost three months before he died. A year-long fight with cancer had slowly reduced the once powerful man, a former police officer, to helpless sinew and bone in faded blue pyjamas. In his final days, he was utterly dependent on morphine to kill the pain.

The old brown swing door looked like it had been kicked hundreds of times. Slowly pushing it open, Boyes found himself in a large white tiled room. Another smell now overwhelmed him, the acidic smell of formalin, so strong it made him cough.

'Arrr... You must be Inspector Boyes,' a rather plummy voice enquired. Bernard Lamb, chief pathologist and resident professor at St. Thomas's Hospital peered at Boyes over the top of his half spectacles whilst continuing to scribble on a notepad. No sooner had Boyes adjusted to the new smell than Lamb led him to another room.

The green sheet was pulled back, revealing the remains of a Caucasian male who had clearly not had a good death. Large chunks had been ripped off the torso and left thigh. Given the extent of the damage, the fact that both hands were missing was not surprising, although it looked like the right hand had been cleanly sliced off.

'What do you make of that?' Boyes asked, pointing to the stump that was the right arm. Lamb looked closer, squinting.

'It could be an attempt to hide his identity. No hands, no fingerprints,' Lamb commented, scratching his chin.

'Yeah, could be,' Boyes replied. He walked around the body, examining it. He was used to seeing corpses. In fact, he rather enjoyed the examination process; he found it fascinating. 'Do we know who he was?'

'Indeed, we do, inspector. Managed to track down his dental records.' Lamb reached for a pile of notes on a nearby stainless steel trolley. 'Our victim is… Jeremy Drake, aged 35.'

'Any way of determining the cause of death?' Boyes asked.

'Most likely drowning, as best I can tell. Been at sea about a week, no more, I would say.' Lamb walked over to the other side of the room and returned with another trolley. 'These are the other remains you wanted to see.' He pulled back the sheet.

Boyes took a step back; the odour was overpowering. 'Blimy! Not much left of him.'

'Yes, poor fellow. Shark attack, judging by the bite radius and the extent of material loss. Leucosia anatum have also had a go at him, I think.'

'Sorry, leucosia what?' Boyes asked, frowning.

'Oh, sorry, hobby of mine, type of crab found in the Indian Ocean,' Lamb replied, momentarily looking up.

'I see.' Boyes then stopped; he was staring at the top of the right arm. 'Good god,' he muttered.

'Found something, inspector?'

'Yes, look at that, the same tattoo,' Boyes replied, pointing.

'Tattoo, you say?' Lamb moved to where the inspector was standing.

'Yes, that other victim had the same tattoo, a red devil with the number '6'. What do you think the chances of that are?'

'Good god, you are right! Missed that one.' Lamb felt rather stupid.

'Have a picture taken of both tattoos for me, will you? Thanks.'

Walking out of the hospital, Boyes took a moment and lit a cigarette. He was now convinced that the cause of death for both victims was somehow linked and he wasn't thinking it was fish. The identical tattoos had to be a clue; Force12 was his bet.

TWENTY-THREE

September 2009. Mogadishu.

McCabe woke with a jolt as his phone rang. Picking it up, he heard the caller trying to introduce himself. But, given it was 3:00 a.m., McCabe was feeling groggy.

'Who is this?' McCabe asked bluntly.

'Sorry, this is Timothy Kent. I'm the head of trade finance at Burrows...'

Before Kent could finish, McCabe interrupted, 'Not interested. I left banking a few months back and I'm not looking for a job.' He wanted to return to his sleep.

'Wait, we are after your other talents, Mr. McCabe.'

McCabe sat slowly up, shaking his head to wake himself up.

'My other talents?' he asked.

'The bank I represent has a situation, one that requires your skills. You have been recommended very highly. Shall I continue?' Kent waited.

'Go on.' McCabe was intrigued now.

'The bank has financed a cargo—you need not be concerned with what the cargo is, but it is valuable to us. The ship has, unfortunately, been hijacked off the coast of Somalia. In short, Mr. McCabe, we need it back. I would add, in no uncertain terms, by whatever force is deemed necessary.'

'Wait, before we get to that, who gave you my name?' McCabe

had heard enough for now.

'A lady, a well-connected lady.'

McCabe fell silent. It seemed his nemesis was suddenly promoting his skills. The question in his mind was why.

'Okay, go on, you have five minutes.' McCabe was now sitting on the edge of his bed, resting his head in his hands.

'The vessel is called *Odin*, a cargo ship owned by Pathos Shipping, now under the temporary control of pirates. So, are you interested?' Kent wanted a decision.

'Leave it with me. Call me back in 24 hours. Now, if you don't mind, I need my sleep.'

Kent knew he had little choice. 'Of course, sorry again. I will call you in 24 hours, Mr. McCabe. If I may add, our fee, I am sure, will seal the contract. Good night.' He hung up.

McCabe lay back down on his bed, now fully awake and trying to work out the connection. It seemed Pathos and the bank were now up against each other for the recovery of the same vessel.

Aside from the fact that he could make a tonne of money, he was interested in the Rain Angel. It had to be her and, if it was indeed her, he had to assume it was a trap. Pathos and the bank's motives were easy to work out—daughter versus cargo, no brainer. It was the infamous woman who concerned him.

There was only one way to find out. He had to speak with her.

Pathos was at first reluctant to release the contact number, but McCabe was insistent and had given him some valuable information; so, he had little choice. Hearing the news, he wasn't sure whether to be pleased or annoyed. Either way, he now knew that Burrows & Co was in competition with him for the recovery of the *Odin*. He now had his own game to play.

Hanging up after his conversation with Pathos, McCabe immediately made his next call. The phone rang just a few times before she answered. The voice was unmistakeable.

'I wondered how long before you called.' She wasn't surprised; in fact, she sounded almost happy.

'So, what's the game?' McCabe enquired, wanting to spare niceties and get to the point.

'Game, my dear? No game. I am just helping out a dear friend. Can I not show my respect and repay a debt of gratitude? You spared my life or had you forgotten?' She loved to tease.

She was stretched out in her bath, sweet-smelling foam covering her modesty as she slid deeper into the hot water. At 42, she was even more attractive than women half her age, her jade green eyes, silver-grey hair and butter-soft skin in perfect condition. She was almost a replica of Audrey Hepburn. Yet, the polished exterior belied the heart of a ruthless assassin.

'Leopards do not change their spots, so you can hardly be surprised if I am suspicious,' McCabe fired back.

'Look, let me be clear. Pathos needs his daughter back, no press. You were a worthy adversary, so I happen to think you can pull it off. I also know that the swine they call the upper management at MI6 are keeping a close eye on you. They have designs on you, McCabe, so look behind once in a while.' She paused.

'The bank, well, I know they have some shady involvement, so I found it ironic that Pathos and those awful stuffed shirts at the bank are now after the same prize. Funny they both came to me, don't you think? But, know this, McCabe, they will want you to kill Alexis and the boy, Daniel, and leave no trace. So, you will have to choose your client.'

'Kill Alexis? Why?' McCabe was taken aback by this.

'That, my dear, is for you to find out.'

'I guess I should be grateful,' he said, his tone somewhat sarcastic.

'Yes, I hear you will make a large sum of money. If you feel you would like to offer me a bonus as a finder's fee?' she quipped.

'Bonus? You want cash?' he snapped.

'The CD you have will be sufficient. Remember the CD, McCabe?'

He had been wondering how long it would take her to mention it. 'Yes, I do, and it got my friend killed.'

'You know as well as I that he killed himself. Careless. I'm sorry for that, but it serves you no good to keep it,' she said, trying to sound persuasive as she stirred the water with her free hand.

'I will think about it and that is all I will do for now,' McCabe said.

'Very well, I await your decision. Be wise, my dear, and good luck.' The line went dead.

At breakfast early the next morning, the team listened as McCabe revealed the duplicity of the mission. It was clear they had two parties after the same goods. Surprisingly, the bank, for some reason, wanted the cargo; and, it seemed, they also wanted Alexis dead. That point alone was alarming, although McCabe knew a bunch of greedy capitalists would go to any length to protect their names and cash flows.

Having sat in silence for at least 40 minutes, polishing off his bread and marmalade and a boiled egg, Mooney piped up. 'There must be something else on board, something they want hidden.'

The other three men looked up.

'What do you mean?' McCabe was curious.

'Think about it. It's a large cargo ship. Pathos said he didn't know his daughter was on board, so...' Mooney stopped, his facial expression indicating the others should really be on the same page.

'So... what? I don't follow you.' McCabe was irritated at his inability to see what Mooney was driving at.

'Cargo ships are not chartered to carry the daughters of billionaires around the planet, are they? They carry goods, goods the pirates seem to want. So, my guess is, there is something else on board. Alexis is a red herring.' Mooney sat back.

'You could be right, not thought of that.' McCabe also sat back, pondering Mooney's point.

Leaning forward, Hadlow spoke up, 'There must be a dirty little secret lurking out there, and you know how you love to expose dirty little secrets, especially when a bank is at the bottom of it.'

It was late morning when the team left the safety of the hotel and headed down the dusty street towards the Bakara Market. Mooney saw it coming first, his reaction was nothing if not lightning-fast, which, considering his size, was impressive. He spun around and stood fast with his back to the wall, his SIG drawn. Seeing this, McCabe and Chaz followed, covering to Mooney's left and right.

A white van had crossed their path. The doors slid open and six armed men dressed in jeans and matching blue polo shirts exited in close formation.

'What's the call, boss?' Mooney bellowed. He knew they were outgunned and surrounded.

'Hold!' Hadlow suddenly shouted. 'Guys, put your weapons down!' He was now standing in front of them, gesturing with his hands to lower their weapons.

'What the fuck?' Mooney raised his pistol and aimed it at Hadlow.

'That's enough, boys. Holster your weapons and get in the van, please.' The voice was not familiar to McCabe, but it was British and his instincts told him who it could be, since Hadlow seemed to know who they were.

No one moved, aside from the local traffic, which seemed oblivious to the scene. After a few moments, McCabe straightened up and dropped his aim. Having observed the six men around them, he knew they had been caught like rats in a barrel and that opening fire would only serve to deliver a large body count, made up mostly of his own team. He also realised their mistake; they had left the hotel without their local protection.

'Okay, lads, let's go for a ride,' McCabe said and stepped forward, his hands slightly raised.

The others, except Hadlow, followed, not without the odd mumble from Mooney. Reaching the van, McCabe stopped and turned to Hadlow. 'Not sure what this is about, but I'm surprised at you.' He then climbed in.

———

The room was small and smelled damp. The wooden table set with three chairs in the middle of the room had seen better days. On it were three white polystyrene cups filled with water and a tape recorder in the middle.

McCabe knew the drill as he entered the room and took a seat. Interrogation would be on the menu; but in what form and by whom, he wondered. Surveying the room, he saw there were no obvious cameras and no fake glass windows, just scuffed white walls and a plastic rubbish bin. He sat back in the chair, prepared for a long wait.

To his surprise, Hadlow entered only a few minutes later, closely followed by the man who had so politely requested his presence. Hadlow sat opposite and looked directly at McCabe across the table, his hands clasped in front of him, his face blank. McCabe returned the stare, not wanting to appear fazed or intimidated. But, inside, he was impatient to find out what this was about.

He then turned to the other man at the table. Harry Ogilvy was 6 through and through. His polished exterior hid his capacity to kill without hesitation. Educated at Eton and Oxford, he later did a stint with the Gurkhas and, in 2005, was recruited by MI6. His fluency in five languages made him useful.

'Now then, McCabe, we have been busy, haven't we?' Ogilvy broke the silence with a wry smile. McCabe said nothing, just held his gaze.

'Okay, now, given I know you know how this works, I won't waste your time, just listen for now. Can I get you any tea or coffee, perhaps?' Ogilvy was nothing if not polite, at least, for now.

Good for what ? (handwritten annotation)

'I'm good, thanks. Didn't know you boys were out here,' McCabe offered up a limited but gracious reply.

'You recently left the employ of Banning Capital, after what I will call a little spat in Mumbai; the folks at 5 called it a ghost operation. You have now been asked by one Mr. Pathos to rescue his beloved daughter from savage pirates and, to cap it all off… shall I continue, Mr. McCabe?'

'Oh, do go on, such a great story,' McCabe replied sarcastically, meaning to provoke Ogilvy.

'I think we all know the rest, McCabe. I have a proposition for you, so let us cut to the chase, shall we?' Ogilvy's tone was now firm.

'And who would we be?' McCabe enquired, shooting a glance at Hadlow before returning his gaze to Ogilvy.

'6, McCabe.' Ogilvy leaned in, his eyes menacing.

McCabe laughed. '6! And what on earth would you want with me? I'm on vacation with a few lads, nothing more.' He stood up. Anyone from 6 made him nervous. His instincts had been right. His interest was more on the association with Hadlow. He had trusted Hadlow, yet here they all were, nice and cosy.

'Sit down, McCabe,' Ogilvy commanded. 'No one is going anywhere until I am done, is that clear? I need not tell you how unpleasant I can make your life.'

'The others, where are they?' McCabe demanded to know.

'Safe, for now. Now, sit down.'

McCabe sat back down slowly. 'It appears I have little choice.'

'Indeed. Hadlow here works for me. You can discuss the way of it all later and I need not remind you to keep your mouth shut. What and how the two of you work this out is up to you. I need you, McCabe, to work with Hadlow and get me that ship, clear as that.' Ogilvy was in full flow.

'Seems everyone wants that ship,' McCabe said, trying not to show his shock at finding out Hadlow was, in fact, a spook, 'so go get the SBS or something. Hadlow, you would like that.' He made sure the last bit to Hadlow was loaded with sarcasm.

'Too much attention,' Ogilvy explained, 'and you, to be frank, McCabe, have the same skills and are far more expendable.' He sounded almost pleased.

'Yeah, how did I guess?' McCabe quipped.

'You in, McCabe?' Hadlow finally spoke.

McCabe looked at him, clearly not at all happy. 'My team is based on trust, you know that. Mooney and Chaz have earned it, now you stick this on me.'

'Come on, it's not like I can just say, and by the way, old mate, I'm now working for 6,' Hadlow said.

McCabe got the point. He knew he would have done the same; he was just being overly sensitive. 'I guess not,' he conceded. 'So, where do we go from here?' he asked Ogilvy.

'I suggest you go and plan. You are on your own, aside from Hadlow here. You will, of course, have access to certain logistics and intelligence, but this is covert, not directly 6, is that understood?'

'How do you figure that one out? Isn't everything you spooks do not you?' McCabe responded flippantly.

'Don't be funny, McCabe,' Ogilvy said firmly. 'You know damn well what I mean. Once you have the ship under control, we will take over. What you do with those on board is no concern of ours, unless they discover what we are after.'

'And that would be what?' McCabe asked, genuinely interested.

'Need to know.' Ogilvy stood up.

'You tell me what it is or you can go and swing in the wind.' McCabe got on his feet.

'Hadlow here knows and that is it.'

Seeing he was not going to get an answer now, McCabe wanted to know what was in it for him. 'Okay, so what's the deal? There must be a deal, right?'

'We turn a blind eye to your adventures in the future, that's what. Can't have you running around playing spook now, can we?' With that, Ogilvy left the room.

Hadlow looked at McCabe. 'So, here we are.'

'Here we are, indeed, you prat.' McCabe broke a smile.

'Sorry about that, my hands were tied. When you contacted me, it was pure coincidence. 6 have had tabs on you for a while, mate.'

'Why does that not surprise me? Come on, let's tell the family about the picnic.'

TWENTY-FOUR

The force of Mooney's right hook to Hadlow's jaw knocked him clean off his feet. McCabe bit his lip, trying not to laugh as Hadlow, after a few moments on his back, tried to stand up, his legs less than firm beneath him.

'That's for not telling us, you bloody spook!' Mooney bellowed.

'Oh, and what the fuck are you, Saint Mooney?' Hadlow retorted, still somewhat dazed and rubbing his jaw.

'He has a point, Mooney,' McCabe joked.

'I meant bloody 6 spook!' Mooney was not happy about being the butt of the joke.

'Okay, enough,' Hadlow said. 'Like it or not, we have a job to do, so can we please move on?' Mooney continued to scowl at him.

'So, come on, what's on board this ship that the brass at 6 are so interested in it?' McCabe thought he would try his luck asking Hadlow.

'I can't say.' Hadlow was now firmly back on his feet and pacing around the tiny room.

'Can't or won't? You tell us what we are walking into, my friend, or Mooney here will keep pounding your head,' McCabe threatened, his tone verging on serious. No sooner had he finished than Mooney started to square back up to Hadlow.

'Do you trust me or not?' Hadlow spat, keeping an eye on Mooney.

'In a word, no!' McCabe's answer was instant. 'Listen, we have two very different agendas, now a third. You think I'm feeling good about that? You know as well as I all we have is each other, no secrets, that's the way it has to be. These pirates are no fools and god knows who else on board is a threat.' He sat down on the sofa, more to ease the tension in the room.

Hadlow was silent. Finally, he said, 'Okay, but if this gets out, I'm dead, I mean it.' He sat down next to McCabe, his face showing his anguish.

Chaz and Mooney gathered around, sitting or leaning on anything they could find. The room wasn't meant for so many guys, but it was safe and clean, so no one was complaining.

'6 have been tracking a shipment of gas centrifuges, used, as you know, to produce enriched uranium.' Hadlow cast a sarcastic look at Mooney.

'Yeah, I know, moron.' Mooney caught the gist.

Hadlow continued, 'This is the second such shipment we know of. It always originates from Malaysia.'

'How do you know for sure?' Mooney asked.

'We have had eyes on the factory for a while. SACAMO Engineering. The source, the real face behind this, is still unknown, but…' Hadlow paused.

'But what?' McCabe asked.

'SACAMO will be raided later today. We hope to find out more. We need to know who the buyer is and where the shipment is heading. That is, until it got hijacked. If those pirates get wind of it, then we really are in the shit. Clear now?'

'Jesus,' Chaz muttered.

'You got that right. Your target, as of now, has changed. Alexis Pathos and the boyfriend are gravy, but the centrifuges are what we have to get secured. Agreed?' Hadlow proposed.

'Aren't you forgetting who our paymaster is?' Mooney stated the obvious.

'What's that?' McCabe looked apprehensive and seemed to have forgotten the cheque from Pathos.

'Pathos just loaded us with cash to have his girl back. Now, we are chasing hardware. I think he may have something to say about it, don't you?' Mooney replied in his typical blunt tone.

McCabe had a sudden thought. 'Yeah, but who's to say he doesn't know about this cargo?'

'You mean he could be a suspect?' Mooney now realised they might have taken the Cypriot's innocence for granted.

'From the checks we have run, he's cleaner than your boxers, McCabe,' Hadlow jested.

'Yeah, very funny, so seems not him, then. But you must admit it all seems too much of a coincidence. Dodgy cargo, daughter of a billionaire, pirates... you could make a freaking movie out of it!' McCabe leaned forward and rested his chin on one hand.

'Do we even know if the pirates have discovered this so-called cargo?' Mooney piped up.

Hadlow got up and walked to the window. 'Not from the ransom demands. They seem to only reflect the human cargo, which is strange. It's like they were tipped off that she was on board. So, we go with our eyes open, gentlemen.' He then produced a case of beer that had been hidden behind a curtain. 'No hard feelings, boys.'

'Like your style, Hadlow.' Mooney landed a firm pat on his shoulder.

McCabe was less interested in the beer. He was trying to piece together the various bits of information he now had. Something did not add up and he needed to work out what.

The sun had long since risen and the heat, as they entered the Bakara Market, was stifling. Mooney was sweating like an overweight dinner lady.

They maintained a tight formation as they navigated the chaotic labyrinth of street stalls. The noise alone was deafening. Dark faces stared out at them from behind the curtains of tattered fabric that acted as screens against the dust and the glare. Westerners were not a common sight in this area and most who did dare to walk around ended up as hostages or corpses.

Duga, dressed in a white shirt, black trousers and a faded pink baseball cap, was their fixer. He was the man; he could arrange anything, get anything. Today, he was guide and babysitter all in one. McCabe had hired him from the hotel at a negligible cost, a mere US$100 for the day. He skilfully brushed beggars and sellers out of the way, shouting in Somali for them to move aside. Four guards came as part of the package, all armed with what McCabe recognised were Russian-made AKs, just in case things turned to shit. McCabe also knew they could ill-afford a compromise, especially as they didn't know the streets. Rats in a barrel would be an understatement.

As they rounded a corner, Chaz stopped. 'Will you look at that, holy smoke!'

The others looked in the general direction. There, perched on top of a truck bonnet, was a boy. He could hardly have been older than 12, McCabe thought. In his arms was an M79 grenade launcher. His eyes were wide open as he observed the four pinkies looking up at him. No sooner had they seen him than he took off.

McCabe felt Duga pulling at him, as if to keep them moving. Then, Mooney, too, felt something tug at his shirt. Looking down, he saw a small boy offering him what looked like a fistful of spinach. 'Do I look like a fucking rabbit?' he muttered.

'No, khat, drug.' Duga tried to educate the big man, whilst one of his men chased the boy away.

They reached a junction. Just across the street was the arms dealer Duga had told McCabe about. McCabe took in the fact that their current position left them exposed.

'Where are we?' he asked Hadlow.

'Hawlwadig Road,' Hadlow replied, having checked his GPS.

'Hell's bloody kitchen.'

'Great.' McCabe was anxious.

Chaz was busy observing the condition of the street, which, he noted, contained more potholes than tarmac.

'Okay, over there.' Duga pointed. They saw a tiny shack on the opposite corner, its rusty corrugated roof and driftwood walls making it look more like a large chicken coop than a gun shop. But there on show were literally dozens of what looked like M16s and AKs.

Each member of his team was getting nervous, McCabe could tell. It showed in their body language, their backs turning to anything solid, their eyes scanning everything around. He could feel his own gut tighten as they waited. Worst of all, they were defenceless, with not so much as a pea shooter between them. To be seen with arms would incite a riot.

The plan was to eye the weapons they needed, posing as journalists, and make a list for the fixer to purchase later. Buying weapons on the spot would be like announcing to every militiaman and pirate in the area that pinkies were in town for a fight.

Mooney and Chaz stayed with two of the local guards as McCabe and Hadlow finally crossed the narrow street. Glancing up, McCabe took in the sight of the twisted phone lines along the street, like mile upon mile of tangled rotten spaghetti.

The shop owner greeted them with a beaming face and open arms, indicating his willingness to trade. He didn't seem to care whom with. McCabe looked at him, thinking it was nothing more than the type of fake smile a few dollars could buy and, if it came down to it, he would turn one of his precious AKs on them.

No sooner had Duga rattled off something in Somali than Hadlow was handed an AK, which he instinctively checked to see if it was chambered. Despite its rather used appearance, it seemed to be well-maintained. It also had a live clip.

'Russian,' he muttered to McCabe.

McCabe took hold of another weapon and also ran through a well-practised routine, checking the breech and sights, sliding a magazine in and out.

'Hadlow.' McCabe warned with his eyes. He had noticed the shop owner observing them, perhaps thinking they seemed a little too familiar with such weapons.

'What is he saying?' Hadlow enquired.

'He is saying two hundred each,' Duga replied, and then turned back to the shop owner. They seemed now to be negotiating.

'Did you hear that? No wonder this place is fucked up. Two hundred dollars and you can have one of these babies,' Hadlow commented.

The familiar crack of an AK sent McCabe and Hadlow diving instinctively to the ground. The screams of people running all over the place filled the air. Another burst hit the shop, sending clouds of dust and debris flying in all directions.

'Shit, you okay?' McCabe yelled, looking at Hadlow.

Hadlow stuck his thumb up. 'You?'

'I reckon our 11 o'clock.' McCabe bobbed his head up. Just then, another burst shook the shack. 'Fuck!' He dropped back down fast.

'Any more bright ideas?' Hadlow laughed. Then, he caught sight of a small boy lying 10 yards or so to his right; the boy was bleeding. 'Damn it, they hit that kid!' he shouted.

'Leave it, nothing we can do for him.' McCabe was used to assessing a situation in which those on the other side played by different rules. There was no doubt that the guys who shot the boy were die-hard militants. A kid meant nothing to them.

More rounds rattled off, ricocheting in all directions. 'Where the fuck is our security?' McCabe shouted to Hadlow, who now had his hands on one of the shop owner's AKs.

Bobbing his head up once more, McCabe could see a white pick-up with three armed men in the rear.

'It's coming from over there.' McCabe pointed to show Hadlow where, just as another burst sent bits of tin shooting around the shack.

'Okay, on three, else we are sitting ducks.'

'Roger that,' McCabe acknowledged, having now commandeered an AK himself.

Gesturing with his fingers, Hadlow counted, 'One... two... three!' Both men sprung up and went loud.

Their return fire did nothing much other than to pepper the tailgate of the truck with holes as it vanished down the street, but McCabe did notice one man reel backwards; it looked like he had been hit in the shoulder.

As Hadlow raised his weapon to put down more rounds, it was grabbed by the shop owner, who let out a barrage of Somali words. Then, McCabe felt a strong hand grab his arm hard; their bodyguards were trying to move them back across the street.

'What the hell was that all about and where the fuck was our cover?' McCabe shouted to Duga.

'Militia, they not want you here, the word is out,' Duga replied, fear evident on his face.

Mooney booming 'Man down!' was the last thing the team needed to hear. Hadlow and McCabe shot each other a glance and bolted across the street.

Seeing Chaz on the ground, bleeding and barely conscious, both men knew it was bad news. The hired guards started pushing the crowd back.

'We have to get out of here, please.' Duga was getting agitated.

'Hang on, we're not leaving him!' McCabe knew they had to try and stabilise Chaz's condition. He knelt down next to Chaz and pressed his hands down hard on the wound to stem the blood flow. 'Chaz, stay with me, okay, hang in there.'

'We have company, 10, maybe more,' Mooney bellowed.

'We need some gauze or clean cloths, and fast. Mooney, keep an eye and get those guards to do their fucking job, else grab their weapons and sort it!'

'We have about five minutes. Then, this place goes mega loud,'

Mooney warned.

A local woman appeared out of nowhere with a bunch of white cotton towels. Hadlow grabbed them and handed them to McCabe. 'How is he?' he asked.

'Looks like he took a round in the lower right abdomen,' McCabe answered. Hadlow knew it was potentially a death sentence.

A hail of bullets hammered the wall behind them.

'What am I paying you for?' McCabe was now completely pissed off. 'Okay, lads, we have to move him, and I mean now!' He stood up and lifted Chaz's shoulders, whilst Mooney grabbed his legs. Chaz moaned as they carried him.

'Hadlow, you keep some pressure on the wound,' McCabe said. 'Duga, get your boys to stop pissing around and put down cover!' he shouted.

Duga let out a few heated words in Somali and the bodyguards finally started to earn their pay, legging it as best they could up the street.

'Here, over here!' Duga shouted to McCabe. He had commandeered a van from a passing tradesman. The team heaved Chaz into the back and piled in around him.

'Chaz, stay awake, stay with me, buddy,' McCabe said.

'Yeah, I'm trying.' Chaz's voice was weak.

'He looks bad, boss,' Mooney blurted out. 'We need medical equipment, and fast.'

'Cannot go to hospital,' Duga immediately said. 'Must head back to hotel. I call doctor.'

'This man needs proper equipment!' McCabe was not happy at the thought of giving Chaz backstreet surgery. But deep down, given where they were, he knew that was the best they could expect.

Duga pulled fast into the hotel compound. Some hotel staff were already waiting there. As the van doors flung open, they could see the floor was awash with blood. Chaz was hauled out and carried off into a small room on the ground floor. To McCabe's surprise, a table had been scrubbed down and covered with a clean tablecloth. Buckets of steaming water were being carried in.

'The doctor here soon,' Duga said. All they could do now was wait.

As the minutes ticked by, the team sat around in the lobby like expectant fathers. Only the odd mutter escaped their lips, and that was to ask for more beer.

When the door to the small room finally opened, the three men looked up. Dr. Aziz, a Somali educated in the United States, shook his head. 'I'm very sorry, nothing more I can do.'

Mooney sprang out of his seat. 'Nothing more! What did you do to him?' He bore down on the doctor. McCabe quickly moved between him and the now shaken doctor.

'Easy, big fella. Come on, chill.' He gently pushed Mooney back. Then, turning to Aziz, he asked, 'What happened?'

'The bullet had entered the anterior abdomen near the umbilicus,' Aziz explained, 'passing through the large and small intestines, before exiting through the lower back. There was massive internal bleeding. I'm sorry. I did my best.' He bowed his head.

'Okay... thanks, doc,' McCabe said quietly. After a while, he turned to Duga. 'Duga, we will need you to take care of the body, ship him home.' McCabe had to focus on the basics; now was not the time to let emotion get in the way. Chaz was dead and that was that; time enough to mourn later.

'Yes, of course. It will cost you.' Duga replied.

The look McCabe gave him was cold. 'Yeah, just get it done.'

'Come on, lads,' Hadlow said, as he stood up. 'Chaz knew the score. Beer time.'

'Yeah, he's right,' McCabe said. 'Chaz wouldn't have it any other way. The mission carries on.'

The three men sat around, picking at their food. The mood, despite the beers, was subdued. To lose a member of the team so soon was not good at all.

Knowing their morale was running low, McCabe started to jibe up what was left of his team. 'Okay, we are a man down, that's life and we all know the score. Any one of us could be next.' He was prone to using painfully honest language; he sugarcoated nothing. 'But this mission goes ahead, clear? In addition, we are going to need weapons, and buying a bunch of AKs off the locals is not going to work.'

'I can make a call, get some gear dropped off, somehow,' Hadlow piped up.

'Should have done that in the first place,' Mooney snapped.

'You two shut it, sort it and no more!' McCabe was at the end of his patience with the tension between Hadlow and Mooney. 'Clear?'

'Clear,' Mooney replied.

'Clear,' Hadlow agreed.

'Good. Hadlow, you sort the gear. Mooney, you and I will sniff out a boat. A nice big fat Gemini would do. There is much to do. I will also try and think of where we can find a fourth member. Four is already light for an assault team.' McCabe headed off to meet with the fixer.

'What's with you, Mooney? Is it my breath or something?' Hadlow opened up.

Mooney glared at him for a while. 'No, it's my fault. Never like you guys in 6. Sorry, let it go. I'm good.'

'Come on, let's make that call, see if we can't get some decent gear from 6. About time they paid up.' Hadlow shot Mooney a smile.

Peter Ryan was a loner. He drifted from country to country, chasing stories others didn't want or weren't stupid enough to chase. He had few friends, and his habitual gambling took what little he earned.

He seemed to most people a broken man. His ruddy cheeks, the result of far too much booze, added to his pitiful appearance. Yet, he hadn't lost his ability to talk. He could coax lunch or dinner out of anyone he came across in a bar with one of his many stories.

Despite his faults, Ryan was a damn good journalist. *The Guardian* needed someone to go to Mogadishu and dig up a story on pirates, a topic of increasing interest in the news, and Ryan was the only journalist available and mad enough to accept the assignment.

Ten years in the field, covering every hellhole on earth, had honed his journalistic skills. However, it was what he learned in his past life that served him best. Ryan had done his time in the regiment, specialising in intelligence. Unfortunately, his addiction got him kicked out.

As he entered the Peace Hotel, his face two days deep in stubble and his linen suit creased from the series of connecting flights from London, it was unlikely anyone who knew him would immediately recognise him. His stomach, now hanging over his belt, had also changed his physique.

'Good god alive, Ryan!' McCabe almost froze to the spot.

'Bloody hell, McCabe!' Ryan seemed just as shocked.

'How the hell are you?' McCabe asked.

'Well, as you can see, not as fit as you.' Ryan ran his eyes over McCabe.

'So, what brings you to hell?' McCabe quipped.

'Chasing a story. I'm doing work for *The Guardian*. And you?'

'Like you journalists, there's two more of me upstairs.'

'Of course, you are!' Ryan didn't believe McCabe for a second.

'Well, let's catch up later. Must run, have to see a man about a boat.' McCabe then dashed off in search of Duga.

TWENTY-FIVE

September, 2009. Northwood, United Kingdom.

Eddie Bates propped himself against the wall, just inside the doorway. As he scanned the large wood-panelled room, hoping no one would spot him, he counted off 10 men, many of whom he knew were the army and navy elite.

'Not hard to work out, given the amount of tin they're sporting,' he thought. And the fact they were seated in high-backed leather chairs around a mahogany veneered table rather than on arse-numbing steel chairs in some smoky old briefing room.

He then counted five non-ranking men who stood somewhat apprehensively around the room, seemingly waiting for something to do. 'Much like myself,' he mused. Having completed a circuit with his eyes, he relaxed, comfortable that he was, at least for now, not conspicuous.

A loud cough, delivered by a para colonel with a poker face standing at the front of the room, abruptly ended the various conversations that had been taking place around the room. He took everyone in with his steely gaze.

For Bates, the seemingly endless round of introductions that followed was boring. He knew pretty much every face in the room. They reminded him of ancient gargoyles—stony, ugly, fearsome.

Except for two; he didn't know the rather stuffy-looking admiral and the woman seated next to him. She had the look of a class-A bitch, he thought. Any woman present amongst so much brass and scrambled egg had to be either a spy or an analyst. His money was on spy—she had that look, feminine yet deadly.

His mind started to wander. He recalled studying his reflection only a few hours ago. It wasn't often he observed the smart figure of a soldier dressed in his Number 2s, with the sand-coloured beret of the SAS resting proudly on his head. It was a far cry from the face he had seen in the mirror prior to getting cleaned up. The baggy green eyes, messy brown hair and two-day stubble had made him look more like the man he was—a man who had just got back from a long mission.

He was pleased to see that his 31-year-old physique was still in good shape; at least, he didn't need to suck in his stomach, which was more than he could say for some in the room today.

Stiffening his posture, Bates focused his attention on the satellite images now being projected on a wall-sized screen at the far end of the room. This, at least, interested him. They were looking at images of an industrial park in Malaysia.

When the slideshow ended, he turned his attention back to the people in the meeting, specifically to the man seated at the far end of the table next to the two strangers. He knew Ogilvy particularly well, given it was Ogilvy who had invited him to the meeting. He was also the only man in the room not in uniform.

'Baker, bring me the files,' Ogilvy said in his clipped tone.

Bates knew Baker, a weasel of a man in his opinion, who worked for Ogilvy at 6. 'Come on, you weasel, no one has time for your shit,' Bates mused. He knew Baker was there simply to kiss arse and aid his boss, and that was that.

Baker nodded sharply and promptly moved around the table, placing a thick buff personnel file in front of each officer, careful not to make physical or eye contact with anyone. Each member of the brass skimmed his copy of the personnel file, picking out only relevant details from what Bates knew would be tonnes of photographs and military jargon in plain black text.

General Parker, a grey-haired, eagle-eyed 22-year-term regiment man, SAS to the core, cleared his throat. He was the only one not bothering to read the file.

'Echo Force,' he said. 'This team is the best. I suspect you're all familiar with some of their work. I doubt anyone knows about all of it. Well, these lads are like Chinooks. They land at night, take care of business and get out fast.'

He lifted his copy of the file off the table and flipped it open to display the name at the top. 'MARK MCCABE' it read, in large, black bold font.

'Except this man,' Parker continued. 'He created and trained the team a long time ago. To be frank, a cold-blooded killer in his day.'

Bates tensed up. It was a name he knew all too well. He was now very focused—so focused, he even noticed the subtle smile on the woman's face.

Ogilvy dropped his file flat on the table, the loud 'thwack' indicating he was about to interject. 'I know of him, sir, and I know all about Echo Force, too,' he said.

Everyone in the room turned to look at him. Ogilvy contemplated surreptitiously wiping the palms of his hands on his trousers, then thought better of it and leaned forward with his hands clasped in front of him, his elbows resting on the table.

'This man,' Ogilvy began, 'has carried out operations in Georgia, Africa, Cuba, Bosnia, Colombia, Iraq, Kuwait, Thailand… pretty much every nook, corner and cranny of the world. I would go as far as to say he has been to hell and back on many occasions.' He paused to work some moisture back into his mouth.

'Echo Force have more than proven their effectiveness as a single unit working in intelligence-gathering, unconventional warfare and direct action capacities. The recent decision to give them greater independence in the field under Major Michael Scott was, I feel, a good one.'

'Skip the PR speech, Ogilvy,' the gravel-voiced para colonel who opened the meeting, a chap Bates knew as Osborne, spoke up from the far corner of the table. 'Can you get to the point?'

Ogilvy held his stare for a second or two before replying. 'Very well. I have a mission that requires the skills of Echo Force. The engineering factory you have just seen images of in Malaysia needs to be taken out, and fast. I draw your attention back to the images on the screen.' He pointed to the wall behind him.

'This factory has been churning out gas centrifuges for 10 years, items that have been sold to Pakistan, Iraq and Korea. A new buyer is now in the market, a buyer we are still in the dark about. The man profiled in the file in front of you is engaged unknowingly in an operation of significant importance linked, we think, with this new buyer. A load of gas centrifuges is now in the hands of Somali pirates and McCabe is trying to get them back for us. He is attempting this mission with a bunch of volunteers. Whilst they are a mixture of former regiment troopers and very good—one man even works for me now—I would like us to sanction Echo going into Somalia as a backup team.' Ogilvy sat back and awaited any questions.

'What, you spooks can't handle it alone?' Osborne blurted out. 'And why have we sent a civilian to recover this cargo if it's so damn important, even if he is former regiment? Explain yourself, Ogilvy.' He seemed somewhat pleased to point out that 6 needed help.

'McCabe was hired to rescue the daughter of the ship owner Christos Pathos. She is on board the ship, so we sought to use McCabe to do our dirty work at the same time. I need not remind you that, if we send in a team officially and the daughter dies, the media will be all over us. Not to mention, if any crew member dies, the accountability will be on us. This man, Pathos, is a big backer of the current government, if you get my drift. And, yes, colonel, MI6 needs your help,' Ogilvy fired back.

'Poppycock!' Parker spoke out. 'Whilst I buy all of that, there is something else you are not telling us, Ogilvy. Come on, out with it.'

Ogilvy looked to his right; seeing the nod from the admiral, he continued, 'Okay, we think the Americans are somehow behind it, but we have no proof, at least not until Echo goes in and finds it in that factory. Even then, we don't have enough time to mobilise another team. To put it bluntly, gentlemen, McCabe is our best hope.'

He took a sip of water and then continued. 'Also, if it goes wrong and the Americans start to point fingers, we can claim no involvement. McCabe is not on our books and makes the perfect scapegoat. It's the game, gentlemen, and you, by the power of the PM, have to approve such a mission.' Ogilvy's eyes darted around the room.

Langdon, the admiral, spoke for the first time. 'And I believe McCabe is the man to get it done, gentlemen. This man is stone-cold fearless and, much as I want to disagree, Ogilvy has a point about his anonymity.' Murmurs sounded around the table.

'If this Pathos is paying him, then he is nothing more than a damn mercenary,' Osborne chimed in.

'He can be whatever we want him to be. My word is final,' Langdon volleyed back. 'If you wish to challenge me, gentlemen, please do.' He stood up. Osborne shrank back into his chair. Even he knew just how powerful Langdon was.

'So, do I have your support, gentlemen?' Ogilvy capitalised on Langdon's authority.

Bates then stepped forward. 'If I may speak?' He looked at Ogilvy and Parker for approval.

'Carry on,' Parker said.

'I know McCabe. I should. He trained me and half the men in Echo. To be frank, I can't think of anyone better right now. He is a man of war, gentlemen, make no mistake.' He eyeballed the room. Then, he turned to the woman. 'May I also ask who the lady is, sir?'

Her eyes instantly bore into his. Her wry smile was almost as good as saying, 'I bite.'

'You do not have the clearance, sonny!' Langdon thundered. Ogilvy eyed each of the officers in succession.

Parker spoke up to defuse the tension caused by the error Bates had made in asking. 'Okay, Bates, noted. Now, stand down. Ogilvy, you have my approval, at least for Malaysia, but the offshore leg is on your books. Is that clear? Oh, and use McCabe.'

Ogilvy reluctantly nodded and then spun around in his chair. He looked right at Bates, who was now standing bolt upright and looking back at him.

'You have your orders, man. They will be confirmed to you in full. Now, get on with it. Dismissed,' Parker barked.

'Yes, sir.' Bates delivered a crisp salute, turned sharply and left.

TWENTY-SIX

September 2009. Kuala Lumpur, Malaysia.

The eight-man SAS team, call-signed Echo One, gathered in the shadow of a building 100 yards to the left of their target area. Bates observed the area of open grass in between that led to a perimeter chain-link fence about 2 metres high. Thus far, it was as they had modelled back at the forward operating point.

Bates hunkered down on one knee, and looked at his men. 'Okay, Red team on me. Blue team, you cover the rendezvous point and the road to the south. Let me know if anything moves.' He then got up and cocked his weapon. 'Stand to.' He checked his watch; he had just 45 minutes to get in and get out.

'Blue, go!' he gave the command to Blue team. Then, he led Red team swiftly out of their cover and across the open land. In seconds, one of his team had cut a hole in the fence, and they streamed through in close formation.

According to their intelligence and recce, there were no security cameras located around the perimeter of the two-storey building. Bates double-checked as he paced across the yard to the far side of the building. On the way, he observed a stack of wooden pallets and a generator shed off to his right. They were the only objects outside the main building that offered any form of cover.

Despite the late hour, Bates could see that the building was still very active, its interior lights on. When he reached the main entrance, his radio crackled into life. 'We have visitors, over.'

The headlights of a car suddenly swept up the road and across the yard. As the car drew up outside the compound gates, the two teams melted away into the cover of darkness and waited.

Bates knew now who the visitors were. His team situated at the forward observation point had picked up the car coming in. He watched as two men dressed in suits got out of the car. Both, he observed, were Caucasians in their early 30s. 'We hold, but are you getting this?' he put out.

'Roger that. Have them in our sights,' Blue team responded.

A sudden slam of a door sent Bates ducking down. He then saw Mustafa, their target, exit the building, cross the yard and start to unlock the yard gates.

'That's our target, over,' he spat out over the radio.

'Shall I take him out, boss?' Chris, one of his trigger-happy men in Blue team came in.

'Negative, hold.'

The men shook hands and started to walk back towards the building and head inside. Bates then moved out from his position and eased himself along the wall towards an open window just a few yards from the main entrance. With his back pressed hard against the wall, he could listen in.

'The cargo has been hijacked as planned,' the taller of the two Caucasian men was saying, 'so it should be in the right hands before long. You need to get the next batch ready.'

'Okay, can.' Mustafa nodded.

'Yes, and then we need you to shut down,' the other Caucasian chimed in. 'The Brits are getting too close.'

Bates noted the accents were distinctly American and, given the two men were Caucasian, wearing suits and had a certain swagger, it didn't take Einstein to work out who they were. 'CIA,' he thought.

'Okay, my friends, I will do as you ask. Just make sure the payment is ready,' Mustafa replied.

The two men then left the building. Seeing them exit, Bates retreated behind the external generator block, 15 or so yards to the left of the main entrance. From there, he watched the two men walk back towards the gates.

Just as they reached the gates, the taller of the two men suddenly stopped and turned, as if something had triggered his senses. He stood motionless for a few seconds, as if listening for something. Then, he started to walk slowly towards the generator block, drawing his 9mm pistol from his shoulder harness.

'Eyes on, I may have been compromised,' Bates put out.

'I have him in sight.' Someone in Blue team had a visual and would go loud, if required.

As the man came ever closer, Bates eased his finger on the trigger of his carbine. He felt a bead of sweat roll down his face, as he focused on remaining calm—not easy when his guts started to knot. The other two of Red team were still positioned in the opposite corner to Green team. Every man was now intently listening, waiting for the inevitable gunfire.

When the stranger was just a few feet from the generator block, he stopped. Bates could hear his breathing and the gravel under his shoes, as he turned slightly. Silence then hung in the air. Bates felt himself freeze; any slight movement now would give him away. He could almost hear his sweat droplets hit the ground.. He hoped it was his imagination and the mystery man could not hear it.

Then, just as Bates let out a slight breath, the other man shouted, 'There is nothing there. Come on!' He was clearly in a hurry.

The first man turned sharply; Bates heard his feet move. After a few seconds, he replied, 'Okay.' The sound of his footsteps told Bates he was walking away. Bates popped his head up slowly, thankful he could breathe again. As the man turned beneath a lamp by the gates and got into the car, Bates could see his face very clearly. A few moments passed as the two men appeared to exchange a few words, and then the car moved off.

'Okay, clear, stand by. Go in ten,' Bates put out.

As the flashbangs came in through the windows, Red team came in hard and fast through the front door and Green team breached the upper level; both teams had hit the timing perfectly. A short burst of fire from Blue team took out the armed guard, who had been caught completely by surprise, blinded by their torchlights and shaken by the percussion of flashbangs.

The two other men on the upper level were now face down and being cuffed. Mustafa was moaning, felled by a blow to the guts. He was cuffed and dragged out of the building.

As Echo One gathered with their prisoner on a large patch of grass to the north outside the gates, two helicopters appeared out of nowhere like ghosts, extracted the nine men and chopped off into the night.

Only six men remained in the yard, writhing, when the Malaysian police arrived. Mustafa had vanished. MI6 would now have their chance to interrogate him.

TWENTY-SEVEN

September, 2009. Gulf of Aden.

The smell was starting to become overpowering, a mixture of body odour, cigarette smoke and sour milk—hardly surprising, given they had been locked up in the recreation room now for four days. Toilet breaks and the odd snatch of fresh air on deck were short and always overseen by two or three armed pirates. Daniel noticed the guards changed over every 24 hours; they were nothing, if not well-organised.

Vandenbrook sat in one corner of the room, reading a rather worn copy of *Kane and Abel*. He seemed relatively unfazed by the entire incident. Daniel, on the other hand, just gazed into thin air, occasionally getting up and pacing around the cramped room to burn his nervous energy. He lived now with the fear that Abshir would somehow discover his dirty little secret and find out that Jeremy was, in fact, innocent.

Just as he felt himself start to sweat and shake, the fear now so intense it was raising the alarm in his brain and manifesting itself physically, the door burst open and two pirates entered. Much to his relief, they walked towards Vandenbrook.

'You,' the smaller of two men shouted, pointing his weapon at Vandenbrook. His tatty black shirt was barely visible under the bandoliers loaded with tarnished ammunition. The ski masks they had been wearing were gone.

Looking up, Vandenbrook could see the pirate's face was heavily scarred with what looked like homemade tattoos. Calmly, he closed his book, placed it on the table next to him, stood up and walked out the door.

Abshir was on the bridge as Vandenbrook entered. Looking around, the captain observed two of his crew had been left at their station to navigate the ship in large circles.

'You men okay?' he asked.

'Yes, captain, we are okay,' the Dutch crewman spoke up, somewhat apprehensively.

Abshir then spoke. 'Captain, you have now only five hours. After that, I execute one of your crew. Get on that radio and ask where my money is.' His tone was unmistakably firm.

Not wanting to react too quickly, Vandenbrook held his stare, as if trying to work the pirate out. 'Do that, and you will have the entire navy down on you,' Vandenbrook replied. 'You have no choice other than to wait.'

After a moment, Abshir smiled. 'You dare to challenge me, captain. I like that, a man with courage and intelligence.' He paused and then got up and walked around Vandenbrook, a tactic he liked to employ.

'But you forget one thing, captain. Pathos will not allow his daughter to be harmed, so do you really think this is on CNN?' Abshir laughed.

Vandenbrook knew he had a point.

The radio transmission was connected directly to an office in London. Pathos had a team on standby 24/7, and he was to be informed the instant any news came in. Vandenbrook delivered the message with his normal composure, ending with the insistence that he receive a reply within the next two hours. He had asked for a firm date for the money to be delivered.

Vandenbrook looked at Abshir. 'So, now we wait. If it comes down to it, you shoot me, understand? Not my crew.' He then stepped off the bridge.

'Very noble of you, captain,' Abshir commented. 'Don't think for one second I would not.'

Vandenbrook turned back, frowning. 'What happened to you?'

'The West happened. It thinks it can treat Islam like dirt!' Abshir was suddenly fired up.

'This is not about Islam; this is greed.'

'You dare to challenge my beliefs?' Abshir stepped forward and pointed his AK at Vandenbrook. The two crew members moved forward but were halted by one of Abshir's men.

'Then, educate me,' Vandenbrook said in a calm voice. 'How can money be a religious calling? Tell me that.'

'It will buy weapons and food to fight the West, that is how.' Abshir's eyes were now raging.

After a pause, Vandenbrook replied, 'I see. Then, I hope you get it.' With that, he turned and started down the steel stairway.

Abshir was stumped. He didn't know how to take such an honest remark. It was as if Vandenbrook had understood and accepted his cause. He lowered his weapon and went back onto the bridge.

The phone call came at 11:00 a.m. Pathos was at his desk.

'Yes,' he grunted.

'They have requested that the money be dropped within 24 hours, sir,' Teasdale announced. 'Otherwise, they will start killing the hostages.'

'I want to know what this Force12 bunch are doing about this situation,' Pathos replied. 'And get me McCabe!' He knew his time and ability to stall was out. He hung up and buzzed his PA.

'Send in Nicolai, will you? Thanks.' He then eased back in his chair.

Nicolai took only a few seconds to appear, being just outside the office, reading the morning papers. His large frame loomed in the doorway.

'Nicolai, I want you to pay our friends at Force12 a visit today, please. Find out what they know. This John Thirway, who is allegedly on board, see what you can find out. Okay, off you go.' Pathos waved him off.

The final call Pathos made to his PA was a simple request. He wanted to speak with McCabe, and fast.

TWENTY-EIGHT

September 2009. London.

Water dripped into a little pool on the ground, sending an eerie echo around the dark brick archway every few seconds. The lock-up garage near Waterloo Station was used to repair and service the cars of those who could ill afford to even run a car. It was a function it had served for many years, evident by the rusty engine blocks, bent exhaust pipes and damaged tyres piled up outside.

The figure in the shadows to the left of the large blue doors blew a plume of cigarette smoke into the night air. He had been there for over 30 minutes and was not at all happy at having to wait. Leaning against the wall, he stamped his feet every few seconds, as if to demonstrate his rising anger.

He looked out down the narrow street, one side of which was lined with carbon copies of this garage, the other a mass of overgrown brambles trying to break through an old rusty chain-link fence that ran alongside the railway line. He could see a man approaching hurriedly. He turned his head to the left as a train thundered past, the noise it made bouncing off the walls of the garages. Then, the stillness of the night was restored.

Stone stopped, took out a pack of smokes, and lit one. Seeing this, Kent emerged from the shadows.

'You're late, damn it,' Kent snapped.

'Easy, I had to make a few calls,' Stone explained, not at all happy with Kent's angry tone.

'So, what the hell is going on? Your man Thirway seems to have fouled this up with his stupid games. I need a solution.' Kent was agitated and jabbing his finger.

'Listen, he knows how to handle a few pirates,' Stone replied, annoyed. 'More importantly, he has no idea about the cargo. I never told him, so calm the fuck down!'

'This savage, Abshir, needs to deliver that cargo to the Libyans, just like the other guy Mohamed did. Is that clear?' Kent was even angrier now, seeing that Stone seemed unfazed by the entire thing.

After a few drags on his cigarette, Stone looked at Kent, his face a contrast of calm to Kent's twisted features. 'Okay, tell you what, you pay me three million and I will keep mum and make sure the cargo gets to where you want it. Else, go to hell.' Stone squared up to Kent.

'What?' Kent was shocked at the sudden proposition.

'The way I see it, you are in no position to dictate shit. I'm the only one who can deal with Abshir and have him listen, and you know it.' Stone blew a cloud of smoke into Kent's face.

'Are you not forgetting your man Thirway? He may have other ideas,' Kent came back.

'Thirway is nothing more than in the way, right now. I can have him taken care of in a second.' Stone smiled. 'If you don't accept my deal, I will blow your sordid little story to the press. Imagine the headlines: "Mercenary turned good Samaritan, dirty banker who is really working for the..." '

Kent cut him short. 'Shut the hell up. It's a real shame you had to take that approach, Stone. You could have saved us a lot of trouble.' He now seemed cold, almost oblivious to Stone's threat.

'So, you are saying no?' Stone asked.

'Yes, you foul little man, I am saying no. You have served your purpose and are now a risk I can't afford.' Kent scowled.

'Risk? What does that mean?'

The double tap to the back of Stone's head caused him to slump forward, his eyes rolling up in his head as he fell. Kent studied the body for a moment.

Then he said, 'Come on, let's get out of here,' as he stepped over Stone and headed down the street, the figure of a well-built man following closely behind.

——— ——— ———

Boyes stepped inside the polythene tent erected around the body. It didn't take a genius to see the man had been shot at close range.

'What have we here?' Boyes asked the crime scene officers in white coveralls.

'Male, 40s, double tap to the back of the head, time of death, best I can tell, around 11:30 p.m. last night, 9mm, by the looks of the wound,' one of them rattled off without looking up.

'Do we have a name?' Boyes knelt down to get a closer look. No sooner had he asked the question than he knew the answer. As the victim was turned over, he recognised Stone.

Boyes now had his suspicions confirmed. Force12 was neck-deep in something and he needed answers fast.

'Have this body sent over to Professor Lamb at St. Thomas's, will you?' Boyes then stepped out of the tent. His mind was on setting up his next meeting and, knowing the attendees, he knew it would not be a fun experience. Even if they did know something, they would not exactly acknowledge the fact.

——— ——— ———

The car journey to Vauxhall Cross was as slow as any in Central London. But it did give him time to mull over the case. His meeting with his contact at MI6 was at 10 a.m. He had met Ogilvy at a training seminar on international terrorism, and Ogilvy had proven to be useful at times.

Boyes entered the glass-walled meeting room and took a seat. He observed the busy tide on the other side; people were moving around with files, or just moving somewhere. He was somewhat surprised at how young and normal they looked, not that he knew what a typical spook looked like. For all he knew, the guy who looked like he delivered pizza could be one of their best spooks.

Ogilvy walked in and held out his hand, which Boyes shook.

'So, what can we do for you?' Ogilvy sat back in his chair.

'I'm working on a case,' Boyes replied. 'It's getting more curious by the day, something you guys may be interested in.'

'Go on.'

'Two bodies recently turned up in the Indian Ocean three months apart, both British males, both marked with an identical tattoo—a red devil and the number '6'—on the upper right arm, both heavily mutilated. Last night, the body of one Trevor Stone turned up with a 9mm double tap to the head. He managed a firm called Force12, bunch of mercenaries, as best I can tell.' Boyes paused.

Ogilvy showed no emotion, in fact, no interest.

'I'm not sure,' Boyes continued, 'but something very strange is going on.' He got up and started to walk around the room.

'Sounds like a few mercenaries working the ships in the gulf fell over the side,' Ogilvy finally commented. 'Not a 6 concern.'

'Yes, that's what I would suspect, but both men were civilian, with no prior military records. Stone, on the other hand, was a former marine.' Boyes sat back down. 'In fact, they were both civy corporate types—marketing and banking.'

Ogilvy leaned forward. 'This Stone chap, let me look into it and get back to you. Send over the files of the other two also.' Ogilvy stood up. 'Nice seeing you again. Be in touch.' He gestured towards the door.

'Okay, soon, please. The body count seems to be growing.'

When Boyes had left, Ogilvy looked up his contacts list and found the name of someone he had used before. He dialled; after a few rings, a woman answered.

'Ogilvy at 6 here. Know anything about a company called

Force12?'

The woman on the other end of the line paused for a moment before replying. 'Yes, it's being dealt with, I believe.'

'Good, it's getting in the way of the other matter, which, to be frank, is far more important than a few pirates and a couple of rich kids,' Ogilvy said. The line then went dead.

———————

Hearing from Nicolai that Stone was away confused and concerned Pathos. It meant he had lost his only link with the men who were meant to be protecting his ship. Knowing Thirway was on board was some comfort. He, at least, Pathos hoped, would protect his daughter. That is, until McCabe arrived.

It was not so much Stone's absence that concerned him; it was the fact that, in front of him, the news story did not support Nicolai's update.

Nicolai had informed him that the Force12 office was closed and that Stone was away on business. Yet, there in black and white, was the report that Stone had been murdered. The police were now investigating. Pathos sat back in his chair, his mind a frenzy of thoughts. It seemed the man he was paying to protect him had a secret agenda.

TWENTY-NINE

September 2009. Gulf of Aden.

Abshir eased down a shot of whisky. He only felt a subtle burn in the back of his throat, which, in his book, made for a good blend. A second shot followed, and then a third. He needed to steady his nerves.

He began to scan the manifest in front of him. His gaze stopped halfway down the third page. He knew it was an anomaly to list items as 'machine parts.' He was now intent on finding out exactly what it was Stone wanted him to divert.

'Get me the captain!' he shouted to one of his men.

Vandenbrook entered the tiny cabin a few minutes later, apprehension on his face.

'Yes, what is it?' he asked, his tone sharp.

Abshir glared at him. 'Do not be so flippant with me, captain. I am not some illiterate fool. Now, what is this?' Abshir pointed to the manifest. He wanted to know how much Vandenbrook knew.

'It's the ship's manifest. Why?'

'Machine parts, captain. Even I know that could mean anything,' Abshir replied, his eyes wide open.

'I assure you that is what it is, at least, as far as I know.' Vandenbrook seemed confident.

'Then, we'd best take a look, hadn't we? And bring that fool Thirway with you.' Abshir stood up.

Entering the cargo hold, they switched on the lights. Their

footsteps echoed as they walked in. Abshir noticed the hold was only half full, with cargo stacked up on two sides. Barrels of seed oil made up part of the cargo. A few yards in and two of the crew members hauled off a large cargo net that had been used to secure the 56 crates in case of rough weather. Each crate was marked with a bold red arrow indicating the correct way up and black stencilled letters spelling 'SACAMO, agricultural machine parts.'

'See, I told you, machine parts,' Vandenbrook said, tapping one of the crates with his hand. Thirway stood a few yards back, simply observing the search.

'Open one,' Abshir said, waving to one of his men. Thirway took a few steps back; he seemed anxious.

The crate was ripped open and the pirate tossed a white manual to Abshir. Using a knife, the pirate slit the foil seal. Inside was a large cylindrical device, held in place by wood and foam packaging.

After studying the 2-inch-thick manual, Abshir walked over to the crate and peered inside. Then, he looked up.

'Take him!' he shouted.

His men grabbed Vandenbrook by the arms and held firm, as Abshir stepped forward. 'You think me a fool?' He punched Vandenbrook hard in the stomach.

The captain doubled over in pain. 'I don't know what you mean,' he spluttered.

'Gas centrifuges. They are used to separate uranium for nuclear weapons and power. You think I don't know?'

'I have no idea. I didn't know.' Vandenbrook looked up. Abshir kicked him in the ribs, which sent him collapsing to the floor.

'How, then, did they get on board? Magic?' Abshir shouted. He then looked over at Thirway. 'You know anything about this?'

Thirway simply looked back at him, his face showing confusion. Vandenbrook tried to get up.

'Bring me one of the crew,' Abshir instructed his men.

One of the crew members who had come down to help was

dragged over, kicking and shouting.

'Tell me the truth or I will kill him,' Abshir threatened Vandenbrook.

'I am. I know nothing.' Vandenbrook got to his feet.

'Very well.' Abshir took out his Beretta and aimed it at the crewman. The shot was deafening as it echoed around the hold. Even Thirway winced. The crewman fell to the floor, clutching his right shoulder and screaming in pain.

'The next one kills him.' Abshir aimed his pistol again. 'I'm waiting.'

A moment passed before Vandenbrook spoke. 'Please stop this. I didn't know the contents of these crates. My crew are innocent,' he pleaded.

Abshir looked at him. 'I know that now. I wanted to see if you, too, were linked with that scum.' He looked at Thirway.

'You mean, you knew about this?' Vandenbrook asked Thirway.

'Listen, it's nothing to do with me. It's between my partner and him.' Thirway pointed at Abshir.

'Yes, it is,' Abshir admitted, 'but I did not know the contents.'

'Come on, what did you think Stone was selling? Candy?' Thirway laughed.

'I will tell you something now, though,' Abshir was very serious. 'The Americans and the British can go to hell. This cargo belongs to me now and I, Abshir, will decide where it goes.'

'Wait just a minute! You had a deal!' Thirway moved forward.

Abshir raised his pistol. 'Back away, fool, or the next bullet is yours. Now, get them all out of here.' He waved to his men.

'You,' Abshir said to Vandenbrook. 'I can trust you. I want you to make a call for me.'

Pathos was seated at his desk, reading the newspaper, when Burrell rushed in. Nicolai was sitting outside, listening to music.

'Bad news, I'm afraid, Mr. Pathos.'

Pathos looked up, the blood draining from his face. 'What is it? What has happened? Tell me.' He felt his heart sinking for fear of news on Alexis.

'Captain Vandenbrook has just contacted us,' Burrell announced. 'The pirates seem to have found something in the cargo hold. They now want 80 million dollars, and in 24 hours. If not, they will kill all on board.' He was nervous and wringing his hands.

Keeping his cool, at least on the surface, Pathos instructed, 'Arrange the funds and get hold of McCabe again, and fast.'

THIRTY

Sepember 2009. Mogadishu.

McCabe had the team seated around a small table in a back room of the hotel. Half-eaten Mars bars and opened packets of salt-and-vinegar crisps that Mooney had thankfully brought along littered the table on which a few maps were spread out.

It was routine to run through the plan of attack many times, each man noting down his role and how the plan would play out. Mistakes could cost lives. Mooney leaned back in his chair and let out a yawn. 'Are we done yet?'

'We are done when I say we are done. Now, from the top.' McCabe wanted a final run-through for the day. He wanted each man to eat, sleep and crap the plan.

'At 0500, we leave by truck, head for Eyl, 400 kilometres north,' Mooney started.

'We retrieve the two RHIBs Duga has arranged. Situated in the blue warehouse, south Eyl docks,' Hadlow followed. 'At 1800, you and I will take one of the boats and move out of the port and rendezvous with *HMS Devonshire* at the agreed point. From there, take delivery of one M107 Barrett sniper rifle, an assortment of side arms, mainly SIG P226, Glock 9mm pistols, our carbines, a couple of MP10s and enough ammunition to start a small war and a few boxes of flashbangs.'

'Okay, enough for today,' McCabe said. 'Let's have a final briefing at 1800 tomorrow evening. We can run through the rest of the plan then. We leave the day after tomorrow. Let me remind you, this is a black op. We are nothing more than ghosts.' Mooney and Hadlow nodded, now exhausted from hours of planning.

'Okay, use the rest of the evening and tomorrow to get some rest.'

McCabe had one last task to complete. He went into his room, pulled on a clean grey T-shirt and dashed out and down to the small bar on the ground floor.

Entering the bar, he saw, as he had expected, Ryan slumped over a pint of warm beer. The man had been at it for some time, given his loud snores.

'Come on, Ryan, jump to it.' McCabe shook his shoulder in an attempt to stir him. The wrinkled face that emerged was not an inspiring sight. McCabe observed the wet patch on his sleeve where he had been dribbling.

'What? Oh, hi. I must have dozed off,' Ryan said.

After being plied with copious amounts of thick black coffee, Ryan started to come around.

'Listen, I need a fourth man for a little jaunt. You interested?' McCabe asked, almost regretting the offer, but he had little choice. He needed a fourth man, and someone that knew how to handle himself, although, looking at Ryan now, he wouldn't think so.

'Jaunt? What kind of jaunt?' Ryan asked.

'The kind that may get you killed. Pirates.' McCabe replied.

'Are you mad?' Ryan almost fell off his stool. 'These guys are no fools, military trained these days.' He was now back in the real world.

'Yeah, I know. Rescue mission. It pays.' McCabe mentioned the incentive he knew Ryan would swallow.

'How much?' Ryan's eyes were now wide open.

'Two hundred thousand for you.'

Ryan sat frozen to the spot. Money was something he very much needed; his debts were substantial, given his inability to hold down a job.

'Okay, I'm in,' he said, attempting to sit up straight.

'Briefing in my room 1800 tomorrow. I will put it to the rest of the guys. Try and clean up, yeah?' McCabe patted Ryan on the shoulder and strode off.

As McCabe stepped outside, hoping to grab five minutes walking around in the hotel compound before getting his head down, his phone rang. Pathos sounded anxious.

'Listen, McCabe, things are heating up. I need you to move fast.'

'What's happened?' McCabe asked.

'There is something else on board, something the folks on board should not be allowed to escape with. This chap Abshir has discovered the ship is carrying gas centrifuges.'

McCabe listened silently, not wanting to react.

'Thing is,' Pathos continued, 'it's now sensitive. My damn bank has financed the deal, much to my annoyance, and it's now clouding our chances of getting Alexis back.'

'Who else knows about this cargo?' McCabe enquired.

'Not sure, if I'm honest, but that chap Stone, the other partner of Force12, has been found dead.' Pathos neglected to mention his concern about Nicolai.

'Okay, from now on, not a word to anyone. My men are ready. We leave in a day, so try and relax.'

'Yes, but please get her back.'

'I will do my best, and that is all I can do.' McCabe knew the risks. He then rang off.

Having spent the day basking in the sun and generally just trying to relax before the mission, the team filed into the tiny room bang on 1800 hours.

'Okay, we have a lot to talk about. First, I have found our fourth man. Ryan.' McCabe announced.

'Ryan, that bloody old drunk! Are you insane?' Mooney barked.

'I know, but he knows the score and we need him,' McCabe responded.

'Liability, if you ask me,' Hadlow muttered.

'Maybe I am. Maybe I will be able to help.' Ryan stood in the doorway. To McCabe's surprise, he had taken a shave and almost seemed presentable in a clean white T-shirt and jeans.

'Come in and shut the door,' McCabe said. Ryan sauntered in and stood at the back of the room.

'Gentlemen, we have an interesting adventure in front of us. Alexis, as you know, is the primary reason for our assault. However, we also have a cargo of gas centrifuges, Hadlow made us aware of this. It seems our pirate friends now know what they have on board.'

'Jesus, when did this happen?' Hadlow jumped in.

'They just made a new ransom demand. Pathos called me late last night. So, the cat is now well out of the bag,' McCabe said.

'I will have to inform Ogilvy about this,' Hadlow said.

'Do what you have to, but it changes nothing, we go.' McCabe made his point clear. 'Thing is, we have no idea who the real bad guys are. Someone on board is dirty and it's not just the pirates.'

'Has to be the captain,' Mooney offered.

'Maybe,' McCabe shot back. 'Our best approach is to board, lock everyone down as per normal MO and wait for orders from 6. One of us can leave with Alexis. At least, that part of the job would be done.'

'The cargo is the priority, 6 won't have it any other way,' Hadlow piped up.

'Funny you should mention that,' McCabe pondered. 'Why is it 6 don't just send in the regiment or even get the Seals to do their dirty work?'

'Yeah, it makes no sense,' Mooney chimed in.

'Listen, I'm just a spook down the food chain. No idea why. I follow orders,' Hadlow responded.

'Find out,' McCabe ordered. 'Now, let's move on to the plan.'

After two hours, they were done.

'Okay, well, I say it's as good as it can get, so we go,' Hadlow announced.

The others nodded. They would leave at 0500 hours.

THIRTY-ONE

The 12-hour journey was somewhat boring, except for the occasional contact with a few armed militiamen. The fixer always managed to convince the armed men, who stood menacingly around the vehicle, that the foul-mouthed journalists with him were not worth the bother. That and a fistful of greenbacks seemed to pacify them.

The roads were dusty, potholed and littered with burnt vehicles, a reminder of the bitter civil war that raged around them. The odd herd of goats and camels the team passed on the way seemed to look at them as if they knew the hell the men were about to enter.

Mooney and Ryan were able to sleep through almost the entire journey, whilst McCabe and Hadlow mulled over plans and boarding tactics, not that it would do any good now. They had to get on with it and their strategy was set.

Ryan was at least sober, a state they both hoped would last. Something about Ryan bothered McCabe. He seemed almost too well-briefed for a drunken journalist who had not seen action in years, and his ability to strip and assemble a weapon was still sharp. Letting it go as paranoia, McCabe tried to rest his own eyes. Tomorrow would be a busy day; rendezvousing with the *Devonshire* at 0600 hours to receive their weapons was vital.

When they reached the small village of Guci, just south of Hobyo, the team made camp. McCabe spread out a groundsheet, placed his Bergen down as a pillow and closed his eyes. He knew two hours of kip was all he could afford. At first light, he would take to the water with Hadlow. Ryan and Mooney would remain.

Stepping out of the shadows, McCabe and Hadlow eased themselves along the outer wall and towards the main doors. The old blue warehouse had been easy to find. The air was still, apart from the odd dog barking in the distance.

As they moved cautiously around the corner, McCabe drew his pistol and held it in front of him. They scanned the area, which seemed deserted. Hadlow slid back the bolt on the main doors, eased the doors apart with his hands and stepped through the gap. The pitch darkness of the warehouse smothered him. McCabe waited outside, just in case.

Moments later, Hadlow popped his head out. 'Okay, seems we have our boat.'

'Bloody miracle, if you ask me.' McCabe eased himself backwards into the warehouse and peered into the gloom.

'Over here,' Hadlow called out. He started to push the RHIB.

'Jesus, we could rupture our balls on this,' McCabe spat. He got behind the boat and pushed.

When they had finally moved the boat out of the warehouse, Hadlow heard a click. Turning slowly, he saw the thin figure of a man, with an AK in his hands.

'Who are you?' the man snapped.

'Easy, fella, we are just moving our boat.' Hadlow raised his arms.

'This is my boat. You steal.' The man stepped forward.

'We buy from Duga, okay?' Hadlow remained dead still.

'No, this is my boat. You...' He didn't get to complete his sentence. A bullet struck him on the forehead, knocking him backwards.

'No time to piss about.' McCabe appeared from behind the RHIB.

'You took your bloody time. Thought I was done for.' Hadlow

dragged the dead body inside the warehouse and covered it with an old tarp. Then, he swept away the drag marks and closed the doors.

The darkness was just beginning to lift as Hadlow heaved the RHIB into the shallow water. The waves breaking on the sand felt strangely warm. McCabe sparked the engine and they moved off, leaving a light blue cloud of smoke behind them.

'The next time we do that, mate, there will be no turning back,' McCabe said, a wry smile on his face.

'Yeah, let's hope so.'

The GPS guided them with pinpoint accuracy to the *Devonshire*. Hadlow could see a bunch of sailors on the port side; he knew their approach had long ago been detected.

'Blimy, if they were pirates, we would be fish food,' he laughed.

'Yeah, thanks for that, matey.' McCabe then realised Hadlow had a point. Getting close to a ship was not easy. It struck him that they needed a distraction, and he knew just who to arrange it.

Like bundles of dirty laundry, five dry bags were cast over the side of the ship and into the RHIB, sending it rocking from side to side. The seamen above didn't seem to bother who these men were. No trumpets, no salutes. They just heaved the bags over and that was all they cared about; their job was done.

McCabe and Hadlow then started back for the shore. That was it; they now had the equipment they needed. Hadlow checked each bag. As he lifted an MP10 and ran it through a check, his murmuring made McCabe smile.

'Is it okay?' McCabe asked.

'Armageddon, mate, in a bag,' Hadlow replied and smiled.

———

The next evening, the band of four eased the RHIB into the water and slowly took off. The black camouflage paint on their faces, coupled with their black wetsuits, made them blend in with the failing light. Only their eyes shone in the moonlight.

The moon was strong and the water calm. An eerie silence seemed to have descended on that particular area of the Indian Ocean. Only the sound of the boat moving effortlessly through the water and the light repetitive murmur of the outboard could be heard.

McCabe knew this was not the ideal set of conditions in which to attempt a stealth attack, but they had to make the most of it now. They headed northeast, navigated by Hadlow. Given his time spent with the SBS, he was the most qualified to take them in.

McCabe and Mooney were crouched down in the middle of the boat. Ryan lay flat at the bow with his M4 carbine at the ready. From there, he could scan the horizon with his night-vision binoculars, just in case they crossed the path of a tanker or, more importantly, were spotted as they neared the *Odin*.

Reaching the 10-kilometre waypoint, Hadlow cut the engine. The boat dipped its nose and then drifted with the current.

'I reckon we must be getting close now, given her last known position, so from here on in, it gets real,' Hadlow said.

As if Hadlow had a sixth sense, Ryan then turned around. 'I can see her, due east, about five clicks.' He pointed.

'Okay, let's get ready. Use the radios from now on,' McCabe ordered. Each man nodded. 'Okay, then, off we go. Stand by.' McCabe waved to Hadlow and the engine fired up. As they slowly moved off, the sound of magazines being slammed into carbines and MP10s and boots slipping and rubbing against the sides of the boat indicated the team were getting ready.

McCabe was running through in his head the boarding routine. Mooney would heave the grappling iron up and snag a guardrail. McCabe would board first. If clear, the others would follow. He could feel his nerves beginning to tingle; he knew the feeling well. Each time he placed himself in a hot zone, his body would let him know. He still got scared; that was the sign of him being fully alive.

Ryan was like a fox on speed, his ears pricked up and his eyes scanning the water ahead. He had dried out—not a drop of drink in two days—and, for the first time, he felt like his old self.

The men were all silent, each saying his prayers or performing whatever routine he needed to, to mentally prepare for what was to come. After another mile, much to everyone's relief, the water began to get choppy. The waves were gaining in size and breaking over the bow, and a strong breeze was blowing across them.

These conditions would help cover the noise coming from their engine—not to mention the fact that the pirates would not suspect an attack in rough seas. The RHIB started to skip off the waves as they went with the surf, and a wave would occasionally hit them from the side as the tide changed direction. It was getting rough.

'That's better!' Hadlow cried.

'Not if we bloody well drown before we get there, it's not!' Mooney replied. He hated boats at the best of times, which was why he had joined Mountain Troop when he was in the regiment. As the RHIB started to arch off course, McCabe looked at Hadlow.

'What's up?' McCabe asked.

'I can feel a strong tide pushing us. If we keep on this course, we will get carried right past her. I need to sweep in wide and come in on her starboard side, but it may get hairy,' Hadlow responded. No one would question his ability.

'There, at anchor, by the looks of her,' Ryan put out on the radio.

'I would prefer she was moving, but it is what it is. We have to keep going now,' Hadlow responded.

'She's lit up like a damn Christmas tree,' McCabe commented. They could all see it. They would be like sitting ducks in the moonlight. Then, suddenly, a rogue wave hit the RHIB, sending Mooney over the side. The others were now splashing around in a foot of water, making sure the equipment was secure.

'Hang on, mate!' McCabe shouted. Mooney was hanging on with one arm. Then, another wave hit, sending McCabe slamming against the side. 'Jesus, Hadlow, keep her out of the breaks!'

'I have to get us back around. You will just have to hang on,'

Hadlow answered. McCabe looked over to where Mooney had been; he was gone.

'Jesus, we have lost Mooney!' McCabe shouted, now anxious. They had a man in the water and that was bad news.

Hadlow swung the RHIB around fast and caught a wave, which hurtled them forward.

'There, over there!' Ryan pointed to the left, where he had seen a dark shape just before a wave rolled over it. Hadlow swerved the boat around again. They were now at serious risk of capsizing. The waves were building and they had hit a major current.

Ryan again spotted Mooney, flailing about in the water about 20 feet in front of them. 'Okay, he is at your 6, port side!' As they drew near, McCabe and Ryan leaned over and grabbed Mooney by the arms.

'Okay, throttle it! Get us out of here!' McCabe bellowed. As the RHIB speeded up, Mooney skipped on the surface of the water, which helped McCabe and Ryan heave him out of the water. They then hauled his bulk over the side and into the boat like a tuna fish.

Spluttering but otherwise okay, Mooney nodded at McCabe and Ryan. A breathless 'cheers' was all he could manage.

THIRTY-TWO

A sudden burst of light illuminated the water around them, which seemed to boil and spit for a few seconds, the effect of a strong downwash. The deep thud-thud sound was unmistakaeble, as the French Panther MK II helicopter passed overhead.

'Right on time!' McCabe shouted over the noise.

'It seems Pathos pulled it off,' Hadlow shouted back.

'We'd best move in fast. The window of opportunity won't be open for long.' McCabe motioned forward with his arm.

McCabe mused as he watched the Panther heading off towards the *Odin*. The idea had come to him when he had approached the *Devonshire* with Hadlow and realised how hard it was to get close undetected. Using the ransom payment as cover would provide just the distraction they needed.

Ogilvy had managed to persuade Langdon to open up a channel of communication with the French Navy, who were, at first, not keen to get involved. That is, until Langdon reminded them of the French cargo ship they had protected from Mohamed. Then, they were more than happy to provide a helicopter.

As the Panther passed overhead, Abshir looked out of the bridge window, somewhat taken aback by its sudden arrival. A few of his men rushed out to take a better look as the helicopter looped back towards them and hovered momentarily off the bow before flying overhead again, as if it were intent on drawing as much attention as possible.

'What is that?' Abshir yelled.

'Unless I'm mistaken, it looks very much like a helicopter,' Vandenbrook sarcastically replied, earning a glare from Abshir.

'Don't get wise with me, fool,' Abshir snapped back.

'Most likely just a routine patrol. It's a French navy bird,' Thirway chipped in. He had been leaning against the wall in one corner of the bridge.

The Panther finally settled on a position, hovering about 500 yards in front of the *Odin*'s bow, its searchlights scanning the water.

Daniel, Troy and Bull were leaning against the bow guardrail, observing the new arrival. Given it was so unexpected, it provided a welcome break from their monotonous supervised exercise breaks.

Alexis was looking out of her cabin porthole to see what was causing the commotion. It gave her a welcome break from trying to call Kent.

As the Panther hovered, more and more of Abshir's men ran forward, compromising their security. It was something even Abshir had not anticipated.

Just as Abshir was about to order his men back to their positions, the ship's radio crackled. Vandenbrook took the message. As he listened, he started to frantically point towards the Panther.

'They are going to drop the ransom!' He sounded almost ecstatic.

Hearing this, Abshir raised his arms. He looked on as a large orange dry bag was dropped into the water. The Panther hovered for a few more moments, as if waiting for something, before finally swooping low over the bridge and off into the darkness.

'Retrieve the bag!' Abshir ordered.

'I guess you can leave now,' Vandenbrook spoke up.

Abshir turned sharply. 'No. There is still the small matter of the cargo. For that, we wait until tomorrow, when I will have it removed.' He then walked off the bridge.

Vandenbrook collapsed into his chair, slightly deflated that the hijacking ordeal was still not quite over.

'Hold up, my friend, almost there,' Thirway spoke.

'Alright for you to say. I have to explain this entire mess to my employer,' Vandenbrook snapped. 'We can't allow him to take the cargo.'

'My advice would be to let it go; we can live to fight another day. What do we care what they do with it?' Thirway responded nonchalantly.

The sea was choppy and the RHIB bounced dangerously around under the stern. Fortunately, the *Odin*'s large propellers were not operating at the moment.

'Okay, let's get it done,' McCabe announced, his voice raspy on account of his throat being dry. He started to ascend the slippery rope, inch by inch, towards the guardrail some 30 feet above. Halfway up, he stopped, his hands throbbing from the tight grip on the rope. Then, he slipped down a couple of feet. It had been too long since the last time he had done this sort of climb.

Mooney just looked up at him, helpless to do anything. If McCabe fell now, he would most likely hit the water. After a few moments, McCabe sucked in a second wind and heaved himself slowly upwards. He reached the guardrail after a few minutes and hauled himself over the side and onto the deck.

Having scanned for any lookouts, he gave the all-clear to Mooney and then moved cautiously towards the base of the accommodation tower, flattening his body against the steel bulkhead. The other three men made the same harrowing climb and joined McCabe in rapid but stealthy procession.

'Okay, Mooney, you with me. Ryan, Hadlow, you take the starboard side.' McCabe tightened his grip on the MP10 he was carrying and headed down the port side. Having made only 15 feet, he centred a target in his sights and squeezed the trigger gently.

A pirate had stepped out of a side door and looked right at him. The immediate result was the gentle thud-thud-thud of three rounds, followed by the metallic clinking of casings being spat out.

'Contact,' McCabe put out on his radio. The pirate lay face-down in a pool of blood. McCabe had hit him twice in the chest and once in the head.

Mooney moved forward quickly as McCabe disposed of the body over the side. Then, stepping into the open hatchway, McCabe scanned up and down for the next target and ascended the stairs leading to the bridge.

Ryan followed close behind Hadlow, his senses on high alert. He could feel his guts churning with each step. It had been too long— 15 years since he had been in action.

The rattle of an AK stopped them both dead in their tracks. They dived for cover as the rounds ricocheted off the steel of the ship, sending sparks flying in all directions.

'Shit, I'm hit!' Hadlow yelled, as he was struck in his right shoulder. He sounded more annoyed than concerned.

Ryan pushed him down and behind cover. 'Let me take a look.' He leaned over to see the extent of the damage. 'Just a scratch.' McCabe and Mooney had been listening and not reacting, given they were slowly walking up the inside of the bridge tower and silence was an absolute.

Ryan rolled over and started to return fire with his MP10, sending the pirate back and behind one of the lifeboats. The rounds peppered the side of the boat with holes.

All hell broke loose as they went loud. Pirates started to run from everywhere, their disarray playing to McCabe's advantage. They were now firing at anything that moved, even at one another; discipline had been lost. Abshir, who was up on the bridge, turned sharply, knowing now that he was under attack.

'Get the men back!' Abshir shouted to one of his men. He then cocked his weapon. 'You two, stay here!' he bellowed to Vandenbrook and Alexis. 'You, watch them,' he told another of his men. With that, he headed out and down the gangway.

The clatter of footsteps descending the stairway sent McCabe and Mooney flat against the wall. Mooney squeezed his trigger; the rounds hammered the pirate backwards and he slipped down the stairs.

The element of surprise was shortlived. Another pirate had been close behind and was now showering bullets down the stairway, sending McCabe and Mooney crouching.

'Fuck! We are like rats in a barrel here!' Mooney bellowed.

'Okay, let's draw them down,' McCabe responded.

Upon reaching the bottom, Mooney took out a flashbang. 'This will sort them.' He tossed it upwards inside the stairwell and slammed the hatchway shut. The dull thud he heard, as it went off seconds later, was nothing compared to what it would have done to the ear drums of anyone inside the stairway. Meanwhile, McCabe was busy putting down fire on two pirates who were running at him down the passageway; both dropped the moment the rounds struck.

'Okay, let's get back in there,' McCabe shouted, as he changed magazines and started firing at two pirates who had their AKs aimed at him from a gangway above.

'Okay, on two.' Mooney then heaved open the hatchway. A cloud of smoke billowed out and a waft of cordite hit him. They heard groans as McCabe burst in and put down fire. Then, moving fast up the stairs, he squeezed his trigger again. Two pirates sitting on the stairs with their heads in their hands were dispatched. McCabe started to cough, given he had no respirator on. Mooney was fast behind him, almost pushing McCabe up the stairs.

***

No sooner had Abshir left the bridge than Thirway leapt on the sole gunman and punched his face. Then, he brought his knee up into the pirate's stomach and snapped his neck. The sound made Alexis scream.

Thirway got up and grabbed her arm. 'Come on, you, come with us.'

Alexis kicked at him. 'Get off me!'

Thirway had no choice. He punched her, sending her flying back. Her head hit the console; she was out cold.

'Jesus, Thirway, you've killed her!' Vandenbrook looked up at him.

'Are you going to stay here and get killed or come with me? I'm out of here.'

'You can't leave her. Anyway, we could be rescued any time now,' Vandenbrook responded.

'Oh yeah, and I'm top of their list. Have you forgotten what I do? I have to leave.' Thirway knew his chances were better taken at sea.

'Your men?' Vandenbrook asked.

'They can handle themselves.' With that, Thirway vanished down the inner stairway, heading for the stern.

The sound of footsteps descending was detected by Mooney, who readied his weapon. Thirway walked headlong into him. 'Don't shoot!' He held up his hands.

'Who are you?' Mooney asked, his tone indicating he had no time for pleasantries.

'Thirway.'

'So, we finally meet.' McCabe stepped forward. 'Where the fuck are you off to?'

'I just came from the bridge. Alexis is up there hurt. I need to get some medical equipment from down below,' Thirway lied through his teeth.

'Okay, Mooney, you head up. Anyone else up there?' McCabe asked.

'Just Alexis and the captain. I knocked out one of the guards,' Thirway replied.

'Okay, get on with it and come back up. Where are your men?'

'On the bow, I think. We got separated,' Thirway responded.

McCabe scowled at him, pushed past him and continued up the stairs with Mooney.

As McCabe stepped onto the bridge, the captain spun around. Seeing him and Mooney, he let out a sigh of relief.

'Thank god! Are you here to get us off?'

'I'm here for her.' McCabe pointed to Alexis. 'How bad is she?'

'Just knocked out. That bastard Thirway hit her,' Vandenbrook said.

Mooney and McCabe looked at each other, realising they had just let Thirway walk right past them.

Suddenly, a spray of bullets hit the bridge. 'Down!' Mooney shouted. Moving to the outer gangway, he started to return fire.

'We need help down here. Where the fuck are you guys?' Hadlow came in over the radio.

'Roger that,' McCabe replied.

'Don't move an inch, you hear me?' McCabe instructed Vandenbrook. 'We will be back. Here,' he continued, handing Vandenbrook the AK that was lying on the floor, 'use this if anyone you don't like comes through that door, and that includes Thirway.'

Vandenbrook took the weapon, somewhat nervously.

Descending the inner stairway, Mooney and McCabe made their way towards the bow. The sporadic gunfire was coming directly at them, which, in some ways, was a good thing; it meant the pirates were contained ahead, off the main bridge tower, hidden behind the massive cargo cranes and bulkheads that littered the deck in front of them.

———

Troy, Bull and Daniel were lying face-down at the bow. Two pirates had guns trained on them. When Abshir arrived, he got them up on their feet.

'You, walk forward.' He gestured, indicating the direction. Reluctantly, they obeyed. Troy looked at Bull, as if to say they only had one chance to make their move, else it was obvious they would be used as human shields.

On the starboard side, Hadlow and Ryan continued to edge forward, putting down fire as they went. One of Abshir's men jumped out from behind a crane and rattled off a barrage of rounds before being shot in the chest.

Hadlow spun around. 'Okay, let's move up.' He then saw Ryan slumped against the guardrail, his face a deathly white.

'Man down, man down!' Hadlow shouted into the radio. Dropping to his knees, he tore open Ryan's wetsuit. Ryan had taken a few in the chest; the burbling blood was not a good sign.

'It's bad, isn't it?' Ryan spoke, his words garbled, as he spluttered and tried to draw in air.

'Hang in there, Ryan, stay with me,' Hadlow said, trying his best to comfort Ryan, who he knew had only minutes to live. 'Man down!' he bellowed again into the radio.

But Ryan had taken his last breath.

Hadlow took the briefest of moments to say his peace. Then, he picked up his weapon and charged forward, sending out bursts of fire until he reached the crane.

'Ryan's a goner!' he spat out over the radio; both Mooney and McCabe heard it.

'Fuck!' McCabe said, not that they could have done anything to help.

Bull made the first move, charging at the pirate to his left. Troy, a second behind him, spun around and grabbed the barrel of the AK pressed in his back.

Seeing this, Abshir turned and fired, his rounds striking Daniel in the chest, before the butt of an MP5 struck him, sending him down hard. The other pirates froze, as four men in black wetsuits stood around them.

Troy and Bull looked up, letting go of the men they had forced to the ground.

'Easy, boys, just stay down,' Bates spoke up. His men then started to push the pirates back against the guardrail. For them, it was over.

Mooney heard the silence and stood up. McCabe followed, as they cautiously walked forward, meeting Hadlow, who emerged from their right. The three of them looked at each other, wondering what had caused the ceasefire.

'Bates!' McCabe spoke, his face showing total surprise.

'Boss, thought you may like some help.' Bates beamed.

'How in the hell did you get on board?' Mooney stepped forward, slapping Bates on the back.

'Well, big man, helicopters can carry people, too, not just money.' Bates winked. His team had dropped into the water at the same time the ransom was delivered, having convinced the French they needed a ride. As soon as Abshir's men arrived to collect the ransom, Bates and his team emerged from the sea. The rest was easy.

'Seems you had a good teacher.' McCabe winked back. 'Good to see you lads.' McCabe nodded to the others.

Their reunion was interrupted when Alexis ran forward screaming, seeing Daniel lying by the rail in a pool of blood. Vandenbrook was close behind her. 'He's gone, miss.' Vandenbrook said gently, standing over her. For Daniel, it was all over. His love of the extreme had, in the end, gotten him killed.

'So, what's the deal with him?' McCabe asked Vandenbrook.

'It's a long story, but, in short, he had paid to shoot pirates. Got what he wanted, too. That stupid club, Deep Six, Thirway's little sideline. It was him that killed his brother.' Vandenbrook shot a glance at Abshir, who was now sitting up.

'He did it?' Abshir's face said it all. 'Thirway lied to me.'

'He did, but he will pay, I'm sure.' Vandenbrook knelt down and lifted Alexis up. 'Come on, miss, let's get you away from here.'

'Mooney,' McCabe spoke, 'escort Miss Pathos here to somewhere less crowded, will you? Get her some tea. Hadlow, call in the heli. Let's get the hell out of here.'

Then, he turned back to Bates. 'So, what's the deal, the cargo, right?'

'Yes.'

'So, why didn't they just send you in? Save me the trouble. I lost a man.'

'You really have to ask? There's the reason.' Bates pointed at Daniel.

McCabe looked at Daniel and then back at Bates. 'Sorry, it's been a long night. Don't follow you. MI6 used you to get a stupid yuppie with too much money and no brains?'

'No, you are the scapegoat, my friend,' Bates explained. 'In the event it all went wrong, you get the blame, simple. The brass can't be tarnished by this. Besides, the cargo belongs to the Yanks and our boys weren't happy about it.' He turned to look at Abshir. 'They used that vermin to sidetrack it to the Libyans. I'm just the insurance to clean up the mess.'

'I wasn't going to deliver it,' Abshir spoke up. 'I made your man Cutter a promise. But, you bastards killed my brother!' He stood up.

'Not us, mate. Him.' McCabe pointed to Daniel.

'So, who was your contact?' Bates stepped into Abshir's space.

'You think me a rat now, too?' Abshir straightened his posture.

'You may as well tell us. Your days are over, caught red-handed.' Bates made the point, one that Abshir knew was right. Maritime law could send him away for a long time. He had been caught.

'A deal, I want a deal. Get me Cutter,' Abshir made his plea.

'Name, or it ends now.' Bates cocked his weapon.

'Stone, Trevor Stone. He is the partner of Thirway. It is Stone who serves the American scum. I only give you his name because he is responsible.' Abshir stood back.

'Blimy, Thirway,' McCabe said, suddenly remembering the root cause of the ordeal. 'Hadlow, with me.' The two men started to head back towards the stern.

'Hold up, McCabe!' Bates shouted. 'Long gone. He took the RHIB you guys came in. We saw it heading off as we boarded.'

'Fuck,' McCabe said.

'Don't worry, they will find him eventually.' Bates looked serious.

Then, as if a film were running in slow motion, McCabe saw the hail of bullets strike Abshir and his men, sending them sprawling backwards and down on the deck. Bull and Troy were also killed in the gunfire. The smell of cordite and copper filled the air.

'What the fuck!' McCabe shouted, running forward.

'Orders, McCabe, orders.' Hadlow stepped in front of him.

'Christ, you never stop, do you, Hadlow? Another surprise you forgot to mention?' McCabe fumed, pulling away.

'And you, I taught you better, Bates.' McCabe walked up to him and stared right into his face. 'Since when have you been a cold-blooded murderer?'

'Things have changed, McCabe. It's more black-and-white, now.'

McCabe then heard a murmur. Turning, he saw Abshir was still alive. He bent down and moved closer to hear what he was saying. 'This man needs help!' McCabe shouted; no one moved.

'When warrior meets warrior, the truth is found,' Abshir muttered. Then, he coughed and slipped away.

McCabe stood up. 'What a mess. Was that really required?'

'Yes, now the mess, as you call it, has been cleaned up,' Bates said. 'In which court, McCabe, would you try his case? A Somali pirate who ran weapons for the CIA? Think about it.' Bates walked off.

McCabe realised, for the first time that the only law was that of the one who held the most cards. It seemed MI6 had a flush. By eliminating Abshir, the chain had been broken for good.

THIRTY-THREE

September 2009. London.

Boyes was ready. The day was dark and cold. The white van parked between the two white lines that signified it was indeed a legal parking slot looked just like any other van—except perhaps it was too well-parked.

The aluminium ladders strapped to the roof, the deep scratches down one side and the fast-food wrappers wedged between the windscreen and the dashboard completed its authenticity. The final attention to detail was perhaps the fact the road tax had expired over a month ago.

Boyes blew warm air into his hands and frantically rubbed them together. 'Tell me something interesting,' he said to the man seated with him in the rear of the van.

The man turned away from the array of monitors he was observing. 'Well, did you know that Blackheath is often referred to as the "jewel amongst the shit" on account it rises above and is straddled by the boroughs of Lewisham and Greenwich?'

Boyes looked at him, somewhat dismayed. 'Is that a fact?'

The other man with them, an armed CO19 officer, rolled his eyes.

'Yes, Blackheath,' the technician confirmed. 'It's actually an etymology that suggests how the borough acquired its name. One popular but incorrect theory is that it derived from the heath's use as a burial ground in the 14th century for many of the London-based victims of the Black Death.'

'Not about the town we are in, idiot,' Boyes said. He was more after an update on the man they were now waiting for.

The technician turned back to the monitors, which reflected four different camera perspectives of the inside of a large semi-detached Victorian house. 'No, nothing, sir.'

What Boyes did know was that his target had been eyeballed arriving at Heathrow's Terminal 4 five hours ago.

The spooks had been busy during his absence, and the bugs they had planted were functioning perfectly, as they relayed the internal noises: doors opening, taps running, a TV set blaring in the front room. No conversation was evident. It was indeed the man they were after; his description matched that in their file perfectly. He had entered the house two hours ago and walked right past one of the four hidden cameras. John Lucas Thirway was now firmly in their sight.

Approaching the immigration counter, Thirway had felt the beads of sweat on his forehead and the clamminess in his hands. Not normally subject to panic, this time, his heart was racing and his guts churning. Every sign any diligent immigration official should pick up, he was now showing.

When he reached the counter, he held out his British passport, which was slowly taken, not snatched. The officer gave him a look— the type of look that you know is working you out. Then, the officer waved him on, much to his relief.

Once in the taxi, he felt himself relax. His mind was now focused on getting to his home in Blackheath, grabbing as much of his personal belongings as he could carry and setting out again. He would not be returning. He had the contact number of a man on the south coast who was known for being able to make people vanish. He hoped he could get him across the channel and down to France, where he could hide out for a while before heading to Morocco.

Closing his eyes for a second, Thirway recounted what had happened. He was sorry Daniel had been killed. He quite liked the kid, but he had to class it as collateral damage. Of all the people to help him escape, Vandenbrook had surprised him. Maybe he just wanted to get rid of the only real evidence that he was involved, at least, to pay a debt of gratitude for Thirway's silence. As for Alexis, he hoped she got all she deserved.

As the cab drew close to the heath, he was woken up by the cabby's tapping on the window. 'Which road, gov?' the cabby asked.

The sight of the meter, which showed a horrific £81, shook Thirway fully awake. He hadn't intended to sleep; after all, he was hardly the man returning from a legitimate business trip who would be entitled to a quick kip in the taxi before arriving home to the open arms of his wife and kids.

'78 Church Street, turn right at the top of the hill,' Thirway replied, turning his head around to see if there were any obvious tails. Little did he know he had, in fact, been followed for the entire journey.

After paying the cabby the second mortgage disguised as a taxi fare, he walked down the path to his front door, cautiously looking behind to see if anyone was watching. The tatty white van parked opposite annoyed him, but he let it go, given he hardly lived there anymore. He had bought the house as an investment 10 years ago during the property slump.

Easing the door open, and pushing the heap of junk mail behind it in the process, he stepped in. A musty smell greeted him. Despite the fact that he paid a cleaner, it seemed she had been skiving off her duties, thinking the owner, who lived abroad, wouldn't ever notice the lapses in her visits. The fact that the mail had not been cleared somewhat reassured him; no one had been there for some time. The spooks had left no trace of their entry.

Thirway hurriedly checked every room. Then, he drew the heavy curtains in the living room and turned on the TV. He wanted to keep an ear on the news, just in case something about him popped up. The phone, thankfully, was still connected.

'It's me, Thirway. I need to exit the country, and fast. Can you meet me in Newhaven?' he said to the person on the other end of the line.

'Get a trace.' Boyes was quick to react. He turned to the technician in the van, anxious to listen in. The frantic tapping of keys indicated he had initiated the trace.

'No, it has to be soon. I can't afford to hang around.' Thirway sounded anxious. 'Listen, I have cash, whatever it takes. I can be there in four hours.' He was now pacing up and down; the camera concealed in the ceiling rose of the living room light followed him.

The technician held up his thumb, indicating the trace had been completed. He lifted his headset slightly off his ears and turned to Boyes. 'It's an address in Brighton, Margaret Street.'

'Good, have the local lads move in and secure whoever is at that address,' Boyes said, and then raised his walkie-talkie to his mouth. 'Tango Charlie, this is Stag. Stand by, stand by.'

The CO19 teams parked a few streets away ran through final checks, ready to invoke an immediate breach to capture Thirway.

Boyes observed on the monitor Thirway entering one of the upstairs bedrooms. Thirway knelt down, retrieved a black bag from under the bed and started to pull out drawers and fill the bag with clothes. This confirmed he was preparing to move out.

Taking hold of his walkie-talkie again, Boyes gave the command. 'All units, this is Stag. Go, go, go!' He got up fast, kicked open the rear doors of the van and jumped out, along with the armed CO19 officer, who was now cocking his MP7. Within seconds, a few unmarked cars screeched up, along with a navy blue CO19 truck. The occupants of each vehicle streamed out and descended on the house.

The tactical teams had been fully briefed hours before. Each CO19 officer already knew the complete layout of the house and had an appreciation of the structural challenges the doors and windows posed.

The red front door was no match for the Remington shotgun—two heavy-gauge rounds removed the hinges. A second CO19 officer finished the job with a ramming device that drove the door inwards and off what was left of the hinges.

Without having to slow down, eight officers piled in through the front door and started to execute their well-rehearsed clearance procedure, visiting each room to confirm it was clear. Three others entered via the rear of the house and set off a flashbang to distract the occupant from the main breach location.

No sooner had the first flashbang gone off and the word 'police' shouted than the power was cut. Thirway had just managed to find an old 9mm Browning he had placed in the wardrobe. He now stood flat against the wall of the second floor landing near the top of the stairs. He knew he had zero chance against CO19, but he wasn't about to go down that easy.

The first shot Thirway fired struck one of the officers in the chest at close range, hammering him backwards. Luckily for the officer, his Kevlar took the round. Bursts of automatic fire immediately followed, ripping into the walls at the top of the narrow stairs. Torchlight beams were now dancing around every corner. Then, a few grenades crashed through the upstairs windows at the front and back of the house, filling the upper floor with choking gas.

Thirway knew he was in deep shit, as he gasped for air, holding his arm across his mouth in an attempt to shield his lungs from the tear gas. He fired rounds in any direction he thought would cause trouble, until he was out of ammunition.

The blinding light that flashed in his eyes forced him to hesitate just long enough for one of the CO19 officers to push him to the ground. He felt a knee hard in his back and a firm hand holding his head down, as the zip ties bit his wrists. It was over, and he knew it.

Hauled out of the house, Thirway stood leaning against the van, still coughing from the effects of the tear gas, his stinging eyes a raging red. The officer who had taken the first round walked up to him and glared at him whilst peeling off his vest. Thirway just looked at him.

Then, the officer turned to Boyes; the look on his face was enough to tell the inspector what he wanted to do. Boyes gave a slight nod, and the officer gave Thirway a hard punch, then grabbed him and drove a knee into his chest. Thirway fell backwards, moaning in agony. A final blow to his nose sent blood spattering over his face. He was helpless, given his hands were tied; in any event, any attempt to resist would just mean a harder beating later.

'Okay, that's enough!' Boyes shouted. The officer shot a look at Boyes, grunted and walked off. No one would have seen anything; at least, that would be the standard response should Thirway file a report.

'Well, we meet at last, Mr. Thirway.' Boyes stood over him.

Thirway looked up, his eyes streaming with tears and his broken nose bleeding profusely. He well understood the provocation for his beating and was grateful it wasn't far worse, at least, for now.

'I didn't think it would be long,' Thirway replied. 'How did you know where to find me?'

'Indeed, off somewhere, were we?' Boyes held up the black bag Thirway had been hurriedly packing before the lights went out.

'Yeah, hell,' Thirway replied, a wry smile on his face.

'Well, Mr. Thirway, you are under arrest. We need to talk, don't we? About two young men washed up on a beach half-eaten and with the same tattoo.' Boyes was blunt in his delivery.

Thirway's smile faded. He was clearly shocked the two bodies he knew full well about had turned up.

'Read him his rights and take him away,' Boyes said to another officer and walked off.

The interview room, as expected, was bare and cold and stank of stale cigarettes. Thirway was sat down hard on a plastic chair on one side of a small table. The two officers who brought him in had taken the liberty to rough him up a bit in his cell.

Thirway knew that, if you were crazy enough to try and slot a member of CO19, you'd best make it count or die trying. He knew he would be in for a good kicking as a result, and it came with his cold scrambled eggs; someone had spat in it.

Boyes noticed the swelling on Thirway's face the moment he walked in and knew he had to put a stop to it before it got out of hand—not that he had any sympathy for Thirway. He at least wanted him conscious enough to stand trial for murder.

'Well, Mr. Thirway, shall we begin?' Boyes announced, his face serious and unforgiving.

'Nothing much to say.' Thirway leaned back in his chair and placed his cuffed hands on the edge of the table.

'Well, let's start with these, shall we?' Boyes slid a couple of photographs across the table. Lifting them up slightly, Thirway looked at them. His face remained blank as he observed the mutilated remains in the photographs.

'And?' he said coldly, tossing the pictures on the table.

'Two Brits, both sporting the same tattoo, both linked to a club known as Deep Six. You are the founder of Deep Six, so let's stop fucking around, shall we?' Boyes leaned in and glared at Thirway.

'Oh,' Boyes continued after a brief pause, 'and we know you were on board the *Odin*. MI6 have confirmed that. We also have you arriving at Heathrow off a flight from Oman. Shall we continue to play games or just let the jury convict you for life?' Boyes smiled.

Thirway knew it was hopeless. The spooks had him. But, it was too early to give in. 'Listen, I didn't kill those men, period. You have no evidence to convict me,' Thirway said in an arrogant tone.

Boyes held his stare for a moment. Then, he said, 'Well, you may not have pulled the trigger, but what you did was illegal and you are guilty by association, not to mention the attempted murder of a police officer.'

'Manslaughter, at best. I could be out in four years. That's providing you even have the authority to charge me for something that happened in Oman,' Thirway said, a sly smile on his face.

'You think you are so clever, don't you?' Boyes then waved to the officer who had been standing in the room. 'Take him away.' Thirway stood up and headed for the door.

Boyes then played his cards. 'Just one small point. The Omani police have asked us to extradite you on the grounds of acts of terrorism in their waters. Who are we to question them when, as you say, we have nothing on you? As Interpol, we have just aided them in your capture. Safe flight, Mr. Thirway.' Boyes looked down at the table and shuffled his papers.

Thirway stopped dead in his tracks and spun around. 'You have to be kidding me.' His face finally showed some sign of concern.

'I hear prison there, as you well know, is a living hell. No better place for you.' Boyes then looked up at Thirway.

'Prove it! I did nothing! Terrorism, that's bull shit!' Thirway shouted.

Boyes stood up. 'Oh, yes, you did. You solicited men onto that ship, men who were hell-bent on killing. You then arranged for them to shoot men who, for all you know, were innocent fishermen, and you can't prove otherwise. Then, you arranged for pirates who had Islamic ties to board. You then sanctioned the execution of one of your clients, when he threatened to talk. So, do not stand there and pretend you are innocent, you piece of crap.' Boyes was now pissed off.

'Okay, I will talk. Just let's all calm down,' Thirway said, realising now he was in a tricky situation.

'MI6, I am sure, can plant enough on you with the Omanis to ensure you have a good vacation. The spooks always need to trade terrorists and you fit the bill nicely. You see, I don't really care, as I can close my case.' Boyes sat back down. 'Take him away,' he said again to the officer.

'Wait, you can't do this!' Thirway shouted, as he was taken away like a man heading for the gallows.

Boyes literally closed his file and smiled. He had removed a truckload of paperwork from his plate by giving the spooks exactly what they wanted: a scapegoat who, for once, was not a Muslim, but a Brit who could be fitted with a suit of terrorism. He would be used to buy favours. Thirway would be placed on a plane within the next few hours; his destination, only 6 would know.

What other way could he close it?! [handwritten annotation]

Across the hall from where Thirway had been interviewed, Vandenbrook sat staring into a vile cup of cold vending-machine coffee. Hearing the commotion outside, he knew he had only moments before he would have to confirm Thirway had been, for the past two years, not only selling sniper slots on board his ship but also giving maritime information to Abshir. Thirway had access to shipping information, given his legitimate position within Force12.

Vandenbrook was tormented by guilt and remorse. The money he had taken to allow Deep Six to function had benefited his family, but he couldn't help feeling deeply ashamed, given the sacrifice of so many lives. His wife had left him after learning what had happened, taking the kids with her to her parents in Denmark. In the end, he had lost everything.

Pathos had placed him on a leave of absence, until the investigation was completed, but he knew he could never return to sea. His reputation was ruined. To cap it all off, he had helped Thirway escape.

Boyes entered and sat opposite him. 'Tell me, captain, what made you do it?'

Vandenbrook lifted his head. 'Greed should be the answer, Inspector Boyes,' he said, his voice low. 'I needed to pay for home expenses. I was not earning enough.'

'You allowed a man to use your vessel as a floating sniper station, to kill people,' Boyes said, his tone harsh.

'I'm not proud of it, but I, too, have been hijacked. I know what these pirates are capable off,' Vandenbrook fired back.

'Yes, I know, but the authorities are the law. Vigilantes are not legal!' Boyes thumped his fist on the table, causing Vandenbrook to jump in his seat.

'Please, I understand this. I am guilty, so do what you must.' Vandenbrook dropped his head.

Boyes sat back and lit a cigarette. Then, he drew a deep breath. 'Listen, your evidence has helped us to convict Thirway. You did the right thing.'

Vandenbrook looked up, his face sallow and strained. 'What will happen to me now?' he asked the inspector.

Boyes looked at him. 'Well, given your willingness to cooperate and the fact that you tried, I hear, to help save the hostages, I think we can close the file.' He paused. 'You are free to go, captain. Get out of my sight.'

'You mean it? I can leave?' Vandenbrook was shocked.

'At the end of the day, yes, you were a stupid fool. But, it happened not on my turf, so I don't really care. A couple of rich men got themselves killed by playing sniper. I do care about the man at the top, Thirway, and we have dealt with him.' Boyes paused. 'Get out of here, vanish. My superiors may change their minds,' Boyes said, with a tinge of humour.

'I don't know how I can thank you. But, thank you.' Vandenbrook stood up, shook Boyes's hand and left.

Boyes remained in the room for a moment, finishing his cigarette. It never ceased to amaze him what the lure of money could do to a man. Vandenbrook had tossed a 20-year career down the drain for a few thousand dollars. Boyes shook his head and closed the last of his files. He, too, was now free to go.

THIRTY-FOUR

Entering number 11, Cadogan Gardens, a comfortable five-star hotel in London's Sloane Square, Kent felt very uneasy. Every shadow seemed to be chasing him; as such, he quickened his pace along Sloane Street and bolted into the hotel lobby. Only when he had reached his room on the second floor did he feel safe.

Tomorrow, he had a meeting with Pathos at his offices in Mayfair. The time would be confirmed only in the morning. It was a meeting that worried him, on account of the news from his headquarters a few hours ago: Thirway had been arrested for running an illegal band of mercenaries on board the *Odin*. At least, that was the official story.

What worried Kent more was the fact that his own cover may have been blown. There was no way of telling if Stone, his only link to Force12, had divulged his identity to Thirway. There was also no news about where the cargo was.

At the end of the day, Kent didn't care about his cover at the bank. He could simply have the CIA create another one for him. The most important thing now was to tie up all the loose ends. By eliminating Stone, he had hoped any links to him were cut. But now, Thirway was in the custody of MI6. Nothing now could be certain; he was exposed and that wasn't good.

———

Getting up from the bed, Kent moved over to the window and carefully pulled back the curtains. The view of the street below was clear; nothing seemed out of place.

He eased himself into a chair and switched on the TV, desperate for news. Feeling slightly relaxed, he let his mind wander to Alexis. For a few seconds, he recalled the sexual passion they had shared. Then, his face changed, knowing she, too, would have to be silenced—not that she knew much about his dealings. To her, he would still appear to be her innocent boss. But, no stone could be left unturned. She knew him and the details of the deal. That alone was enough to spell her doom.

He picked up the phone and dialled a local number, his fingers visibly shaking as he punched the keys. He got the voice mail.

'It's me, Kent,' he said. 'Call me urgently. I need protection.' He then slammed down the phone.

The sight of the two fried eggs and rather greasy bacon on his plate did nothing to settle his nerves. He could only toy with his food. Scanning the morning papers, he found the only news was the usual paparazzi trash and stories on the ever-rolling world economy. Then, it occurred to him. If the story were splashed across the front pages, he would hardly be enjoying a fried English breakfast. That thought marginally cheered him up, as he sipped his tea.

The phone finally rang at 11:00 a.m. The woman on the other end of the line informed him, somewhat abruptly, that he was to present himself at the Pathos offices near Green Park by 4:00 p.m. As Kent put down the phone, his mind was already making plans. Pathos had to be retired, and fast; he knew way too much.

Pathos was seated like an Armani-clad peacock at one end of the oval boardroom table, his hands clasped in front of him. Kent sat across from him and stared at him.

'Well, anything to say for yourself, Kent?' Pathos erupted.

'Say? About what? I was hoping you could tell me what the latest news was,' Kent responded, calm and collected.

'Well, you must have heard they caught that chap Thirway,' Pathos enlightened Kent. 'Not sure what happened to the damn pirates. Dead, I would hope.'

Kent was now curious. Pathos had not mentioned the one thing he thought would take priority—his daughter. As Kent shifted slightly in his seat, Pathos leaned forward, his face deadpan.

'So, what happened to your daughter?' Kent finally blurted out. Pathos remained motionless; he almost seemed vacant, as Kent eyeballed him.

In his mind, Pathos was thinking about the meeting he had with MI6 just two days ago. His close friend, the Rain Angel, had been at his side.

Taking her father's expensive lawyer's advice, Alexis told Ogilvy and his team everything: how Daniel had met Thirway and how her boss had insisted on the deal being struck. Her claims of innocence did little to help her.

When quizzed about Kent, she explained she had met him in a bar over two years ago, and they had hit it off, based on a shared interest in making money. The torrid affair that went on between them had been nothing more than lust.

What Alexis hadn't known was that Kent was, in fact, CIA and that he had been leading a sordid plot to get arms and bomb-making technology to certain factions of the Somali militia to keep them in the game of war. Instability benefited the Americans, whose attempts to help govern Somalia had repeatedly failed.

Kent, knowing Alexis had developed a strategy for acquisitions that the bank well respected, had wanted to use her talents for his less scrupulous trade financing deals—not to mention the fact that her father's company could provide the logistics and she could cover the tracks.

Abshir had also been under the wing of the CIA, his expulsion from the Marine Corps nothing more than a smoke screen. His roots were what the CIA had wanted to use—who better to run the onshore aspects of the operation than a bona fide Somali pirate leader? He had arranged for Stone to act as his informer. What the CIA had not counted on, was the death of his brother. It turned him against them.

Alexis was now looking at a prison sentence, if convicted, of at least 15 to 25 years, for what was termed an act of terrorism.

In the eyes of the law, she had aided Daniel and the others in the planned assassination of Somalis, even if they had been pirates, which, in any case, could not be readily proven. The acts were said to fuel political anarchy, which endangered the lives of UN representatives trying to administer aid in the country.

Furthermore, she alone had closed the deal to fund the cargo, which was to be directed to Libya—not that she knew about it. But, the law had no place for fools. She and the bank should have practised greater diligence.

It was up to the courts to decide what to do with her. That is, until the Rain Angel entered the conversation. Pathos had looked lost until she had spoken up. Discovering his only daughter had been involved in such a plot had been bad enough; what made it worse for him was the fact that she had everything she could want. He was devastated, but he could not bear to see her convicted.

The Rain Angel offered something British intelligence wanted: the name of a known assassin operating out of London, his employer none other than the good old CIA. The Americans often paid for covert operations to create chaos and fuel hatred for extremist groups. Foreign targets were often taken out on British soil to cover their own foul deeds.

The next thing the Rain Angel offered made her smile to herself. It was the CD McCabe had so skillfully acquired the last time they had met. The disc contained information that would expose a group of individuals known only as the 'Shadow Men'. They controlled not only drug-related activity across the United States, Latin America and Europe but also money laundering on a titanic scale to finance the development of biofuel technology. The disc was worth years of intelligence work on the part of both MI6 and the CIA.

In return for the disc—should McCabe be persuaded to release it—and the name of the assassin, Alexis was to be allowed to walk away and vanish.

Then, just as Ogilvy and Travis Colt, the rather strained head of the CIA in London, were about to accept the deal, the Rain Angel added one more condition.

'I want Kent retired,' she said sweetly. Both men agreed to the terms.

Pathos had not expected such a deal, but he was glad to have been able to help secure a second chance for his daughter. He now knew the part he had to play in order to ensure the plot would play out.

—— —— ——

'Are you okay, Pathos?' Kent gently tapped the table.

'Yes, sorry, zoned out for a few moments there.' Pathos drew a deep breath. 'My daughter was never recovered. It's too painful to discuss.' Pathos could lie like the best of them when he had to. He observed Kent, who seemed relieved.

Kent was indeed relieved to hear the news but faked sympathy. 'I'm sorry to hear that,' he said. Whilst he had liked Alexis, she was one more link to him he could do without.

Pathos stood up and started to walk around his office. 'Listen, Kent, I will play my open hand. I know damn well you were involved in this deal along with my daughter. She is gone and beyond paying the price for her actions. To be frank, I don't care what you do, as long as you never step foot on my turf again.' He glared at Kent.

Kent paused for a second before speaking. 'What makes you sure I was involved?'

'MI6 have been tracking you for a while now. They want your connections. They know you have the identity of a known CIA assassin working in London, so I suggest you vanish. Unless you have nothing to hide, of course.' Pathos gave a sly smile.

This information made Kent freeze, his face now white. 'How do you know this?' he asked.

'I'm not without my own contacts, Kent.' Pathos held his ground.

Kent stood up. 'I see. Why are you telling me this now? You could have me arrested or MI6 pick me up.' He was suspicious.

'Like I said,' Pathos replied, confidently carrying on his story, 'Alexis must have seen something in you. I know the two of you were... well, you know, lovers, so I guess I'm giving you a fighting chance. She was my flesh and blood, all said and done.'

Kent seemed to be buying it. 'Thank you,' he said. 'I'd best be on my way.' With that, he hurriedly left.

Pathos smiled, not only because Kent had swallowed the story, but also because he knew who was listening at the door.

———

Darkness was falling when he entered the park. The majestic trees were coming alive with the chatter of crows. Kent took the narrow tarmac path leading towards Green Park underground station, despite the fact that this was not the most direct route.

He needed some fresh air to calm down. The stress from the mess he was in was eating away at him. Kent tried to clear his head, but the brand new handmade Church's brogues he had on made it impossible for him to relax; the savage blisters on his feet were hell-bent on depriving him of any peace of mind.

The air was damp and cold. He buried his hands deep in the warm pockets of his thick blue cashmere overcoat and raised his shoulders in an attempt to keep the wind from nipping at his ears. As he breathed in the evening air, he finally started to feel some of the tension in his shoulders ease. Small brown leaves were dancing in the air like fairies, whipped up every few seconds by a gust of wind. There seemed to be no one in the park, given it was late; the rush hour had long since ended.

Kent's thoughts kept drifting back to what might happen to him. To make matters worse, Tate had arranged for him to give a presentation to the board members in the morning to explain how the bank had ended up financing such a sensitive cargo—not that he should bother masquerading as a banker anymore, but it was his only cover and he hadn't the authority to break it right now. A good night's sleep was in order to help him think.

As he quickened his pace to head home, he was unaware of the figure that stepped out silently from behind a small brick hut where the gardeners stored their equipment. The figure followed Kent at a safe distance of about 20 yards. The wind whipping the branches of the trees that lined the path covered any sound his footsteps might have made.

Just 100 yards from the Queen's Walk exit, the path narrowed, running down a steep bank and then tight against the black iron railings that surrounded the park. Kent slowed down; he could see the path was slippery and covered with fallen leaves from the overhanging branches of an old oak tree. He knew his new shoes simply would not cope.

As the shadow of a man loomed up close behind him, the crows high above suddenly broke into a deafening chorus. Then, all was calm again, as if their co-conspirator had ordered silence.

———

Blue light danced along the black iron railings around the park. The police car lights seemed almost hypnotic in the early morning mist, which was only just dissipating. It was going to be a crisp yet bright blue start to the day.

Yellow tape with the words 'Crime Scene' cordoned off an area around the body of a man lying face down at the bottom of a steep bank, almost completely hidden by the branches of a rhododendron bush. Police officers were busy keeping joggers and commuters away and searching the area for evidence.

Boyes had seen more crime scenes than he cared to remember, each one loading him with stacks of paperwork and endless overtime hours. His crumpled look bore testament not only to the fact that he had been awake most of the night working on closing a case, but also to the fact that he lived alone and had no time for clean shirts and pressed trousers. He had been called in on account of the probability this was the victim of a professional hit.

Bending over with his hands on his knees, Boyes scanned the body. It was something he liked to do before the boys from forensics—those sterile white-suited ants that captured every hair, thread and drop of blood from the crime scene—took over.

The double tap to the back of the head, delivered at what must have been near point-blank range by a 9mm pistol, confirmed it was a hit. The top of the head was now nothing more than a lump of shattered skull and mashed brain matter. Boyes estimated that the time of death was about nine hours ago, given rigor mortis had set in and the blood had congealed. The flattened flowers and muddy skid marks indicated the man must have been on the path above when he was killed.

Boyes then noticed the soles of the victim's shoes, which were obviously new. 'Jesus,' he thought, 'poor sod had barely time to break them in.'

Tate was drumming his fingers on the mahogany table. The 12 board members had promptly sat themselves around the oval table at 8:00 a.m., having caught the early train into the city, their eyes baggy and their stomachs rumbling.

They were eagerly awaiting Kent's arrival, keen to hear how the bank had managed to get itself involved with the financing of a cargo of gas centrifuges destined for, as the papers reported, 'Islamic militant extremists'. Needless to say, they were less than happy with the situation.

'I have asked my secretary to chase him down,' Tate announced, his tone hiding his own annoyance. 'Very sorry about this.'

Just then, the doors of the boardroom opened. Everyone around the table turned, expecting to see Kent. Instead, the skinny figure of Irene Jones, Tate's secretary, appeared. She scurried over to her boss.

The board members were now looking intently at Tate. One, however, seemed relaxed in contrast to the rest. Ogilvy knew a problem had been eliminated, ironically by the man who was next on his target list. Kent was one less CIA puppet on the streets, and that was a good day's work. As for the bank, he didn't care how they dealt with the issue internally.

In the silence of the room, Irene's whispered words could almost be heard. But, it was Tate's pale face that perhaps gave it away; one could almost see the blood draining from his face. With his hands flat on the table, as if to support his weight, he slowly stood up. His mouth was dry.

'Gentlemen,' he announced, 'I am sorry to have to inform you that this meeting will have to be postponed.' He swallowed, trying to gather some spit. 'I have received terrible news. Kent was found dead a few hours ago in Green Park. The police have just called.' With that, Tate sat back in his chair, realising he would now have to take the blame alone.

THIRTY-FIVE

The individual pieces of the Glock 22 semi-automatic pistol were carefully laid out on a piece of white cloth in front of him. Deftly selecting each part in turn, he ran through a well-practised cleaning routine.

The smell of gun oil hung lightly in the air, and he breathed it in deeply through his nostrils; it was a smell he loved. He paused and leaned back in his chair, allowing his thoughts to drift back to his childhood.

As a child, he spent hours on his father's lap, helping him clean his shotgun. The smell of gun oil and the feel of the cold steel in his tiny hands made him happy. His father would puff away on a pipe whilst humming a joyful tune, as he polished, brushed and reassembled the gun.

The memory made him feel warm and safe; he could now almost smell his father's pipe tobacco in the air. But his smile faded fast and his eyes dilated into cold black pools, as he remembered how his father had died.

His father had been behind on paying a gambling debt; farming didn't support his growing habit. That night, two strangers burst into the house. He vividly remembered his father pushing him aside in an attempt to conceal his presence. His mother had died years before, and his elder brother had been killed in the Russian army.

He could now still hear his father's voice begging for more time. A single shot felled him. Emerging from his hiding place after the killers left, he saw a stream of dark blood on his father's head and across the cold stone floor. His attempts to revive his father were futile. The blood that stained his clothes took days to wash away, but the memory of the killing never went away.

The years that followed saw him being sent from relative to relative until, finally, he was deposited in a children's home 200 miles from his own house. His rebelliousness made him difficult to handle. The death of his father caused him to withdraw and become very angry and bitter.

It was only at age 15, when he met a young man by the name of Yorgo Constantine, that his character began to change. Yorgo was on his way home from a bar on the east side of the city when he came across Nicolai in an alley. The sight of the boy, shivering beside a pile of boxes, his hair dirty, matted and tangled around his pale face, was enough for him to stop and take the boy home.

Over the next five years, Nicolai grew into a confident boy, strong and fit. He also acquired another asset, one that would ensure his destiny—or fate, depending on how one looked at it. He was the best Yorgo had ever seen. His eye was keen, his senses razor-sharp and his agility outstanding. Nicolai became an assassin.

Yorgo, himself an assassin of some repute within Russia, had learned his skill serving in the infamous Spetsnaz and later selling himself as a gun for hire to the organised crime gangs of Moscow.

He had lost his little brother when he was 12. Gunmen had burst into their tiny home and shot his entire family. He had been playing in the alley behind and so escaped the slaughter. Perhaps this was why he took pity on Nicolai; the boy reminded him of his younger brother.

Yorgo died, as most assassins do, by the bullet of another. A contract hit had been placed on him via a disgruntled gang that felt he knew too much.

Nicolai made short work of the man who took out his master. He waited 14 hours, perched high up on a Moscow apartment block, for his mark to appear. The round that left his sniper rifle burst open his target's head, splattering blood across his plush apartment walls and his girlfriend's lap.

Nicolai spent the following years on the run, given he also now had a contract on his head. He worked as a hired gun and, like Yorgo, did a stint as a Spetsnaz officer. Ironically, he found his way onto the A-list of assassins used by various governments that needed a ghost to carry out their dark deeds. He was simply known as the Cossack. The British and American governments were frequent buyers of his talents.

Nicolai snapped back to the present, his eyes once again focused. Off one side of his disassembled Glock lay the photograph of his next mark. It was a face he knew well. Having overheard his boss's conversation with Kent, Nicolai now considered Pathos a potential risk. He had to assume Kent had blown his cover.

Once he was satisfied the Glock was clean, it took less than 40 seconds for his experienced hands to reassemble the weapon and prime a round in the chamber.

Everything was ready. The suppressed sniper rifle was packed, waiting for use. He knew Pathos was scheduled to attend an important investors meeting at his office in Mayfair. Being his bodyguard had its advantages; he knew his schedule. Monday at 10:00 a.m. For Nicolai, that was the 'kill point'.

———

Stepping out of the steaming shower, she wrapped herself securely in a thick white towel. Her thoughts were focused on her breakfast meeting at 8:00 a.m. She was never late.

The Savoy Hotel, which stood majestically near the banks of the River Thames, accorded her with the five-star luxuries she had grown so accustomed to. Glancing at a magazine on the bedside table that proudly detailed the hotel's history, she marvelled at the building's design, as envisioned by the impresario Richard D'Oyly Carte in

1889. She appreciated the opulence. It was a stark contrast to the poverty-burdened, extremist environment she grew up in.

Born to a Lebanese father and a Basque mother in June 1962, she was raised in a small two-room apartment in the heart of Beirut. Given her parents' extremist beliefs and loyalties, she learnt to handle a gun at a young age. Her father, an active Hezbollah bomb maker, treated her like a son.

She recalled their scouting missions and trips to steal supplies and set booby traps for UN convoys. Her mother, a young and very beautiful Basque separatist from the town of Ermua, was fiercely loyal towards her roots and taught her daughter the ways of the world and how to hate.

The neighbours often spat and hissed at her. She was expected to behave like a Lebanese woman, which meant staying hidden and undertaking the work of a woman. As such, and with her parents' help, she would disguise herself as a boy, keeping her hair short and wearing men's clothes. She had fire in her heart and her parents loved her passion for life.

When she was 12, a bombing raid initiated by the Americans killed her mother. She swore vengeance, which, given she was half Basque, was to the death. She hit the streets and ran errands for her father's friends. By her 18th birthday, she had become an accomplished assassin for the Hezbollah.

Frustrated with the slow progress of the organisation's cause, and becoming increasingly ostracised as she developed into a vivacious woman, she started moving from one cause to another, selling her skills to the highest bidder who accepted her feminine form.

At age 22, the Rain Angel was born, so named on account of her unique interrogation techniques, which often led to her victims drowning. Over the years, she served with the Basque separatists, the PIRA and various other groups that had a war to fight.

Only after meeting the wife of the notorious Khun Surat at a party in Bangkok did she start to calm down and transform into a society lady. The string of *tai tais*, wealthy ladies of leisure, who became her new friends inducted her into the world of ambassadors and rich businessmen. She integrated with ease, as if she had always been destined for a life of champagne and caviar. Her marriage to a senior Lebanese diplomat in London completed her transition into a different, affluent world.

In later years, the CIA and MI6 grew curious about this multilingual, multi-talented woman and started using her to infiltrate the very groups within which she already had complete access and trust. The Rain Angel used this double agent status, at times, to her own advantage, making money from highly illegal deals with people most would call terrorists. She also enjoyed sparking trouble between the two intelligence agencies; it had become a sport to her.

She had met Pathos at a party in London. His charisma and charm won her heart. He knew a little about her past but decided to let it go; she was a good friend and that was enough for him.

———

After towel-drying her hair, which took no time at all, given it was only shoulder-length, she put on, as she so often did these days, a smart grey suit and sensible flat brown shoes—a more becoming style, she thought, for her 47 years of age.

'Will he be an arrogant bastard or a polished operator?' she wondered to herself. She didn't have his name, just a detailed description of his physical appearance and a rather bad code name, Mr. Friday.

As she left her room, hanging the 'Do not disturb' sign on the door handle to keep unwanted visitors away, she checked her watch: 7:50 a.m.

'Perfect,' she thought. She didn't like being too early or too late for an appointment; being too early was a sign of insecurity, whilst being too late was a sign of being ill-prepared.

As she entered the restaurant, located on the mezzanine level of the hotel, she took in the atmosphere. She mused at the guests buzzing around, all trying to decide if fruit and yoghurt should be their choice of fare, or the less healthy option of eggs, bacon, sausage and hash browns.

As she scanned the crowded room, her eyes locked onto one man. He fitted the description: athletic, mid-30s, short dark brown hair. He was wearing an open neck blue shirt and seated, as she had expected, not by one of the large windows—that would have made him too easy a target for any sniper—but in a quiet corner on the far right of the room. He had his head buried in a morning paper, but she knew he would have seen her the moment she entered; that is, if he were any good.

'Good morning. I see you have eaten,' she said as a way of introduction.

As he slowly lifted his head, she saw his steely dark brown eyes first. His features were strong and his complexion olive and clear.

'Good morning. Yes, I have, but please join me.' His accent was North American. He gestured to a passing waiter, then turned back to her. 'Tea or coffee?' he enquired.

'Tea, please. That would be nice. Thank you,' she replied. 'Black, no sugar,' she instructed the waiter. As the waiter scurried off, they stared at each other, as if doing a final sizing up. Then, leaning forward, Mr. Friday rested his elbows on the table and clasped his hands, his stare becoming stern.

'I will get to the point, as we are both busy people. You have done a deal with MI6 and a senior member of my team. You want a certain operative of ours retired. In return, we allow Pathos to walk.' He paused for a second. 'We will require that you hand us a CD—a CD that contains valuable information.'

He took a sip of coffee before continuing. 'The operative you wish to be retired was found dead yesterday in Green Park. The man who did it, we think, is a rogue kite of ours. But, I think, you know that, right?' He gave her a broad smile.

They were silent as the waiter, who had returned with a pot of fresh tea, poured her some. Then, slowly and deliberately, she took a sip, not breaking her stare for a second.

'First, Mr. Friday, or should I call you Mr. Jasicki, Mr. Paul Jasicki,' she said, with a wry smile, emphasising his real name, 'I would like some proof that you are indeed who you claim to be. Second, if I were to help you obtain this CD, yes, Alexis Pathos walks, but I also have another request.' She paused.

'Nice, very nice,' he replied. 'You are good. You know my name. And you, madam, a.k.a. the Rain Angel, Mrs. Chamat, wife of the Lebanese ambassador to the UK, have just escaped death at the hands of British intelligence. So, let's drop the crap and get to the point, shall we? What else do you require?'

Content with his reply, she sat back in her chair. 'Very well. I want this kite of yours also retired. I know who he is.' She held her gaze.

'Why, may I ask?' Jasicki was now perplexed.

'I have it on good authority that he may try and assassinate his own boss, my dear friend, Mr. Pathos, and we can't have that.'

Jasicki shifted in his chair. 'My bosses at Langley would like, in fact, to keep him alive, that much I know. You would have to guarantee the information you claim you can secure for us if I am to have any leverage.' Jasicki sipped his coffee and waited for a response.

She was slightly taken aback by his request. 'Listen, sonny, I do not have to give you any other guarantee than my word. Your bosses know my word alone is good enough,' she hit back, with sarcasm in her voice.

'No, I need proof or the deal is off.' Jasicki held his ground.

She looked at him, her face showing no sign of emotion. She also knew that a further moment of silence would unnerve him.

'Well, let me put it in a way even you can understand. MI6 would love this information, so I could simply dance with them. You not agreeing really doesn't bother me. I only came to you first because I hate the stuffiness of 6. But, beggars can't be choosers, now, can they? Second, if you do not accept my kind invitation, I have certain information on your wife that would cause one hell of a stink. You would be a laughing stock back at Langley.'

She observed his now taut face and knew her delivery had had the desired effect.

'My wife?' he said.

'Yes, your wife. The information I have would greatly embarrass you.'

Jasicki sat in silence for a moment, looking back at her. Then, he said, 'You have nothing on my wife. This is all rubbish. Now, if you are done, I have other business to attend to.' His tone was harsh, almost angry.

'Very well. These pictures are not of concern to you, then.' She produced a brown envelope and tossed it across the table at him.

Jasicki gingerly picked it up, almost knowing what would be inside. He carefully opened the envelope and slid out three 8x4 black-and-white photographs. As he studied them, his face showed no emotion, apart from turning pale. However, inside, he was close to the boiling point.

'It is a shame, is it not, Mr. Jasicki, that our partners in life often expose us to weakness and social embarrassment. A shame, given your life is the richer for knowing her and the benefits they afford you. She is rich, I hear.' Jasicki knew she had him over a barrel. He also knew she was highly dangerous and very well-connected.

There, in front of him, were pictures of his wife snorting lines of what looked like cocaine off a glass coffee table. The woman with her was naked and looked like she was engaging in a sex act whilst his wife was busy.

Swallowing, he composed himself. 'It appears you have my attention. So, what is it you wish me to do exactly?' His tone was now calm and accommodating.

'Good, then, it seems we have a deal,' she replied.

'Not until I know the exact terms—what I have to do and how these pictures vanish—we don't,' he snapped, wanting to reestablish some authority.

She took note of his retort, respecting the fact that he was no fool.

'Very well. Listen carefully. Mr. Pathos will arrive at his office tomorrow at 10 a.m. sharp. He has an important meeting there. Your man will make his move then, I am sure of it. If I were him, I would take up position in one of the nearby apartment or office blocks to get a good vantage point. You will need to know which one. Before he takes his shot, simply remove him. It's very simple.'

'How do you know all of this?' Jasicki looked puzzled.

'Because that is how I would do it—clean,' she replied.

'Will he not be suspicious of where his bodyguard is?'

'No, he thinks Nicolai is on leave,' she lied, knowing full well that Pathos was in on the plot to expose Nicolai and that MI6 were involved. Jasicki didn't need to know. He was unaware that 6 would be very happy to have the Cossack terminated, ironically, by their own team. The question in her mind now was, would they do it.

'Ok, I will see to it,' Jasicki finally agreed.

'Good. I will deliver my side of the bargain once you have delivered yours. On that, you have my word.' She smiled.

'I think we are done, then.' He stood up.

'Yes, for now, I think we are.'

He held out his hand. She stood up and gently shook it, then turned and walked out of the restaurant.

———

Once outside in the crisp morning air, she took out her mobile phone and dialled an international number. After a few rings, it was answered.

'It's me, the Rain Angel. I want verification that Jasicki is one of yours and he does, in fact, have the power to deliver what I have asked for.' She waited for the response.

She had used this number many times before; it gave her direct access to her CIA handler, a man by the name of Peter Johnson. As the voice on the other end of the line confirmed her question, she knew her job was now almost complete—just the small issue of the CD to contend with. She then walked off towards the river.

Inside the restaurant, Jasicki was also placing a call on his mobile phone.

'It's Jasicki. The Cossack needs to be retired,' he said, his tone cold. Then, his face started to show his frustration at being challenged by the person on the other end of the line.

'Because I said so,' Jasicki snapped. 'Now, get it done.' With that, he hung up, gathered his things and left.

THIRTY-SIX

At the austere offices of the SIS at number 85, Albert Embankment, which he called 'Lego Land', McCabe sat in one of the soundproofed glass-walled meeting rooms. He was still, leaning back in one of the two very uncomfortable chairs at the table, his legs stretched out in front of him and his arms folded.

Every so often, he raised his eyes to observe Ogilvy, who was standing, studying the various documents and photographs contained within a well-worn beige file. Given the file had 'MARK MCCABE' printed on the front cover, there was little doubt as to whose it was.

Ogilvy sighed every once in a while, as if to inform McCabe he had read something of consequence about him—not that McCabe cared. He knew the tactics of spooks well enough to expect they would toy with him for a while. As such, he would not rise to the bait. In his mind, he had the theme tune of *The Great Escape* playing, with images of Steve McQueen.

McCabe suddenly broke into a smile, as he remembered Mooney being told to fuck off at Heathrow. It was either that, or risk getting hauled in with McCabe for questioning. Technically, Mooney was on a sabbatical for six months. There was little doubt his superiors would want to know how he ended up helping a civilian capture a cargo of gas centrifuges and take out a few pirates off the coast of Somalia.

Mooney had reluctantly obliged at the airport, but not before uttering the word 'pricks' to the MI6 welcoming committee and breaking wind right in their faces. The smell of rotten eggs around them was gagging; long flights had that effect on Mooney's bowels.

The welcoming committee, dressed casually in jeans, T-shirts, trainers and bomber jackets, had pinged McCabe and Mooney the second they cleared Heathrow immigration. Mooney had spotted them first, as they slowly closed in.

'Your 10 o'clock. We are about to get lifted,' he had whispered to McCabe.

McCabe had confirmed the tag with a nod and simply walked on, until he was taken firmly by the arm and told to come quietly. He knew there was no sense in making trouble and, given Ryan had been killed, it was obvious they would be picked up at some point for a chat.

'Something funny, McCabe?' Ogilvy spoke for the first time.

McCabe looked at him and shook his head, then tilted his head back as if to show his boredom.

'Well, you have quite a file here, McCabe. Seems you have seen your share of action. Falklands, Northern Ireland, Middle East, Bosnia, East Timor, Nigeria, Sierra Leone and on it goes. You must have enough air miles to rent your own damn plane, McCabe,' Ogilvy said, pulling out the other chair and sitting down.

McCabe remained silent, his face showing no sign of concern or stress. His shoulders just hunched up for a second as if to convey an arrogant 'So what?'

'Brian Stowe rated you, I hear. He was about to join us, you know, cross over from 5. That is, until you got him killed, McCabe, on that jaunt of yours in India,' Ogilvy said. He then waited for the reaction.

'You have no idea what happened, so don't even go there,' McCabe retorted, much to Ogilvy's delight.

'So, you are human,' Ogilvy quipped. 'You have buttons to press, just like the rest of us.' He leaned forward. 'Okay, what Stowe did to get himself killed is not, in fact, my concern here. That chapter is closed. The idiot most likely rushed in all headstrong and macho, I shouldn't wonder.'

McCabe frowned, knowing Ogilvy was right—not that he would ever admit it.

'So, how did Ryan die?' Ogilvy asked, getting to the point.

'Yeah, another plant. Nice disguise you gave him. Had me fooled,' McCabe bit back.

'Details would be good at this point.' Ogilvy was now slightly annoyed at McCabe's reluctance to talk. McCabe detected this and decided he may as well be helpful; the hard man act was getting boring.

'He was caught in crossfire, simple as that. Your man Bates then executed the prisoners,' McCabe snapped.

Hearing this, Ogilvy eased himself back in his chair. 'Okay, look, firstly, you trained him, not us, so don't give me the high and mighty. No matter how idealistic you think we can be, they had their orders, McCabe. It was cleaner to terminate them. Otherwise, we would have a bunch of refugees on our hands; that, or a number of expensive trials to conduct, and for what. They hadn't really done anything on our soil and we couldn't exactly throw them back into the sea to start all over again. We only cared about the cargo not being delivered, much to the CIA's annoyance. The rest was collateral damage.'

'They were still human!' McCabe spat. But, deep down, he again knew Ogilvy had a point. After a long pause, he reluctantly admitted, 'Yeah, okay, I know.'

Ogilvy then continued. 'There was no place for Abshir to go once he had unknowingly placed himself in the middle of an intelligence service clash. And he would have been further used as a hired gun for the CIA's own objectives. They would have used him, bled him dry and killed him the moment he was done.'

McCabe pondered on that for a while. 'Okay, I get your point, agreed. Now, can I go?'

'No, I have something else to discuss with you.' Ogilvy seemed to relax; in contrast, McCabe looked puzzled. 'I will cut to the chase,'

Ogilvy said. 'We have need of your skills. I have been cleared to bring you in, working for us in 6.' He paused and swallowed. 'You... you can even bring with you that brute of a man Mooney. Seems you two make a good team.'

McCabe jumped in his chair. 'Are you serious?' He was completely surprised.

'Come now, don't look so shocked. You have all of the right credentials. Don't think we haven't noticed. In fact, the suits over at 5 have had their eye on you for some time now. We simply want to steal you away before they get their fat little fingers on you.' Ogilvy leaned forward. 'So, are you interested?'

McCabe's mind was racing. He indeed loved the action, but a spook? He had never considered that. Did he, in fact, have any choice? His civilian working life was all but over, and he detested the thought of being branded a mercenary, a gun for hire. Whilst the pay was good, he still preferred causes he could relate to. Saving the spoiled arse of some billionaire's daughter hardly advanced world peace.

His thoughts turned to his daughter. Whilst he knew she was okay, he missed her. Being a lousy father didn't help make his decision any easier.

After a few moments, he looked at Ogilvy. 'I'm in,' he said. 'But, what exactly would I be doing?' McCabe was intrigued as to how his talents would be used.

'Good,' Ogilvy said, beaming. 'That's good news. In fact, we have a little task for you right now.'

THIRTY-SEVEN

His pace was quick, but not hurried, as he turned the corner and walked the few yards up the side passage to the fire door. Glancing back, he confirmed it was clear. His fingertips gripped the edge of the door and tugged. It was as he had left it, disabled.

He slipped inside and pulled the door shut behind him. Then, he paused for a moment, standing stone-still and listening. Only the clanking of the lift could be heard, as it ascended the building.

As if performing a well-rehearsed series of actions, Nicolai placed each foot carefully and silently down in turn, making his way cautiously up the stairs leading to the roof. The musty smell that hung in his nostrils made him feel better, given it meant lack of use. His ears were alert, straining to detect any sound. He was beginning to perspire, and his adrenaline levels were rising. Such is the state of an assassin on the move.

In his right hand was a soft black bag. He could feel the weight of the suppressed Remington 700 inside. One shot, one kill; it had to be that way, no room for error. He would aim for the head, pass the .30 round through his mark's skull and end it right there.

As he counted off each flight of steps—he had 10 to climb—he wondered how the shooting would be reported the next day. 'Cypriot Billionaire Gunned Down,' he imagined and then told himself to focus; he had a job to do.

The abrupt slam of a stairwell fire door below caused him to freeze.

His senses once again on high alert, he desperately tried to detect any sound of footsteps ascending the stairs after him.

It came. The sound he didn't wish to hear—footsteps heading his way. One person was his guess. Instinctively, he reached inside his jacket and pulled out the Glock that had been secured under his arm. He moved slowly towards the handrail and peered down, just in time to spot a shadow, he guessed, on the third storey.

Just as he began to steel his mind for an encounter, his finger on the trigger, he heard another door slam below. The footsteps were gone. He peered over the handrail again—nothing.

He continued up the stairs at a hastened pace until he reached the top. The door offered minimal resistance, given the locking plate had already been jimmied. He hesitated for a second, his ears alert, before easing open the door. As he stepped out, two pigeons suddenly took flight, jolting him. Then, he crossed the roof.

Peering over the parapet on the westward-facing edge of the roof, he could see the pavement below just in front of the Pathos building. Nicolai calculated the distance as being no more than 100 metres. He could see people clutching their coffee and morning papers already beginning to file in through the massive revolving doors at the entrance to the building. Checking his watch, he noted it was 8:00 a.m.; he had exactly two hours to go.

Unpacking and assembling the rifle took but a few moments in his experienced hands. Once finished, he turned around and looked up towards the spot he had selected during his reconnaissance. The large black water tank above sat on a second roof, accessible via an iron ladder in front of him. It was the perfect position, given the tank would protect him from the wind and prevent him from being seen from the eastward-facing office buildings.

He had one more thing to take care of. He took out a nylon garrotte from his bag, crept back towards the stairway door and stood flat against the wall. Instincts were telling him something was wrong. Whilst he had heard the door slam a second time earlier, he thought he had also detected something else just as he reached the top floor.

The figure that emerged cautiously from the doorway moments later confirmed his suspicion that he wasn't there alone. The suppressed handgun in the man's right hand told Nicolai he was not from building maintenance. In one swift movement, Nicolai moved out from the side of the doorway and dropped the wire over the man's head and around his neck, drawing it tight by pulling on the hand grips.

Almost instantly, he felt the butt of the man's pistol thumping hard into his side. With his other hand, the man tried to break Nicolai's hold on him. Then, Nicolai felt the man drop his weight in an attempt to knock him off balance.

Having expected this reaction, Nicolai had kept his knees bent in order to strengthen his balance. His powerful arms were too much for the slight assailant. The choking sound coming from his throat as the wire cut into his neck, and the weakening of his thrashing indicated his stamina was failing.

Then, a sudden pain in his leg brought Nicolai down on his knees; the man had stamped down hard onto his shin. A stray punch caught Nicolai in the side of the head, causing his left ear to ring, but he held the tension. Nicolai then forced himself to fall backwards, pulling his victim down with him. He wrapped his legs around the man and gripped tight. This was enough to finish the man off; his flailing legs quivered and then went still.

Rolling over, Nicolai gasped for air. Despite being of a smaller build, the man had put up more of a fight than he had expected. He kicked the body over and observed the man's tongue hanging out and his eyes wide open. Checking through his pockets, Nicolai found no identification. Someone, though, was onto him and this man had been sent to kill him.

With no time to waste, he retrieved the rifle, heaved himself up the fixed iron ladder and got into position. Pathos still had to be removed. He took out a sand sock from his pocket, placed it in front of him, squeezed it a bit to heighten it and then rested the barrel of the Remington on top. It made the perfect perch for his weapon. Taking a look through the scope, he gave the sock another squeeze; the adjustment gave him a good angle.

Once comfortable, he slid a round into the chamber and closed the bolt. A tree just a few yards to the right of the building's entrance came up in his scope. An area of dark bark about halfway up the trunk marked the position of a former limb that once hung over the road; it made a perfect target.

Nicolai drew in a breath, narrowed his eyes, steadied himself and focused his mind. Then, he squeezed the trigger, absorbing the kick. He took in the fact that the round had struck 6 or 7 inches below the target, sending splinters onto the road.

He made a few adjustments to zero in the scope and once again gave the sock a gentle squeeze. Then, he sent off another round; this time, it hit within an inch of dead centre. One last tweak was made to the sand sock. He exhaled slowly and then inhaled and held his breath. His finger squeezed the trigger, and the round arrived dead centre with a dull thud.

Dropping the rifle, he proceeded to load a hollow-point round. Once again, he closed the bolt and took up position. But now, something else was disturbing him. He scanned each office block and the roof area—nothing seemed out of place. Dismissing the feeling as nothing more than nerves, he settled himself down. He was ready.

Pathos was trying to read the *Financial Times*, but he kept raising his eyes every now and then to note his location. He knew he had at least another 10 minutes before he arrived at his office.

The Bentley was nothing if not comfortable, and he appreciated the fact that he could be driven almost anywhere he wanted to go. Trains and taxis in London were not a form of transport Pathos subscribed to. But, today, he was not his normal relaxed self; despite the luxury of his car, he hadn't really taken in anything he had read. His mind was on what might happen.

He knew Nicolai was going to make his move; it was a case of when. If the spooks fucked it up and failed to find him in time, Pathos knew he would be a dead man. He broke into a sweat at the sudden thought that maybe MI6 wanted him dead. After all, he now knew way too much. They could simply use Nicolai to carry out their foul deed. The thought made him feel sick; he dropped his paper, reached for the window switch to open the window and took in a deep breath.

'Are you okay, sir?' His driver caught him in the rear-view mirror.

'Yes, fine, just tired,' Pathos pretended.

As the Bentley drew up outside the office and the doorman dutifully opened the car door for him, Pathos hesitated. He could feel his stomach knotting up, his legs turning almost to jelly. Was this where Nicolai would make his move, or was he simply being paranoid?

Finally, he placed his foot on the pavement and climbed out of the car. He started for the entrance, ignoring the doorman's tipped hat and cheerful 'Good morning, sir.' His pace was hurried. It was a distance of maybe 10 yards; today, it seemed more like 10 miles.

Pathos was now in Nicolai's scope, the back of his head almost dead centre in the crosshairs. Nicolai drew in his breath, tensed up his body and moved his finger to the trigger.

———

No sooner had the trigger been pulled than it was all over. His head had taken the full force of the round; death would have been instant. A large section of the skull lay in a mass of bloodied hair on the ground a few yards away. His life had been ended by a single shot from a sniper's bullet; ironic, considering his own intentions.

McCabe looked up and let out his breath; his job was done. Just a few minutes ago, he was bolting up the staircase—20 flights, three steps at a time—not easy when carrying a 30-pound weapon. He had been given only 40 minutes to get into position. His orders were to finish the job and secure the deal Pathos had made with MI6.

McCabe packed away his weapon and handed it to the waiting CO19 officer who was there as back-up in case McCabe missed the target. Nicolai had been completely unaware McCabe had him in his sights from a nearby building. His body was now being retrieved by a swarm of police officers.

The other body, that of a CIA agent, would also be removed. But, his identity would be vigorously denied. He had been ordered to terminate the Cossack but had failed his mission. MI6, not wanting to risk anything, had sent McCabe, on his first official mission as a sanctioned spook.

Pathos had walked into the building, unaware of how close he had come to death. As he took the lift up, he was informed of the events that had gone on around him.

EPILOGUE

'That is one hell of a cheque!' McCabe said, as he stared at the row of zeroes on the cheque Pathos had so effortlessly slid across the veneered surface of his desk.

'Payment for a job well done.' Pathos seemed strangely happy.

'Forgive me, but you didn't exactly get what you wanted.' McCabe was frowning.

'Depends on how you look at it. It opened my eyes and you saved her life in many ways.' Pathos broke into a slight smile.

McCabe recalled the events of the past few weeks. He felt the cost of life had been too high, and he wasn't convinced the members of the MFF should have paid the highest price. After all, they had helped the British in a strange way. Whilst they were, for sure, no angels, they did, at least, deserve a trial and not be slaughtered in cold blood like pigs.

The bloody execution played on his mind. Bates, admittedly, had simply been following orders from, no doubt, some stuffy colonel. But, the sight of surrendering men being gunned down was never a good thing. In fact, it was the ugliest face of humanity.

McCabe could only surmise what Abshir's last words meant. 'When warrior meets warrior, the truth is found.'

In his view, Abshir was in a way admitting that he knew that what he was doing was wrong. But the cause he fought for was justified.

McCabe looked at Pathos. 'If it's all the same to you,' McCabe said, 'I won't take it. I'm not normally a hired gun and, given the events of the past few weeks, I don't feel right taking your money.'

'But you have earned it.'

'Your daughter was not so innocent in all of this. She paid for Daniel to take part, Mr. Pathos. He paid with his life. I feel dirty enough for being paid to save her arse. Sorry, but that's how I feel.' McCabe then stood up, turned and headed for the door.

'Wait. Was it you who saved my life a few hours ago?' Pathos enquired.

Turning slightly, McCabe said, 'I wouldn't know anything about that.' With that, he left.

Pathos said nothing further. He remained seated, staring blankly at where McCabe had been standing. His heart was torn. Despite his wealth, he could not ensure his daughter knew right from wrong. That thought caused him grief. Yet, despite the disgrace she had brought upon the Pathos name, he could not bring himself to disown her. In his heart, she was his own flesh and blood. He loved her no matter what she had done.

He thought only briefly about Daniel, a foolish young man, in his opinion, whose love of the extreme finally took his life.

The morning papers were placed on his desk as they always were. As he read the headline, his eyes widened. 'Pathos Shipping Goes Deep Six,' it said, in large black bold type; it was hard to miss. It seemed a young journalist by the name of James Cutter had a story to tell. As he grabbed the papers, his heart sank. There, on the front page, was a photograph of Alexis and Daniel. It seemed things were about to get a lot worse. Cutter, whilst at Eton, had a close friend; his name was Daniel Spencer.

———

Mooney greeted McCabe with a big smile as he stepped out of the Pathos building.

'And what the fuck are you so sad about?' Mooney boomed, seeing McCabe's face.

'I just turned away two million dollars. I would have felt like a highly paid prostitute. So, I am asking myself why I do this.' McCabe looked at him.

Mooney paused, slightly unhappy McCabe had turned away a small fortune, but he understood his reasons. 'Well, I will tell you why, my friend. Because tough men stand ready to visit hell and take on violence to protect the innocent as they sleep in their beds, that's why we do it.' Mooney slapped McCabe on the back.

McCabe gave Mooney a blank stare. 'What a load of tosh! You would have taken the money, you old sod.' McCabe smiled.

'Yeah, maybe, but it made you laugh,' Mooney joked. Then, he suddenly grew serious. 'Hey, did you ever hand over that damn CD to the Rain Angel?' he asked.

'Nope. It's the property of my new employer, and she will just hate me for that.' McCabe smiled.

'Come on, let's get out of here and visit that renegade Stowe, crack a beer or two over his headstone,' Mooney said.

McCabe nodded. To him, that sounded like a good end to the day. As they started to walk off, McCabe felt his phone vibrating in his pocket. He took the call, not bothering to stop.

Mooney stared at him, curious as to who was calling. The words McCabe was mouthing told him it was Ogilvy.

McCabe then stopped in his tracks. 'Okay, sure, give us 30 minutes,' he said and hung up. 'Seems Stowe may have to wait for that beer,' he informed Mooney. 'Ogilvy has need of us.'

'Us?' Mooney asked, his face showing a mixture of concern and confusion.

'Yes, us. Didn't I tell you? You work for me now.' McCabe gave Mooney a wink and hailed a taxi.

Mooney simply shook his head, smiled and followed.

The lady who watched them leave smiled. For her, it was just the beginning. It was about to RAIN.

If you enjoyed
DEEP SIX
another recommended McCabe title is:

QUANTUM BREACH
ISBN-978-981-4276-38-2
www.markpowell@markpowellauthor.com